*Swordsman and Seer*

Warped and rippled above the fire-heat columns of other illusory tents beyond its ragged flaps, dark clouds rode the wind, twirling, boiling up and fading, knotting and unknotting the sky in alarming haste. Thunder weather in a dream! I thought, bemused. And *smells*. The dream-mist reeked of illness, stank of every refugee camp I'd ever visited. Forked white lightning-fire flared to the top of one tent, consuming the hides in a flick, leaving only the painted figures from its sides dancing and fading into space.

As I blinked in the dim light, I saw in the shadows, among my own tent's painted symbols, Upai faces and narrowed, dark eyes. Chants wailed. The voices swirled about the tent, wailing from the totems painted upon all the hides, bags, and boxes. Though the painted faces were flat pigment, their eyes glistened liquidly, focused hard on me with the glossy, fathomless black of living Upai eyes. The like of my dead mother stared from the bony shadows of every one.

"But you died," I whispered.

### BLOODSTORM
### The Song of Naga Teot
### Book Two

*Books by Heather Gladney*
*from Ace*

TEOT'S WAR
BLOODSTORM

THE SONG OF
NAGA TEOT ℰ BOOK TWO

# BLOOD STORM

## HEATHER GLADNEY

ACE BOOKS, NEW YORK

This book is an Ace original edition,
and has never been previously published.

BLOODSTORM

An Ace Book / published by arrangement with
the author

PRINTING HISTORY
Ace edition / April 1989

ISBN: 0-441-74957-7

Ace Books are published by The Berkley Publishing Group,
200 Madison Avenue, New York, New York 10016.
The name "ACE" and the "A" logo
are trademarks belonging to Charter Communications, Inc.

PRINTED IN THE UNITED STATES OF AMERICA

10  9  8  7  6  5  4  3  2  1

Call this praise, thanks, or dedication, aid came from many friends patient with my questions: co-librettist Tim Randles, who can read that musical bog Teot calls his mind; Beck, toughest of critics, and my family, bedrock when crunch week hit; Ladyhawke zine's joyous wolfpack, Terri and her kith, Pat, Joy, Leona, Brian, Michael, Sally and Joe, Jerry and the Kendo Monk, all of them fierce on the path of research; Jim Bradley, saint and connoisseur; Van, engineer and inventor; Kris Anderson, who binds and cherishes books; Mary Lou, fighting the good fight; Rosemary, Dutch, and Bob—for the next generation's literacy; Damon Hunter, maker of mail and swords; Charlene, poet; Captain Janis and crewmen of the Starship *Defiance*; Hal Holding, area rep; Will, Marc, Jan Stirm, Andrea, Jim, Kirk, and Debra, who put up with me before any book; Teresa and Mischa, with love, thanks, and talismans of luck; and most patient of all but too modest to admit to the virtue, Alan, coming in from the strange cold ranges of the desperado's song with eyes full of desert moons. My work improved by knowing Margo Skinner and Fritz Leiber, citizens of the world, and by Janny Wurts's advocacy and Gail Van Asten's clear writer's sight. Others whose kindness to me can only be repaid to other stumbling youngsters: Dave Smeds, Loren MacGregor, Mary Mason, Jacqueline Lichtenberg, Stephen Goldin, Donald Robertson, Melody Rondeau, Raymond Feist, Sarah Goodman, Clint Bigglestone, Karen Joy Fowler, Steve Boyett, Paul Zimmer, Lillian Stewart Carl, Diana Paxson, Frank Robertson, George Barr. For fans who write letters, discuss in-genre and out learnedly, who hatch exciting ideas: my deepest thanks.

## "This Is Tan"
### (From *Teot's Warning*, Act One,
### book by Heather Gladney and Tim Randles,
### music by Tim Randles;
### based on *Teot's War* by Heather Gladney)


Sidereal
And allegorical
Who could say the truth
Of events perfumed
By the dust of years
Words wrought for world
Of ax and mace
Opposed to world of
Steam and flame and fear

No magic near to spare our champions
Price of honor dear
May be head on pike
And a vulture's grave
Their glories are
But half-heard feats revealed
From dusty scrolls
Invoked across the years

Faint flutes' and drums'
Dance discerned through the smoke
Fading melodies
Upon drifts of fog . . .

# "The Living Fire"

(From *Teot's Warning*, Act One,
book by Heather Gladney and Tim Randles,
music by Tim Randles;
based on *Teot's War* by Heather Gladney)

Osa of the living fire
Drawn to the greatest source of all:
Oil from the Altar Tan
Here where the Goddess Sitha stands

Clinging Osa fire
Like clothes that live upon its victims
Bitter earth and oils
Combined in arcane distillations
Alum salts will jell
To vomit wands of forty paces
Pumped from witches' guns
It burns on water, wind, and souls

Caustic Osa god
With savage hand compels its people
Cross unaided lands
Consuming tribes of gods unlike it
In its callous wake
Remains a profaned blackened region
Holocaust to slake
Its dark incessant thirst to reign

Now I am left alone
Alive to give
This warning song,
I offer what I know
A chance for you to turn this fate.
With single-minded rage
They killed my clan at Redspring Hold
The Upai scattered wide
To flee the monster-makers' flames . . .

# CHAPTER

# = *1* =

THE DISASTER STRUCK in my first winter at Fortress. Sea fog snagged among Fortress towers in vague streamers and lay low about in stray corners deceiving the eye about patches of ice. I rode the slushy streets on a newly trained mare gana: a beast with all the sly wit of a wild goat, twice the tricks, and a hundred times the mass to hurl into it.

Since shying at the stable gate at dawn, the horn-headed idiot pretended to be big, bad, and flighty. I'd extracted the biggest cactus hooks and glochids rubbed in her hide this morning by juvenile malice, but it hadn't helped. Since no one would name her tormentors, I dared not leave her there in quarters so insecure; and after their pranks she lashed out at all stableboys. Desert-bred, she was as alien to the stables as I was; the alienness wore at us both.

Normally inflected in my native Upai, my primary name was Naga Asaba Imuto Teot, Beautiful Gold Dance of Knives—though I had other names and other skills. The ruling Tannese nobles, who truly were golden, could not distinguish desert Upai clansmen like me from the dark blade-faced Sek fishing tribes they'd conquered and impoverished.

Tannese called us all by the same spitting words: *spechei*, natives. Or they yelled *epstacchei*, refugees. Both words were usually true for Upai. That I fit neither word made little odds to any except the innermost councils of power. There, no one commented on the color, length, or root-pattern of my braids. I was a Sati of scaddas in the service of their Liege Lord, Tanman Caladrunan—and for all their disdain, I was helping these con-

1

quering blond farmers and sailors fight against the next, newest
wave of invaders poised over Tan's rich grainfields and water
meadows.

Dun fur flopped over my saddle leathers at my gana's jumps
and starts. The mare's antics didn't amuse me. Very little did
these days, with tensions toward spring warfare escalated so
sharply at court. Though Caladrunan was the only one entitled to
be called by the name of the land—to be titled Tanman—plenty
of others felt a fresh dynasty could better rule that land and its
future.

My beast swung her black-banded horns in saber sweeps and
whistled in amazement, demanding firm hands and good seat to
keep her from bolting the length of the morning market. Robes
flapped in the fog. The shell-within-shell razor-edged whorls of
her horntips whistled past my ears as I ducked, and harness
rings—piercing the shell-edges—jangled and squealed together.
Merchants shouted; market girls laughed; beggarboys and refugees screamed for jade chips. A man snapped out a brocade in a
crack of silk before us. The mare kicked, shrilled, swinging her
hindquarters like a pinnace on an anchor, while ice on the
cobbles shattered under split-shod hooves. Neck arched, she
snorted, rolled an eye at Fortress towers, at pale slate roofs and
green copper lightning wards, and raked yellow tusks at painted
stalls.

Embarrassing. Instead of leading a squad of Tannese officer
trainees along the steep streets, my antic mount rather cleared the
way well ahead of them. Caladrunan would give my trainees
assignment personally, while I'd stand about picking shed hair
and irritating glochids off my robes . . . or so I intended.

A ragged child scurried past under my beast's nose. The mare
honked, humped her back, bogged at her lines, kicked a food
booth and reared, pawing air. "Ride a wagon next time!" a
pie-cook yelled up, waving a fork at my mount. A bucket of
black eels sprayed across a screaming matron in our wake.

My gana drove her saddletree high in the air, swerved aside,
and clicked her tusks with a bucketing, pile-driving landing on
rigid forelegs. So much for the respect due me as Caladrunan's
liegeman . . . She swiveled her hindquarters airborne again,
swapped end for end in the air, and jolted down stiff-legged.
Swinging wide about a pile of turnips she had me down over her
right shoulder, but I kept my balance, stood high in the braces as
she twisted under me like a snake, and I heaved back into the

saddle. Being a Sati of scaddas did not help me now—the curved scaddas merely thumped about my thighs. I unlatched my discipline strap.

Eyeing it, she shied, blatted in her nose, bolted away straight at a low slop alley whose oak beams would brain me. I tapped her near shoulder with the hated strap and spun the beast smartly about by her nose-lines, skidding in sprays of ice. She threw her head high, hissing breath odorous with bean-hay, and trotted along farting loudly every other stride; laughter faded behind me as we caracoled down the street.

I cursed mutely. My patience, even with beasts, had gone.

It was not just Tannese politics that did it. I was a Harper, too, with a trained memory; so when I rode into Tan with my warnings of war, complacency was the last thing I'd expected of future victims of the Osa.

I did not know then that I would have to fight just to make the Tannese listen.

The Lord of Tan and I had worked long days through the winter to keep his country lashed together. Caladrunan was well aware of sly links between the two war fronts: At one side Crag, the southwest province of Tan, and unruly as my mare gana, threatened rebellion. While their nobles disputed Caladrunan's authority, their avowed Liege—even as they hindered recruitment and allied among pirates—the border I knew, at the north, gushed bloody fluxes of open war like a thrashing red deer crippled in the woods. Call them *Osa'aae'ii*—murderers and evil luck ride that name—the Osa bled us in a hundred ways.

Multiple bandit armies raided Tan's northern provinces like ugly clouds spun far before the Osa storm. My people, straggling south into Tan as refugees, had long fled that grinding wall of metal: The Osa had pursued them from the Upai homeland over the Salados, those glaciated mountain ranges, and beyond the ice across the Po Desert and the old Tannese border where I was born.

With their early secrecy abandoned, the Osa brought a war of machines that the Tannese had never drilled for. Waves of bordermen stumbled into Tan's refugee camps—hungry, stunned, and sick—while the pious Osa lines advanced in crushing, slow increments . . . advance by genocide, by burnt earth.

For all the Upai clans slaughtered by the Osa and gone to clamoring ghosts in my memory, I worked hard. I waged my own sly war against Osa theocratic massacres: I drilled Tan's

Army officers against Osa methods; I yelled at stubborn part-time farmer-officers and engineers; I drilled languid sons of nobles, while Caladrunan cajoled funds from his factional and suspicious War Council. Such tides no longer ran with us as at the excited first declarations of war in the fall. These days, supplies and troops failed to appear in pledged strengths. We allotted thirty men to one garrison, two hundred to another, when we wanted six hundred at each site. And weapons! We longed in vain. Of course the Sharinen sold weapons to dream of—but at a price too stiff for a War Council in complete agreement. As it was: impossible.

All the measurements at the huge scale of Tannese war showed Caladrunan's resources shrinking. Despite our best labors, the struggle had become a series of fading retreats to conserve strength, fighting only where we dared not give way. In the field of war, the Tannese officers—so frequently beat back—grew as restive as the half-rebel Cragmen. We'd hoped harvest would quiet Crag unrest, that storms would mire the Osa machines; but not this year, not as much as we hoped. Caladrunan paced nights, and wrestled with wild schemes.

Mine were wilder yet, fueled by my Upai blood. Upai legends told that eating desert red spice in childhood made us rovers. Thus, we sought new forms in the folds and hills of our camps, despising Tannese-style walls that only lay petty arbitrary lines across the wastes and impaired sight. We knew walls did not stop Osa machines. And so, I fought a restlessness within the cramped Tannese walls that rose hard beneath my breastbone—that throttled my vocal cords with impatience, but never quite broke my self-control.

Fighting the Osa through the brambles of Tannese politics took all my energy. How was I to know that I must fight a much more personal war among all the larger killings?

*Now.*

Approaching a blind corner, I drew the mare's lines hard right. She took such turns badly in any weather, bogging her head. Hooves clattering and skidding on icy paving blocks, the beast spun round the corner and grunted the belly-deep heave of startled animals.

Light flared wildly off fittings on her horns. She flinched violently, jerked her forequarters aside, and threw up her head, whistling—"praying at the sky" like a beast struck in the face. I wrenched my head aside. Light rose over ice-slicked slate roofs at a strange angle and blinded me. Green-white fire seared my face. I flung up one arm, but the thick leather of my armor made no difference in the fiery shock bouncing within my head—the stinging glare remained under my lids as I turned my head. My mare screamed, heaved. Something thudded hard between my shoulder blades; warmth and needle pains shot through my legs. In horror I heard someone—myself—utter a thin and distant screeing like a bird, warning, warning those callow children behind me of disaster. In my ears I felt a swooping, falling sensation—then my back took a thump that rattled bones. Whirling Fortress towers crashed on me in brilliant shards of light and blackness.

I dreamed.

I heard music, my eyes were open, my body floated. It was dream-dancing, as Upai seers danced ancestrally with the wise animals and totemic spirits in the ghost lands inside men's minds; but I drifted alone in this strange dark place. Grim the music I heard, keening high over deep drum-pulses, music of such power that heavy sulfurous draperies of air—stinking as only the Altar oil caves below Fortress stank of gas refining, iron, and lime—parted cleanly before my face.

Dreams had always had a disproportionate importance in my life, for seizures of hideous memories opened the ancient sha-man's gate. I never chose it thus, but relivings of Osa flames took me anyway. And on bad days, greater powers.

This nightmare took me deeper into the smell of rot and oil. The somber music in my head helped. The hard, acute beauty of it held back the acrid odor. Sacred oils were refined in aged pipes in Fortress' caves; a pity that its guardians had gone ambitious. The Devotees sold kegs of Altar waste chemicals—sulfur, soft metals, poisons—to enemies. Knowing *that* in the dream, I felt terrible urgency—a need to warn Caladrunan of its hateful, unseen threat. Carvings, runes, Upai symbols, crawled past me on cave walls, leaping like sand-devil laughter.

Elusive symbols teased my eyes, dazzled me. It was a Upai people, come as traders and settled about the greater harbor in Tan, who built the Altar over the cave refinery and began the kernel of Fortress—so long ago they were another kind from mine.

When the dizziness passed, I thought I stood in an empty Upai tent, low and round and marked by my own clan's totems. It was thus a tent owned by the dead, used only for guests.

Warped and rippled above the fire-heat columns of other illusory tents beyond its ragged flaps, dark clouds rode the wind, twirling, boiling up and fading, knotting and unknotting the sky in alarming haste. Thunder weather in a dream! I thought, bemused. And *smells*. The dream-mist reeked of illness, stank of every refugee camp I'd ever visited. Forked white lightning-fire flared to the top of one tent, consuming the hides in a flick, leaving only the painted figures from its sides dancing and fading into space.

As I blinked in the dim light, I saw in the shadows, among my own tent's painted symbols, Upai faces and narrowed, dark eyes. Chants wailed. The voices swirled about the tent, wailing from the totems painted upon all the hides, bags, and boxes. Though the painted faces were flat pigment, their eyes glistened liquidly, focused hard on me with the glossy, fathomless black of living Upai eyes. The like of my dead mother stared from the bony shadows of every one.

"But you died," I whispered.

The Upai wind roared up like a fire in reply—a burst of force, keening high into chants wailed for the dead. Rain drummed on hide. A voice spoke out of the heat-runneled air above the firepit and the sparks. "Dance with us," a wolf's jaws said in crisp, aged accents.

"No!" I cried out. The wind made a tight cone, swirling dust, and dispersed in a willful snap of air up the smokeflap. The portraits on the tent walls faded. I grabbed after them while wind keened chants outside. Under my scrabbling fingers the old ochre and earth-red marks evaporated . . . black, alive eyes lingering last of all, as I faded with them into grayness.

When my eyes opened, Fortress stonework spun nauseatingly around my head. My arms lashed out, struck stone. Blurred pale objects swung over me. My left hand stuttered over ice, grabbed a heavy chunk, hurled it with a vain cat-scream of rage; a spray of snow flicked my face. My tongue tasted of leather, blood, and dirty snow; elbows, hips, hands, bumped on icy cobbles and jerked hard together.

"Get him!"

Past scattering fragments of thought, I heard alien shouting: "Get his leg!" Rope slithered on cloth.

Someone yowled wordlessly, echoing in my head. I wondered fuzzily, How did they—?

*Think!* I exhorted myself.

They gave me no chance for it. My braids yanked and my head went up despite my body's stiff unwillingness. I stretched my eyes wide, forced one blur into focus: pale skin, copper freckles, a narrow arched nose. Teeth, thin lips . . . *smiling*. Caladrunan's staunchest ally—or so he claimed. He was as foreign to Tan as I; he was a Cragman.

Keth Adcrag was called loyal, though most powerful of all the Crag lords. Out of the chaos of his wild province he'd risen to Commander of cavalry in Tan. Cragmen were famous for their brutish lack of skill with ganas, so Keth's riding competition prizes, training formation cavalry drills, were unique. Much as Caladrunan valued that uniqueness, it didn't make the Cragman general likable.

Keth tapped a riding goad against his boot, smiling; tap-tapping his big ugly hook of a gana-killer. The goad bore a broad black scrape-mark from my black riding leathers.

Keth and I were enemies the moment we met on my first harbor-damp dawn in Fortress. More contact just made our mutual loathing exact in its details. A wisp of nasty doggerel about him flitted past my mind. But my braids twisted back, forcing me to see a blank veil of white gauze fastened in place by long gemmed skewers: a Tannese noblewoman. The woman's large gloved hand dragged up my braids while iron held down my chest. Knobby iron.

I snapped my thighs and chest together in a fold-up—or tried to. I failed utterly. My chest and ankles jarred violently in a rattle of chains. The woman jerked me higher, gripped my head at a hard angle. With more force than intelligence, I spat out a dockside word, slurred and blurred past numb lips. Silk dress or not, hers was no noblewoman's grip. She laughed and let go. I was ready for that. But something slashed at my eyes, and my skull smacked on stone into a thousand bright bits.

Wavering in uncertain dream-light, a tall Tannese noblewoman held out gloved hands to me. A clear icy wind swirled about her as from an opened door and came to me scented with glaciers and mountain earth, a knife's breath across the heavy oily air of the place of nightmares; and the wind fluttered white robes stained pink and orange with torchlight . . . clothes vaguely like those of Capilla, Lady of Fortress, Lady Wife to the Lord of Tan, yet of another age, antique. Dream-music thundered along my bones and whispered high harmonics in the snail-curls of my ears. From the wind stepped out a grim gaunt guard-woman holding a thick copper wire.

"Look for this," the White Lady murmured in a voice harsh as silk rasping on silk, and as quiet. The prickling glacier gusts made more noise. "Rigged in the Lord of Tan's most private chambers, on his possessions, to carry the living fire to him from a tower lightning ward. They only now attach this wire to the lightning ward, and that, in a place where none but Devotees pass safely; seek the end in your Liege's chambers. The wire is carefully hidden, believe that."

"Murder with a lightning ward and wire," I murmured.

"Lightning strikes living men rarely now, so well warded they build their towers," the strange Lady sighed in her cool, remote voice. "They believe falsely that if the Lord of Tan and his cause is holy, he will survive the direct touch of the Goddess."

I started. "Spring storms come soon—"

The Lady said, "Of old we call it Kasin's Wind—cones of wind that destroy all, in this season, and lightning, and dry thunder." She inclined her head once and whispered, "Tanman Kasin fought the Osa. Tumult he brought us, along with his ruling sword, the weapon later made into your Lord's sword, Devour. His wind is aptly named, is it not?"

The figures of both women wavered in the darkness, retreating each step but never turned from me—and seemed to erode to gusty shreds of white. Then, along with the chill wind, they were gone as if never there.

A voice came back first: hearing, my first sense. I was vastly surprised that I woke up at all. Struggling up amazed from the deep gray pit of the Goddess, my next sensation was of cold—of dull weights dragging from a central heaviness, a body with too many intensely unpleasant connections to me and a drumskin surface, all vibrating to the rolling bass notes of that voice.

"He can't be roused out of it. Unusual events trigger it. Early signs come in a bow-wave effect; he's told me he feels it rising. I've written down what he says in these spasms, and I expect all of you to do the same." I heard footsteps, the ringing of swords in scabbards. The noises banged about in my head and hurt. "As these fits answer solely to Sitha, Goddess of the Flame, I consider that this expands his duties as a commander. That will be all. Admit the Council.''

I didn't open my eyes. I was sprawled on my back. I finally sorted out that a hand was tangled in my hair, one big finger stroking across my forehead evenly, repetitiously. The hand extended halfway around my head: a huge hand. Gently this cradle lifted my skull as if it were an egg and lowered it onto a robed arm—and as the hand wiggled free I lost all sound in a wild roar of noise and blinding sparkles under my eyelids. For an instant I thought I saw dancing figures prancing through the starry roar, animal heads bent over Upai spirit drums and their black goathair robes flying out as they spun and chanted.

A sound crashed across the music, and it was gone.

A bell tolled the change of watch; boots scraped on straw floor mats. I heard a soft, close ringing of metal: Caladrunan's odd pale sword of state, Devour, sang as he shifted weight. Even that whisper of sound was painful to my ears. Something inside me winced when I heard rustling brocades with the unique rasp of Tannese silk. I held in breath, waited. Gradually past my own roaring head I heard the screeching of some witch-lore jumping about me, and muttering court voices.

I opened my eyes. Firelight flickered over my dazed sight, glints of orange light spun by, a jumbled flit of impressions past my eyelashes. It had a real name, this place; but to my sight, the tapestries of the Fortress Great Hall blurred, refocused uneasily. Embroideries and metals glinted queasy underwater lights. Drafts of air played with torches which shimmered away like fish. I felt no warmth from the flames. I was cold. Utterly cold. The arm under my neck went rigid and hard.

Beneath my cheek, silver threads crackled; the wiry patterns scratching my jaw were sewn into silk. Blue sheen lapped about my chin. As the wrestler's arm within the sleeve tensed, it became familiar. My neck lay across Caladrunan's corded forearm, and he was yelling at someone.

"*Human!*" the Lord of Tan shouted over me. Pain jabbed within my skull. His face shifted fiercely above me, all sharp lines angling and cross-focused and harsh as a cut gold mask in that firelight, while his arm cradled the back of my head. In weak protest at the roaring in my head, I shifted fingers. I was surprised: My hand moved freely.

It broke some outer tableau. Caladrunan looked down at me, eyes a blur yellow as topazes above his beard. His eyes were often as pale as his hair, but that blaze meant his pupils must be drawn tight shut in rage to show the irises—I'd never seen his eyes gone so quartz-brilliant. Something darkened, melted, opened, in that glow as he looked down; his forearm cradled my head more gently. "Naga, rest."

Others protested. "Unholy fits! Ungodly—"

I squinched my eyes shut.

"Look well on him, Councilmen, and think again! Witches, what utter nonsense! Do you listen to silly witch-lores above *my* word?" His voice shook stones and shattered my head like the herd-roar of a gana bull. Murmurs tenuous as fog answered him, far away.

"Nonsense!" snapped a woman's voice, followed by a brisk slap of cloth on stone. "Fits—absolutely common, you thick-headed lot bash about so flaming often. Get that howling witch-lore out, Pitar, I can't think past such a backwoods haze of ignorance. Let me have a look."

Cold touched my neck. I opened my eyes. "Pergo," I grunted, feebly pushing the herbalist's hand away. "Fine. Go 'way."

She ignored it. Pergo and I had had our disagreements in past moons. "Charmed to see you join us again, little menace," Caladrunan's personal herbalist murmured. I blinked at a blur of leathery color. For all she was a Tannese woman, nobly born, Pergo never veiled, and no one had ever braved her temper to make her. Her voice sounded as unmoved as when she studied the dead. "Follow my finger with your eyes, don't squint. Now, Pitar, the light about his eyes, thus."

She sighed and straightened. "His eyes are a bit off. Minor epilepsy—his unconscious fits are bet upon in Fortune Street. Brain damage does cause unique symptoms like his hallucinatory spasms and convulsive speech. I can't judge any prophetic remarks he might make. Impossible to guess at damage in the intertwining of nerve and muscle energies until I examine his brain after death."

I rasped, "Soon?"

Pergo answered cheerfully, "No, not soon—though I'd love a peek inside your skull. Might not find anything grossly damaged; the ancients recorded many tiny parts too intricate to see in all that gray slop you're abusing, young man. Liege, somebody else can candle-check his eyes tonight. I'll be out at refugee camps."

Caladrunan's hand disentangled itself from my loose hair and withdrew. Confused by the hollow roar in my head and by his bass bellowing, I had thought he was in the great black dais chair where he gave Judgments; but as he shifted, my shoulders dragged with him across straw matting. And I realized he was on his knees—the Liege Lord of all Tan knelt on floor mats for me!—and voices murmured at this unprecedented act. I ought to warn him.

Pergo's voice murmured. I blinked against the ache in my head, moved my lips, trying to tell Caladrunan about Keth's veiled woman and the White Lady who spoke of lightning. He leaned closer and lifted my head. I gasped. When I heard past the storm in my head, Caladrunan was saying, "Rest, Naga. We'll proceed here."

He looked up past me. At Councilors, no doubt. His voice changed. Bits of bitter music drifted in my head, describing it. He overrode their voices through the vague firelit distance, saying, "If it's a true prophecy, we're saved from a surprise assault by the Osa—yes, *Osa*, flame their greed and their Nando spies and little machines!"

I could have remarked that the machines of the Osa were *not* little. I didn't.

Closer, crisper than the murmurs, spoke out a dry rustle of a voice. Strengam Dar said, "It wouldn't harm to send patrols to check that area early and in greater force." That voice, soft as reeds twisting in wind, spoke for Caladrunan's oldest, canniest general. He must have just ridden in. He could placate Councilors, reinforce decisions. My eyes drifted shut in relief. The floor did not tumble about so wildly if I shut my eyes. Vaguely I heard protests, but the thunder and water-roar in my head spoke louder.

"*Fit*, nothing!" Caladrunan snapped above me. "Think what you like of Naga's fits, his advice is worth taking. It's always been accurate in the past!"

A white-fire fit, I thought sadly, ravings. Natural enough after a head blow. But the pain was new: A skinny whiplike weal had dried into a tight scab across my nose and right eyelid, which had swollen near-shut. The infuriating part was, *I* never knew what I had said during such convulsions; I had no idea what my "advice" might set off. I had warned Caladrunan against it, but people listened, calling it prophecy or sometimes sorcery. Apparently I could answer questioners in their own language—real discouragement to rational thought. Gibberish to scribes, too. Caladrunan simply changed the subject when I demanded he ignore such fit-ravings.

Now he roared, "We were warned—dare we ignore it?"

"But *if*, when given active duty, the Sati has seizures . . . "

*Unsuited for field duty*, I thought bitterly. After such a public fit, the conservatives would never vote me on the active list. I shifted limbs stiffly, aware suddenly of how unnaturally I had been laid out. My mouth was bloody where somebody had tied gags tightly across it; my wrists had torn, through sleeves, under chains or ropes. And all my riding leathers had vanished.

Yet recently I'd been handled with more thought than usual for my comfort: I wore thick baby rags under my rumpled inner robes, which must have been a chore, and I was grateful. They couldn't have known my precise discomforts, my old muscle binds, strains and tensions—fun, getting the big muscles in my back and thighs to work again. I tried to ask about my weapons. Caladrunan ignored my husking noises; he was giving orders over the protests of hostile Councilors. I whispered, "Please—no litter for me. Too many rumors. Keep it among top guards."

His gold blurry face nodded. I heard soldiers' voices as they departed past us, saying, "So who gets to check Spring Hill Pass? Can't send Keth's favorite cadre; he'd scream like a henyard cock."

"Don't yell so loud! Ehé was beaten up at his house in town, last moon, after talking that way unwisely at a drinking party."

"And died of it," Strengam was saying as the doors creaked. "I wonder what Oldfield is doing in exile these days. Did Isaon fix those gas surges in the Altar flame supply?"

The voices faded until only Caladrunan's personal guards remained. When the Great Hall was quiet, Caladrunan himself lifted me and draped my weight, with a grunt, across his shoulder. Muscles burled under me. My equilibrium whirled. I rasped, "Where are my blades? My mare—she went crazy when that weird green light hit her—"

Caladrunan lowered me into a pile of fur. I opened gritty eyes, groped out. A goblet rim touched my lip; I gulped down watered wine. Then he lowered my head by careful degrees. His six-foot tawny hunting cat stretched out heavily at my feet and purred; Caladrunan's hair caught the same golden lights as the cat's while he took off my boots. "Rest, or you might make another visit to the Goddess. Stop asking! *I* have your scaddas. Your gana mare was all right once her panic was past. And yes, you told me, you were both attacked with this mysterious brief blinding.'' He sighed gustily. The Lord of Tan, the Liege I had sworn the Great Oath to serve past life or hope, slumped down and sat on the furs beside me. His hand checked my throat pulse.

''What . . . ?'' I asked hoarsely, spreading wide my hands.

A grunt this time from him. ''Something triggered off a fit while you were riding, maybe that blinding you got. Your trainees followed too far behind to see much, but Keth told me that in a market dispute with a merchant, you fell off and landed on your head. Some unpleasantness was involved.''

Gingerly I touched a melon-soft mark on top of my head: a deep bruise. My braids, coiled as padding under my metal cap, should have protected my skull; and I distinctly remembered landing on my back, not my head. I said so. Then the nauseating memory of faces returned. ''Keth Adcrag was with a woman dressed exactly like the Lady of Fortress, your Lady Wife.''

''Well, Keth took you away from your trainees—*he* said for your health. But Strengam Dar and his sons, at market buying harness, took custody of you and your mare when commoners— mostly women—swooped in from all over to protect you. They objected violently—call that, near-riot—to Keth's care. Strengam didn't report any woman with Keth.''

''She hit—dropped—my head. Deliberately. *Why?*'' For a long time he sat next to me, saying nothing. It was his bed, his furs, I lay on. Scattered shreds of music spangled my thoughts in random puzzled chirps. The dreams had warned of some awful danger, but I couldn't retrieve any of it but the vague image of the White Lady, an avatar of the Goddess Sitha. I turned my wrist upward. ''Why this? Why tie me up and not kill me? Why hit me?''

The anger leaped so vividly across that blurred broad face that I flinched. He touched my arm lightly, apologetically. ''Keth insisted that your fit was so violent he had to bind and gag you. Not at all the thing, for prophets.''

''Not a prophet!'' I growled rather sullenly. ''Just have stupid fits, you know that, Drin—didn't mean to. Sorry.''

He petted his cat. ''Ah well, Keth didn't succeed. You . . . *talked* when I got you untied in the Great Hall. Upset people a bit.''

I snapped, ''So the Council wants me sent to some House of the Moon as a madman.''

Fingertips tapped my arm. "Seemed to be Keth's idea—which rather put me off it." He smiled, a widening of teeth and lip color in his beard. "These Harpers, can't keep them quiet."

"Fit-babbling!" I said in disgust, closing my eyes. The Lord of Tan drew furs over my body. I shifted my left arm restlessly.

"Before you ask, I won't return your scaddas to you. Yet."

I swore at him. "The security mirrors in those tunnels—"

"Rest, my hawk. I'll check any mirrors and trouble myself."

"That's what I was afraid of," I snapped, and watched the dancing, dipping span of his mouth smile. I said fiercely, "Don't you let the silk clan merchants in without a searching. Remember—the guard watch won't be thorough on fancy nobles—"

He pulled more furs over me. "I'll remember. Can't put off those meetings, so I'll have food sent up when your head eases. I want you to eat it all, Dance of Knives. All."

"Try," I murmured. He touched my shoulder, rose, and went silently away. The cat yawned and sprawled happily over my bruised shins.

The changing guard watches outside Caladrunan's huge tower bedchamber marked the passing day. Pitar diffidently mulled me some wine and nibbled his mustache while he helped me drink it. And he wrestled expertly with bedding and slushpot, which surprised me. Pitar was always so stiff, so proper; an utterly unlikely nurse. Then I remembered his wife was invalided, and felt less humiliated about causing him such chores.

"I must look like something the dogs dragged upstairs—you're not yelling about protocol. Yell so I'll feel normal." Even fingertip support dented my skull too hard. Aside from the expert's duties of a Sati of scaddas, I was a guard commander like Pitar, a bodyguard, and a Harper with far too much to do. I said, opening my eyes wide, "Won't sleep. Work. I want—to—get up." The bed spun about horridly.

A knobbly hand planted itself on my chest. "You just get better," Pitar muttered while he tucked extra furs around my ankle. Later, in the guardroom outside, over a hundred feet away and muffled by sandstone walls, he bellowed, "Need those speaking trumpets open—Army here never hear it—negligence—" I winced, surprised afresh at the real anger in his tone, fierce as for a good friend's sake.

I got more surprises. I was awakened after noon by a formal

note on a tray of food. I blinked at the note: Capilla, Lady of Fortress, Tanman's Lady Wife, sent the food to help heal me.

*Me!*

Her slate, countersigned by Caladrunan, commended my strength and valor—though I hadn't done anything valorous in falling off a mare gana in the street. Since she and I cordially loathed one another, the food would prove she was trusted; if I didn't touch her tray, servants would have the news all over.

Trust the Lady to make food a display-piece, I thought. I gazed at Pitar, who was tormenting his mustache again. But Caladrunan might have suggested that ploy to force me to eat; oh, he was that subtle. I chose a goblet. Perhaps the thin soups and juices, pressed of unusual fruits kept in the women's quarters roof gardens, had medicinal qualities; I drowsed the last daylight away, waking only when Caladrunan swirled in late at night.

He led officers into his personal quarters. Though it was clearly not a private, secured meeting, he pointed, and his guard dog lay down quietly, nose on paws, at the door. As he shrugged out of a mist-glittered outrobe, a curt wave of his hand kept me in bed. Officers crowded near the hearth talking; preoccupied men strode right past the gauze bed draperies where I lay. I was annoyed that my body felt so distant, as if I were floating away. Not a time to drift into some Goddess-inspired state, I told myself irritably, but I could not focus. I squinted blurrily across the chamber at Pitar and Rafai.

Pitar saw my harpcase sitting nearby on a stool; he frowned and nudged it into shadow. I smiled within my huddle of furs. He disliked having the proprieties upset. Yet Pitar, the scarred old veteran, privately approved what he would never presume to do. I often slept here, with my scaddas unsheathed beside my head to defend Caladrunan's life . . . but never so publicly.

Whatever anyone's wishes, all winter I'd stayed close to Caladrunan's side, both on-duty awake or off-duty asleep. In old chambers riddled with secret passages, I was deterrence. I was properly grateful when Pitar slipped two curved lizard-leather sheaths onto my furs, directly against our Liege's earlier orders. I held the cold viper-skin grip of my right scadda and listened.

The Lord of Tan paced furiously. His blue and silvered robe swirled out as he turned, folds of black in that orange light. His face pulled in taut lines. Tension rode the other men, too; Pitar sat now rigid as a carven figure. I thought, Caladrunan sent heliographed word out to that pass I mentioned in my idiot fit, and now they all wait for news. I wondered which pass it was, perhaps Spring Hill. Messengers stinking of gana sweat clattered in with slates, back out to the guardroom. Abruptly Pitar waved the other officers to go, too, all but Rafai.

Caladrunan bent over the slates. His lips thinned, his eyes shocked pale, one fist strained white. His hand whipped up and slung aside one slate to crash into a chair. "*Flames* Above and Below! Naga was right. Osa treadmarks, a burned village—had Keth's force been in place, they'd have been in time to—" He read slates, swearing, while Rafai scrambled to catch flung slateframes before they crashed to shards on the floor mats. "Rafai, if you're too flamed slow—"

I frowned. It wasn't like the Lord of Tan to vent temper on any man. A huge pup barely grown into his paws, Rafai worshiped Caladrunan, and he was a gifted officer. Partly my fault, that: I had brought him to Caladrunan's attention. The Head Armorer's boy had grown up with weapons; wasteful to let such massive potential go unused. So Caladrunan promoted Rafai to watch command and watched him grow into the job. Now Rafai and Pitar must split my watch, keep the boys out of the wine barrels at night.

Thinking about it made my head hurt. I plucked irritably at bedfurs. What if the Osa had blasted a larger force through that pass than Keth's men admitted when confronted, in their retreat, by Strengam's field officers?

Caladrunan dismissed Pitar and Rafai. Expressionlessly they glanced at my perch and left. The Lord of Tan clattered slates and scowled; one slid off and smashed, while he scowled deeper.

I whispered, "I can harp for you, if you like."

He snorted. Then, parting the bed curtain, he sat down with me. His fingers swirled dark seal-fur nap until it shone in the gauze-filtered light. Gold hearth lights prickled on his hair. Eventually his hands slowed down. Tension drained from the set of his shoulders. "How's your topknot?"

I waved lazily at the tray on a bedside table. "Better."

He read the Lady's note and tossed the slate aside with a clatter that made me wince. "Sorry." He ran fingers over my head, examining lumps. I closed my eyes to endure it. "Pergo's off working in the refugee camps, so I called my Lady Wife to substitute as herbalist. You did say *she* hit your head?"

I frowned past his arm, squinted my eyes against his heavy

silk sleeve. "I'm not sure. The woman with Keth was dressed just like her, gems like hers, the scent . . . but something was wrong. Not enough motive. What if it wasn't her? It seems more likely it wasn't. And why now?"

"Other women might like you better dead," he murmured. He had told bitter stories about the women's quarters to warn me fangs lay under the placid surface. Ambitious seductresses tried for his bed, to displace his son Therin, while their noble husbands plotted against Caladrunan himself.

I was no threat. I'd never rule pale-born Tan of the Seventeen Houses, so haughty over defeated native tribes. He still made friends where he enjoyed their company; but perhaps it made him easier with me. Because as a boy he'd been sent out for toughening to an outlying Hold and because my clan camped there, he became *kigadi* among my clan, brother to my eldest brother. Through years training in the desert, I clung to that. On the strength of it, I swore the Great Oath to him sight unseen, and swore it once again when I met him—no light test of character. But the trust existed on both sides anyway . . . unjustified, mysterious, inexplicable. I'd never seen him relax so entirely near anyone but me. It was true of me, too: I felt best in his company. We were of a kind, whatever the different structure of our bodies.

He frowned. "My Lady Wife, Capilla, sent you that food as a peace offering, you know. She agreed to treat you with simples." His voice went grim. "None of the court herbalists would do a thing. They squalled to the Devotees of Sitha about prophecy and fits, and I got nowhere. Only Capilla and rude old Pergo seemed to understand that even prophets can get dented heads."

I smiled wryly, fingers stirring near my chin on warm seal pelt. "Not even any bloodshed. Ought to get up and work."

"Pitar told me you fell on your face trying, this afternoon."

I grimaced. "How did they blind me off the mare?" I fell silent, remembering that icy glaring light. What had it been? My trainees would've reported a huge flat mirror.

His face went taut and smooth and very cold. He looked away while his hand stirred the nap on the furs. "No idea, my hawk. You're put off work but not actually murdered, all an accident, so sad. There were rumors about witch-contaminated cuts on you—I had to reassure Council you showed no plague signs, they were so concerned for your health. Those attempts on my life last fall taught them: Lock *you* up safely beforehand."

I agreed. "Set up to keep me off work, prevent me from finishing some job, perhaps. But what?" I yawned.

Caladrunan said, "You should sleep. You're unfit for duty."

I should get up and prove him wrong, I thought, with my eyes shut—and proved him right by dropping from consciousness like coal from a Cragman's bucket.

# CHAPTER

# = 2 =

BECAUSE I FELL uneasily in and out of sleep, the mist of dreams mingled with odd memories, and at last joined in a continuous sound too crisp to be solely imaginary. I hoped so, anyway. "Grandson."

The Upai word grated harsh on my ear. I struggled within the tangle of dream. If any of the water blurry figures were real, then a stranger spoke to me, my last and only kin.

Then, squinting, I saw Isaon the scholar near Caladrunan's gold blur. Odd: I always saw Isaon's white head bent over carvings in the Fortress caverns, among the gas pipes that fed the Altar holy Flames with fuel, for he repaired those pipes and gauges and sent up tart-spoken reports on rock movement in the deeps. Beyond him I saw Upai women staring at me.

My eyes lingered on wide, age-leathered faces—dismaying how slight, how tired, they looked. The tallest was a hawk-fierce woman who tapped upon a slate, translating runes aloud for Isaon. Bright silver spirit beads hung from her shoulder. She was shorter than I, with broad squint-folds around her eyes and wings of white streaking back from her temples. And her face!

I lifted my two hands together to her as my kin. Royal kin. Orena é Teot, mother of my mother.

Carved in portrait throughout the gas pipe caves, painted on Upai tents, the distinctive face of my people with its broad eyehoods and sharp-boned nose stared at me—while her true self hid behind eyes as black and secret as tarn pools.

Too familiar a face, exactly as I saw it in my relivings of horror, nightmares where I watched my mother die of Osa flames. The skin drew tight along my cheeks. Images of my mother ghosted between the strong bones of Orena's face and my own, mirror-seen, oddly reflected. Echoes of the past, young-old, gone-alive, myself-alien, reverberated between us with queasy strength. For her, too, a vanished dead breathed in my flesh. Her brows crawled back in shocked horror just as my mouth pulled flat across my bones. Head high, she examined me with quick flicks of her eyes, sure sign of a spooked Upai.

The Osa, far distant and hated kin, too, looked thus.

But our shared blood came of rulers, and desert pride was there in her eyes. The hostility, too. I wasn't going to be automatically admitted into her confidences simply for my breeding. In that instant I read into a tight, scarred, rigid soul so acutely and precisely it was painful, and I felt a horrible sinking pity. I looked steadily at my grandmother. "Orena é Teot, how many of our people have gone out to boats in the harbor, out into the pirate islands to scratch for shellfish—how many people have you led through Fortress caves and tunnels?"

She looked at me. "This one, he's sharp." She lifted her head high. In Upai she said, "Not us—we're old women, too weak to climb caves, to hide in wet holds, to sail." The others threw back their heads and cackled, slapping hands on thighs.

Caladrunan's blur seemed to study all of us. "They're couriers, Naga. They run messages for my Lady and Fat Nella. They get paid for information when they find out things for Nella, the pirate queen herself. I imagine that's where Orena unearthed the fancy steam-pressure gauges Isaon asked for."

"Does Isaon also work for Nella?" I asked mildly.

"But of course. The Devotees don't even make sure he gets fed down in the caves—at one point I thought him dead! Watching the cliff-root is important work."

"Nella thinks research on pipes gives practical benefits?"

"It certainly led our ancestors a long way," Isaon murmured, lifting his white head. "Research requires patrons. So do hungry refugees. You know Histories and ancient dialects as a Harper, don't you? Orena doesn't know this variant."

I peered at the scroll while a Upai held an oil lamp close. Caladrunan said, "Goddess help you if you overtire him, Isaon, he's not recovered," and departed.

I squinted hard at the markings on the slate Isaon held up before me, and I picked out words and characters while he wrote down what I told him in Tannese. When I had done what I

could, he thanked me absently and departed. Caladrunan returned, murmuring in awkward Upai about resting me; it angered
Orena. Jerking at the folds of her black goathair robes, she said
in rapid Upai, "Not the place *I'd* choose for a reunion, indeed
not, in this Tannese rock—and *you* sworn to serve the likes of
the Pale People! I should have died with the others of the clan
before I saw this day."

Distressed, Caladrunan said, "Really, this is too much—"

I stiffened with outrage: *I* had never profaned the dead thus.
Nor could Caladrunan, her Tannese host, follow her rudely rapid
speech. Hardly the behavior I expected! My pity for Orena
vanished in a flash. In Upai I murmured, "They make it hard for
the Lord of Tan to be our friend, Old One, difficult to uphold
trust. Do not make it harder."

She spun away, turned back again. "Can any Tannese ever be
a 'friend' to us? Whatever they tell us—and few of them at root
believe we do pray and feel and think—they always, *always* go
to their own advantage in the end. They back away hastily to
save themselves when they fear they have gone too far helping
us! Why, think you, do we distrust what they all say? When
have kindly blow-away wishes scattered like cattail-down ever
saved us?"

"The Lord of Tan is not like that."

"You are young," she said coldly and precisely, in the most
ancient mode of Empress, of priestess.

I looked up with hot burning power building like rage in my
head. In her own precise and ceremonial mode I said, *"That I
am not, and have never been."*

Orena snapped at me, "The last time I saw *you*, you were
messing diapers—so, *choose* the Tannese above us! All Upai
must have children; we have grown so few with wild ones like
you, gone mad just like your father's kin. What good can you do
us *here* as Tokori, Warleader, one with a child's name still
because you lost all the kin who would rename you adult—I
certainly won't! Keep your child-name forever!"

That was too much.

"The last time I saw *you*," I retorted like a hot boy, without
thought or hesitation, "you had my mother in tears! And you
were never with my mother again, not once! before my mother
died. When the Osa came."

Her voice dissolved into spirit rage and roars of lightning and
red sparkles in my head. She and I yelled furiously at one

another, hammering kin-curses like sword blows. The walls rang with slashes of Upai.

I snarled, "I watched her die!"

Her eyes flinched. "You could not possibly recall—"

I looked deep into the rock. "There are things I remember," I said very softly. "I have a name."

"Such a young man to claim the burden of my clan's name. Indeed, your accent *stinks* of the border and of Marshman Nandos."

I felt a painful tide of heat flow into my ears. The other women stared, not averting their gaze as Tannese would have; I had not taken such scrutiny for a long time. No Upai raider had told me that I sounded to them like a border outlaw; no one had dared. But it explained Orena's instant mistrust of my claim to be her kin. I said, as evenly as I could, "If you examine the tattoos you gave me when I was a child—"

"I don't think of examining your body like fool Tannese," she rasped. "What do nicks and marking prove, these days?"

I blinked and looked at the others. None of the blurry forms moved. "So being of the People is not proof against traitors? I had not heard that before."

"Now you have." She narrowed her eyes, coming close to peer at me. "And yet there is something different with you. Are you one of us? Or are you something else . . . a thing risen like a haunt from what should never have happened—that should have stayed dead when the rest of them died? I hear strange things of you, child. Indeed, I see strange things now. I was glad when I learned of the Warleader Tokori Efresa, when I discovered his past was indeed my own blood's past—glad that my line had not died out. It gave me hope for children, for the Upai royal line—until I learned the truth of that crazy Tokori."

A vague fluting of tones rose among the women, and a tentative, hesitant stranger's voice said, "But, Orena, we can't yet feed the children we already have—I can't teach any to read runes if they're all starving—"

Orena gritted, "Your clan—you scared widow—has need!"

I saw Caladrunan move, a blur of blue robes; the words were awkward Upai. "That's enough shouting. Any more and you'll all be taken out and dumped in a camp. If this widow-woman can read, she should teach, not breed more mouths you can't feed. Does she need help for a school?"

The timid shadow shrank back in abrupt, fluting alarm.

"Coward!" Orena snarled, eyes glittering black. "*You* start a Tannese school under this great Tokori, you can both bleed white with Tannese blood. Oh, we can use a white-blood Upai here, none of *us* could stand it so long." Then, with soft, trenchant contempt, she added, "Pity it had to be my once-grandson."

I felt another flush heat my ears. They thought I had humbled myself to get them aid, and though they needed it, Orena loathed me for that. I drew in a deep breath. "My task was laid on me by Reti—the People trusted him. Just as he did, I fight the invader that drove us here, dig it at the root."

Orena's mouth smiled, but not her eyes. "The burning enemy—the Osa—you dare much, child. Stronger men than you struck that viper, and were killed by it. That trainer, Reti, did not choose idiots to make into Satis—do not fall into Tannese ways and risk our entire line, not for these blind fools." Her hand waved contemptuously about the walls.

The blur that was Caladrunan now looked very angry indeed.

I said, "How far can we run, Old One? We stand above the sea now. Can you fly over it?"

Her eyes met mine unblinkingly. "The ancients could."

"We stand in Tan," I said quietly. A cold ringing seemed to infuse my words, a belling echo in the rock. "*Stand or die.*" And I inclined my head as to an equal, in dreamlike gravity.

She slanted a glance at me, at the others—as if to say, *you see how strange he is, look at him, this child-named man.*

Caladrunan coughed and tapped my wrist, sign I must translate precisely for him. "I'll make the widow-woman an interpreter between your camp children and some good teachers, so your children learn all the Tannese they need. These are Devotee teachers of an Order I trust; you needn't worry. With the teachers' help, this widow-woman could run a Devotee service Order; much easier to give aid. I know, Naga, you'll yell about feeding the children first. I can justify food to the Council. But someone we all trust must run the service Order to receive it—"

I heard a soft murmur that sounded tired, confused, and then, slowly grateful. Orena snorted in disgust. "The widow says she will begin a service Order for *all* refugees—Upai or not—Tall Man, because your words are so fair and generous." Another snort.

Caladrunan reached out and tapped my harpcase, hugged under my left arm. "The service Order will get its supplies from a noblewomen's group that my Lady Wife organized to help Tannese refugees. With that link, I'll hear more directly how you're doing, and the Order will protect you better from other Devotee harassment. Let's call it 'Women of the Harp.' "

" 'Women of the Harp,' " I muttered.

"We'll name it that because *you* and your nasty temper, Harper, got me to think of it!"

But the Upai eyes were still wary of me—except Orena, who watched me aloofly: The look of a woman who made demands. For a moment my heritage flew up hard in my face, and choked me. The totems began singing again in my ears.

Caladrunan said then, "*Kigadi*. Brother-self."

Insidious voices muttered, "He was never one of us." Over the rising rasp and wail of the wind, "*Kigadi?* What right has he to that word!"

"No more!" I screamed.

Caladrunan's face was the most astonished of all in the mass of flames and faces and shocked voices, shouts, torchlight. I fled away from their demands into the dark inside me, and it all faded to silence. It seemed wiser. If any spirits dream-danced there, none spoke.


" 'The Lady of Fortress' women, come to serve her here, Liege." I woke with a start and blinked, disoriented, across bedfurs: Rafai's burly form had appeared in the opening chamber door.

A woman's voice snapped, "The servants stay outside there." By the time my eyes focused adequately, I was squinting up at a Tannese noblewoman. Immediately after my fall, I had seen just such a woman with Keth: long pale hair braided into immense coronets topping her silk-robed height, the veil, the gems, a scent of violets. Yet something had been different . . . perhaps the blurring, the head-blow sparkles, had distorted my sight.

Capilla, Lady of Fortress and Caladrunan's Lady Wife, sat down then with her back to a brazier, staring at me unblinkingly. She did not look so grand as Keth's woman had. She drank from a goblet of wine; her veil was simply a gemmed circlet holding a plain gauze, which was thrown away back upon her dressed cone of hair. The hair was less tidy than usual, the blond locks and ringlets spilling loosely down her back.

But stately as ever she stared at me with strong, calm eyes so

pitilessly wide open that all the bright stone-blue color had gone
oddly neutral by firelight. I stifled a sharp desire to pull furs over
my bare neck. Her fingers twitched on her goblet, languidly
straightened a crease in her fashionable robe; she only looked
that way after Caladrunan had lavished special attentions on her.
It was never enough. Her eyes flicked to Caladrunan, sitting on
the bed next to me, and dismissed him with the contempt of old
demands unmet, failed, given up.

I felt dully cold. I knew, with a sick sense of humiliation, that
after their latest rapprochement she'd come here grimly to watch
me surfacing from unconsciousness. I turned my face away from
her. Which was a mistake. I lay still, riding it out.

She said, "I've never seen anything like these fits."

"Neither have I, Lady. Did your searches among the Archives
unearth anything? No? A pity. I never understand a thing from
the Devotees. It'd be nice to know what causes it."

"Damage to the brain, likely," she said calmly. "The visions
must be wild distortions of facts you've collected and half-
forgotten. No, it's brain injury."

I closed my eyes.

"In the old days they would have skinned you for a witch."
Her voice had no obvious disdain or contempt to it, only the
distant precision of a locksmith intent on his work. Or perhaps
the tones of the old scholar Isaon, busy with his tangled Altar
gas lines—an intellectual interest, as if I were a strange insect.

Another, lighter woman's voice said crisply, "I hardly think
Naga fits that fool superstition—"

Capilla never turned her head. "He deserves the label better
than any of the recorded cases I researched to understand his
condition. 'Fool' is correct—odd old folk who were harmless,
most of them. And Naga is not harmless. Why do you depart
from your day's schedule, Lady Girdeth?"

Venom replied to venom. "Aside from concern for my friend
Naga, *I* assumed our Liege, my brother, called me here because
he meant me to be an advocate for a man injured in our service." A figure brushed rudely past the Lady's chair, flung aside
bed curtains in a flurry of blue silk robes. Yanking off her veil,
Caladrunan's sister Girdeth plumped herself down on the bed
beside her brother and me, and peered over cheerfully. "You
look horrible, Naga."

I wished they would stop talking about me. Change the subject. Weather, dogs, parties—anything. But no, Capilla's calm

naked face kept staring dispassionately at me. If she meant to prove how very civilized she could be, she was succeeding.

*I hate her,* I thought, and felt only dismal.

Girdeth waved. "Give me that goblet of water, would you, brother dear? Thank you." She sifted a parchment packet of powder into steaming water, stirred it with a wooden spoon. I made a face, which made her laugh. "I brought you some willow powder straight from the women's quarters Apothecary. This will taste as horrible as you look, so it'll work."

"Do you know," I said rhetorically from somewhere down in the gravel of my most bass voice, "how tired I am of the Tannese love for overstressing a word unable to carry the weight? Great Hall, Great Altar, Great Oath, Lady this and Lord Badbreath's Quarters that— Don't you people know any *other* flaming words?"

Capilla rose. "I see no need for my presence." She lifted her chin, staring down at me. Her nose looked longer. "Drink the willow extract."

I stared back, unmoved. They all knew I took no orders from anyone without Caladrunan's consent—but, actually, I didn't lift my head because I'd be instantly sick.

Caladrunan understood the problem then. He reached forward, sliding his hands under my head, lifting me. Between my teeth I grunted, "Thank you." His hand lifted the goblet, and I drank. After he let me down I lay willing the red and white spots away, trying to make their faces come into focus. When I could see them, their faces had changed expression. Girdeth was no longer smiling. Caladrunan took Capilla aside in a rustle of silks, saying, "I wish you hadn't stayed. Shaming him like this is cruel of you."

"Is it?" She sounded genuinely surprised. Then she went on in those scholar's tones, "Granted that he may have seizures if you are away, I need to know what to command when panicked soldiers run to me for orders about him. And he *must* finish his tasks here as you promised me."

Caladrunan adjusted a lamp wick, squinting at the flame. "Nobody can make Fortress' secret ways as secure as you'd like."

The Lady fluttered one gloved hand. "So much depends on the guards, on the commander's acumen. Bind him on his honor to finish securing the ways, and I will be satisfied. As long as

I'm content with Naga's performance, our voting friends in the silk- and iron-trading clans will be, also.''

"Agreed," he said flatly, as if it were a market deal. My throat went tight: He did not lightly give up my service. Demanding a battered Sati's labor in exchange for forcing her iron-trading kin to cooperate was reasonable from her side—humiliating from mine: unfit for field command but good enough for garrison duty. Odd, how often contacts with her meant pain. Gossip said that she reserved her best punishments for me since I usurped her traditional place in Caladrunan's closest counsels. That she did not care for his company, and that I enjoyed it, was irrelevant. Appearances were all to her. Or so gossip said.

Looking at her now, I wondered if court gossip missed most of the Lady's subtleties. She ruled court life. Her personal dislike of me could rest on a simple, stark judgment that I was politically dangerous to her husband-ally. For all her stiff, conservative mien, no woman was less like a flighty, silly, traditional Tannese female than the reigning Lady of Fortress.

She moved closer. From memory I heard again the hateful veiled woman laughing in the street. I drew up my lips, hissing. Flames danced in my head. Relivings of flame. She backed away. In a milder tone she said, "Rest and time are the only cures for a cracked head— I researched such injuries among the Devotee Archives when I heard of his accident.''

Caladrunan said, "Do you know the examination Pergo gives?"

Girdeth lifted her chin. "*I* do. I read about it today."

He glanced over at her. "That gives you little experience."

She nodded at me. "Either you or myself, brother, can touch Naga if he chooses. I think few others, today."

His jaw muscles leaped in anger. "Somebody *did* touch him." And he nodded permission to the two women.

The Lady drew from her robes a small wax candle, lit it. I'd rarely seen herbalists' tools before, and I didn't like the look of it now. She swung the candle about, with a rustle of her robes, and handed it curtly to Girdeth. As she stepped aside, a whiff of wood hyacinth followed her movements. Girdeth had the better sense to approach slowly. She knelt beside the bed, put up her empty hand to my face, and cupped her fingers lightly about my jaw to steady it. She smelled of soap and girl and honey powder. "Look straight ahead, please. Don't close your eyes." She held the lit candle before my left eye. "Be very still, it's important."

I swallowed. "Don't like it," I admitted.

"I know," she murmured. She flicked the candle away, brought it close again, flicked it away from each eye, peering at the swollen one. Her gaze was close and intent, a slight frown marking her pale brows. The Lady of Fortress leaned close behind Girdeth, narrowing her brows in sudden interest. I clenched my hands into the furs. But Girdeth was skilled enough. "You saw it, Lady?"

Capilla inclined her head. "My Lord Husband, the Sati's head blow causes his pupils to open and close unevenly, one remains wider than the other. Not a thing can I do, nor any herbalist. If the Goddess grants, it will heal. If he doesn't injure it again before it is grown sound. Bed rest is the Archive wisdom. Falling as he went unconscious . . ." She shrugged. "The damage was compounded by how he was carried after."

Girdeth looked up. "Surely it wouldn't have hurt him that much, trained as he was to fall correctly. He was struck."

Caladrunan pulled irritably at his beard, rested his palms flat on his thighs. Briefly he rubbed his hands up and down his silk-robed legs. "Naga said that a woman who looked like you, my Lady Wife, was with Keth Adcrag. And she knocked Naga's head."

The Lady's hand seemed to hang in midair. Then she linked her fingers over her silken waist garter. "I see."

"You heard a rumor of that, my Lady Wife," he persisted. "So you sent Naga food as a public proof of trust, a peace offering."

She stared at me. "From an innocent tray of food, you—"

"Oh, he warned me of it long before you sent him your note and food," Caladrunan murmured. "Someone heard it. And you have your spies."

"Stalemate, as usual," Girdeth said in disgust, rising. "Well, none of this helps figure out what happened."

I opened one hand sharply. "Wait. It might. Lady Capilla—you aren't wearing the scent of violets."

She put up her chin indignantly.

Girdeth chuckled. "Her supply of that scent ran out two moons ago, which is longer than most of us had. This scent is—"

I waved one hand. "Wood hyacinth, yes. That other woman . . . could anyone have stolen some scent from you, when you had the perfume of violets?"

Their eyes glittered. "You think someone dressed like Capilla to implicate her.'' Girdeth jabbed out a pointing finger at her sister-in-law. ''That Crag bitch you threw out.''

The Lady said, ''Possibly. I dismissed a Cragwoman for poor conduct. She looked very like me, even caused one incident which I understand you yourself held against me, Sati. She made endless trouble and thought she would never get caught.''

''Turned her out in the street without a shot of silk on her!'' Girdeth agreed with relish. ''Oldfield fled into exile last fall and left her patronless. That one had a temper! It's been boringly peaceful without her.''

The Lady threw the girl an irritated look. I'd never seen Tannese noblewomen talk unveiled before; it was enlightening. Capilla said with freezing dignity, ''It is possible the Cragwoman found a new patron down in town; she had nothing when she left, certainly no gems! She will rue the whim that made her try such a coward's revenge. This impersonation is a direct attack on me, not your pitiable self, Sati. *You* were simply the tool.''

I squinted harder, studying her curiously rigid face. She seemed in the habit of controlling her expression strictly, in or out of veil. ''Did the woman stay as local agent for Oldfield?''

Capilla straightened to her full height. ''How would I know? *I* have never stooped to subverting my husband's officers nor endangering his safety with plots to kill his bodyguards. This imposter shall suffer when I find her hiding place.''

Girdeth said, ''But why did they knock him about? It can't be just an attack on you, Lady, though that angle's most ingenious.''

Caladrunan's face turned to me. I knew very well he'd put an interesting chameleon he called the spymaster to such a task, not me. He probably already had, with reports back in a half-day; but perhaps he felt his Lady Wife or his sister could let slip to wrong ears the fact of such remarkable speed. He said, ''So you can't do anything with simples for Naga?''

The Lady said, ''Oh, we could compound cupflower drug for him, but that addicts unto a bad death. Our Liege, my husband, make this man rest in bed, or he may hurt himself again. If that happens, he might die of it without an outer mark on him.''

Caladrunan's brows lifted. Girdeth nodded.

I said, wondering, ''I thought you hated me, Lady.''

Her eyes were proud and cold. ''*Your* idea, Sati, not mine. We must unite strengths—as my Liege often says, we have a war upon us. None of us benefits from this attack, only our enemies.''

I whispered, ''But if I can no longer guard our Liege?''

She tossed her veil in place with a flick of one hand. "That is undoubtedly what the imposter planned—which is enough to make me wish you healthy, Harper. That woman seems not to have allowed enough for your hard head or your stubbornness. But I know better: Cautious exercising in ten days, no sooner!"

"Yes, my Liege," I said obediently to Caladrunan's reinforcing gesture. Staring at the overhead stone arches and joists, I said hoarsely, "Who commands me, my Liege, and who obeys, if I stay here?"

No one had mentioned Keth Adcrag's involvement with the woman imposter. That was too dangerous a connection to speak of, since Keth was one of Capilla's fashionable court friends. Keth was a much-befriended man because he happened to be a key voting bloc; he was as close to dictator of Crag as that unstable land was likely to come with his old rival Oldfield still in exile—and more powerful for it than any other single noble. The Lord of Tan knew my opinion of Keth and what he risked when he used Keth's political power and recruitments to strengthen his own forces.

Caladrunan shifted, making a swift rustle. But his voice said calmly, "If I decide that you secure Fortress in my absence, you command the Household as my armed presence. The best economy sets you to Girdeth's personal defense in any violence."

Capilla snapped, "And that only because *I* have a trusted guard corps I chose myself, but Girdeth does not. She may need such defenses, as careless as she goes." The Lady turned and parted the curtains and sailed out, slamming the bedchamber door with rather more force than necessary. I winced.

Girdeth looked at me, trailing her fingers idly over the furs. "Well, brother, it seems your Lady Wife does not lack honor in this, much as she despises our Sati: She didn't do it. That's a nasty set of rope burns, Naga. Best wash them."

Caladrunan examined the raw marks on my wrist. Head bent, he murmured, "*Try*, Girdeth, not to offend her more than necessary. She can make life difficult for a lot of other people."

"Including *you*, of course," Girdeth said sweetly. She grinned at me, flounced a brief salute at her brother royal, and went off waving her veil. At the door, she turned. "It was fun, Drin—the two of them are oven and ice!" She ducked out in a flurry of giggles, while Caladrunan growled after her.

"She knows flamed well Capilla has not damaged her honor in this." He snorted. "I think it's impossible for my Lady to act against her honor." He glanced at my wrist and sighed, brushed stray hair from my forehead. His weight lifted from the bed; I felt his hands pull furs close over me. "Sleep, my hawk. Heal."

Caladrunan went quietly to his slate table, where stacks of work awaited him. He lit the rack of oil lamps, picked up writing chalk, and lifted a leather slate-cover. I lay watching him, squinting hard, with my hands on my scaddas. Lamplight darted over his face, while the dimmer light from the hearth glimmered vague sparks on silver embroideries in his robes. Shadow shapes wriggled all around him.

I never thought Capilla lacked honor; I thought she lacked the deep inner fires of her Lord—the passion that brought warmth, humor, and kindness to his rulership. Perhaps she kept unlady-like feelings where no one expected to find them and caged her soul in thickets of ice to protect it. Whatever honor she might give him, she never let *anyone* look past those glacier bastions— poor, rigid woman, afraid of toppling from her narrow noble perch. Then I thought, yet don't we all balance as carefully?

I blinked, but sharp sight was too hard to maintain, and my eyelids relaxed. Caladrunan had rested his forehead in his hand, reading; he snorted to himself as he wrote a reply. Imperceptibly my eyes closed on the golden blaze as he moved, and my fingers relaxed on my snakeskin scadda hilts, and I slept.

# CHAPTER

# = 3 =

"WHAT—?" I said, lifting my head. Dreams of screaming mingled oddly with the reality of the quiet chamber air.

Caladrunan blinked, frowned, his nose a handspan from mine. He was warmly tangled in furs, eyes bleary. "I didn't hear—"

"*Flames!*" I grabbed him, snuffed the only lamp, and rolled us both in one great untidy heave out of bed, flapping the bed curtains and tumbling furs into a heap behind us on the bedstraps. We fell with a thud behind his black working chair. Through the communicating wall's ear-trumpets we both heard steps running along the main corridor, rising fast toward the guardroom just outside. I lifted my head: The panic door to the secret tunnelway was too far away for safety. A dog barked once—a single cry, ending in a short high screech. A voice made a sharp trumpet-carried gasp and screamed, piercing incoherent sound, as instantly cut short by silence . . . then I heard just a babble of distant, confused cries.

"*No,*" I hissed as Caladrunan squirmed and almost reached up for my scaddas, left beside the bed. I pulled him down, covered his head with my shoulder. I wished I'd enforced more viciously my rule that Caladrunan's brace of dogs *stay* with him—nervous guards were too quick to use them outside to investigate noises.

The door shattered and vanished in a glare like noon sun, even the door bars exploded in sprays of wood. Deafness boomed in the stone chamber. Splinters shot past our shielding chairs. Like arrows, shards of wood shattered brass lamps, skewered cabinet veneers, and shredded the bed curtains. They had used a petard,

32

a bomb five times the power of the hand-bombs we called kukkie-grenades. The blast knocked all sense from my head; red twirling figures became dancing totemic animals spinning under my eyelids.

My ears roared. I held my head rigid, fighting tears of pain. Acrid dust stung soft linings. I still held my arms protectively over Caladrunan's face. We cringed together at another explosion that shuddered our bones and rocked the shielding chair heavily onto my spine. The chair's ponderous weight jolted oddly—slowed—halted in crushing me and my old injuries, and tumbled away to rock back upon its legs. Dust rolled. Thrown-up unidentifiable bits pattered on our heads.

I thought all the pain meant my hearing had gone, until I heard past it the distinctive scrape of boots on stone. And screaming, outside. I looked slowly up: A long shred of door bar protruded like a ragged sword through the chair's split back. A matching segment still vibrated, driven rigidly into matting and stone grout, a bare handspan away from my ribs. That shard had stopped the chair smashing my ribs during the second blast.

"Gone," a thick Marsh accent snarled in Tannese.

A Crag-accented voice snapped, "*There,* that hump—the bed shifted a bit, they're still here—damn this dark, find a torch." A crossbow racheted, string thwacked; wood thudded behind us.

"Waste of a good shaft," another Marsh voice grunted. "*I'm* not carrying a torch, not with your reload powder on me. They're gone, secret passages. We made enough noise!"

Two different Marshmen, I thought, and a Cragman. Odd. My hand scooped up a fallen necklace bead amidst the blown dust: coarse heavy jade strewn by Girdeth. Had to be—Capilla was too tidy to wear such jade, much less lose it. Caladrunan gripped my other wrist with such furious intensity I couldn't move. I tapped his hand: *let go.* When an alien metallic click echoed in the chamber, I felt his body flinch silently against mine, uncontrollable physical flinch. Then we both hunched, holding our heads. A shred of curtain plucked free and flew across the bed.

The sound of the gun hit.

My skullbones seemed to thin out and vibrate and then to shimmy unevenly like a bathing room soap bubble. In a blizzard, my one experience with a Tannese ice storm, frozen bark had exploded from trees in deafening reports just as loud and sharp and echoing, while wind hurled glass-shrapnel sleet and screamed on helmets with all the burning laughter of a frost-witch.

Then hearing, and pain, returned. Single-shot Sharinen guns, probably stolen—two guns to each man, make sure of us, I thought, straining to hear clearly. There was no pattering debris to fear from a Sharinen small-gun, only death when the soft lead bullet splattered a body. Hard as I strained, my hearing faded in and out with each heartbeat. Through waterfalls of roar and surges of blood tides, I made out mechanical noises punctuated by clickings.

Three identical explosions followed, slow with rustling and curses at the failed click of parts. A jolt vibrated the chair. One bullet ricocheted, whining from stone, and someone yelped. A bed pennon crumpled, dropping in veils of curtain gauze and explosion dust; a bedpost shattered. Caladrunan's ribs were absolutely taut-still against mine; but then, I wasn't breathing much myself.

"That's it for mine," a Marshman shouted, faint through the deaf-roar in my ears. He must be equally deafened. "Got them with the first kukkie-bomb. Ricochet went through that chair—nobody alive in here. Get out *now* and reload later. We got to go; garrison'll be up." Caladrunan's grip eased on my wrist. I drew in a breath and picked up a second heavy bead from the mat fibers.

"*Search!*" the Cragman shouted over metallic grating of parts.

"Scaddaman left his blades here," the other Marshman shouted back, going around the far side of the bed. "No blood. Furs are warm yet. You big, brave Cragman, used up shot on nobody! Better use big messy kukkie-bombs to save you if guard-watches come!" Marsh contempt, that, too subtle for any Cragman to read past so thick an accent. He shifted rent gauze and silk about, peering.

I tensed. When the curtains were drawn aside to reveal the man, I'd rise and . . . but it didn't happen. I waited, listening. Boots rounded the bed, approached us. Caladrunan's arm slipped on a mat with a rustle of straw. The boots stopped. Fittings clinked.

As Caladrunan and I stared upward, a sword extended stealthily across the gap between bed and chairback. The edge almost brushed my bare shoulder. Tilting down, the tip poked the chair, and as slowly withdrew to some new target. I looked down at Caladrunan. In the dim light I pointed at the dust-floured space beneath the heavy bed. He nodded very slightly. I gathered myself, gripping my bare toes into the floor mats for traction.

The Marshman growled, "*Gone*. All trouble to nothing gained."

Crag rasp: "Had it of the guard they were here. Search!"

"Place is too full of holes," the first Marshman yelled. "They gone to tunnelways by now. We did what the master said, it does not work. Garrison coming—we get out before the guards."

"They'll get us in the back; you don't *know* this Sati," the Cragman shrilled hysterically. "Search, flame you!"

I smiled in my hiding place. I did have a reputation.

"So, shoot shadows. *We're* leaving." Two sets of soft Marshman boots slurred on stone.

Odd, I thought, two Marshmen agreeing like this on anything. Odder yet that a Cragman was teamed with them for a delicate job.

I judged the footsteps. I tapped Caladrunan's arm, rose up, and threw both jade beads with all my force. In the same throwing motion I went down on my shoulder and rolled aside behind a scroll cabinet. The echoing report this time was single and slow, briefly obliterating screams. Loud panicky Cragman swearing covered the screams and was covered by a sixth wild shot. Now he *must* reload his two guns to shoot— A new sound startled me.

"OoooOoo . . . ." Hollow, echoing, eerily directionless moans.

Flame it, Caladrunan, I thought irritably, you've *no* right to risk silly stuff. I squinted around the cabinet as the Cragman was distracted, and drew back with a clear sight of the enemy. One Marshman wallowed in pain on the mats, screaming with a bead-burst eye; the other, hit on the temple by my second bead, had stumbled and fallen straight backward onto a wood shard that impaled a scroll cabinet. The free end impaled him as well.

I reached for my next weapon. My hand extended into stronger light: I moved in frozen stages, grasped the base of a spare oil lamp, and drew it to me in a single smooth shift into the shadows.

"What? What?" The Cragman turned, high boots thudding. I heard him work a gun sloppily. Metal parts clicked. He fumbled for something in a pouch, undoubtedly his precious kukkie-bombs. Another big bomb would clear the chamber. My hands moved over the lamp, found the clay wick-pellet with a hole which held the wick at proper trim. I removed the wick from the pellet, put the lamp pot gently on the floor, and blessed the quiet of naked skin.

"Get up," the Crag accented voice snapped at the wounded

Marshman. His accent was colder, less panicked. I heard a
ratcheting noise: probably the crossbow he'd used so well on
guards outside. "Get, lump!"

I dared look around the corner. *Clack*-twang-twang, ritch-
ratch, twang-*ratch*, twang-scratch-*twang!* I whipped back and
cringed as splinters peppered my shoulder. Loud chunkings of
wood on wood shuddered my shield. Repeating crossbow, too, I
thought sourly. The best equipment for *our* assassins! Perhaps
one of those noises had been a kukkie-grenade dud, but getting
more duds was too wild a hope. Given enough time, too, he'd
retrieve and reload all those scattered guns. I looked up the tall
back of the cabinet.

I'd done this before at leisure, as a precaution. I grasped the
thick decorative wood scrolling, gripping the clay wick-pellet
between my teeth, and I climbed rapidly in shadow, toes grabbing, up the cabinet back. My body moved as silently as training
and my imperfect ears could enforce. The Cragman wasted a
crossbow bolt on a fallen chair. Then I heard him approach in a
slow scrunch-crunch of straw mats.

The cabinet rocked very slightly under my weight. For a
moment I clung there dizzily, locking my teeth on the pellet. I
reached the cabinet top, looked over, and climbed swiftly onto
the narrow top shelf. As I watched the Cragman below, my feet
stepped gingerly among explosion-tumbled piles of scrolls.

He rounded the cabinet's side without looking up. He fiddled
with something in his hand and his crossbow was hooked at the
back of his belt. He was not panicked now: He peered among
shadows and the dark recesses among the cabinets. Light flared
between his fingers. The ceramic bulb—a kukkie-bomb—rolled
to the foot of my own perch. The brilliant fuse flame twirled
once and sputtered, disappeared, before the Cragman had even
turned to run away. Dismayed, he took a step toward it. Another
step and he might see Caladrunan's tracks in the dust.

I turned stealthily above him and hurled my clay button at the
wounded man. The screams stopped.

The Cragman spun about.

It put him beautifully into position. I dropped on him, grabbed
his hair, and threw his weight into striking the cabinet as we
tumbled. Before he thrashed once, I had snapped his neck.

Unhooking the Cragman's crossbow and pouch, I rose from
the kill, dropped the emptied bow inside a cabinet, and padded
across the floor. The two remaining ceramic bulbs in his pouch

had cloth fuses sealed with wax. I sank to my belly, protectively shielding the grenade pouch against the heat of a coal brazier lit to fight drafts of cold air. Then I peered cautiously into the guardroom, my face at the base of the door pillar.

A Marshman outside swung about and glared into the doorway. He, too, wore pouches bulged with kukkie-grenades. He cradled an arm's-length metal tube. Long gun, that; more dangerous in a large guardroom than single-shot guns. "Get *out* of there, damn your red rockhead stubbornness," he hissed furiously into the air above my head. He squinted his eyes to peer into the dark with a curiously reptilian weaving of his head.

I snaked a hand to the brazier beside me, picked up a live red coal in my fingertips, and dropped it onto a kukkie-bomb's twisted cloth fuse in my pouch. My other hand hurled the pouch out at the gunman.

It made a nasty mess.

It deafened me longer this time. Things pattered on the mats, on my feet and calves. I lay quite still in the dark, which was good; I was at less risk when I heard a reaction to the explosion.

"Plan Three," said a new, laconic Marsh voice in the guardroom beyond my view, muffled through my damaged ears as if underwater. "They're in there—get backup and torches, black as a minepit in there." Faint bootsteps ran about. They were cautious; I didn't see them. Guards' bodies were strewn in the corridor outside, very few stirred. I saw neither Pitar nor Rafai. I had more hope that Rafai, off-duty, might bring up reinforcements.

*Time!*

We needed time. I grimaced. I knew what I faced now. A commoner's blunt ax haggling at a side of pork hit far more cleanly than Cragman swords. Stupid trade to specialize in, I thought, and shook my head clear of bad memories. I crossed the bedchamber, snatched up my scaddas, buckled my weaponbelt hastily over my nakedness, strapped on bracers and kneepads. I wondered when exactly it was I'd simply voided my guts like a scared hound, and never noticed. Everything smelled horrible. "Out," I hissed at the bed, and then whirled.

Rampaging like riot trumpets, a mob with torches raced up the guardroom outside: Marsh mouths open, all howling-set for individual glory—they all promptly jammed together in competition at the chamber door, heaving and shoving.

No way out *there*.

Caladrunan scrambled up, grabbed his sword Devour from its

bedpost sheath, and ran in a flurry of robes for the secret way.
The first ring-walls, absorbed by a growing Fortress, were built
with two dressed stone faces over a rubble coring; within those
walls the rubble had been picked away by conspirators tunneling
through the ages, building crazy rickraw bracings of scrap timber. Half the guard watch duties were to keep alert for signs of
fire.

He lifted the hidden latch, put up his foot to step in.

The Lord of Tan jerked back, and the panic-door swung wide.
Another torchlit mob screamed in the secret way. *This* mob
waved clubs and swords about the tunnel ladder—and likewise
wrestled one another furiously for the glory of getting in first.
Fireglow reflected on fox-red hair: Cragmen. Caladrunan slammed
the door shut, but the attackers' bodies slammed it open again.
Hands clawed out at him. Devour's tip swung up, smacking
away something that was lost in the confusion, and the Lord of
Tan backed away into a corner.

I ran in front of him. *Time,* I thought, fight for *time* to let the
other guards get here. Caladrunan was protected along two sides
by solid chamber walls, on another by the imperfect barrier of
his wrecked and splintered bed, and on the open side by me.
They'd have to come through *me,* and across the tangled bed, to
get him. Scanning the two mobs, I saw mostly clubs, as if their
leaders didn't allow them costly tools, and only two crossbows—
which four or five men had grabbed at, jostling one another's
grip and aims. Already they were fighting over the bows. A
wild, awful hope bloomed in my tight chest. *Go away,* I told it;
this was no time to get silly.

Any decent bowmen could take us in our corner, spit-spat,
like rats. Where were the inevitable Marsh archers, spitting our
reserve guard watches? If they had none, maybe we could . . .
no. I'd punish them horribly before I went down; asking for
anything better was absurd.

I gripped my scaddas in cold hands. For armor, I'd got leather
strapped on my forearms, my knees, and my belly. It wasn't
much. Deep in my chest, muscles were drawn up so hard it
overrode the other pains, and my mind kept trying to fold up my
entire self into nothing, and vanish. I greatly wished I knew
how. I never said I was a brave man.

Dark Marshmen fought viciously among themselves at the
main door, ignoring all else for the satisfaction of interclan
blooding among themselves. The Crag mob looked like a little

interracial blooding of former allies was next. I glanced swiftly
from one spreading lot to the other: One richer-looking Marshman
wore a green armband slapped with the black sigil of the exiled
Crag noble Oldfield. It seemed Oldfield had fled east and hired
rival Marsh clans just as competitive and unstable as any of his
old alliances had been.

"Marshman didn't take out the garrison at all," someone
muttered in Tannese with Crag accent. "Better if we came in by
ourselves from the start." So, with Marshmen rented by Cragmen
and Crag clansmen, we faced two warring Crag schisms, once-
allies fallen tonight to battle for open prizes. The two huge Crag
sea bass meant to eat the other upon our death—oh well, they'd
tried it all before. In the summer, Keth had maneuvered Oldfield
open to charges of treason, and hasty exile had been expedient
for the fat man. Whatever his joint plans and promises with
Keth, Oldfield never gave up old grudges.

The Crag mob heaved, craned fearful heads around, and parted
like water before a wedge of massive bodyguards. Keth Adcrag
stepped through the secret way. He smiled at us. "A fight,
Naga? You're bleeding."

I didn't glance down at *that* old trick. The Marshmen were
flowing forward again, avoiding the Crag end of the chamber. I
didn't let my eyes rest on Keth too long; I must watch them all.
The spreading Marsh mob looked as hostilely at the Cragmen as
at us. They could smell plunder, and the risk; shouts rumbled
among harsh olive Marsh faces as they surged past the dead
assassins on the chamber floor, and halted. The mobs eyed one
another. Caladrunan's feet shifted on mats in pitifully small
space behind me.

The cocking rasp of a crossbow did it. I hurled myself back,
twisting and falling in a protective sprawl across Caladrunan's
body as I took him down, or he pulled me down, or we both fell.
Something hot stung my left arm and knocked it wide, while
with my right arm I felt Caladrunan rolling with me. Gripping
both scaddas left-handedly, I scuffled along on my belly, and his
body gathered forcefully ahead of me, sweeping his sword ahead
of him. A dagger rent blue cloth past the gap of my bent knee
and jerked away before it opened Caladrunan's flesh. Cruel
gloved fingers slithered on my sweat, trying to grab in quarters
too close for swords. I slid free like a wet piglet, tumbled nearly
onto Devour's quillons. Caladrunan heaved free beyond me as
all the competing hands fought. We went under the bed together,

shoved among broken timbers, and scrambled underneath to the far side.

I peered out. In the narrow corner they were a thick shadowy confusion of clubs and knives and swords—so sure we were at the bottom of the heap that most of the chamber was actually empty. When the last of them joined the melee, we wriggled from under the twisted bedframe, Caladrunan dragging his sword along behind. He clove the hand off one clever man who reached far under the bed trying to grab my foot. As I scrambled free, I gutted a Marshman who jabbed across the shredded bed curtains at Caladrunan; something smacked across my back and left a line like a hot wire, and I stumbled forward. "Run," I gasped, snatching up rhythm again.

We darted out of the chamber in precise tandem and pounded down the long guardroom. I heard a shrill yell, muffled, in the chamber behind. Together, spurred by that yell, we pivoted sharply to one side into a dark meeting room. I scrambled after him behind the door and stood still.

As we both held strained breaths, running steps thudded the length of the guardroom, past, and away. I bent. At floor level I peered out; fights had spilled out in various directions.

*"Now."* We lunged across the guardroom into a storage chamber. Caladrunan pulled the door shut silently, rather a feat in itself. I felt about in the dark, whispered hastily improvised instructions. Panting, we pulled a heavy, footed chest away from the wall. I lifted the trapdoor beneath it, while he slid Devour into the back of his robe belt. Thumping the naked sword incautiously on the stone floor, he climbed downward; I followed more quietly, my scaddas in one hand. With the trapdoor propped barely open on Caladrunan's head, we grabbed the feet of the chest and pulled it in place across the trap to conceal the secret opening. It seemed to take a long time, straining together on the ladder in the darkness.

Finally I latched the trap against intruders from above and looked down into the old tunnel of the secret way. At the very bottom, at a muddy cross-passage, a torch burned—which should not have been there. We were standing inside a major Fortress wall, between its two dressed stone faces; its core rubble was dammed back by old mine struts and wooden braces, leaving a bore barely wide enough for us to stand together on the ladder. I touched Caladrunan in warning—new shadows jumped and flickered at the bottom.

At shouts, we flattened desperately against the dark rubble sides, tried to get thinner. Lights brightened in the cross-passage a hundred paces beneath our feet. Faces squinted up, holding up torches at our sweet darkness, and withdrew, shaking red hair. They went away along the passage. I heard thuddings, bangings, doors slamming, yelps of fury in Crag dialect. I tapped code on Caladrunan's arm, *forty paces down right danger noise.*

*Go,* he tapped back.

I went halfway down the ladder, scaddas in one hand, heart thudding as it had in the upper rooms. My sight spun nauseatingly now, worse than during the fighting. I fumbled in the dark past rubble and braces, found the round door plastered to look and feel like a rock face. I worked it open, and listened.

All quiet within. "Come," I whispered, and slid into the door feetfirst. I turned about slowly, dizzily, on the bare rubble floor of the inner hole and reached out blindly to help him. "Here," I said. He slid down noisily into my arms. I strained in the tight hole past his body, closed the door, and dropped the bolt. I touched my hand to his mouth to warn him to stay quiet, and I strained to listen at a chink in the door.

I froze at a rasp—a rasp of friction, then hissing, vicious and loud. Metal ratcheted in the hole with us. My reflexes seized at the sudden flare of yellow-green light. I twisted violently, and with blind accuracy spun Caladrunan underneath me. *Goddess!* totemic voices screamed in my head, but there was no lightning explosion, only the hiss of burning. The light was the same amplified greenish glare that took my mare down easily in the street, and me, too—a glare that here chased around the hole after our heads, sought our faces, crippling us. Then it was gone, and I heard a softer hiss of burning gas instead—Altar oil burning. My free hand fumbled at the door.

"That's of no use, Sati," an oddly urbane woman's voice said. She even sounded now like the Lady of Fortress. But she had stood with Keth over my body in the street: *cold* voice. "Such a pleasant surprise, your popping into my command post. Sharinen guns penetrate the strongest flesh. Won't you move aside, Sati, and save me killing you? *Your* sacrifice is not necessary."

"No." My fingers unlatched the door that I couldn't see. All tonight's guns had been stolen. Sharinen scientists and soldiers did not approve of rebellions, they had consistently favored our side rather than rebel Cragmen in arms negotiations. The ambassador for Sharin would be furious if he ever got true report on tonight's events—the Sharinen hanged thieves and gun smugglers as renegades.

"Sati, move aside or I shall shoot you. Relax. Cooperate." And she laughed. Talkative woman, with us pinned. "Afraid of a little word like *traitor*? For your dismissing my fiancé from the watches—for that bitch Capilla dismissing *me*—oh, we found *many* weak ones in your watches, so we take down your puissant lord, that great Lord of Tan who cowers under you like a draggled fur! His Lady Wife will come toppling down after and beg for pity."

I almost laughed: not Capilla! Not even standing on an execution mound to die, I knew that clearly: *never*. The cold blue-white glare of Altar gaslight kept blinding me. I bowed my head over Caladrunan's curly hair and wished fiercely there was more of me to spread around to shield him. If I had to die, why couldn't I save what I cared for! Whatever I decided to do, live or die, pinned under my weight he was helpless to stop me. That angered me.

Dismissing instead of arresting them: That old mercy of Caladrunan's could kill us now. But the woman had gotten back into Fortress with help. I began making chains of political guesses to support her presence—which felt exactly as if my boot thrust through a rotten log into grubworms. I snapped, "Such a brave lot, unable to fight in open Council or in a challenge-fight."

She purred, "One shot would end *you,* but Oldfield would be unhappy. It spoils the main event to lose such a prime treasure."

I felt my back crawl with revulsion. I knew what Oldfield wanted *me* for.

"But then, Oldfield isn't a very good patron. My other friend gave me a message to leave you." Her voice twisted into memorized language alien to her. It was Upai stripped of inflection and larded with strange hill slang: It was Osa, recited from a true source. Even Caladrunan stiffened on hearing it.

"Abomination, know your sacrilege-give-giving-gone sacred hidden things to outlanders just as your dog bastard family always used to do, know the hand of the godly shall strike-smash-kill-soul-dead you and all gone-gone." Two voices, above us in the dazzle, laughed eerily; two, not just her one voice.

In the blind glare something tapped my leg, hitting me at the extreme range of some tool. I said, "I won't move, you bog-spawned haggishead." I slitted my eyes into the dazzle. A vague blot perched behind it.

"Even," she said, "if I remind you we've tapped into the Goddess' Altar fires here, and for many days it has been mine to command? To store, to sell? To—burn with?" Hissing multiplied into many flares. "Quiet, Biree, good servant. Yes, those fools crashing about tonight know nothing of power. Show the Sati your power, Biree."

Something—whatever it was, it was ungodly hot—brushed against the sole of my left foot, scalded my heel, trying to drive me to shift off Caladrunan's body. He jerked under me. My leg muscles knotted, fighting it. *She can't shoot him through my body,* I thought, or she wouldn't try so hard to shift me.

"Well, Sati," her voice said lightly from somewhere in the blazing white glare overhead, retreating, "you'll regret it," steps ringing away hollowly as of boots climbing a metal ladder.

Fire lashed across my foot, and I went rigid against it.

Pounding shuddered the door of the hole from the other side. Tannese words came dimly through wood.

"Open up!"

I twisted my head, trying to ease my eyes. Did *everyone* know our boltholes?

Caladrunan's ribcage heaved. "Code thirteen!"

*Code thirteen,* an idiot voice jabbered in my head: *Fire!* Crew emergency, get bucket crews, get men, lots of them!

The woman shouted, "Biree, I give them into your hands—evil men, as I said!" A slapping of leather on metal retreated upward.

My eyes were filled with fading gold and purple spangles that resolved into three burner tubes alight with gas flares like those of Tan's Great Altar. The tubes poked out of the rubble braces overhead, high up, next to a metal ladder. These were burners for Altar crews' tests, and always snuffed afterward. Metal pipes snaked down a passageway at our feet.

Gas thieves, I thought suddenly. She'd been here, when we tumbled into her hole, to siphon oil from the Altar lines to storage barrels, then smuggle it out. All of it was recent, for this bolthole had been untouched at my last inspection. Blinded red wheels and suns still floated over my eyeballs; I blinked past glare, twisting to bring up my scaddas.

Robed in Devotee black, a skinny man crouched like a bat on

a wooden ledge above us, cradling a wine tun as good as any shield. I knew it didn't hold wine. He gave a soot-streaked white mad grin and upended the tun. I braced under the gush of oil. The tun's rim rolled agonizingly over my thigh, down my calf, and bounded away at our feet, shuddered timbers at impact, and blocked a passage for oil lines. In a grand gesture, the Devotee reached up for a lit burner, his robes splashing more oily fluid over us.

My right scadda whipped up and hurled the man into the wooden brace behind him. He made a horrid gasping noise, clawing out. My left scadda cut the fuel line of the burner above his hand, the flame guttered and died. Black fluid sprayed out of the thin metal tube, whipping about under pressure.

One moment I'd gained, while the spray spattered—the open flames would ignite that fan of oil, I had to throw scaddas at the remaining burners. Desperate to cut all the lines, I heaved about, lunged upward, grabbed, jerked my scaddas free. Biree's slack body tumbled into me, fell limp over my legs, impeded me, slopping over in a viscous pool of oil and blood. Caladrunan heaved under me. The tunnel door came open in his hand. The flames flared at an angle, and a line of white-hot roar raced along an oily wooden brace. Caladrunan grabbed me. The two of us, wrapped about each other like a Tannese pastry, shot out the hole into the dark tunnel.

Together we flailed, overbalanced, and nearly fell. He got to the ladder first; I clung onto his middle with one slippery arm and both legs, gasping. My scaddas dangled down his side against Devour, all of the weapons banging and clattering together. As he surged up the ladder my back thumped and scraped against braces and rubble, but I was too dazzle- and smoke-blinded to duck juts of rock. I yelled that we should've gone down, but fire-roar drowned my voice.

''Here!'' A bellow above us yelled for a water pump. Something hot exploded past my feet. My ears rang, my lungs sucked for air in the searing smoke. Even as Caladrunan surged upward away from the tongue of flame that had just been our escape door, the ladder ignited. It became a flare burning away beneath his scrambling feet. Flames chased us upward. Rafai's smudged face screamed at us, his arm stretching down.

Caladrunan braced his feet on the rubble, grabbed my slick body, and handed me up past himself like so much sacking.

Then I was tumbled aside, my scaddas clattering on stone, while
they pulled him out. Smoke billowed out of the hole. Soot-faced
men sloshed buckets of water at the ladder in great billows of
black steam. A soldier ran past me dragging a heavy cloth hose
with a brass nozzle. "Pump!" Rafai bellowed, and men braced
to hold the stream of water. Smoke choked the room.

Caladrunan sagged onto the overturned clothes chest, body
heaving for air. "Oil fire," he croaked. "Altar oil is pouring in
down there. Rafai, get sand. Pour sand into that bolthole, quench
it—find the other tunnelworks, get at it from all sides."

"Altar oil—! It's too dangerous here, my Liege, you're—"
Rafai handed off the hose. He held up a lamp brought him by a
soldier, peered at us. *"What . . . ?"*

Caladrunan gasped, "Never mind, you wouldn't believe me
anyway. If a fire starts through the walls—"

"Wood braces," I agreed hoarsely, ribs aching, and coughed.

"Naga's hurt—and you, my Liege?" Rafai said.

"Few hot spots, that's all." Caladrunan stood up, limped
away, and by the door breathed deeply of fresh air. Heavy gray
billows of smoke rolled about the storage room. He wiped at his
grimed face. He looked terribly old. "They burned Naga."

I sat up and held my head; my sight spun with red flickers. I
felt a shuddering start in my arms. So close, so close . . . I had
no idea how I'd run or fought in such pain. Stunning pain.
Caladrunan looked no better. Streaks of oil and soot and shit and
blood smutched his wretched bedrobe. His knees were bare
along with his singed feet. Devour hung unregarded, stuffed in
the side of a robe belt cut half-through. But he came at me with
startling speed, dragged me up.

Red haze crept into the edges of my sight. *"Mmnngg,"* I
gritted, staving off the thing I felt coming.

"Later," he said urgently, gripping my arms. "Hold it off!"

I nodded jerkily. He handed me bodily to someone. My feet
dangled. I blinked up at a grim young face: Ben, once my own
underofficer on the first guard watch. Caladrunan, stepping jerkily as if his footsoles hurt, asked about casualties, riot control
crews, fire crews. With one hand hustling us all out of the
storage room, urging his Liege Lord to a near trot, Rafai reported. Caladrunan clapped his shoulder in thanks and added
more work. "Get a mason crew to trace the new diggings where
they tapped the oil lines down there."

I spoke hoarsely, abruptly, each breath jolted by Ben's steps:

"Isaon needs a fire crew to help him switch the whole Altar complex to pumping water. At normal air-type shutoff, a smuggler's abandoned opening could let air bubbles through the partly emptied pipes—carry ignited fumes through the whole of Fortress. And if the Flames have gone out before Isaon's shutoff, let no man approach Her Altar with torches or lamps or any flame. The legend of Sitha Goddess' fumes of wrath is true. The Altar chamber will become a ball of Goddess-fire." How did I know that? I wondered blankly. Oh yes, Isaon's lectures about gas safety.

They stared at me. Then Caladrunan said, "You heard what he said, Rafai. Very good, Naga—first thing we'll do."

Rafai bobbed his head. "The assassins used Sharinen guns, my Liege, smuggled from Sharin. The Sharinen ambassador wants to help us, insisting he'll take the heads of the guilty, demanding to see you. *Very* angry."

Caladrunan said, "Good, I'll borrow some of his Lawservants, flamed good soldiers. I want their doctors up here, too—I'll talk to him about that. Rafai, I want Naga kept by me. He may go into a fit tonight, and I'd better be near him when it hits."

They propped me up in a chair while Caladrunan talked to the Sharinen ambassador. I was too dazed to be much surprised at the diplomat's size and bearing, or that of his Lawservants: huge men equal Caladrunan's size. All were of darker coloring than I myself, with tight curly hair in clouds and mats of black. As soldiers they were famous; mere Osa invasion had not stopped them. For that, for their scholarship on ancient skills, and for shrewd trading they were granted great respect in Tan. Nobody was surprised the Lord of Tan took time for soothing the Sharinen, worried that they might be accused of the attack and shamed by the renegade trade in guns. Their technologies and abilities were legend, and invaluable any aid they might offer us in war.

One of their doctors examined me in that meeting room. I stared blankly at his eyes, while he looked at mine by an odd mirror-reflected lamplight. Living so much among Tannese sea-colored eyes, I had grown unused to eyes as dark as my own. The room moved queasily at the edges of my vision.

The doctor muttered over what he found, and turned to cleaning, sewing, or covering burns, knife nicks, fingernail marks and rock rips. He probed the dent mark left by the rolling oil tun. "How did you walk on these feet?" he asked in melodic, accented Tannese. Pleasant, like the singing voices of Upai . . .

I blinked at him. "I don't know."

He told Ben sternly, "Concussion, chilled, clearly impaired hearing, and probably smoke damage in the lungs. Should be washed of this filth and put in bed. Going into shock."

"Not surprising!" Caladrunan snapped, striding up. "The ambassador has waived the usual Sharinen neutrality to compensate us for the offense of unsanctioned import guns. Would your crew of doctors look at other men also? I'd be grateful."

I lifted my eyes. Spacing breaths slowly, I said, "Hurt?"

He blinked. "I'm fine, aside from a scorched dignity!"

"Liar," I whispered, hunching down. I was growing cold; which probably meant that only now was I coming out of the deathly cold that held my bones since awakening this night.

Then I saw a relief guard salute briskly, snapping about clean robes. Against any pressing urgency of duty, the man had changed clothes. Now, of all times! For an instant the man's gaze flickered toward me. I straightened, staring. His face came back clearly to me: That man, in Marsh clothes, had jostled among the mob in the bedchamber, arguing with other Marshmen.

*But he was no Marshman.*

I dropped the blanket they'd wrapped me in. But for my few filthy leather straps snatched up as armor, I was naked; it rather got everybody's attention. I walked, feeling the burns on my feet, the rips, and the tearing pain in my head at an odd distance, not at all like part of my body.

Soldiers parted before me and melted away from him without a word. I lifted an aching arm and pointed. "Traitor."

# CHAPTER

# = 4 =

THE GUARD'S CLEAN FACE drained of color. He reached out abruptly
The door slammed shut under someone's white-knuckled hand.
Men came up behind and ringed us both. I said woodenly, "You
thought I would not remember you."

"Me? What—you mistake me for somebody—I did nothing—"

"Yes. Nothing at all." My hand came up, arched stiffly.
"*You* let them in. *You* guard a corridor beneath the secret way.
*You* let conspirators in there to dig, to smuggle away oil, while
could not go on regular rounds of inspection. I make one guess
on their plans: The Osa agents would light the wooden braces to
burn Fortress while we all slept helpless as sheep. Children
women, servants, all of us."

"No, I did nothing like—" His terror was plain.

Mutters rose behind me. The sounds of rage, of a riot murmuring to a start. Hands smacked, slapped at the man.

I glared round, hands flexed. My nails stood out in claws.
"*He's mine*," I whispered, and they drew back.

"I didn't know—" The man went to his knees, pleading with
me. "They made me, they made me—"

I felt no real interest or anger over his excuses. No surprise.
Just an odd, distant curiosity. "How?"

"They held gambling notes my uncle wrote—they took—on
the notes, they own my family's land, I had to do what they
said—" He babbled what he knew, delaying, repeating it over to
absolve himself, and found nothing to stave off the judgment in
all the eyes upon him. It was a very silent moment.

I said mechanically, "I failed you, my Liege, in not learning

48

of this before." Then I drove my knuckle into the bridge of the man's nose. A grotesquely intimate act, putting a hand into somebody's brain; I felt his bones move and his flesh flex sickeningly under my skin. The force of my blow lifted his body back and dropped him in a huddle ten paces away. Puddles made it clear he died instantly. They didn't always do that; just a final petulance to finish off an obstinate life. The leathery calluses over my knuckle were cut by his nasal bones, a trail of blood ran down my fingers. I closed my eyes.

Then I opened them. I said gently to the huddle of fallen robes, "Pride is never so big you can hide under it when the truth comes to look at you. Forgivable mistakes; if you told any of us of such gambling debts, we'd have helped you. But of such pride gone a *traitor* . . ." I closed my eyes. "I'd never suffer a traitor to live, if I struck from the valleys of the dead." Then I lifted my head and squinted at the other men slowly, consideringly. Idly I checked faces against my memory.

The other one broke and ran before my head turned toward him. Hands grabbed him. They wrestled him forward. He screamed as he was thrown down before me. "No, *please*, merciful Goddess—"

I looked at the other guards. I looked at dry grief in the eyes of bereaved friends; I looked at the cut and burned faces of the weary. He filled the silence with shrieks for pity, screamed out names, dates, places, in vain search for mercy. I looked at the sons of nobles, at the sons of farmers, and wondered about pity. Tannese pity.

The Lord of Tan spoke quietly, but his voice rose like clean water. "Naga, you have killed enough for my sake tonight. If you want him, he's yours. But you need not. Say your wish."

I looked at the traitor, at the soldiers who held him. His former friends looked as if a viper had crawled up from a drain near them; the others looked murderous. Distantly, very calmly, I said, "So, this one is yours." They took him away into the corridors, shrieking, until his cries faded with distance and we could no longer hear him.

I blinked. I must have swayed as if I was drunk. Caladrunan drew my fallen sooty blanket around me and steered me to a seat in an arrow loop, a long slit to fresh air. He sat down on the cold sandstone bench next to me while I took deep breaths of clean, cold night air. My breath rasped. "Just . . . tired."

"Rest then," he said easily. What I saw in his face was an

exhaustion equal my own, but he'd summoned the energy for an unworried tone. When I was steadier, he smiled, let go, and beckoned the soldiers waiting to report. I put my head on the stone wall and rested, floating in a cold, vaguely delusionary calm while they spoke in low tones. Rafai performed efficiently, though he was anxious until Pitar was carried up.

Pitar snapped, "Well, Rafai, get on with it! Doing fine so far." He was cross. Pitar had been stranded with a thigh wound in a corridor. After treatment by the big Sharinen doctor, Pitar sat rumpled and dirty beside me; I had never seen him so rumpled. He looked at me, and at Rafai's anxious hovering face, and whuffed his mustache irritably.

I lifted my face from the wall. "Rafai, someone should relieve the riot crews. Shift new fire crews to riot control if the danger from that tunnel fire is past," I rasped in a mode of polite suggestion—I wasn't in command. I felt very light-headed. Hard to think. "Are the oil lines switched to water?"

"Yes, Noble-born," Rafai said respectfully.

I lifted heavy eyelids. Finally I gave up the effort to modulate politely; he'd understand. "Secure safe quarters for Caladrunan's rest later. Check with Isaon on the stability of the gas pressures. Find the smugglers' fuel line tap—"

"They're trying," both men chorused. "Rest."

I put my head on the wall, closed my eyes. I kept seeing the tunnels and runways beneath the Great Altar—lots of places to search for that gas tap. Deep shuddering twitched my body.

Caladrunan rested one hand on my hair. He frowned. "It's easy to forget my Sati is barely twenty summers old."

I opened my mouth to refute but my jaw trembled.

Pitar sighed. "Aye, catching up with him, same as me." Caladrunan nodded and went back to the reports. Pitar waved Rafai's hovering face to go off and manage business. He said briskly, "Heard about your heroics."

My teeth danced. I stuffed my hands against my mouth to stop it; Goddess, I felt so cold. "Tell yours."

Pitar's pale blue eyes crinkled at the corners. "Not much to report, really. Headed up to relieve Rafai's watch. Somebody must have come up behind, knocked me on the head. Woke up in the middle of a blazing racket in the dark, gunmen and a bunch of Marsh bowmen—I had to figure out which side was whose. Luckily, found fallen gear, shot a few of those rat-eaters and their damned metal noisemakers before they punctured my leg. My boys finished the lot, aiming for the flare those toys give off—hard to gauge range in the dark. Of course they couldn't see us at all, just stray chance I got hit. I figured archers could pin your lot up in our Liege's chamber, so I told my boys to chase down every flamed last bog-spawn and *then* go up to reinforce your fellows. No use myself then, just slow them down. Seemed a long wait to me!'' He laughed, bristling his mustache.

"Sorry," I chattered, hugging the blanket closer. Caladrunan turned around from the Sharinen and looked at me in concern.

Pitar said, "Sorry for your battle-chatters or my wait?"

"Both," I gritted, but the shuddering grew worse.

"You need to warm up. That's the first thing, roast and toast. Here, Ben, carry him over by the fireplace. I want two more braziers and another blanket, warm it and wrap it around him. Quick now, get a pot of fresh mua boiling. Why isn't the doctor treating him, Ben? Because he's busy working on bootheads like yourself, that's why. Get to it!" Men ran under the crack of Pitar's voice. Caladrunan, in conversation with Sharinen Law-servants, nodded once to Pitar as if thanking him for the care. Pitar snapped, "Goddess, Naga, you're cold as a tomb. Haven't you got battle-chatters before?"

"Only saw it," I admitted. Even my feet were twitching.

"You a Sati, and never had the chatters before!" Pitar snorted. "Get those leather straps off him, wrap that blanket on him, get some hot mua in him. Careful of that head, now!" Then Pitar asked, "Think you'll have a fit, Naga?"

I stuttered grimly, "Don't know."

Calmly, swiftly, Ben's fingers unlatched the cold leather armor from my forearms and knees. "Can you move a little, Noble-born? I can't reach your belly band there."

Pitar said irritably, "*Flames,* run all over the Fortress naked, no wonder you're like a codfish on ice. You, Esgarin, go get clothes for him and for Liege. Do it yourself if you want it done right, but this flamed leg has me pinned down—Naga, you should go to bed. Come, we can—"

"No!" I said fiercely, gripping the blanket.

"At ease now, no one's *hauling* you away."

"No," I slurred warningly. "Stay."

"Goddess, he is far gone," Pitar remarked. "Flip that blanket on him. Nervy little bull. Get shot at, it's flaming enough to make me get a fit of the chatters, let alone these inbred lines.

Don't toss that blanket on him; he's a damned hero and a royal and don't you forget it!''

I blinked. Well, I was a Teot, the Upai Imperial House, which was nothing here in Tan. Pitar said he disliked natives. Always had, he said. If he'd ever before defended me as a blooded noble, I was the last man to know. I'd heard plenty of abuse about flamed slumgutter black-haired native slatterns, slovenly thieves, and dirty mare-mop refugee children. Pitar, defending *me*! Dumbly I endured the jostling of being rewrapped. Flicker of red darted at the back of my eyes.

Caladrunan put his hands on his hips. ''Pitar, did I hear something on royals and inbreeding?''

Pitar grunted, ''Not stupid, am I? Sati must be bred to it. Don't know who else could pull live bodies through that mess in your bedchamber. Look at him! Nervy as a bull getting a yedda lion's scent, keeps trying to follow you. Flames, my Liege, can you make him calm down?''

Caladrunan said, ''But he was calm all through the fighting—''

I lifted my eyes to his and turned away again, shamed. The blanket rippled; I knew I hardly looked like a man who could walk coolly through any attack. Caladrunan bent, gripped my elbows. ''Naga, I have to attend to some things, but I want you to stay here, talk to Pitar.''

''No,'' I said, struggling to push aside the clumsy blanket. ''No—'' Red began to infuse my vision. ''—must guard—'' My face twisted as I fought it. ''Won't let it happen.'' My teeth clenched. ''*No*. I—no fit—'' The red became flames, firelight flickering over Caladrunan's worried face. Then his face began to melt and flow. ''Won't,'' I gritted, squeezing my eyes tight shut. Then I blinked, and tears flowed down my cheeks, and his face settled like a little puddle into its familiar patterns. Behind him, other men were staring at me. Their eyes followed a tear as it ran down my face and dropped onto the blanket at my chin. Two of them made witch-warding signs.

Caladrunan asked, ''Naga? *What?* Tell me what you see.''

Red surged at the back of my eyeballs. ''*Nnng*,'' I gritted. My nails lifted out and my fingers curled backward. Rafai's eyes, looking at my hands, went round and horrified. I was not able to tell him it was a perfectly normal ability for any Harper to flex back his fingers so far. Flames surged over my sight.

''*Nnng*,'' I growled in my throat. Red dancing figures twirled across my gaze as if visions strove to speak symbols to me.

through my blurred eyes. I struggled through the red haze. Something clicked in my ears, and then I heard what others heard during my relivings: Hoarse and urgent and very fast, some stranger's belling voice tolled: "Send a squad to the eastern gate to catch the Osa double agent, the woman Agirode, who flees to Marshman allies because she dares not bring her patron back to Crag to challenge Keth, who controls the province now, for all of his stories of warfare—" I struggled against strong hands. "—they set the Altar to burn through the bones of the walls!" My body began to thrash and writhe against Caladrunan's grip.

"Where's the tapped fuel line?" Clear and harsh in my ear.

"In the passage one level beneath the Altar stone," I gasped senselessly, "with the help of Devotees who know not what they have done. Look for the round stone with a jagged Goddess key mark—behind—the tap is behind the stone—"

Rafai's voice said, startled, "What—"

Caladrunan snapped orders and boots went running. I writhed against all the strong hands. The odd voice shouted from my head, "Round stone in the fifth corridor roof! That mark—it burns—"

"He'll reach it in time," Caladrunan soothed.

"It burns!" I twisted, and then many hands were holding me down, and I screamed in rage at being restrained.

Pitar said, "Flames! Look how he hit Esgarin."

A hand slid over my shoulder. No dream! I thought wildly, flailing out. My hands stuttered over cloth. Caladrunan grabbed me. "Naga."

I held onto him so tightly my own ribs ached. I gasped into the strong cords of his neck—it unraveled the wind-whine of those voices. I gasped, "Drin. Drin . . ."

But his hands tapped my back in harsh, impatient pats. "Drin," I grated, wanting more help than this. Needing it.

"You're too strong, Naga," he said. "Ease your grip. Tell me." Hands tugged at me with impatient force. I rolled away onto my side, struggling to contain rage. He sighed. "Please, I have to meet an envoy very soon. Can't put it off, Naga."

Something about the brisk use of my name did it. My muscles went rigid, flattening my spine against wood. Hard-pressed temper snapped and sang along my bones like overdrawn harpwires.

"Free me." Low, quiet, I said, "An Osa, isn't he? You must be very careful of that Osa."

"Naga, you'll be all right once you get some rest—" His
mistake was patting me like a dog again. I came off the floor in a
crack of clothes and leather, rolled him over twice, and pinned
him in straining hands gone sweat-cold with rage. My lips pulled
wide to show teeth a handspan from his face. He hiccuped for
breath with tears of startlement in his eyes; the light skin and hair
made him look terribly vulnerable. Which was bad.

That way lay madness.

The cords in my neck drew taut as cables. He stopped breath-
ing as he stared up at me. My lips writhed, stretched wide, until
I forced them down to talk. "Caladrunan, whose name means
Heart of Iron, beware Kasin's Wind."

His eyes stared into mine, wide and shocked. It obviously
meant nothing to him, and I was shaken like a rat in a dog's jaws
by the force gripping me. My hands clenched and strained,
pinned him without actually hurting him. Much. "I *warned* you
of this flesh: Be very careful, *Kigadi*, yes— I warned you about
the walls you break asunder to free the mind of this flesh." My
voice echoed distantly in my head as if it spoke from an increasing expanse—night winds squalling through a cavern, hollow
and far. "You Tannese dismiss all without fear. I warned you!"

He gasped, "I never meant to give you pain, Naga—"

I glared at him, threw him aside with one hand. Something in
me despaired—*useless,* such warnings: He had not understood!
Something cold jabbed my shoulder, infused the flesh of my
arm, made it numb. Then the coldness was spreading, and the
whole torchlit ring of faces spun once, slowly, around me. The
hands released me.

"He's still conscious?" The Sharinen doctor leaned close
above me, holding a silver tool.

Caladrunan said, "Naga, can you hear me?"

I slurred, "Don't bind me—hate that—just you."

"All right, just me. You won't kick or scream?"

The words took a long time to form: "I do what you say."

"Will you go to sleep now?" Caladrunan asked.

I scowled. "No. Kill—pig-face men, I kill—"

"Yes, we know. Rafai! Keep Keth away now, I don't care
what he says, or we'll never calm Naga. No more, Naga, I
promise."

"Don't tell me that pig-shit!" I yelled. "See any more, I
kill—I see Keth and I eat his liver with my two hands!"

Caladrunan's face, over me, was a puzzle of moving lights and shadows. Then, gravely, he told me, "Yes, you do that."

"I will!"

His hand touched my face. "Go to sleep now. We're safe."

"You'll make me . . . I know you will if you want . . . all right." I blinked, and the room spun graciously. "You?"

He smiled. "We're safe now. Go to sleep."

"If you say. Kill them if they come. I will. You hang that Keth, or I do," I muttered, and the Sharinen tool poked my arm. Strong hands gripped my arms, lifted, and I felt a flash of pain. Blanket-felt folded gently around my shoulder; I was troubled briefly at an odor of fresh soot. I tumbled over, and there were no more dreams, just the woolly darkness of sleep.

When I blinked awake, I was curled up naked in a wrinkled, smudged expanse of blanket on a briefing room table. At the other table end was a tight wheat-headed clump. Caladrunan's bright hair lofted high in their midst. I rubbed a throbbing temple. These men were the morning watch: All the assaults and mad confusion filled a single night, no more. Soldiers were still hunting assassins, tracing oil lines through the walls, and treating injured.

I sat up on one elbow. Nearby, Pitar had fallen asleep half-dressed in a chair, his head thrown back, loudly snoring. His wounded leg was propped on a stool. On the floor, Rafai whistled instead of snored. I stared at my bandaged self. The blistered feet, a swollen ankle, the rents in my skin, hurt a lot—along with my head. "This running about naked has got to stop."

"But why?" The light, trained voice lilted behind me.

I looked. Gingerly. "Who's running the watches—you?"

Lado Kiselli, fellow Harper, gossip, drinker, skeptic, sat with long legs table-propped; he fingered the harp in his lap. "I am designated to attend you," he said grandly, flourishing a salute.

"To watch over me with witty verse and musical charms, to soothe the madman's rage?" I quoted a History dryly.

"You don't look very mad to me," Lado said. "More like a bird after a lousy night and some singed feathers."

I grunted in agreement. Lado's eyes dropped. Thus prompted, I pulled up the dirty blanket around my shoulders.

Lado said, forthrightly, "Sorry. I must say, our Liege's sculptors would argue like street women over you."

I yawned. "The exercise. Chasing about getting feathers singed. Builds up the frame. Good for growing boys."

"Too much hard work," Lado said, as he always did, and we both sat content with these habitual quips between us. Then he spoiled it by adding, "Would all that running about getting singed feathers and visions of plots be that hero I hear about?"

I pointed my toes—my good toes—at him. "Don't you *dare*!"

Lado made a pouting face. "I wouldn't! Of course not. I *never* carry stories about you, not even one tiny little verse for my own pleasure . . ."

"Not one!" I said sternly. "Stop it, or I'll—"

"You'll what?" Lado pounced, sitting forward. "What rhymes with—ah—gouged—or slayed—or the Lady of Thunder Veils—"

"I won't," I warned him. "No verses!"

"But our Liege *asked* me to compose a song about—"

"Mmh," I grunted, disbelieving every word, and climbed carefully off the table. Definitely I wouldn't ask what had happened during the fit. Or fits. My feet hurt, and I couldn't find a way to walk on them. Awkward.

Lado startled me by picking me up. "Isn't this," I said, feeling ridiculous, "just a little too much work for you?"

"Not at all! I must consult an authoritative source on yesterday's events, namely you, for my versifying." He grunted and put me down in a chair. "Now, may I present you with robes, my dear naked Ruler of the Imperial Line of the Upai, Tokori of House Teot—you remember screaming at us?"

"You're a lousy servant," I said crossly, and put on my rumpled and mismatched set of robes. Definitely I wasn't going to ask about the fit.

Lado said, amused, "I was wondering where you were going to stuff all that impressive manliness of yours. Most informative."

I said, "Stable muck! That's two pieces of flattery out of you at one sitting. I must look like vulture pickings."

"Worse," Lado said. "Your eyes are all sunk in. I heard you were frightful even before this latest batch of fireworks. Of course I'm afraid calling in your grandmother that one time didn't help. *She* started yelling back."

Nice of him to fill in fit-blanked spots; yes, indeed. I sighed. "Do you suppose if I rolled over and went back to sleep, it'd all go away—"

"That's not the Imperial Ruler of the Upai speaking, surely."

"No," I agreed. "The pigeon with the singed feathers."

Lado stood with his hands on his hips, studying me. I could see him thinking about giving me a talk—a cheering-up talk, he called it—and discarding the notion. "Last night Oldfield himself was in town! But he got away. They did pick up a few of his men, rented Marshman Nandos, and a woman who was apparently in charge. Couldn't question any of them—Keth Adcrag got them. Carried in the sack of their heads, claiming he was, of course, trying to *defend* Tanman when you whisked our dear Liege Lord out of sight."

I scowled and said a few rude words concerning Oldfield's intimate relations with a field sow and Keth's resemblance to ferret vomit. Lado cheerfully added a few remarks on both their ancestors and carried me in my chair bodily over to the busy end of the table. Caladrunan looked up from a parchment map and smiled. He asked my opinion on an ambush at Bada's Well at the border.

"Ferret vomit," Lado said, "that'd rhyme perfectly with—"

I turned and glared at him. He smiled and went off humming something under his breath. "Flame it," I muttered. Somebody chuckled softly. I rather suspected it was Caladrunan, so I didn't say anything. And although Lado hadn't given me one of his interminable cheer-up talks, I did feel better about the world, and my particular place in it, when I pointed out an error in the border map they were using.

The length of three difficult days following the fire and my subsequent seizures—long days of repairs and questioning men, of proving myself fit to command, to organize despite injuries—I looked into the twilight of Caladrunan's spare bedchamber. This chamber roosted in the highest Fortress tower directly beneath a Devotee observatory.

The air stood eerily still. Nothing stirred the clouds that hung in heavy, sooty ink-washes outside. One band of sunset light glowed on the stone wall from the arc of tall slits.

A shaggy guard dog, gray-dark as the hard clouds, snuffled the air and studied me with patient dark eyes. A chair grated wood on wood against the scrape-shield beneath the table and creaked under weight. From the dusky shadows Caladrunan replied to my unspoken address, in a voice so deep the hair stood on my neck, "Oh, drop the title, Naga. Had enough of it today. And sit down."

The guard dog slunk away quietly to the door, lay down nose

on feet. I lifted my head high, alert to the Lord of Tan's extraordinary tone. I was as close to fearing the man then as I'd ever been. "What title would you prefer?"

"*Kigadi* might do," he said, with deep notes of iron grating on one another in his voice. "Or perhaps just Drin."

I flinched. Compelled by the pain humming like harpstring beneath the words, I reached out—but I didn't, quite, dare.

"*Don't touch me,* I might blight you! I'm in a foul temper."

My hand jerked away as if burned, rested on his silver-inlaid chairback. At every attempt on his life Caladrunan suffered intense anguish: What had he ever done that they hated him enough to risk their own lives at snuffing his? No answer I made was answer enough. There must be an answer to such pain. I scowled down at my chair, my feet. Silly hallucinations of White Ladies did not count.

A storm was coming. Certainty breathed sudden and cold on the hairs of my nape. Gripping the chair's arms, I said in my calmest tone, "A white-robed Lady spoke with me of a plot—"

"*White Lady?*" He jerked forward, staring. "A *real*, white-robed woman?"

"I don't know if this was a real woman or not. She warned of a threat to your life." It was true. Or parts of it. I looked wildly about the chamber. *Wires,* the White Lady had said. Wires, where would they hide wires . . .

He stared, two fingers extended over his mustache, while I spoke of lightning wards, hidden wires, and hallucinations. The real test of the danger, I told him, was in how often this tower's iron ward was storm-struck: Five reports came from the Devotee observatory above, last season.

"Lightning!" he muttered. "But we can't direct it—"

I rasped, "The ancients did."

The Lord of Tan startled me by saying, "You *remembered* that, out of a fit? But you never remember—"

"Yes." I lifted my head. "Dare we test your life, my Liege?"

He looked deathly tired. Wearily he stood up, resting his hand on the chair; he pointed his thumb at my feet. "*I* saw you run, Naga. In warning of plots, I must trust your judgment."

"Perhaps your Lady Wife warned me, my Liege. In antique veils it seemed like her—but her voice wasn't—"

"Why wouldn't she warn me directly? Must've been another woman. A warning—even from within the Devotees—yes, perhaps—"

He'd think me irrational if I pressed the idea of his wife in disguise yet again. "This chamber may be the next line of attack on you."

He didn't stir. In that hung moment, suspended in stress, my mind made an almost muscular leap of intuition. I said sharply, "Drin. Come away from that chair. The ancients used precious metals and glass for their powers. Perhaps *that* was how." I pointed at the chair inlay, fantastically lined and accented with wires of silver.

Startled, he said, "Pitar checked—"

"Pitar did not expect what I do." I knelt down, stiff as an old man, and wrenched aside a straw foot mat. Beneath was a circle four feet wide: two wooden semicircular shields, inlaid with extravagant old silver. Scrape-shields traditionally prevented the legs of ruling chairs from wear on stone flooring; the inlay was folly from past Tanmen, for Caladrunan never indulged thus. Still it angered me, and kneeling, I hurled aside the heavy ruling chair. Caladrunan rolled aside the matched table—and flinched away from touching it, at my fierce gesture. I jerked up half the scrape-shield, grunted, twisted. It came away very reluctantly in my hands. I felt cold all over.

"Flames!" he muttered, staring stricken at what hung beneath it: a spray of corrosion-brilliant green copper wires encased in oiled new leather wrappings. The hole seating it went through to the shield's silver inlays. Matching rent ends thrust out between stone floor blocks, having stained the mortar green with bright recent corrosion.

Caladrunan clicked fingers, brought the guard dog to him, and bawled into a connecting wall-trumpet, "Call Pitar!" Half a guard watch crashed in, swords drawn. "Get masons—I want this wire traced. Rafai, cut a sample of the wire and leather for your father, see if he can identify its source." The Head Armorer, Rafai's father, had the best knowledge of old manufacturies. Caladrunan ordered fire crews on duty.

"Kasin's Wind comes soon," I said curtly. They all nodded.

That power was too great for any Tannese harness; if the tower ward got hit, the wire would ignite—even thick tower wards failed sometimes under such strength. Devotee attempts to shackle Tan's frequent storms, as the ancients had done, always failed. The plot: Immolation for the Lord of Tan; but igniting all Fortress to mass inferno was the most likely result of this folly. Red trembled at the edge of my sight. I dream-danced, *yes!* in ignorance of the real stores of my own knowledge!—while human tools danced to the Osa puppetmaster's touch yet again—but I would not give in to the twirling red figures.

Pitar hobbled in, swearing horribly, wielding a knobby black holly cane like a sword as much as walking with it. Proud man; he was stubbornly ignoring the limits of his wound. He looked ill. "Lightning is random, my Liege, they'd try to rig more chambers. May the men search the observatory overhead, by this evidence? We *must* stop them before the storm—"

I scuffled across the chamber on my knees, bent over the massive bed, grunted, and shifted it aside. Pennons broke and draperies tumbled about me. I wadded them impatiently aside, yanking down the silver-embroidered gauze and tossing it at men to dispose of as more danger.

Caladrunan lingered near the doors despite my fierce signed warnings, and even for his life I couldn't *order* the Lord of Tan out. I frowned. The bedposts were blank of inlays, while the bed frame bore just isolated silver emblems with no connection to one another. I was unsure if lightning would arc that way.

So it must be more hidden wires, I thought. I rummaged about in the leather bedstraps and felt along the frame: nothing. I stretched out on the floor, threw aside straw mats from beneath the bed, and found nothing. Then I slid bodily under the bed and ran my hands over all the revealed floor and wall surfaces and the few broken pennon posts. *Nothing.* I said a few nasty words and climbed out. Leaning on a bedpost as I knelt, I stared about the chamber while Pitar yelled at men grunting and shifting scroll cabinets.

"Check Liege's private bathing room," I said absently. "Once I saw lightning dance over a waterhole; it killed all the fish." Caladrunan stood motionless, palely staring at me. Pitar turned and bawled for more men.

I gazed up speculatively: Silver-traced gauze bed curtains hung in a canopy on pennons and draped next to them. Wire entry had to be in a wood-lined pennon socket, but *then* where did storm-fire travel to find its earthing in stone? I ran my eye up an intact pennon and realized curtains were not the only route for the bolt. Caladrunan always kept Devour close to hand at night, hung on a bedpost hard by a pennon. Its ancient scabbard bore silver. And he'd grab it at any disturbance in his sleep; during alerts he kept it in hand all night long. I read the connections:

pennon, scabbard, man, bed, stone floor—and once connected in line, *death*.

I broke off one of the nearest gilded pennons in its socket and let its heraldic banner flop on the floor, to a shocked gasp from a guard. I glared at the splintered end. Solid wood. No wire, nothing. Then I broke the next pennon, hard by Devour's usual bedpost. Sanded and gilded as if solid, when cracked *this* pennon revealed two different colors of wood glued together. I snapped it again lower down—broke it sharply against the bed frame— and watched the halves part in my hand.

From its socket in the floor, the pennon's hollow core carried a dull brown copper cable thick as my thumb, which terminated at scabbard height in a silver plug and an exterior silver design. Easy to calculate the silver plug would lay squarely under Devour's harness, all easy to Caladrunan's hand. The cable had not even corroded.

Pitar nodded grimly at me and yelled for reinforcements to move cabinets. Caladrunan's master stonemason, a bald burly man named Gidas, selected chisels to delicately check the stone around door latches and hinges for hidden wiring. I said, "Who let the Black Robes in? Devotees are *always* going up to the observatory, we'd hardly suspect them in that very corridor outside. With help, they could slide in unsuspected."

Pitar said grimly, "If you recall the traitor you killed, Naga— well, he also substituted here during my watches. Perhaps he didn't name all his masters." Protocol-stern even now, Pitar let me think about all the information I'd sacrificed by indulging in such rage. I thought about it. Hard.

Gidas muttered, "Aside from digging ways, Black Robes always were plotters."

Pitar said, "Oh, we'll trace the wires to their observatory— where we're never allowed to desecrate holy air. Be sure we'll search it well."

Carefully, thinking of how the legal case would read, I said, "Perhaps they wore disguises. That smuggler Biree wore Devotee robes. We'd need absolute proof to arrest true Devotees."

Caladrunan said quietly, "It's starting to blow outside."

I wasn't fooled by his thin, calm tone. "Best if you go to safer quarters, my Liege. Now."

He murmured, "If they could do *this,* they'd find out where I've set up other reserve chambers."

My lips curled back off my teeth with a soft hiss. "Yes. So

we set ambushes to catch eager visitors. I think Rafai can carry messages home to his parents, close, convenient, just the place for you. How are you with toddler girls?''

He blinked at me, opened his mouth, and closed it.

My smile didn't change. "And I don't think," I said gently, "the Devotees will have thought of wiring family quarters. Pitar, do the men know what to look for in here?''

Pitar thumped away past me, swearing biliously at his cane and shot leg and the world. "You'll suggest what we missed?''

"Depend on it," I said grimly.

Caladrunan spoke; a pair of guards picked up Pitar in a chair-lift grip—which the old warrior protested in a roar. Caladrunan looked thoughtfully at Pitar as if the swear words were merest rain, and Pitar's noise grumbled away to mutters.

I went by way of Rafai's bearlike grip and I held doors; Rafai grunted. "Ulp," he said, almost bumping into his master. Returning slowly from some miserable internal space, Caladrunan looked at us under bristling brows.

I folded up my robe hood, shivering. Wind whistled about statuary as we crossed courtyards; dull rumbling echoed among the dark towers, around a sky blotted black of all landmark stars. The outside storm, and Caladrunan's gloom, were well matched by our squalid new quarters. We looked at the Head Armorer's vacated chamber in silence. Even the hearth smoke smelled odd. The Lord of Tan gestured absently. Rafai grinned and put me on the bed.

Fuming, I settled into rumpled furs, scattered scraps and toys. I knew that silly, anxious Tannese grinning—since the Lord of Tan was alive, what was the fuss? Unlike Upai, who'd scream furiously at one another, Tannese farmboys at heart wanted placid pretenses that nothing was wrong.

"Stop grinning," I told Rafai crossly. My head ached.

"You look drowned in such big furs, Noble-born," Rafai said, grinning. "Sleep well!" He saluted cheerfully.

"Flamed unlikely," I grumbled at Rafai's departing back. The door closed us into soothing quiet. I breathed a deep breath, let it go, and lay flat on the Armorer's sagging old bed. It squeaked under my weight. I rubbed my hands into my hair, gripped at the roots of my braids.

"Rest," Caladrunan said flatly. His eyes looked bloodshot.

Flinging back bed curtains, I snapped at him, "Ridiculous! It's only dusk, I have work to do—''

"Oh, so I've offended your sticky desert pride!"

"Is that what you wanted?"

"No," he said, and slumped down onto the bed and put his head in his hands. "No." He suddenly sounded utterly miserable.

"What was in the report slates today?" I demanded.

He kicked a broken toy viciously with one boot toe. "Bear Clan and those bastards Berry Clan are backing out of their commitments, so I won't be able to send their troops to Edan Dar's son. Edan wrote me that things are going badly again on the border; he lost two companies since last report, he's outnumbered, he fell back to Black Pebble Ford. Goddess, the clan names going down out there . . . And recruitments are dropping badly. More trainees giving up."

"It's hard to like someone who steps on your neck and says nasty words for your foolishness. We spoil all their silly ideas about noble combat." I snorted. "Halfway through my classes they all want to go over to Keth, whose boys do pretty mounted maneuvers and shine and tinkle in parades."

"And get their crisp little behinds picked off in border skirmishes like flies," Caladrunan grated. "One of his pet officers lost a half a troop for nothing, *that* report came in."

I cocked one eyebrow. I had little sympathy for Keth's lot; Keth's pets deserved their fate, though I had no proof of their offenses—as yet.

"I drafted my Lady Wife's brothers and cousins, and she was *not* happy about it. My *dear* Lady Wife. Pitar should escort me to Great Hall tonight while you rest. I've still got to put on my flamed silly court robes. I don't know where Rafai dumped them."

"I'll find them," I offered, waving my hands in bitter jest.

He laughed sharply at that quip, rising. "You're a mess—I've got my day's work out of you." Silk rustlings and the clink of metal fittings were drowned in a sudden boom of thunder and the rush of wind on slate roofs outside. Fastening robe loops, he looked critically at me. I could adopt a thin cheery veneer, or collapse tiredly into myself. And I refused to give way.

"You look nice," I said, admiring him.

"My Lady Wife spent enough on these clothes."

Such bitterness, seething so close to surface!

His expression changed. In the gentlest imaginable tone he said, "I do care about her. She'd wither, away from court life."

I leaned outward from the noisome bed, twitched his outrobe

straight—pulling the cloth carefully with my rough calluses. "Why do you not choose another wife?"

"Her clan might murder her, failing their interests so far."

I tilted my head. "Did she hurt you that much, Drin?" A guess: His flinch told me I was right.

He made a harsh inarticulate grunt, scrubbed wearily at his face. "When we first married, I wanted her. *Needed* her. But she—well, her brothers starved her until she agreed to it. I didn't get to see her during *that* part. They chained her feet to keep her in place for the wedding ceremony."

After an instant's horror, I asked, "You didn't *know*?"

His face twisted. "She had her pride. That haughty silk and iron clan pride. I never guessed. Oh, yes, it was true." He was silent awhile. "I was such a young fool! She may have saved my reign. I wanted to strip away Devotee properties, give it to somebody who'd use it better—never have got away with it, of course. She insisted on my appeasing the Cragmen and the Devotees, or she'd see to it that iron stopped coming through her clan."

Rumpling his silks indifferently, he sat down with me, leaned his chin on his fist upon my shoulder. "She told me I was a plowclod with mud on my elbows: insulting *me*, of the oldest clan in Tan—aside from really ancient native families like yours."

"That was another land. Different." My throat felt tight.

He sighed, lifted a low-lidded, hooded gaze, and drew away. Fidgeted with his robes. "Do you know what the men think of you?"

"I don't know, after all the traitors!" I was as twitchy as he was. So I took my scaddas from my harness where Rafai had left them, tugged out my cleaning box. I set to work on my blades, scowling. The only reason to ask was that he might leave me alone in some command. Perhaps Fortress itself.

"You're looking bad. Headache?"

A memory shadowy clear, I still saw his face as it had been contorted under enemy guns, which, in my mind, distorted his actual quiet expression. I glanced away. Something Upai in me flinched from memory. Let Tannese remember things, I thought. "No."

He leaned toward me, speaking from his earnest island of Tannese privilege, trying to penetrate my mood, to explain why opinions about me were so important—leadership in war. Firelight moved over the planes of his jaw, glinted on the straw-pale twists and curls of his beard. I stared past him.

Once I had seen a child, its hair just that color, caught by Osa. The Osa had bathed the child in their fire. The tragedy was how long it took to die. When I had dug the grave, no one could tell what color its hair had been. *War*. I hunched my shoulders, shrugged away the image, shrugged off Caladrunan's hand. *War*. I felt as far from him as from another shore, him and all his sea-eyed Tannese.

*"Naga,"* he said.

I lifted my eyes and we stared at one another. What did the men think of me? I felt my lip curl. Flames, I was an educated man: a Harper no less, not some frozen Sati with the opaque stare of the border. He had a right to ask. If the men thought me too mad, they'd defy me. I reached for my left scadda to draw and clean it. Why even discuss it? I thought—then, I must be more tired than I realized. But if talking to me let Caladrunan think calmly, neutrally, past the attempts on his life, I must make the effort. I dug for and discarded answers, which tired me and made me irritable. Neither of us was in fit state for discussing anything.

Finally, while examining my left scadda's outer curve for oils and fingerprints, I said, "What do the men think—well, what about all the interesting rumors: I may be a woman in disguise, a Kehran boy, a monster. No one blames *you!* Who wouldn't take advantage of an easy ass if it were offered?" And my temper escaped me. The scadda flicked up and around, spinning fluidly around my arm in full extension, sharply up in salute. Caladrunan drew in a deep breath. I turned the blade, wiping it from guard to slender tip, checking the fire-sheen on the metal. I frowned at a smudge and wiped it away. I glanced up. "They'd be fools to say so to my face."

I plucked a hair from my braids and dropped it across the blade. It fell, drifting like feathers, in two. I put away my rubbing stone. Then I said, "I do see need for crisp drills. I make them run roadwork. Maybe eventually they'll be able to do forced marches hard enough to surprise bandits. Won't help against Osa machines. But I never had to teach a desert boy how to fill a waterskin or catch rabbits—and these numb-kukkies are nobles! My old Master Reti would've carved these overgrown children like bean-curd cheese."

"You're a hero, Naga. Don't you think they look up to you, that they listen to your warnings? Or that they just *like* you?"

"Nobody has ever liked me, as far as I know, until you." I snorted like a pig, ruckling my nose hostilely. "I know you could recite faults about all of us, your top officers. Strengam is old and hard to rouse, Keth always starts fights, Rafai is young and silly, Pitar worries too much. And I'm crazy, I get in trouble."

He looked into the hearth fire. It was misting snow outside; icy rime piled on the outer window ledge in the screech of wind.

I brooded. "Poor Strengam Dar—one of his sons, in my officer class, is brilliant. The others are hopeless. They're slow in the mental works."

"Well, their name is worth something in leading troops."

"Drin, you're thinking like a ruler, not a general! Will diplomatic flattery help incompetents in the field?" Then I sighed. "But you know that already." I sheathed my scadda and put away the cleaning oil and soft abrasive; I sat staring away from the hearth fire into the shadows lapping about the chamber. It was hard to keep up the words for him, keep away the image of that spray of wire. I grimaced at the one slit-window.

He said softly, "Officers tell me you can mold a trainee like beeswax. The men think you're a powerful witch who can read minds—which only raises my reputation with them as a holy force, since I command you, bend you to my whims."

"A witch is no friend to the right-side-up world!"

"But I *control* your witch powers, you see, aiming it for good. Or they get confused: No, you're a prophet and I aim the holy force you transmit. Isn't superstition comforting?"

"Bull vomit," I growled. "In all the confusion, you still haven't told me everything today."

"What else did you want to know?" he said, straightening, and then winced at old injuries. I reached out to massage the heavy muscles that always pained him under such tension. Abruptly agreeing to it, he stretched out on his back on the bed, staring up at the stone overhead.

"Did you also recall this *is* a Feastday? I have a state entertainment tonight. I had to reinstate it at the last moment because my dear Lady Wife absolutely obligated me to entertain her guests. It is a Feastday, don't you know, and we should show solidarity, prove the whispers wrong: *Sorry,* I'm still alive."

"And security for this Feast?" My fingers probed his sword-arm muscles, expecting tensions to have knotted them painfully. I was right. His whole body was shivering very slightly.

I was about to grip his shoulder and rotate it when he said, eyes shut, "I don't expect trouble tonight. With the conspirators imprisoned from tonight, everyone will be afraid to sneeze in public. Especially with more arrests to come out of this wire plot."

"That's when I'd strike, after a big event. Slack guard."

"You're a Sati, my hawk." He put his fingertips together, looking upward thoughtfully at the stone-ribbed arches of the chamber. "But I think you should come to the party unofficially. You'll find out a great deal more than I could buy from spies."

I sighed and dropped my hands. I wasn't going to coax out many knots like this. Perhaps as well if I quit.

He said, "Were you trying to relax me into jellyfish, Naga?"

"Harder than I thought," I said dryly, taking his legs across my knees. I stretched his foot tendons. Tension! He felt like a collection of rocks and string. I grunted, "You should let me do this right after practice, so the knots don't set in the muscles."

He snapped the back of my hand with a fingertip and ruffled my hair. "If you go in the field with me, I was thinking of making you my general of unconventional forces, use troops like those guerrilla riders given Edan Dar's son. Keep you busy. You've earned it. Saved my neck last night and today."

"So I *can* come with you if you go off to war—" My head jerked up. Big mistake, that. I went dizzy. He promptly grabbed me and put me flat. I didn't object very strenuously. I grunted and snapped, "I'm *not* sick—" I tried to sit up. Unsuccessfully. He had very large hands.

He stared down in my face. The Armorer's bed squeaked slightly under his weight as he eased closer. "Swear you'll think of your health before you do silly things like overworking. I need you well." His voice wavered oddly. "Swear."

"All right," I said. "For a while. Got work to do." I knew what he needed. Yet I ached as if my soul had been thoroughly beaten, and I didn't want to talk. Still, however it dragged my insides and pained me, I gave it to him. Struggling with the words, I said, "It's hard to watch you risk things. You—surprise me, knowing things about me without being told."

He shifted his head.

In a flat, tired tone I said, "You always did. It doesn't matter how I deny it or push words around, my whole being is warped by the damage the Osa did to me, and I cannot speak straight-grained. But twisted and drift-bleached as I may be, I still love you, *kigadi*. I can't lose you. I can't.''

With those words out, in that dispassionate tone, with so many dangerous emotions strained under tight discipline like harpwires—then the *real* sense of the words came to me. ''Not me who saved you. Sheer blind luck, the Goddess' Hand.''

*Luck.*

Emotion stumbled over the word that cold intellect uttered and found that chilly assessment hit with searing, acute pain. All my self-control blew away with a pop like a snapped rooftree blown away—rolled all my Sati coldness to shatters and knocked me helplessly into the grating shingle and tidal wash uproar, the pent-up terror surging through my body. *Flames.* I'd done everything I could, and we had barely survived it.

I curled up. It was all I could do not to scream with it, staring past my knuckles. My fingers pressed hard marks in my face. My ribs shuddered. By any rational chance we should have died. I had always known the Goddess was a cruel power, and to be beloved of Her might be the greatest curse of all: one fierce test after another, life-long sentence. I shouted, ''I never felt anything before—let alone this—this. What did you *do* to me!''

''*Don't*—don't twitch like that. I never did anything to you, I swear it. Oh, Goddess, Naga. Would it help to keep talking?'' he said, with his voice breaking hoarse in his throat.

My body shuddered convulsively. I grabbed him, or he grabbed me, or we tangled, in a painful hard hug like frightened boys.

It took awhile before the terrible blind wave passed; slowly the violent shudders slackened to a clenched ache. Living, breathing strength practically flowed like healthy blood from him. I noticed the rasp of his sword calluses on my back, and then the heat inside my body eased back into its normal reach to my fingers and toes and brain. Peculiar sensation—my soul slowly stretching out from its tight shocked chill. My eyes blinked, focused. Even as I felt knots loosen inside my guts, he said, ''Are you all right now?''

Rather clumsily I patted the hair and his robe smooth again. Puzzled, I said, ''Now I'm—all right.'' And, aside from a few stray hiccups, I was.

Something changed, lifted, in the set of his mouth and eyes. Tiny facial muscles relaxed. ''Rest, I think, would help us both,'' he said. He gripped my shoulder with a shaky hand until

I stretched out, and he lay down close beside me. He didn't shiver so much with leftover shock as long as he could keep some grip on me. My body relaxed into his greater warmth, and the nauseating pain in my head eased. I closed my eyes. I mumbled, "You're a pretty good holy force yourself."

His voice smiled. "You're a horrid patient. Just horrid."

So I asked him roughly for my harp. Better to practice my music now, especially since I was in danger of dissolving into a puddle of sticky, annoying emotion. Caladrunan looked at me and shook his head. Perhaps the sticky-soft parts of me were showing in my eyes. He tweaked my ear and pulled furs over me. "No harping. Sleep. We've got that Feast; I want you rested for it."

Maybe I could sleep; I was trained to nap wherever I could. I muttered, "Such a tyrant," and felt my eyes dropping shut.

# CHAPTER

## = 5 =

OUR HOPES OF changing the terms of the war had died in the lone, long moon since the attacks, so the Lord of Tan was going to war himself, and so far doing it without giving me my orders.

The afternoon of the final briefing, Caladrunan pointed over the expanse of the sand map built on a broad table. "Strengam, we'll move during breaks in the weather, meet there in ninety days." He assigned officers to new garrisons, to scouting forces.

I waited patiently. Perhaps he didn't want everyone to know my task; Keth's forces made up a third of the Tannese army. I listened while officers entered, received their orders, and filed out. Caladrunan was advancing wings of his army into the last teeth of winter, digging them into border garrisons where they would be ready to move out at spring thaw. Finally Rafai leaned forward and asked, "Liege, do we have a special job this season?"

Caladrunan stared blankly at him. His eyes shifted to me. "You two hold the Fortress while I'm settling troops."

I opened my mouth but no sound came out. I shut it. Rafai said anxiously, "But your guards—"

"I'll take some of Pitar's men. You two will be busy here, and I don't want Naga getting his head damaged again. When Pitar's leg finishes healing, he'll ride out to me." He turned to a new batch of officers.

Rafai looked at me. He plainly expected me to nod, yes, I knew it all along. The effort was beyond me. I got up and went out in a blind daze. Then Rafai gripped my arm; I went where he tugged me to go and blankly held a goblet of wine he gave me. He said, "Are you all right? You don't look well."

"Fine," I whispered, staring at him. I blinked. He'd steered me to one end of the long practice hall used in winter for trainee arms exercise. I said, "Open the shutters. Get some air in here."

Rafai hurried, glancing back over his shoulder. *Slam, slam, slam*, the shutters admitted bars of cold winter light across the wood floor. Rafai crossed the light shafts to me and hovered— absurd that such a big presence could hover—at my elbow with one big paw out to catch me if I fell. I must look like flamed hell, I thought. But I wasn't falling down yet. "Go away," I said.

"Noble-born, I don't know if—"

I lifted my eyes and looked at Rafai. He turned about and left. The door closed so softly after him I knew he was going to creep back. To drop that plan dead in its tracks, I turned in one smooth motion and hurled the goblet at the door with an attack-scream. I heard his running steps fading away outside. I opened my mouth, straining for another scream, unable to sound it for the tightness of my throat. I went down on my knees, clenched my fists in the remnant sanding dust on the bare plank floor, and watched the sunlight glide closer to my fists.

I was stiff and gritty-eyed when I rose. I shook my muscles loose and began attack-dances across the use-polished floor. The planks echoed the slightest rasp or thudding carelessness in footwork. I had drilled myself, with great control and precision, to make no sound whatsoever, but injury had impeded my skill. I was midway through a difficult slow sand-dance called Bloodstorm when Rafai returned. He ducked his broad curly head in the far door, then made way for a taller figure than himself: The Lord of Tan swept in, thundering, "You were not to exercise for thirty days."

My head gave a punishing throb of pain. I gritted my teeth. I completed my series of movements and sheathed my scaddas, whisper-whisper, at my sides. I saluted then, chin high.

Caladrunan waved Rafai back and closed the door in his face. "I put off telling you so I wouldn't ruin your recovery, but surely you guessed I'd leave you. I can't trust Keth here, I desperately need Strengam in the field—"

I folded my arms. My leg muscles trembled; I hoped it didn't show. "I guessed nothing," I said coolly.

"Oh? You guessed a lot about that gun attack!"

"Then take Keth's word, arrest *me* for conspiracy in that attack and believe *he* was just trying to protect your life."

"No—Flames, Naga, I know better than that—I'm just saying I need your foresight to keep this flamed rock under control."

"*Stones.*" My voice dripped contempt. "In the desert movement is the only control. To defend stones is to die."

"It's different here," Caladrunan said.

"Is it?" I said. "Your court certainly pretends so."

"That's why I'm *telling* you, not asking you," he said.

Rage blurred my sight. I lifted my chin higher, suppressing the blur. My head hurt in savage counterpoint to my heartbeat. I said, "You tell me to stay because I am weak, I might fail you."

He said levelly, "You'd serve me too well—at cost to yourself which is too high. I rest wounded men and beasts until they heal. I've made my decision. And I'm presenting Girdeth at her court party before I leave, too."

"I'm not a blank slate you write whatever you like upon me!" I yelled. "Roast her party—no more! No more assassin gifts—"

He stood at the far end of the practice hall while long arches of sunlight barred the floor between us. He replied mildly, "Since your injury, you haven't been able to go out riding; maybe that's why you're getting a little—"

"—crazy, is that it?" I paced. "I *was* something before you got hold of me. This trying to make me snap into a tin shape, to make me Tannese, I hate it. Flamed parties—nobles and guards I never saw before, always crawling with extra servants with every last bit of food some damn fish paste—" I sputtered, for once in my life as a Harper lacking words to describe how furious I was. I loathed the fish paste dainties of diplomatic meals. "I'm tired of the risks you take!"

"Will you wear your weapons tied into scabbard for the party? My Lady Wife's women requested that."

I exploded. "*Idiots!* As if I'd sully my skill playing party games! Do they think their stupid restrictions will stop a palace coup?" I added something anatomically unlikely that such people could do with their respective bodily ends. I made a rude face. "There, is that crazy enough? Do you want me to stand on my head, run about barking like a dog and howling at the moon?"

"You always throw such tantrums when you decide I lack decent protection."

"Tantrums!" I yelled, tossing down my armor cap with a clang of metal and flinging braids about. "Tantrums! Near-killed and next you want to play war without bodyguards and go to parties!"

"I knew you'd throw a tantrum," he said in a regretful tone. "I have to go. Rumors about my death are flying thick and wild."

*"Let them!"*

Rafai poked his head in. Not at first aware of me, he said, "Is Naga done throwing things? About the party—"

I let out a noise that started *"Bawwhh—"* and degenerated into an incoherent roar as I charged down the practice room. Rafai squeaked and slammed the door shut in my face. I raked it in a double strike of razor spurs, *thump-thump*, and spun away. Panting, midway in the room, I clenched my fists.

"You really have a horrid temper," Caladrunan murmured.

I grabbed at a loose braid and yanked. I wanted to yank it out and throw it down, but it didn't come. Caladrunan grabbed out, gripped my wrists. *"Stop that!* Don't damage your head."

I growled, pummeled his chest, while he hugged my upper arms hard into my ribs. I jolted my feet downward, arching my back, and hurled us both over backward with a spin on it so he landed safely enough on his side, the wind knocked out of him. We ended up flopping on the floor, twisting, gripping each other's wrists. "I'll squeeze the piss out of you," I grunted, with my legs wrapped around his middle.

"You would," he got out, gasping for air. Our arms jerked; I didn't let him twist his wrist free. He held my forearms in an equally fierce grip. "Settle for a truce?"

"I'd win and you know it," I grunted.

"All right. Ease up, you're killing me!"

I let go a little bit. Just a little.

He drew in breath. "I'm letting go. No, don't run away."

I sat up, breathing deeply. So did he, rubbing ruefully at his middle. Then he looped his long arm around my shoulders and hugged me to him, hard. I wasn't objecting much. He said, "After this latest attempt on me, you've every right to be suspicious of a public event. But I also have to show myself to the people, let them see what sort of job I'm doing, keep up my popularity. No parties or events at all means I'm hiding my head in some hole afraid to show my face. As for war—our men were so green in the beginning the Osa won some minor battles, and then every thumb-sucking coward in the Three Countries ran off to them. So they and their Nandos have an artificially puffed-up army, where ours is bedrock small and far more dependent on the Cragmen numbers than the Army of Tan has ever been before. All of that could be reversed if I go out in the field, get morale up, and we start winning. I have to do it without looking a puppet tool of anyone's—including *you*. That's aside from needing somebody I trust to finish securing this flamed rock so a garrison can hold it even if my Lady Wife is the only commander.''

I said a few nasty words, with my head lodging somewhere near his belly button. I knew all that.

He put his hand on my back. ''You really should be too tired to hate me for it.''

I flopped over like one of his dogs, with a dispirited growl, and rested my aching head on his knee. His hands felt dry and pleasant on my hot temples.

''I know you're not a blank slate,'' he said, with his arm resting over me. ''But I don't *always* know what's already there.''

I pushed myself up. My skin prickled and pounded. ''I can't lose you. I'd—I can't let those—'' my face contorted.

He squeezed the back of my banded neck-leather. ''Small risk of that when you're so fierce to defend me.''

''I'm not perfect!'' My body shuddered with the force of it. ''Not enough. Nobody's good enough if you take silly risks—''

He said, ''You have been. I know: good enough, *so far*. Come, now. You do as well as the Goddess could expect. Anything more is in Her hands, not ours. Hush now.''

The shaking eased. I said, very low, ''If I lose you, I'll go insane—and I'm so afraid I won't see shadows jumping—''

''That's just the nature of the work you do for me.'' That *wasn't* all of it, and he knew it. I hadn't fooled him a bit over the past moon, pretending I was normal, past the dream-dancing figures, the nightmares, and the odd occasional fit. But he had let me pretend. Maybe he had no other stratagem to try. ''I need your help now. Hold Fortress for me.''

''*Bastard.*'' I drove my body hard against his, felt his arms clench my leathers into my ribs. I snuffled a little, he relaxed his grip, and we sat cross-legged side by side.

''Come to the party with me.''

I glared. ''You know I will, flame your silly pig hide!''

''Good.'' He took it as a good sign I was swearing again. He sat up suddenly, eyes wide, jolted a finger into my shoulder. ''I know what you need: a talk with an old friend of mine.''

He led me to a chamber behind Fortress's main Altar room. I

glanced up apprehensively. "She'll be here soon," he promised. "She's different from most Devotees. I've known her since I was a boy. She isn't a fighter, she doesn't speak against her own Elders. But she . . . listens." And he hurried out, talking to the guard escorts who met him outside the door.

I turned about uneasily. It was so much a Devotee chamber. The flame symbol sculpted on the wall, the small brass traveling bowl with its burning twigs, made me uneasy. I knelt and made desert salute to the little bowl of fire, and said the words, and felt better. I tried to meditate, but my body itched to move; I paced before the rows of oak benches. Harsh dream-words flew like crows in my brain. I turned about several times—and then I knew someone spied on me. I could feel it. I stood still, feet apart, nearly in a fighting stance.

The observer came into the open, waited quietly at the door, neither challenging nor bowing to superior force; the figure wore a plain black robe with the brass mask of a Devotee just come from a ceremony. To say the figure was sexless would be untrue; but in the mask it was not a person to me at all—odd effect, since I was used to reading past Nando face wraps. The air swirled with the scent of pine resin, a ceremonial incense far too humble for most Devotee Orders. A woman's low voice came from the mask: "Would you like to sit with me and contemplate the Goddess? We are alone."

That calm voice soothed many suspicious and nervous impulses. Though the words were crisply noble Tannese, her voice had the rich soothing timbre of every Upai lullaby I had ever heard. I had loved my mother's voice very much.

The woman sat on a bench with weary, careful gestures. I could not even see eyes under the mask. I sat down near her, staring at the intricate brass plating. Finally, timidly, I reached out and touched it. She didn't stir. Even her hands rested in utter repose. She said, "Does the confessional mask disturb you? It often frightens the children I work with."

I said, "Children often have *very* good instincts."

She chuckled. "I hear another teacher's knowledge! I'll take off the mask for you." Her hands drew it off. She wore a black face cloth beneath it, showing only steady blue eyes. She unwound that and revealed a dazzling pale skin, the porcelain blush often found among the Crag beauties—and she had the bright red Crag hair of legend and ballad. A Cragwoman! She gazed at me. "I mean you no harm, my friend. Talk seems the least I could do for the man who saved my Liege and kin in his own chambers."

"You're kin?" I blinked.

"Indeed we are. Cousins, despite this outrageous coloring of mine. I am his Great Aunt Agtunki's youngest daughter. I came to court with Caladrunan when he escaped confinement by his Regents. He says Girdeth's escapades are beginning to resemble mine!"

I stared. Her red hair and Cragwoman beauty seemed all the more astonishing.

"What do you teach?" she asked, tilting her head. The shadows in her bright red hair lay dark as nutwood.

"Killing," I said flatly.

"Ah," she said. Her gaze remained steady. Those eyes had seen a lot, by the lines around them, and one nervous Sati seemed unlikely to disturb such hard-won tranquillity. "Would you be more comfortable walking while we talk? I, unfortunately, must rest my feet, so I will stay here."

I glanced at her booted feet. "Too much sudden exertion after too little exercise," I said critically, remembering how she'd moved.

"Exactly," she agreed, with another sigh, and rested her riding boots on the bench before her. "It is nice to be so informal with a fellow-teacher. Are you good at your work?"

"Yes. Politics—" I moved irritably. "That's not why I'm here. Liege suggested your guidance. He knew I wanted to talk—to clean some of the mud out of my mind. From the danger, the politics. I feel—" I moved my shoulders unhappily, as if to shrug off a dirty robe. "While others say I am some sort of prophet, I—I do not feel I know much."

"So you can be tart, too," she said mildly, lazily. I could have listened to nonsense spoken in such a wonderfully soothing voice, but it wasn't going to be nonsense. Not from this woman.

I said sardonically, "It would be natural to be confused. *I* am. Forgive my rudeness. I have met too many demanding women lately."

"You want the Goddess. You want to talk to Her with the ease of a child, without all the Tannese elaborations. There is a lot of the child in you yet. Indeed, in us all."

"Not the innocence," I said quietly. "I see—too much."

"What is it you *see*, Upai dream-dancer?"

My eyes went wide open. Such was the strength of the woman that she looked in and read the horrors there, and never flinched. "Yes," she said softly, regretfully. "As a sign to you of his trust in me, Liege said to ask you about the cave of machines that saved you from the Osa."

I turned abruptly, flattening my hand on one wall. Harshly I said, "I know very little about that place. Consciously."

Her face did not change at the bitterness in my voice. She said, "Liege told me you would not. He then instructed me to report something you said during a fit, thus: 'I alone survived the fire of the Osa to reach the cave of the machines. It was a holy place among the rocks, and the ancients filled this place with talking machines of many and various design, filled a space that could have saved a thousand fleeing people from the Osa—filled it so full of their machines that my people knew only a small child like me could jam into that cave. No one else escaped with me into the rocks that far before the Osa flames got them. I was tested by the machines—and by the ancient dialect and codes given our children, I gained safety. Great voices spoke there. And the machines talked, many marvelous alien sounds among themselves. Many machines had died and decayed. The lifeblood in the black veins sputtered and sometimes died out completely . . . and then fell an utter blackness in that place, silencing all there.' "

I leaned on the wall, scrubbing at my sweaty cheeks and chin. The chamber felt unaccountably hot. I took deep breaths of heavy stale air. "Fit-babbling. But I thank you for this report."

"Do you remember where the cave is?"

As smartly I turned at her and snapped my hand to my weaponbelt. *Do not forget*, I told myself, *she is still a Devotee.* "I do not know."

She tilted her head to one side, studying me. "But what if, because we do not defend that ground, the Osa happen upon this place during their invasion?"

Rage burst out of me in hacking laughter. *"Wish* that upon them—they'd never survive the tests of that place! Oh, they would *die*, many and many, for a discovery useless to them!" The words exploded from me without doubt, pause, or understanding. And only puzzlement remained.

She studied her boots awhile and smiled. "You would never tell me where it is, you hardly know me."

"I rely on Liege's excellent judgment." I moved stiffly.

"His judgment has improved since you began running security. Definitely, we—all his friends—appreciate having that whole assassination business sorted out."

I paced. "I would prefer that no one noticed my attempts . . . except the ones sorted for prosecution."

She smiled again. "He said you'd be a hard one. But I'll tell you a secret. Our Order is very independent. *We* just haven't screamed as loudly as those Orders suppressed by the Elders. Yet." Her face tilted downward, distressed. "You are not alone in having dreams, my young friend. Other seers speak of ill times. I pray."

I laughed harshly, flung my arm out toward the Altar. "Will that stop what I dream, night after night, O Devotee? Liege wants to cure me of fits—if you want prophecies of me, you're no help at all. Oh, yes, Upai had a skill called dream-dancing. It takes an old man's wisdom, years of training and wrestling with inner voices, to interpret such visions. I am just come twenty summers, no more, and even if it is true dreaming, I have no training, nobody alive to ask. My people would call me *kapopi*, insane with visions, useless."

"Is that why you are afraid of the Altar? Of the Flames?"

I snapped about toward her, then flung away again, and paced. She'd seen *that* in me as I moved. Finally, trusting Caladrunan's judgment, I said, "I hate flames. My clan was killed by fire, in war. That cave was how I—how I believe I survived." It was much to admit to a stranger, for me.

"Yes," she murmured, looking distant and thoughtful. "In some places they use a sheaf of grain to represent Her. Here in Tan we use the Flames. Dramatic, attracts the eye, encourages reverie. But you don't have to accept guidance from a symbol that makes you unhappy. She comes to you as you can accept Her, not some cosmic rapist."

I lowered my head.

"Do you love Her enough to pray to sheaves of grain, and perhaps feel a bit silly for it?" she asked.

I said passionately, "I do pray, that's why it—why that—" I waved my hand at the bowl of Flames, "—that feels so wrong to me. To me, fire is a thing of—" my hand made a repudiating gesture. "I am of a Upai royal house. Praying over grain is a thing no true ruler would ever feel ashamed to do."

For a moment her brows lifted as if she contemplated that along with a lot of other things she'd heard about me. "If you accept a Devotee like myself as your spiritual counselor, with Liege as second sponsor, then training as an acolyte could permit your worship to conform to the needs of a different spirit than one Tannese-raised. Liege thought educating you in orthodox practice might protect you as a prophet. Joining my Order brings you within accepted religious bounds and sanctions your actions.''

I caught at one slippery difficulty. ''You said that my spirit is not as Tannese are—''

''How could it be Tannese? And did I say lesser? No. Different. Could a teacher of killing perform the devotions of a teacher of sacred texts or of a busy noble? We aren't the ancients. We haven't learned how to give everyone what they need in one all-purpose ceremony. The great celebrations, we partake equally, but I never find that my extended periods of worship interest laymen.''

I smiled slowly. ''And you still manage to get along with your Elders?''

She sighed. ''Other counselors would advise you differently. I have always tried to advise first as my conscience required, second as mercy begs, and lastly as doctrine demanded. Those are the priorities of my Order. There are other arrangements of belief—and, yes, at times I must defend my views.''

''I guess it hasn't been easy of late,'' I suggested.

''It has never been easy,'' she said harshly. ''Ease is not my purpose.'' Then her face and voice softened. ''Were you a child of hunger? I noticed that you hoard food.''

I glanced down. I had been fingering, unconsciously eating, bits of baked, broken cake of kinash as I talked; the crumbs were visible on my fingertips. I glanced up. ''Habit. I can't eat much at a time.''

She nodded. ''Many small meals. Yes, the refugee children, when they need food, they need it that very instant. I've had them faint of it in classes.'' The lines of her face drew into sad and distant lines.

I sat down next to her. ''You go out to the camps. Then you must work with the Upai widow who coordinates the Women of the Harp. Are many fellow Devotees willing to teach there?''

''A few,'' she said softly. ''I do. And my acolytes do.''

''Then I choose you my adviser.''

Her eyes became intent, staring into mine. In an odd tone she said, ''Liege chose to send you to me. I must trust, and so must you, that his judgment has always been sound.''

I stood up. ''What? What is it?''

''Would you keep listening when She comes in the convulsions of a seizure, when others must record what you have uttered?''

I looked away, fidgeted. "Liege knew I was troubled. There is a man who plotted against Liege, but I cannot act against him, prevent him from new plots."

"Ahh. So you are considering disobedience to your Oath."

"Liege bound me by it!"

"And you would disobey him?"

"He trusts too much."

She watched me sit down. "In my Order there has always been a special respect for private conscience. It got many of us in trouble in the past and will continue to do so. As with you—a conflict between your conscience and the world's."

I lowered my head. Chin in hands, I said, "Did you ever feel so strongly about a person you couldn't even speak of it—"

"Yes. He fell while supervising a roof reslating and was not properly cared for in time. I became a Devotee after. Long ago." She flicked one hand, and I saw she was older than I had estimated, by ten years or more. "And you?"

I looked at my boots. "Yes," I whispered.

"Others may bicker on theological grounds, but I speak as I see. And I have seen altogether too much to object to real and selfless love. The feeling goads me that Liege is far more important than he knows—that we have a duty to him, especially *you* do. But he thinks it only a personal love. Loyalty. He doesn't realize the smell of doom and judgment it truly has. Or perhaps . . . he simply trusts in something larger than any of us."

Something struggled in my chest, came out in a hoarse sound. And suddenly, absurdly, I felt tears well over in my eyes and spill down my face. I sat unmoving, astonished at her, astonished at myself, and after awhile the tight feeling in my throat eased into an absurd comforting warmth, and the alien, bewildering tears stopped. I lifted my hand and smeared awkwardly at my face. "Thank you," I said at last.

She turned her head. In a deep, soft voice, she murmured, "But with all this, it is not done yet."

"*White Lady.*" I stood up, one hand rising. At last I felt the hair come up rough all along my spine under my robes, and I knew. I gasped, "It was *you!* In the dream, you—"

Her head angled to reveal a bright blue eye under her coppery brow. "Yes," she said, with no pretense at ignorance. "I learned, very late, of dangerous and unconscionable plans. So I spoke and dressed that way to frighten away observers—I guessed *you* would not back away! I broke serious vows to warn you, and I do self-imposed penance for that transgression.''

"But you *saved* him," I said in the lipless mutter that died out inaudibly, sooner than any hissing whisper. "You saved him from a lightning storm—''

"Pray, never again." Then, gravely, "Sati, poor counsel if I decided your conscience for you. So I say, study a sheaf of kinash grain as you meditate. Recite that desert prayer I heard you singing, very suitable. Do you so choose my counsel?''

"Yes," I said and smeared at my face, rubbing away the last salt tears. I stared at the brass traveling bowl, at her mask mute and shining beside her. "I'll do my best."

She slapped her knees once and rose, taking up her black wrappings. "So. By all the signs you'll make a good acolyte of the Goddess. I'll check your progress as I can. I'm tutoring Girdeth until her presentation preparations."

"Oh—" I caught back a swear word. "She *loves* parties."

"I'm sure Liege does not. I think it rash; but her formal presentation to court is already far delayed. Fortress will be secure enough if the event is kept brief. Despite my faith in prayers, Naga, it's reassuring to have a Sati on our side." She wrapped her black face cloth, lifted the mask, and made herself anonymous again. I looked into the inhuman filigree eyes. "Naga, remember some of your friends at court maintain as stiff a face as this. You have more help than you know. And pray."

I inclined my head to her in salute. She turned about and walked away with a wide and hasty stride. She hunted irritably in her pockets as the door closed behind her—hunting for a list of things to do, written on a scrap of parchment, just as her cousin Caladrunan did it. The cool scent of pine mountains swirled away with her, and was gone.

Three days later I saw dull red robes move through chaotic party preparations in the Great Hall. My thoughts instantly left prayer. I slid behind a pillar, watching. The Osa ambassadorial party passed, heads fixed, eyes front in rigid attention. Even with their offers rejected, they had not given up. Hoping for a peace treaty, Caladrunan tolerated their presence. I thought, let *me* throw them out.

Therin, Caladrunan's Heir and nine summers old, came along the gallery and moved quietly beside me to see what I was staring at. In one big rush he asked, "A lot of your people have

become Army scouts or servants, haven't they, Noble-born? Yet
Lado told me you'd make a terrible servant." With that sage,
childish look he hurried on, "My Lord Father agreed! *He* said
you were too mean—and Lado told me that no born servant
could kick a camp robber silly and bite his ear off and drive him
away. Then my Lord Father said you always *chose*, like his cat.
That he never got obedience of you. Is this so?"

I blinked, disconcerted, and stared at Therin. At last I couldn't
help myself; I grinned wolfishly at the picture they'd made of
me. Goddess forbid I must live up to all of this!

Therin looked almost as surprised at my reaction as I was.
Sitha, I thought, this boy has courage. The whole Fortress knew
how I felt about Osa! I said, with proper gravity, "Your father is
right. And Lado is a gossip."

Therin grinned. He knew I'd never admit his father gossiped,
too. The boy's smile made me feel good; but then, he had all his
father's charm. As I was his tutor, I had never expected Therin
to like me. *Nobody* liked arms trainers, no matter how good, and
it was stupid to expect him to appreciate it. But I liked him,
always had. Pleasant, to talk to him with the same freedom as
with his father. Then I realized the Osa were gone—and my
focused hatred had been scattered.

Deliberate, I thought. I looked at Caladrunan's son, narrowing
my eyes. His face was little boy bland, but *he* knew where the
soft streak in me lay, and he'd used it to prevent my rage. I
nodded once, acknowledging the ruler in the child, while he
looked at me unblinking. I said, "I bit that bandit's ear in half,
not all the way off."

Caladrunan's sister drifted up to me during her presentation
party that evening, trailing a hand on the rail of the upper Great
Hall gallery. "You must stop looking half-smothered, Naga. I
met your friend, the Devotee, and the Upai translator for the
Women of the Harp."

I glowered at Girdeth. She was, like her brother, much taller
than I was. Covered by the royal chaos, a day ago she'd escaped
her quarters, run away to the camps and Goddess only knew
where else—alone. But the women had taken tomboy Girdeth in
hand tonight. She was completely veiled, becomingly gemmed,
swathed in voluminous robes—almost anonymous. But I knew
that irreverent voice too well. She *knew* I was angry. Royal
apologies were implied in giving her attention to me. I looked

away at two nobles conferring behind the screen of a cluster of pillars. They weren't as well hidden as they thought.

Her fan fluttered archly, riffling her veil in a fashionable way. "All those scheming minds!" She waved her fan graciously over the rail at a lady, who waved back, but only because she couldn't hear Girdeth. "And how bitchily elegant."

Caladrunan had granted his sister a privilege of me: Just as I did with him, upon her pointing out anyone, however obliquely, I murmured information. *"She* wears two pairs of wool socks to bed, kisses her husband's house dogs, which may account for any doglike qualities, while her gaunt friend with her has a passion for confections of cupflower drug, which make her vague—not all bad, since her husband smuggles. Very bad if she hears too much. Both the ladies frequent the fighting pits, losing substantial sums gambling. So their Houses are purchased votes— for a price."

"Dog pits are illegal!"

"Quite," I said dryly. She was still young. "Well, they stimulate the economy." At her expression, I laughed.

Girdeth said, "I didn't know you ever laughed."

"Doesn't everyone?"

She gazed at a lady whose very robes disapproved of us, of the company about her, of the food. "No."

I followed her gaze. "Well, one can guess what *she* needs, and frankly I'm not brave enough to offer it. My poor manly parts might scorch and fall right off."

Girdeth smothered a snort of laughter behind her fan, which was as rude as my words had been. "I ought to find someone— aside from *me*—who's up to tempting you! Aren't you even interested?"

My lip quirked. "No." Of course she was only teasing, and well I knew it. But I was in an utterly foul mood despite Girdeth's efforts. I glanced around the upper gallery and Great Hall, checking guards among the pools of gold lamplight, hunting for the flash of their metal fitments in the confused deeper shadows. I hate guarding in this rockpile, I thought. Sharply I turned my head away, and we both fell silent, watching the stately progress of Capilla, Lady of Fortress, in full ceremonial regalia, across the main floor. She whished past us.

"I bet she kisses her dogs, too," Girdeth muttered darkly. "She has that look to her. Or maybe vipers. Escort me? Nothing's likely to happen to my brother with so many guards about."

After a quick scan, I agreed. "For your safety—I can't escort you as a noble."

She flicked her fan and laughed. "Of course not! *You're* not Tannese. Horrors, I think I'm not supposed to talk to you—you impose those silly old rules on yourself, you know." I paced beside her toward Caladrunan's marble dais. Her silk-covered arm lifted gracefully, furling air over her veil with the batting of the fan. It looked like a huge butterfly in her gloved fingers. "Do you *like* me, Naga, I mean as a friend, not guarding and all?"

"Be careful! I can't prevent hostile ears from—"

"So you *do!*" she said serenely, fan fluttering.

I stared at her. Her light manner had jarred me into a careless rebuke—I'd forgot the mind within that veil, diagnosing my preoccupations. She'd just seen into me and jerked me up short, as deft-handed as Therin. Or Caladrunan. Which was disquieting. And she'd *meant* it thus. Were my nose-lines so obvious that a young girl could yank me about? "Thank you."

Her voice sparkled with hints of laughter. "You're the *only* one who thanks me for pointing out frayed holes in your robes."

"Or in my armor. Or my mind," I muttered.

We both saluted. Caladrunan turned his head and smiled at us. "So here's the girl who caused so much uproar yesterday," he said, smiling still. Ironic lights danced in his eyes—and caution. He sat in the great black chair on his Hall dais, surrounded by guards—and at respectful distance, by his court. His yellow eyes were watchful.

"Naga won't answer a question!" Girdeth said.

"What question is that?" he asked indulgently.

"He *won't* say if he likes me."

Caladrunan slapped the dais table and roared, and pointed at Lado Kiselli, who grinned back from the harp stools below the dais. Lado strummed his harp grandly, gave a horrible mock Upai growl, and chuckled, saying, "That, dear Lady Girdeth, is a sure sign he's your prostrate slave. He'll never admit it, never!"

The Lord of Tan said then, "Ah! Girdeth, here's a new friend Lado brought. This Lady runs an orphanage that just moved to Birchwoods Hold. Lady Yoyu educates orphaned children from all over, her alumni do very well for us. I believe the Master of Scaddas, Reti himself, sent children from the border, didn't he?"

The slight woman at the foot of the dais bobbed her head in agreement, clutching at a veil that threatened to come out of its hairpins. Her gray robes looked severely practical and faintly stained, and the cut looked oddly archaic. She was clearly unused to the court's requirements, and she was nervous.

"Well met," Girdeth said pleasantly, surprising us all by adding, "I've heard of your orphanage. One of my lady-maids came from you and spoke highly of the training she was given there."

But Lady Yoyu, beginning to thank Girdeth, looked past her at me and stuttered. Her hands flew up, clapped together, and lost the veil. Her eyes, revealed, were wide and gray and astonished—young eyes in a middle-aged face. She pointed at me while the veil fluttered unnoticed away. "But I know you!" Her mouth opened, her face all delighted smile.

I blinked rather stupidly.

"I do! Little Treasure. You didn't know your name or how you came to be lost; you were seven summers, you had a young mare gana you kept close. Distinctive face—I beg your pardon, my Liege—such an unusual child. Reti sent you, do you remember?"

I tilted my head. "I do not remember any orphanage."

"You know your name now—"

"Reti trained me. He knew my name." I folded my arms.

"So he did find out, by that tattoo on your temple there—I recall he remarked on it when he brought you. Do you recall, you went with the group who needed clothes." She lifted her hand lightly toward Caladrunan. "Oh, my Liege, he was pitiful. His ribs showed, he was patched up with dog bite wounds in rags, never washed, when they brought him in—desperately small for his age, but so fierce for his mare. He was just darling when we got him cleaned up, but aren't they all? He slept two days straight!"

The Lord of Tan slanted a look at me. " 'Little Treasure'?"

"Yes," she said eagerly, "that was the name I gave him when he came. He was so quiet—quick to learn, too, he audited accounts for me! I preferred that name to Scratch; they called him that after he got in some nasty fights. They will bully without supervision, you know."

Caladrunan smiled slowly and said, "Why would Naga not remember being at your orphanage?"

"Oh, whatever lost him his parents had injured parts of his

memory—he had terrible nightmares. And Reti took him out only a year later.'' She smiled at me. ''Well, you've turned out so well, Liege's Sati, you know who you are—it's so gratifying one of my children has grown up so well!''

The Lord of Tan said dryly, ''He wandered ragged and starved into the middle of my fall hunt, threw himself on my mercy, and ended by telling me what was wrong with my Fortress security. I wonder if it's a habit of his.''

I felt heat flare in my ears. ''I didn't—''

His eyes met mine. ''He also had not washed for days and made a bit of a fuss about doing so. Naga, do you remember anything of Lady Yoyu's orphanage?''

I wished I hadn't escorted Girdeth here. But Lady Yoyu had kind hands; she meant no harm. Something about her eyes, the tiny dry wrinkles about her brows, was familiar. Maddeningly familiar. Something surfaced from the hash of my past. I pointed at a gold bracelet on her wrist. *That*. A woman's white hand, with a finger ring just like that, giving me cheese. Her hand smelled of soap. Bean-curd cheese—it was good. I thought I dreamed it.''

''He always remembers food,'' Caladrunan said. He looked at Lady Yoyu, and they both smiled.

She said, ''And who could blame him for it, my Liege? Not I. All the refugee children react like that—my Liege, we're just desperate for more help.'' Yoyu blushed. ''I was going to sell this bracelet; the ring already has gone for orphanage funds.''

Caladrunan said, ''We will arrange for you to meet the Women of the Harp, who will be coordinating refugee aid efforts.''

I studied her. The tiny lines came of weariness and concern, not age. She was barely above Caladrunan's age, young to be running an orphanage that had sheltered me at seven summers. Abruptly I dipped my hand to my belt, jerked my robe belt free, flicked my wrist. With a sliding gesture of the small chest-knife in my fingers, I slit free the belt buckle from its leather strap. I set down the white jade inlay on the dais step. Caladrunan bent and retrieved it, looking at me. I'd won the buckle as a prize in a challenge bout that did much to settle my right to be Caladrunan's bodyguard. I pointed. ''Begin by breaking up and selling that.''

She stared at me, then at Caladrunan, who held it out to her. Slowly she accepted it. ''But this is a Feastday prize—''

''It is a gift now. I may not remember your orphanage.'' I pointed at the buckle. ''Use that for refugees. For other children who don't remember what happened to them.''

Her fingers gripped tight around the milky-pale prize jade. "I will," she said, and nodded fiercely.

"I applaud you, Naga," Girdeth said suddenly, her hand extending. A string of black pearls dripped suddenly from her gloved fingers and pooled into Lady Yoyu's hand.

Yoyu blushed and paled. "You're all so generous—"

Girdeth gave a low, soft chuckle that was not funny at all. "We can afford to be now. If we were border-lords, it might be *our* children you cared for, Yoyu. Do well with it. You may be working with me in the Women of the Harp."

Lady Yoyu inclined her head deeply to all of us, repeatedly, and gesticulated as Lado Kiselli led her off, exclaiming with every step.

Caladrunan smiled broadly. "So you got the pearls you wanted, sister. How *did* you end up in the market a day ago?"

"It was quite fun," Girdeth said blithely. "Your Lady Wife nearly ruined a perfectly good pot of mua when I told her!"

"I should think so!" Pitar's mustache bristled in horror. "Royal women traipsing about the market alone!"

"Oh, it was fun," Girdeth assured him, waving her fan gaily.

"Mmm," Caladrunan said, looking at me with a bleak eye. "How did Girdeth get *out* of the quarters? More important, why?"

I said flatly, "She climbed out a neglected guarderobe shaft. I smelled it on her when she returned."

Somebody gasped, Somebody else tittered. Girdeth's fan slapped on robes. "Not true!" she exclaimed. "I *never*—"

I looked at her. Caladrunan looked at her.

"Well, just part of the way," she said.

Her lord brother sighed.

"My Liege, I repaired that breach—" It wouldn't help much, but I tried anyway.

"Mmmh," he said quietly, eyes shifting between his outrageous sister and myself. "I'll talk to you both. Later. In my chambers. Might as well go on up to yours now, Girdeth, you've been flaunted in the public view long enough. Naga, escort her."

Girdeth made as if to throw a tantrum, stamping her slippered foot. I grasped the edge of her fan and turned her about—never once touching her person—by example more than tugging. She found herself walking away before she realized how I'd done it. We picked up a squad of female guards and were out of the

Great Hall doors before Girdeth could speak. "You're very mean! You know I went out there to the camps to pass funds to your Upai teacher— "

"Liege, *your brother*," I said, in a tone which made the listening guards flinch back out of earshot, "can be meaner. Neither of us would ever ask you to take such risks and then to talk openly about it in front of half the court!"

"I suppose *you* want to thrash me for escaping—well, the place is too—" She flung up her hands. "I don't know, I needed fresh air anyway. I have to get out sometimes!"

"You could run away and become a commoner if you wanted it enough. I don't promise you any joy of it."

"I hate it when you use that ugly flat tone." The hands flung up again. "I thought it would be *fun* living here, but everyone is so touchy and tense—"

I checked the first of her private chambers in the women's quarters before admitting her. I stood in the middle of silk floor cushions, looking about at an impressive scroll collection. As Girdeth rustled in, I adjusted the metal bands over my glove knuckles. Girdeth waved for her women guards to withdraw, and sank down on a cushion; her favorite lady-maid avoided me— with a small witch-warding sign—as she adjusted the heavy headdress on Girdeth's brow. By that sign's country origin I knew she must be the maid trained at Lady Yoyu's orphanage. Girdeth said, "What does it matter? Silly veil."

"It matters," I said harshly.

Girdeth waved the girl off. The maid sat down just past earshot. I fidgeted with my gloves. Girdeth's voice went low and rough and sounded years older than it had in the Great Hall. "You say I'm watched? I know it. I went to the market after I met your Upai teacher. It was dangerous maybe, but I wanted to get away a little while. That's all."

"Then go home," I said gently. "Go back to Lake Hold."

The headdress moved sharply. Low and thick, she said, "No. I'm staying. Drin needs me. Somebody has to make the traditional charitable aid groups help the Women of the Harp. And I'll act as I think right!"

The door sailed open gaily. "Our Liege sent me up to retrieve a lost Harper," Lado said.

Girdeth flapped her hand. "Go—I'm terribly cross and maybe I won't speak to anyone for days."

Lado hooted in disbelief and dragged me out. In the corridors he said, "Mustn't cause rumors, Naga. I heard people wondering if you—" He yelped when I gripped his arm punishingly hard. "Stop! It certainly wasn't your friends saying that. But don't give them any more substance to talk about!"

I let go.

"Flame it, I'm just trying to protect your reputation. I know, I know, you say I gossip too much, but I worry—"

"You're right. You talk too much. But I thank you for your concern. You should've just punched the flapping mouth."

"Me, hit a gossip source? You're dreaming. Goddess, you *are* in a foul temper. When I got that package of Army funding authorizations voted our way in Council, are you pleased? No, you just grunt at me and ask for more. Always more! When Liege told me you were supposed to stay, I warned him. I said you'd be *horrid,* and you have been."

I said, between closed teeth, "Let's just say I have a weakness for seeing that members of Lake Clan remain healthy."

"Of course, Little Treasure," Lado said.

I turned my head and looked at him. Lado fell abruptly silent. Then slowly he began to smile, his eyes anxious, but his grin growing wider. "I'm sorry, but it really is such a funny name. I can't help it. There's a song in there somewhere, I—"

I smiled back at Lado. "And if you sing it publicly, I have no idea what I might do about it, Lado. Remember that *charming* lady you went to see the other night—"

Lado said hastily, "You wouldn't. Her brothers are three times my size. You know it wouldn't be fair."

I patted his arm. "I knew we'd understand each other."

"Blackmailer," he grumbled. "Little Treasure!"

I growled a bit myself as we strode into the Great Hall. None of them realized how often I chose to do the Lord of Tan's bidding above my own free will—and how I felt the weight of that constant choosing.

# CHAPTER

# = *6* =

AT DAWN I stood in the garden roof of the women's quarters.
Reserve troops marched through streets, shouting cadence; the
roar echoed along alleys. Crowds shouted below Fortress' walls,
complex whistles of appreciation followed street women.

Everywhere else, silence.

For all the parade noise, the tower-cluttered Tannese sky
seemed empty without hammerblows echoing down stone streets.
I'd grown used to the jagged din, to dodging blasts of furnace
heat and water puddles shimmering out of the smithies Caladrunan
had collected over the moons, used to metal screaming and
carpentering echoes in odd corners. Now they'd gone. The training courtyards below were also silent. Within its walls, Fortress
seemed too quiet. Behind me the soft silent rooms of the wom-
en's quarters seemed eerie, alien.

It was just dawn; the air hung cold and foggy around me. A
strangely colored fog, this—pink-tinged with dawn light, it lingered over the garden trees in a smooth glow, obscured the
proud Fortress towers, cut off the tops of gates, pooled and
eddied along courtyards outside the siege walls, and collected
woodsmoke in long, flat, sooty sheets. Men marched into the fog
and vanished. As an omen it made my spine turn cold.

Caladrunan's honor guard formed in the main square and
marched out in the crisp lines that only parade competitors
mastered. The real march commander, Strengam Dar, had long
since departed—taking along a ferment of ideas I explained to
him in the early morning dark. Strengam could repeat them
during the ride outward, which was far from good enough for

me. If I were there, I'd tell the Lord of Tan more as I saw the
terrain. The air hung cold and wet about my face as I looked
down. I raised my fist and brought it down softly, controlled, on
the crumbling stone merlon in the battlement.

I spun around, hands out, at hearing a light skipping step.

"Oh, *Father's* friend!" a frilly pink creature said.

·I stared for a moment. It was a girl, a noble little girl in full
ceremonial regalia, but lace dragged about one ankle and her lips
and hands were muddied. Her eyes were brilliant turquoise,
which marked her as Caladrunan's daughter Vopi. All the golden-
eyed monarch's children had startling and varied eyes.

"I wanted to see Father—they told me he's going away." She
scowled. "I didn't get to see. I had to run away from the ladies.
But you're here, so he can't be going—"

"He's with the Army." I pointed into space out a crenel.

"Can I see?" She danced for the battlements rising on the east
end of the gardens and added earnestly, "Really, I won't fall
down." She knew that rise gave the best view.

Walking east, I asked, "Do you get dizzy on heights?"

"Not the times I try," she said, skipping beside me. She
seemed absolutely fearless. I saw animal scratches on her arm
and large muddy rips in the robes at her knees. The girl's nurses
would suffer if the Lady saw the child now.

I said, "I'll lift you here next to me, then you can see over."
She lifted up slender, fragile-looking arms. I picked her up—she
was perhaps half my size—and set her gold slippers on the seat
of an arrow loop built into a buttress in the parapet. She stood up
on tiptoe, craning forward. "Steady? Lean on my shoulder if
you get dizzy. I'll catch you."

"*I* know, silly! Father told me you were very fast. Very, *very*
fast!" She rested a muddy hand on my shoulder and touched my
braids. "You talk funny, but you have nice hair. Shiny."

"Thank you. Your father should be down there any time
now." A sudden blare of horns from the street made us both
jump.

Behind us, from the quarters door, Lado Kiselli's loud
cheerful voice rang out and bounced lightly in quips among
servant women. He trotted excitedly past us, pointing. "There
he is!"

I followed him with one hand on Vopi's shoulders. I leaned on
the wide tooth of a merlon and strained out a crenel to see past
an intervening wall buttress. A small hand crept into mine; I

turnéd and helped Vopi step onto my crenel's ledge. I watched the shining snake back of the honor guard marching through dimming patches of fog—buckles clanking, pennants snapping on poles, jade and tin ornaments jumping and tinkling regularly at every step in a mass musical note, muffled strangely in the sea fog.

Then Caladrunan was riding four stories below me in his glittering Sharinen-made armor. His son Therin, shining in matched armor, rode beside. The girl-child beside me squealed in delight under my hand.

Lado said, "*I'm* not trying that perch."

I glanced over my outstretched arm at my fellow Harper. Then I unpropped myself and stared away down at the honor guard.

"Cheer up, Black Man, he'll be home soon enough," Lado said flippantly. "He can't *really* go risking his hide—"

I stood perfectly still. "There are times when your humor slides into an irritating overcompensation to make up for surviving the unfair murder of your elder brother by those Marsh raiders—at such a young age, too."

"Down to *that*, eh." He lodged his robed bottom on the crenel ledge at our feet and jiggled his boot toe at the parapet walk. "*Oooo,* you sneer so well. Are you always so vicious to friends?"

I glared at the offensive landscape, at the troops still marching past. "Often worse," I snapped. It was that or hit him, and even poor jokes were better. I knew his eyes were skipping about examining my mood, my stance, thinking how to defuse it.

I didn't much want to be defused.

"Do we Tannese exasperate you to quite *that* degree?" he asked.

I gripped the merlon with one hand, and felt sandstone crumble under my fingers. "Flamed rotted-out pile of—"

"Don't kick it," he said hastily, "you'd knock that stone stump onto some bystander. Besides, you might break your foot!"

I glared. But my hand stayed moth-light on Vopi's shoulder.

"You *do* have a nasty temper, don't you?" After surveying me for a moment, he added, "Really, you're the last man I'd pick to make into a Sati. If that temper rips loose, there's so many more pieces to pick up."

I took a deep breath, drew Vopi back from the crenel edge, and released her shoulder. I rubbed my banded gloves together with tight squealing sounds of metal on metal. Vopi studied me with grave bright eyes. I challenged angrily, perhaps to them both, "Then it *does* bother you that I could kill you if I decided to, Lado—if I lost my temper, and you couldn't fight."

He flushed. "Fighting just got me beat up in the past, and it isn't likely to change now, is it?" He waved a crooked Harper's hand. "Come, there's limits to paranoia. You've proved yourself friendly too many times. You even got me off when Tanman questioned me on that misrecalled History line the other day. How many Harpers would do that for me?"

"Oh, *that*," I said. "Lado, you can't drink and perform—"

He held up his hands. "Oh, I remember it clearly, I swore—"

"You're distracting me."

"You're brooding, not planning, so I felt free to."

I glared.

"Look," he said, "you've already kicked pebbles on the heads of two guard watches this morning. I hardly believe you kick things when you're thinking tactics—"

"Strategy," I snapped. "Tactics is fieldwork. They're entirely different!"

"And you weren't doing either," Lado flared up. "Sorry. If I had something for punching practice, I'd toss it to you. But I don't. Just me." He spread his hands wide.

"You've got courage," I said in a calmer tone than before.

He fluttered his hands, dipped his chin in mocking salute, shrugged. "Thank you, but don't flatter me, it might give me delusions of safety."

I herded Vopi toward the parapet. Once we were back at Lado's level I stared out an embrasure and grumped to myself. Vopi folded her little hand in mine, offering comfort. The calluses surprised her, and she examined my hand. I half-closed my eyes. "Do you know, Lado, how many ways there are to kill a man?"

Lado, out of the corner of my eye, shook his head.

"Good. Because I don't even know that myself. But I know there are plenty to wipe out one little Tanman who's getting in the way of the Osa." My thumbtip ground a speck on the embrasure wall into dust while I stared at Lado.

After a suspended moment, Lado said, "You're afraid you'll go mad if he dies. That he's the only one who can help the fits."

I waved one arm a little wildly. "That's just the start of it! If he's gone, then what happens to his wife, his son, his House-

hold, this little child—to you and me, Lado! To Tan!'' I waved
the arm at the landscape cut by the embrasure.

Lado smiled. ''Well, I've a great speech about repentance,
praising new rulers, pack full of abject groveling.''

''Fifth History,'' I said.

''Absolutely right. What better model to adopt than a failed
usurper trying to save his neck?''

''Oldfield's messages last fall.'' Said very dryly, that.

''I'll have to study them for proper humility.''

''It won't help. You're a Harper. The Osa condemn all secular
music as the sign of an unstable mind. Their priests consign it to
the forbidden arts like witchcrafts, navigation by stars, and
mathematics. Illegal except for priestly use.''

Lado blinked. ''They must be a singularly humorless people.''

''I rather thought so,'' I said grimly. ''Priests of the Iron
Sword. Their men are organized as tightly as ants from tiniest
childhood; the less competent officers end up at the edges, which
is what we see. It's not how they began, but now they march to
the same music everywhere, and they pray for the same rulers,
and they have the same paintings of holy faces in all their
buildings—'' I gestured in frustration. ''They're like nothing in
Tan.''

''Not even Devotees?'' Vopi asked.

We both looked at her. I dropped all notion of insulting her by
simplifying my conversation. ''They make Devotees look like a
rained-out parchment copy.''

''Oh. *Bad* men.'' She frowned, pinching pearls on her robes.

Lado said, ''Well, neither you nor I could stand rulers like
that, Harpers or not!''

I tapped my forehead tattoo. ''This—this alone—would see
me flayed alive, Lado.'' I turned away in a violent movement,
thumped the battlement viciously with my boot. ''People are
packed in everywhere here, bawling like cattle, and the Osa are
coming. The Osa are sick, Lado! I pray every day that their
empire collapses from its own weight.''

''We're trying to give it a good push in that direction,'' Lado
said. ''Would a long ride outside the walls help your mood?''

I shook my head. ''Too much temptation. Ride off and simply
keep going until I reached the war camps.''

''But Fortress is important, too,'' Vopi said anxiously, tilting
her head up. Her eyes seemed very blue.

''This rotting pile!'' I snapped. ''The Osa want the site to rule

Tan, but they won't bother about the walls. Burn it and watch it come down. Or pay someone to blow up the gas mine. I hate fixed defensive positions—they don't work, especially when they're so primitive, against Osa.''

"Should we all run away very fast?" she asked. Her face was calm and still as a brushed porcelain portrait mask.

"No. *Stop* the Osa before they reach Fortress at all."

She spoiled the exquisite mask by squinting through pale curls at me. "*I* can throw rocks at them! Big rocks."

I brushed back the pale curls. "Thank you."

Lado said, "Most commanding officers never reveal doubts."

"Tanman is the commander here, never doubt that!" I said fiercely. "You precious Tannese would never take orders from *me* independent of his authority."

"Oh, we'd do it if our lives hung on the quality of our commander."

"*It does,*" I flashed at him. Then, "I hope you're right." I paced up and down the parapet. "I can't get the silk traders to free up their wood contracts. The cutters and burners in the hills stopped working because the silk men don't think they'll need any more charcoal this season—but *no,* the silk men still won't release those flamed exclusive contracts, so *we* can buy wood for channel scaffolding—"

"I've some relations in the milling and sawmill business," Lado said. "Why don't I see what they suggest? If nobody's hauling charcoal or firewood, the cutters will be hungry. They'll gladly sell wood to another outlet—though, mind you, charcoal and milled timber are such different specialities—"

"We've got old Household mills idle on the Tejed River down there now! We can take this year's limbed rough green trunks—"

"Oh, good. That'd be cheaper. Now, transport—some drovers will yell swear-breaker, but the hungry ones will negotiate. Teach that snobby silk lot to be less high-handed with other people's trade. I've heard complaints about them for years."

"How do we make sure the cutters aren't taking too much; how do we get them to obey the replant laws? Liege said if we let it go, there won't be any woods for their grandchildren to cut."

"Make it a condition of payment. Best way to enforce the law would reward the drover loading the limbed trunks—but graft—"

"Lado? Thank you. I was too angry earlier."

He glanced up. "I guessed as much. It's difficult not having Liege here to discuss things, yell and shout and get over it. One of his strengths, that. Well, you probably know him better than anyone, for all you've only been here a short time. Remarkable how he's relaxed, and grown perhaps as a ruler, since you've been here. When he dealt with Manoloki and the Nando mercenaries last fall, just after you came, he was masterful. Before, the very thought of Manoloki paralyzed us all."

I said dryly, "I think I've just been the victim of one of your cheering-up talks."

He grinned. "And you didn't see it coming?"

Vopi glared at Lado, flouncing her finery. "You made him *sad* again!"

Lado spoke to her sober gaze. "We all are sad. We'd all like your Lord Father to stay here. Tannese never have liked wars so dire that Tanman himself must take part." Lado's voice changed. He said to me, "And you know he must."

I gripped the stone in one hand. Lado looked at me. I stared at him. If he had had pity in his eye, I would've kicked him. But he said, "Why don't you make yourselves useful? I've got a melody I want shouted down there, and you've got lungs enough to help me!" He unslung his harp.

More slowly, I drew my own harp from the case under my left arm. "Give me tune," I said.

We sang Lado's music. I'd never heard anything like it before from the master of pastel tones and silken verse. We played until dust flew off our robes, while Caladrunan's daughter clapped her hands. Giggling, the girl climbed into a crenel and beckoned Lado. He finally climbed into the crenel next to hers, all the while his arms pumped wildly at his harp. Vopi was steady as the rocks of her perch. I stood on top of the merlon tooth between them and bawled down verses at the marching honor guard. When we ran out of words, Lado and I made up new ones—every rude soldier's phrase intact and pristine. I saw heads down in the crowded street turn up toward us. The second honor troop picked up the melody and carried it as they passed; the song rose in a blurred wave both ways down the column.

Jumping from crumbling merlon to merlon-top, with Vopi safe under my hand all the way, we yelled Tanman free of the gate of his Fortress, we yelled him out to battle and overran his enemies in glorious roars, and we yelled him back safe again. We bawled his honor guard and his friends along until chickens in the street

coops crowed and pigs ran about squealing against the cacoph-
ony. Then we climbed down to the big eastern arrow loop and
sat on the bench inside its wide embrasure.

Our girl-child shaded her eyes at the slit aperture. "I don't see
him now. Mother said she didn't know why you couldn't find
something better to do, Father's-best-friend, but I told her everybody wanted to see Father leave. She cried, really. It was so sad.
I can't see him anymore. Did you see him leading them all? He
did!" She leaned; I watched her, finally brought a firm hand
around her chest, but I didn't stop her looking. The child shaded
her eyes, shaking her head.

Behind me I heard a whisper of slippers. My back muscles
went rigid. I held Vopi securely; but I knew exactly how I could
be punished for it. There was a sharp gasp, and then silence, a
tautly drawn, a nervous, silence. I drew the little girl back gently
and pointed out the different divisions. She clapped her hands.
She liked them all; she waved at the elaborate banners. Lado
drew away quietly. Behind me, more silence until the child
wanted to get down, and I lifted her off the wall and set her feet on
the grass. She ran off gaily, muddy hands outstretched. "Oh
Lady Mother, I could see far and far; I saw Father ride out!"

I looked around. The Lady of Fortress lowered tight-clenched
gloved hands and spread them, and hugged the draggled child-
finery to her. In a deliberate, careful tone she told the child,
"You must never climb up there alone, you know."

"Oh, I didn't! Father's friend held me so I could see, and we
all sang. Can I show Father's friend the birds?"

"Your nurse is here. Go play with her." The girl scowled
ferociously; but her mother brushed some mud from the child's
lips, suggested a song that made Vopi smile, and waved her to
go back into the women's quarters. Vopi twirled in circles,
singing as she went, and slammed a door shut with a loud,
healthy bang. The Lady let out a long, slow breath; her veil
fluttered. Then she gestured sharply for Lado to go entertain her
maids—but that *I* was to stay.

I turned away to the fog, streets, and towers cut by mist.

"Odd," Capilla, Lady of Fortress, said quietly, turning her
veil up to the flat gray sky. None of her servants would hear us;
the women had scattered westward, chattering loudly and waving
to the troops passing below. Lado spoke to the women, smiling—
and he kept his back to us as he clapped his hands, waved, and
got them all scurrying away eagerly inside the quarters.

The Lady looked at me through her thin private-quarters veil, a somber set to her body. She said, "Makes you afraid, doesn't it? And you started it all."

I said, looking at the troops, "As much as the voice that cried out warning to the prophet Rapnam from a glowing cave in the very cliff beneath us."

She turned away, rasping her brocaded sleeves on the stone. "You and your fatuous Harper prattle."

To keep from answering her as she deserved, I twisted my boot toe on the lip of the giant lead soil pan that drained the garden.

She pushed away from the stone and said, "I realize, Sati, that you were climbing everything in sight from the time you could crawl, and with your speed of reaction you might snatch a falling child in time to save her. But in one respect you were an utter fool just now—Vopi will be climbing all over, alone or not."

In surprise, I thought: So the Lady does not rebuke my simply putting native hands on her child, but the safety risk! I looked at her veil, utterly opaque at this angle. It must not be easy to restrain offspring with Caladrunan's leonine vitality. I said, "Tell her I'll cane her if she climbs without help."

The Lady's hands came together in a shocked, negating gesture. Repressively she said, "Her nurses could not save her a fall. I do not believe in striking any child. In any case, asking servants to strike her would never do."

"Let her climb solely with my help," I said abruptly. "I'll punish her myself if I catch her at it alone. She'll climb about somehow—anyhow—she has no fear. It's a bit awesome."

"Awesome!" the Lady snapped. "Yes, she'll try anything— her father's gift. So she will not climb at all. Don't expand her world like that again, Sati. She'll get herself killed."

"Can you hide the world from her? Much safer, begun under your supervision than invented on her own! She has heart. The child wasn't afraid of me—and most young children in Tan are. Properly channeled, that courage could—"

"Of course she's not afraid! She's seen you with her father many times, and she's overheard enough gossip to last a lifetime. Courage! How Upai you are. We are women; what use is courage to one of *us*?" Her voice made bitter quote of some fool's opinions.

I looked out the arrow loop at the men marching past. "The whole world is changing, Lady."

She tapped the great wall with a ringed hand. "Liege told me you would be staying, training more of those hapless idiots down there. But he'll take the field himself, lead the troops with just Pitar as his shield. He told me he needed your analytic abilities saved. *Yours!*" I heard a whole world of scorn and pain in her voice. I had never heard any emotion there before.

"Liege is the one to judge the best use of my talents, not me." I looked at the vine-draped walls of the women's quarters and down at the marching troops, adding, "But you're right about those hopeless idiots. Too few trained officers, no battle experience, recruits with a moon's training at best—" I looked at her and sharpened my fingernails on stone, rasp-*rasp*-raaasp. "It could have been worse."

She seemed to stare through the embrasure of the arrow loop at the line of march. "If I were a man, I would go with him."

I felt something catch in my throat. After a moment, flatly I said, "If you were a man, you'd do what he told you."

Her shoulders jerked slightly.

"I wish you talked him into taking me!" I told her fiercely. "I wish it more than you know. A rattle-trap mob of farmhands with pitchforks for weapons—I wished devoutly to go with him!"

Her veil turned down toward the marching troops. She said, in an arid courtly mode, "I have rarely seen you so moved, Harper." She spoke crisply, with such exquisite courtesy it stung like nettles. Leaf-green speckles of light slid over her veil as sunlight flickered dimly through the fog and the garden trees.

I glanced about at the sky, down again. Bitterly I said, "What would you prefer, History recitals?"

"*My* wishes!" she hissed. "As if anyone ever asked. Do you know what pain you have caused me?" Grief lay in her deep voice.

I said seriously, "I meant only to do what was best by him."

"Oh, Goddess, don't you think I *know* that!"

I wondered suddenly—shocked—if she wept under her veil.

She went on, "He was so careful to explain necessity. I let you teach my son because my husband—" her voice wavered, found itself again, "—my Lord Husband judged you the best tutor he could find. I reconciled myself to it. He said that you were—that you—" she could not utter the words. Her head rose a degree higher, she turned rigidly away, an iron tower wrapped in silk. I heard a discreet rustle of cloth. Then she said in a voice renewed and hard, "I'm aware of your *wishes*—your competence—or I would never tolerate your presence. Oh, I know the causes; he was careful to explain them. You go down and do your duty to this pile of rock. I do not wish to speak to you again." Her voice grated bitter as desert frost underfoot.

I moved a few steps away from the wall. "Do you have any message for Therin before I post today's work? It would save you sending another rider after them." I could needle her, too: I knew she didn't write to the boy as often as she used to.

She lifted her head higher yet. "Give him my love," she said. Cold blue eyes glared through the translucent veil. Then she whirled her robes close, spun about, and left.

I inclined my head and turned away. *"Kigadi,"* I said to the free air beyond the walls, as if to a direct order of his. I went stiffly down to my quarters.

I had work to do.


For all my rages against his carelessness, Caladrunan had known what he was doing. Fortress was quiet in his absence, all peaceable workmen silently doing what they were told, as placid as their pigs in the town. I had wondered if the quiet came of the enemy's disinterest or of a lag in messaged new orders from the Osa. They might just be busy watching the uproar of all the Tannese courtiers bickering in the field of war. Caladrunan came back with half of them in a moon's time, muddy, scratched up a little, sunburned across his nose. He'd lost his nervous anticipation, he'd hardened. Tan's forces had swept away the enemy at Black Pebble Ford with little trouble, considering their numbers, machines, and our raw troops.

The Lord of Tan told the crowd that Keth's gana tactics had cut the enemy up severely before the masses of footmen grappled. The enemy deployment began masterfully, but in action some inept apprentice scrambled their troops. Strange, I thought. The true master had been off somewhere thinking up better trouble. Cold thought, that the Osa could afford such losses, but I had seen it before.

Caladrunan said over the heads of the crowd, "Just raw Marsh villagers press-ganged or promised a jade chip a day, every one, except for a poor lot of Nando mounted. I'm thirsty for decent wine! What, we leave and you all mope about and forget to eat?" He loved the attention after his victory. I had no place there in the sunburned crowd of officers, courtiers, and messengers. I found an empty bench and sat down, waiting. I heard Rafai tell his subofficer Ben, "Naga's about to storm off to find trouble to sink his teeth into—"

Therin sat on a bench beside mine. "You look much better Noble-born—only a bit peeling on that burn spot on your brow."

As Heir, he had the right to comment. I grunted.

Therin said, "If only you could have gone . . ."

I turned away, which stopped that line of conversation. Orders were orders, after all.

Therin looked wistfully to his father. "Maybe he'll have time for us later. I can wait," Therin said hastily, and squirmed on his bench. I looked at him under my lids. After a moment he added, "Noble-born."

I relented on the stare. Caladrunan was drinking new beer from a goblet and spilling out events as fast as he could get the words out, while Devotee scribes wrote madly across slates. He was like a vetted boy. After a moment I thought, that was what he was, really.

Caladrunan did talk to his son; he was still excited, and Therin was eager for his father's attention. Then the Lord of Tan called together the War Council, and they all went off for a formal closed session. Caladrunan grinned conspiratorially and waved me off to other duties as he went. It was dusk, almost time for last meal, before he got free of courtiers.

*I* was in the kitchens.

"*Look* at him!" the cook shrieked from the door behind me. Newcomer come from army service with Caladrunan, poor fellow; the Fortress cooks ignored him. "Eating our meat and killing things!"

I whirled. Caladrunan surveyed me. "What *are* you doing?" he asked mildly.

"Kitchen duty, my Liege. Sharpen up my eye, keep in training. Doves—been awhile since I made dove pie. You'll like it."

"I'm told you terrified the potboys, drove off a pack of runaway dogs, killed innocent birds, and sent my new cook into hysterics. So I guess you must be glad to see me, you terror."

I just grinned and ripped a piece of smoked meat from a hanging carcass by kicking out and stabbing it whap-whap-crack with my right razor spur. Not, I knew, the way to run an efficient kitchen, but I needed the practice; and the Fortress cooks, outspoken mixed-blood commoners, had always wel-

comed me as a partisan of their arts. Bits of kitchen dust drifted
off my boot. The meat tasted delicious. "Want some, my Liege?"

He looked at it, and at me, threw back his head, and roared
with laughter. "Did you really hit doves with rocks?"

"Dirty little birds." I picked up a chunk of tinder wood,
weighing it as I watched another dove settle on the wall outside
the grain-bin delivery door. *Ffffwhack,* the bird went down over
the wall like the others. I said happily, "I wanted three, and I've
got a good dozen already."

"What would you scrounge if there weren't any birds?"

"Oh, if the place was empty? Stray animals, wild dogs. Rats.
Vegetable gardens gone wild. Recent garbage, maybe—amazing
what you can find. After I ran through stored stuffs here, out to
the fields. If I had to stay under cover, leave minimal spoor—
into the oakwoods, hunt log-worms and beetles. I used to catch
oasis frogs in the desert, and the big wolf-ants that come out at
night. Snakes, of course, were the main thing. Sand-death vipers
taste the best, but they're risky catching, they spit venom as well
as bite." *Fffwhack,* I nearly missed; the bird fluttered, spun, and
thrashed before falling. I scowled. "You really don't want anything to eat?"

"I'm . . . not hungry. Why don't you fetch your doves," he
suggested gently.

I took a running leap at the wall outside, jumped over. I
gathered up the broken birds into a leather cook-sack and tossed
it back; I leaped the wall again and dusted off my hands.
Caladrunan blinked. At the kitchen hearth I set about making pie.
Same as for trainees, I explained myself. "Normally I'd save
intestines, the down, vane feathers, tendons. But—for instance—
dove feathers are too weak for fletching my long bow arrows.
Now the gut goes for gana feed—seeds in it are good for beasts."
The burning feathers smelled horrible. I sorted through the guts,
adding the good stuff to the sloshing green hide cooksack. Caladrunan watched without moving; his nose wrinkled slightly, once.

"You don't waste things," he said quietly.

"Not if I can help it," I agreed, and wiped my hands on a
chunk of bark before throwing it on the fire. From a comfortable
distance, of course. I never strayed too close. "The Goddess
doesn't like it. This cooks until the wine is all gone and it's a flat
cake in the bottom. Mix grain with it midway and it becomes a
travel cake. Stop looking like that, the bones are good for
you—they go all soft by then."

He gave another slow smile. He lifted from a fold of his robe a greenish fruit. "More food that's good for you. Imported, I just received a box. Would you like some? I wagered the rest of the boxful on Isaon's fourpeg tonight."

I accepted a chunk he cut from the fruit. It was juicy and extremely tart, like other scurvy-fruits I'd eaten, but I managed to get the rind down. He watched me, smiling that faint smile; perhaps I wasn't supposed to eat rind. At my expression he said, "Medicine for your teeth."

"Certainly tastes like it. Fourpeg?" I managed to say when my mouth was empty.

He cut another chunk and gave it to me. "A marathon tonight while my men are here. Are you going to play?"

I began to chuckle, chewing rind, and winced at the acid. He walked out of the kitchen with me, cutting another chunk, and handed it to me. "What kind of game is Isaon running?" I asked.

He glanced at me. "I don't know the game well enough to know what variant he does."

"Mmm," I said, doubtless showing a gleam in my eye. "I've got a few ideas for a new variant—"

He opened a gate and passed through, dismissing his other guards with a smile.

We went into the long, warm sculpture garden. Caladrunan strolled, head down, hands linked at his back, along the slate-paved pathway past summer-dense bushes. "I'd like to hear your thoughts on a choice of War Council chairman."

I plucked a thorned stem, scratched the great red hooks against my harp calluses. Not enough harp practice of late—my calluses were peeling; the scrape of the thorns felt wonderful. I said moodily, "I'd appoint Swan. This other one, Whitmill, won't even give us a good argument on tax laws."

Caladrunan looked at me astonished. "How will we get anything done if we spend all our time arguing with Swan?"

I scowled at the red hooks on the stem in my fingers. "Swan is strong, he's smart, but he has a lot of other work—if he were chairman, he couldn't argue any but important things. And he's capable of using logic. So neither of you will waste time on things that don't matter. If you lose to him, it's more likely to be all right—neither of you are stupid, just disagree violently. And you do need a strong voice for the conservative side."

He glanced at me, brushing aside a ferny purple branch. I

went on, "Your method is a straight-ahead full charge. Should you hold back your own young bucks when they're getting extreme? No, your style needs a strong opposition to hold those points where the opposing view is right, and because of political alliances, you're dangling out there, maybe wrong. Now, you told me Whitmill's a weakling, a sneak. He'll pick all the wrong places to stick at, not the genuine issues where their views might be better for your country. With Swan you can always look like you're fighting vigorously, no softening your punches."

"I'd be fighting for my life! Mere punches with Swan, ha!"

Caladrunan looked at me and shook his head slowly, smiling. "Just when I think I know what you'll say, you come about and surprise me completely."

"Training technique," I explained, and punched a cork-oak's corrugated trunk with the savagery of a kitchen cat at a feather. "Lazy training doesn't build any strength."

"It's a very Tannese chain of reasoning you just gave me," he said, reaching the end of the walled garden. He paced back the way we'd come, boots whispering on the slate path. "Swan holds disastrous opinions about Army supply costs—"

"Prove it to him," I suggested, duck-walking as drolly as I could, imitating Swan's posture. He smiled. "You know Whitmill would enrage his own conservatives into going to other methods. Violent ones." I whipped a wrist-knife out between my fingers, sliced an innocent flower stem, and left it standing in place, looking untouched, while my knife went sheathed.

"Save trouble in the end." Caladrunan agreed mildly, lifting the flat yellow bloom as if accepting it directly from my offering hand.

I stared at him. "You planned it that way all along—you were testing me!"

"Well, I wasn't sure you'd understand—you and your Sati dislike of rank-and-file battles. You always slide in on weak spots, pinch out the strong sites—"

"That's battles! That's not ruling a country. Surely you don't think I confuse the two."

"I've heard merchants confuse paying taxes with war—and these Councilors are near fighting pitched battles!"

I snorted. "Not the same at all. Flames, you're all trying to work out the right thing to do while keeping an eye on personal and local benefits. You're not really enemies."

"Except for some who've allied with the real enemy."

I flashed him a grim look. I grunted, "They may think that is the only course left them, if they're honorable men. If they're *not,* it's my job—and Pitar's and your spy network's—to root them out as enemy. We do our best. It's difficult to read between the two types once they've tangled with Osa and Nandos."

"Yes," Caladrunan said, assuring me that he hadn't meant any criticism. I dipped my head in half-salute.

He halted before a large-leafed tree trained up on a sun-wall, reaching through the light green foliage to break off a spike of large bluish bells. The tree was covered with them. He stirred the bells with his thumb, briefly gloved his fingertips in blue, looking at me. Then he tucked the spike into the braids behind my left ear, brushing bell substance and fragrance about my earlobe. "There," he said, his eyes assessing the effect. "Makes your hair look blue-blacker."

"The tails are faded rather brown," I admitted. I adjusted the blue spike. My hand checked quick retrieval of the garrote wire tucked in a braid underneath and the draw of a tiny knife. I grinned. "Swan will hate any praise from me. I think it's because I have such a different idea of nobility and manhood; to his sort, I look neuter. At best. Or a witch."

"And you *like* alarming them that way!"

"Use any means I've got. My job, to scare people."

"I knew our court thinking didn't work among Upai," Caladrunan said. "It doesn't disturb me—I must have absorbed attitudes from your brother when we were boys. But if I thought like Swan—I'm beginning to think you apply logic more often than it seems on the surface."

Beyond the wall of the garden came the squealing of a pigskin pipebag puffing up preparatory to playing—a very Tannese, and very common, instrument brought out for Feastdays and summertime music. I thought it sounded sad, more suited to funerals—but the Tannese used drums for that—and to the pipes danced on meadows outside Fortress in whirling, laughing gangs. Lado played the pipebag wonderfully well. If it wasn't him out squealing there now, it was somebody with huge lungs. Caladrunan looked wistful. "I used to be good with a flute and the reeds," he said.

Commoners bound a fan of hollow tubes together and blew over the ends, much as they blew over the mouth of a clay jug, its frequent fellow instrument. Neither was an instrument a noble often admitted to knowing; and the flute wasn't much better. I grinned at him. "Ever try playing a stew kettle rigged with a stick and a harpwire, sometimes scrape it with a string bow? We could play as a pig-band."

He swatted my shoulder. "Shame on you."

"I get bored harping to drums all the time! Start a new fashion, give your reputation a whiff of the common touch."

"Swan would have a fit!" He started whistling with puckered lips. The piper on the other side of the wall gave an astonished squawk and then repeated Caladrunan's tune. I leaped at the rough granite wall, caught a grip, climbed, and popped my head over the top. Straddling green rows of kitchen delicacies on the other side, Pitar stood blowing with great concentration, eyes shut, pipe sticks splayed at all angles around him. Caladrunan's head popped up beside me, and for a moment the royal mouth gaped open. Then he smiled, and the smile widened, and finally he let out a bellow of melody. Badly off-time, unfortunately.

Pitar opened his eyes with a jerk. I chuckled while Caladrunan sang soulfully—and rather out of tune—over Pitar's failing squeal of air. It was a song about a farmer, a traveling pleasure woman, and a pig—and it was obscene. Pitar went redder yet, which I had not thought possible. I sat up, cross-legged on the capstones of the wall, while Caladrunan leaned on his elbows beside me and finished the verse with a flourish of wobbly grace notes. The Lord of Tan grinned down beneficently. Red as beets, Pitar mumbled, "Didn't realize you were in the garden . . . happened to be off-duty . . ."

"Entering tonight's piping competition?" Caladrunan said.

"Well, Liege . . . not under my own name of course . . ." Pitar shifted the pipebag uncomfortably under his arm. We both laughed, waved him luck, and dropped back into the garden.

We strolled into Caladrunan's newest Household tower, collected Lado Kiselli from some errand. Having been experimenting happily with distilled wine spirits, Lado chattered all the way up flights of stairs past guard posts, through the guardroom, and into Caladrunan's private chambers. A bell pass later he was still chattering and had exhausted my patience. Lado jabbed his pointing finger at me. "Naga—"

I said, "Would you *stop* pointing? I know I'm here."

"Why should I stop pointing?" Lado said, unsteadily but persistently pointing.

"Because it's bad luck." I felt silly the instant I said it.

Lado slapped his finger on the table, looked exaggeratedly shocked and burst into screams of laughter. "Upai bad luck!"

"Umm," I said uncertainly, wanting him to stop.

"You're being bad, Lado," Caladrunan said in friendly, tolerant tones. "Shall I send you off to bed?"

"Anytime, anytime for bedtime," Lado sang out.

Caladrunan sighed and called guards to carry Lado away to his quarters. Lado laughed maniacally all the way out. The Lord of Tan looked tolerantly after the noise, shaking his head. At my questioning gaze, he told me, "There are nights Lado doesn't sleep well, especially in the winter. He stays up and gets drunk and gets in fights, or he gets a laughing fit. Of the two, laughing is better. This is the first time I've seen it this whole winter. Not an easy matter, the care of a full raving Harper."

I glanced down. "Then both your Harpers are plagued by—"

"—nightmares," he said. "I wonder if it's always like that for the good ones. Drunks, the lot of you."

"I'm not drunk," I said.

He smiled. "Good. You ought to go to bed. Seems I've another Harper to talk into what's good for him tonight. What was his name—Little Treasure?"

I spluttered and swatted him, and got chased across the chamber. We rolled genially across his bedfurs, kicking the gauze canopy curtains and wrestling.

When we had wrestled ourselves out, he shed outer robes and sprawled across the bed, grunting as he stretched out his arms; he looked drowsy. I leaned against his knees. The fire in the hearth roared at a gust of wind outside.

Caladrunan's gaze burned with energy now; he stared off at the dogs as if calculating figures. He meant to ride back to war in the morning. His son was to ride with him partway. Newly authorized troops would follow the Lord of Tan; he'd dumped off slates of contingency plans on that both with me and the Council. Aside from the selection of Swan, he had told me nothing of the Council's actions, and he wouldn't if their debates were sealed under a war security vote. And he clearly hadn't thought of resuming arms practices with me while he could. I'd missed that. I waited, slowly picking tufts from a scuffed fur under my knee. He stirred.

I said, "I like sitting up with you."

He smiled. "Fortunate."

I sat up and smacked his chest. "Now you're teasing."

His smile widened. But while I looked at him, the smile faded. Shadows filtered, darkened his bright gaze. He studied me a long time, moving his thumb gently in the loose tail of my hair. "Our friend the spymaster reported sightings of suspicious fires around the Tejed headwaters two days ago."

I sat up with a jerk. He only looked at me as I grabbed up outer robes, snatched up my banded gloves. I adjusted the hang of my scadda scabbards as I fumbled to my knees; my tongue suddenly felt sour in my mouth.

He stopped me with a gesture. He said, with a sad, wry smile, "Why rush? The Council wouldn't give me your full commission. You're commander of Fortress, yes. But they specifically prohibited you from active fighting. They were muttering about once-Nandos being always-Nandos, the fools."

I stared at him open-mouthed, kneeling next to him. If they thought *that,* they shouldn't give me command of Fortress—but I guessed they merely wanted their own choice field officers to command troops to glory. *And much glory I wish them,* I thought savagely. I said, "What about the Sharinen proposals?"

"All postponed."

I fumbled my gloves tighter. "Keth got it *all* today?"

"Let me get the Army moving, and I'll use Keth to mop the sewer channel out there. He had his day today blocking your commission. His Councilors were prepared, oh, yes." He grabbed my arm, pulled me over, lightly tugged a tail of my hair. "You make quite a friend, my hawk. A shield-brother. It is hard to order your staying here. But I *must* leave this rockpile in trusted hands while Gidas' masons get those secret ways rebuilt."

He felt my muscles jerk and my body tighten. I stared levelly into his eyes; then I forced the tension down. "Well," I said hoarsely at last, "soldiers. We never know when the time for jokes might be over. I knew—I *knew* that. But to go alone on the battlefield without enough guards—"

He smiled. "Oh, I'll take plenty of guards. But none like you." His hand loosened the last weave of my braids, slid through the falling tangles of black. His eyes were very grave. "I feel like I'm tearing off my right arm—we can't be so dependent, Naga! We have to be strong, strong to hold both Fortress and the Army, or it'll be for naught." He yawned suddenly, sitting up and shaking his head. "After Fortress is secured and you rejoin me, we'll know if we're just feeling the comfort of habit."

I looked at him. Habit! Then I lowered my eyes. I rubbed my hands over my head. Goddess give me strength, I thought. "What will you do with me after the secret ways are secure?"

"I haven't got it all worked out yet. But don't go chasing off on any wild Upai expeditions. Wait for my message."

"Who is going to shield you in battle? I have to fight."

He looked at me.

Softer, I said, "Liege, I have to. *I must!*" I used the vocal mode for conviction, for absolute duty—for Oath swearing.

"I'll take Pitar. He's not as good as you, but he's adequate for bandits, Marshmen, and rebel Nandos. I do want you with me for the real Osa battles."

I grabbed his robe. "If you catch one—"

Caladrunan stood up. He said grimly, "The first Osa we catch in battle—" he touched my jaw with his thumb, "—you get him all to yourself. Leave that Osa ambassador, Ungoro Tinadi, alone. On your Oath: You leave him alone. And his whole party!"

"On my Oath," I said, rather slowly.

"Say that again, more like you mean it. All right. If it helps, I'll admit it's been a long moon out there without you to kick my chairs and tell me Histories."

"But you know the Histories already—"

"It's not the same as listening to you. But that's enough futile bathos, I've got work to do."

"Please let me go with—" I reached out to him and he caught my hand.

"No," he said gently. "Meetings now. This is my rest—and restful it was. My thanks." He rose, stretched, and waved me off when I'd have followed him.

I turned silently to duty slates instead.

# CHAPTER

# = 7 =

WHEN GIDAS THE stonemason pronounced his crews had completed their order slates on the secret ways, it was time for me to finish mine. Not that it would free me from commanding rocks, of course. I trotted through Fortress on a long early guard watch check, so I was in the secret ways when I heard it.

*"Let go of me!"* a woman's voice said, in the most freezing tone I had ever heard one take. Trapped in the wall, unable to see through a blocked spyhole, I heard noises I did not like at all: An alien blurred sound became a man roaring like a beast. As I ran—bumping and scraping scabbards, harpcase, razor spurs, and lamp along the tunnel braces—the woman's high, ragged shriek echoed into the walls. Then more screams, punctured by tearing cloth and hard, wet slapping sounds—each cry rose wilder after the smack of impact.

I plunged into a side passage, unlatched the heavy exit gate, and plunged facefirst into a lacquer screen that shattered under my knees. Lamp oil spilled about. I came up scrabbling, slewed around in torchlight—lunged through the door of Girdeth's room. I was not quiet about it.

Driving forward, I jumped the hurdle of a fallen body, twisted face, maid's plain robes, then I hurdled a tumbled red-stained heap of white brocade. As I landed on my feet, I glimpsed Girdeth's face in the brocaded heap behind me. The girl clutched a small silver dagger, broken; rent lace dripped from her headdress. Her eyes were huge and dazed and hypnotically blue.

I rolled my head aside from the sight and hurled the thing in my hand—a vase plucked up from somewhere unnoticed. A man, huge in metal and leather, laughed and dodged for the far door, which let into a dead-end bedchamber. Bright vase shards exploded across stone and tapestries; he spun and threw an unlit torch at me. I dodged. My right scadda dropped into my hand.

He gave a great pleased bellow, and a fighting ax leaped from his belt to his hand, shedding its bitsheaths in a lazy fling. He was Rafai's size, but faster; his mustache through the breath-holes in his leather mask was Cragman red. The bedchamber had a secret exit very few knew about: Either he was ignorant, or he first emerged there informed and dangerous. He circled past the long canopied bed at one wall, his heavy boots scuffling over rugs, backing for the secret way. *Informed,* I thought grimly. And armored under those rough leather robes.

In a jab my left hand grabbed the chamber rug, heaved the thick weave off its straw floor pads, and snapped it at an angle from under him. The rug thudded into a heavy roll against a nearby wall. He roared, rolled slightly in the air as he lost his balance, and came down again poised like a cat on the straw mats—laughing.

*Not* an easy fight at all, I thought grimly. He hadn't thrown that ax because he knew I'd dodge and he'd lose it. He waited silently to close with me on clear floor. No roars now: none of the irritating Cragman yells, none of the obvious Crag school signals, so I had no firm clue about his training. He might not have come to molest Girdeth, only to make me fight. Disaster for us all if he won, though Girdeth and I would be too dead to care about it if he did.

A distracting splash of color, Girdeth crawled into the door-way. Her hand clenched and unclenched on the dagger's hilt. Its blade was broken but her blank stare never saw it. "Call guards," I shouted at her, circling rapidly as the Cragman pounced into my divided attention.

The ax whistled past my nose, twirled about the man's grip in a flat overhand loop, and tried a long forehand sweep for my arm. I twisted aside, drawing my left scadda—and with that drawing motion punched my scadda pommel into his wrist as it swung past. His full leathers blunted the strike, but he grunted, jerked; he'd expected my left arm to be the weaker in timing and force. With any luck I'd crushed his tendons.

I spun about, snapped my leg up, and sank the outside of my right boot into his kidneys. The fighting spur built in the boot made a cracking report on his leathers. The armor beneath his leathers impeded the gouging slither of my spur razor. But as the impact of the spur jolted his balance, I posted my right scadda through a defensive gap between his rising ax-hand and his shoulder.

I wanted his throat, angling up between his metal bands, but I knew I couldn't get that. I managed only a shallow messy slice at his mask before his arm lifted in a massive counterswing.

Dragging my blade free with me, I spun away behind him, breathed deep, and ducked an anticipated outward strike—but as he spun toward me, his whole arm twisted abruptly in a tight startling little arc. The ax came shearing straight in for my middle.

My right scadda tip stabbed his knuckles in a wild attempt to divert his aim down, while I skipped back on one leg away from the double-bitted monster. The ax only wobbled, turned flat, and grazed my retreating thigh with a *smack!* of stunning force.

Had it hit squarely with the flat, it would have broken my leg. The grazed blow was plenty. I fell back off the numbed leg in surprise as much as pain and recovered with a shaky step forward. His arm still moved away in wild swing, leaving an opening. Expecting and defeating his reflexive jerk, my left scadda darted like a snake snapping in a strike, the tip lifting in a hooked gesture.

His eyes were not armored against a point. In a swift hand, scaddas could penetrate under the brow-hood of any helmet; those types made resistant by wire netting or extremely narrow slits blinded the wearer enough to make him vulnerable to other sorts of attack. Scaddamen were feared, sometimes loathed, for the ability.

I had no time to punch the tip into his brain, for he had other reflexes, too. Even as he jerked on the blade, binding it on bone and his helmet-edge—even as he screamed in pain, his axhead spun back in that absurd tiny arc and slammed flat—on into my hip. Force exploded in my pelvis.

I was flying. My left arm wrenched out full length, but I didn't lose my scadda; it came with me. Then I was tumbling over and over sidewise on the floor, scaddas extended safely together above my head. I rolled up, got my feet under me, vaguely surprised they worked. My side was numb. I crawled into a limping crouch.

I'd been very lucky, again hit by the flat. The edge would've laid me down in two pieces. And half-blinded, he couldn't follow to smash my rolling body while vulnerable. Oh, he saw me *now*, with his one eye. The man roared, both hands swinging that ax in tight, whistling arcs, and staggered after me with blood spurting in gouts over his mask. His ruined eye was a mess; still it didn't stop him. He was as mindlessly, dangerously, berserk as a wounded gana bull.

I sidled away, testing my leg gently to see if I had the strength I needed from it. My hip socket was still so numb it alarmed me, but my eyecorners caught no blood spewing down my thigh, no flapping robe or cut leather. My bones held together because he hadn't got up the force of his full swings. He made gobbling noises that hurt my ears.

I backed along the curtained bed, dragged him closer to it, trying to tangle those flying iron edges in the bedposts—perhaps even give me the chance to knock him out. But I didn't want to get killed either hanging about waiting for guards to come. I heard a vague gabble of noise out of sight—incredible how well I heard it, given the keening, bubbling noise of the axman. Babble . . . blue robes . . . guards. A rope flung lazily at the Cragman fell slowly short as he screamed at me. I realized about then that no one could help me. *We were both moving too fast.* When the Cragman lunged at me, rolling awkwardly in the motion with his damaged depth perception, I feinted my tip at his sighted side, the side away from the bed.

Instead of shying away into the bed as I wanted, he turned into my motion. I faded back hastily, deflecting the axhead with a poke at his wrists. The high choked noises he made at that were not even animal. *Revenge.* He took a single long step forward and cocked the ax massively over one shoulder with both hands, entirely losing his training, and I backed hastily away around the corner of the bed. He swung after me across the bed, slashing into the draperies' multiple layers of thick tapestry. His well-wrapped blade crashed deep into the wood of a bedpost.

I leaped at him, ribboning my trailing right edge to cut around his knees as I skated circularly behind him. Then, leading the whole arc of force in my body, my left wrist snapped outward. With the entire driving force and momentum of my weight I thumped him pommel-first on the back of the head in a clang of leather-muffled metals. His helmet dipped forward under the force of it. As my left hand swung down, my trailing right scadda twirled upward, smacked a pommel-blow into the under-side of his masked chin. Gore splattered from his eye as his head snapped backward. The left hand down-blow caught him all the harder for it.

My strength should have killed him. At the very least it should have tumbled him backward over my lowered left edge—but no. The big Cragman just staggered a little, flung gore from his head, tugged at his trapped ax, and brought the tall bedposts and draperies crashing down on himself. I dived away barely in time to avoid becoming entangled with him. I went tumbling over twice and coming back up ready on my feet, scaddas poised. He roared and thrashed and heaved the ax about under the cloth, slitting it into worse chaos than if he'd simply wrestled the stuff in his hands. Swiftly I wiped and sheathed my scaddas. I threw more bedfurs over him to increase his difficulties, and then I thumped a broken bedpost on his head. Twice. He stopped moving.

After a moment, staring at him—rather in disbelief that I'd actually felled this beast—I felt a warning tingle of sensation in my thigh. I heaved for breath. There were voices, noises, uproar at my peripheral senses. I looked. Eight blue-robed guards stood around the room's perimeter, swords up. Rafai sheathed his blade and told me, "Runners are checking the guard posts for any other assault reports. Nothing so far." I nodded. Silently I accepted a cloth that Rafai held out, wiped my hands. Then, carefully, I let my fingers drop to my hip.

I prayed in silent relief. My hip felt perfectly normal from the outside; the flesh was just swelling under my intact leathers. So was the lump on my thigh where he'd grazed me. I moved stiffly past guards into the other chamber, turning my head to find Girdeth; and in the motion, found my numb spots were no longer so. I rolled my shoulders, stretched—finding other strains and bruises. Even my finger tendons hurt from hitting so hard.

Then all thought of myself left my head.

Girdeth crouched against the bedchamber door. Her veil was gone, blood splashed her rent and tumbled robes. She stared at no one and gripped the broken silvery knife, ignoring the cries of her ladies. The serving girl struck aside by the Cragman lay limply nearby, cradling a bloody swollen cheek, tears silently running from her eyes. She was the only one near Girdeth. A woman came holding a cloth out to Girdeth and got a vicious dagger warning for her effort. I gestured the other women to back away. Gently I touched Girdeth's sleeve.

She looked at me with wide blank eyes as her body shot

upward, erect in one fierce motion. The broken dagger slashed at my face. I got a stinging slap across the face and then a standing kick intended for my crotch. I let that slide past my bruised hip rather than absorb it, while I grabbed her wrist, took the dagger away from her, threw it out of reach, and released her. She writhed, clawed my chest, lashed out. Her strength astonished me. I didn't try to stop her; she seemed to need it, and it didn't hurt me—much—after all the other damage.

"Girdeth— I'm so very sorry," I said, and meant it. I let go of her.

"Don't you say my name!" she gasped, "—*you*—but that— your accent." She paused, stared at my face. "You're not—*him*, the one that—"

"No," I said, rather glad she'd halted the pounding.

She gave a great huge blink with both eyes and said, "Naga?" I smiled in tired agreement.

"Don't," she said, shuddering. She closed her eyes. "You— all that gore— Don't smile." Her body shook. In one violent heave she huddled into herself. And swayed against me.

"All right." I felt her hands curl up between her body and mine as if she were cold. Her hands twisted, one inside another, back and forth, in a bizarre pulling gesture. But I made no attempt to stop it, nor to hug her, nor grip her arms, nor even touch her. I just stood close. I murmured, "Shall I call an herbalist?"

"He tore my earrings out," she said, as if puzzled why anyone would do that. "He just reached up and took them."

"Why—"

"There were two of them. Two men. He hit my maid, knocked her down, gave my earrings to the first one, who got away when *you* ran in."

I tilted my head, looking. Blood flowed down her neck; I saw crusting barely begun where her earlobes had been torn. But I knew better than to grab to stop it. "Do you want your ladies to bathe it for you?"

She shuddered violently, shook her head in another convulsive shudder. "Those men hurt my maid from the orphanage—you'll see that she's all right?" I nodded, lifting my arms to hug, to offer comfort—impelled unbearably—and in time checked the impulse. She would remember, if I touched her against her will now, that I was a man too.

"You're *looking* at me, aren't you," she said very low.

"No," I said. "Do you want me to close my eyes?"

"You can't guard that way," she said, and swayed in place.

"That's true."

"Well, open your eyes. But don't look at me."

I couldn't see much of her in any case, she was standing so close to me, and I didn't like the hysteria under the words, but I said, "Your maid will be cared for; Rafai will see to it. I'll stay with you if you want."

"Hurts," she whispered. Girdeth bent her head onto my shoulder, turned her face into my robe, and cradled her bruised hands between us. Something wet ran down my neck. Blood or tears, I thought, and stood motionless. She whispered, "You can't even hold me."

I turned my face slightly into her hair. The limp strands smelled of sudden rank sweat and terror. "Not unless you say so," I said evenly. "And only when you say."

She sniffled, lifting her hand. She drew the remnant of her veil across her uppermost eye; the other was hidden against my outer robe. "And you won't? You won't—touch—"

"Only if you say," I murmured.

"You don't sound like him at all," she said. "I don't know why I thought that." She shuddered. "A bath. A hot bath with perfume and lots and lots of clean cloths."

"Good for you," I agreed.

"You aren't asking me if he—" she drew a deep hissing breath against my neck, sagged a little, caught herself.

I tilted my head closer, shifting her hair lightly with my cheek, once-attractive red and gold hair like her brother's. The bruised servant girl uttered a sudden, sharp groan of fear, pulling herself away on her knees. The guards carried the Cragman prisoner past, gagged, bound with straps, while his body heaved; grunting sounds punctuated their efforts.

At the sound Girdeth's body went rigid, her head pushing hard into my shoulder as if to hide for a moment. Only a moment. Then she straightened, gripped my upper arm, and turned to them. Her fingers on my arm were shaking hard, and her voice went harsh and deep as a man's. "Why?"

Rafai looked up. He said, with great gentleness, "We'll try to find that out, my Lady Girdeth. Shall I call an herbalist for you or your hurt maid here?"

She lifted her eyes to Rafai's face, glanced briefly at the other guards, and said in that odd deep tone, "Call one for the maid.

Carry on. And thank you.'' She turned back and stood very close to me, but this time standing rigid, with her arms folded under her breasts. Fine tremors moved the tendrils of her hair. As the men clumped out, she closed her eyes. I saw muscles jump in the line of her bloodied jaw and cheek. ''You still haven't asked.'' She blinked open her eyes. A slight frown marked her brows. ''He hit you. Are *you* hurt—''

''Just bruises. Girdeth, are you faint or dizzy? Do you want someone in particular to attend you?''

She shuddered. ''Great-aunt Agtunki, but she's not here. You don't know what it's like.'' She rolled her eyes open again. Her gaze went to the nervous women hovering about the edges of the chamber, lingered on the crying servant—the only one who'd been hurt. The others clung together in knots, silent, staring fearfully at Girdeth. ''You couldn't know. The only one I trusted is hurt and—''

Softly, very softly, I said, ''Where were *they* when he came?''

She looked up in a sharp, startled motion to meet my eyes; then jerked her head away from the intensity of my gaze. Her lips looked pale. ''Nobody came but my one maid even when I—''

She felt me flinch, too. ''I'm sorry,'' I said, again looking into her eyes. ''I'm very sorry I wasn't here sooner.''

She drew in a breath. *''Don't* think about what you'll do to him. Not—just now. It frightens me.'' She shivered, tightening her crossed arms. Her fingers picked and plucked at her robes. She sucked in a great breath, let it out raggedly. ''I could see his eyes. He looked—looked at me like I was dead. Don't let them paw at me. I can't—I couldn't stand it. Just you.''

''Girdeth,'' I said. I wondered if I could get her calmed and treated before she lost blood and went too deep into shock. It could kill her, that much I'd learned from Sharinen herbalists. ''Shall we get you that bath?'' I added hastily, ''Of course I'll stand guard outside the room.''

''You'll stay with me until I'm not a shaking wreck,'' she said in that low harsh voice, ''if you have to hold me up in the water naked.'' Another deep breath. ''I have—a court to face. I have—responsibilities. And all those eyes—all of them thinking—''

''All thinking that we came far too close to losing someone we love very much,'' I said. The words stuck funny in places.

''Damned smooth-talking Harper,'' she said, gripping my arm as if she might fall down, and half-swallowing the words.

"Come," I said, drawing her gently along by that grip. "You bathe; we'll find some clean clothes . . . Would you rather have a lady attend you?" I asked patiently. "Maybe Rafai's wife—he tells me she's very nice, and—"

She gulped. Tears rolled down her face. "Maybe."

Granted that permission, I nodded a fierce signal at Rafai, and I unlatched the door to the women's bathing rooms. She stopped in sudden terror; the place was dim. Steam rose from the warm pool. I glanced around swiftly. "There's nobody but us here, Girdeth. Don't worry, Rafai will take your maid safely home to his family; they'll take good care of her. Do you want me to wait outside?"

She sat gingerly down on a bench. "*No.*" She was shivering. "Could you send for Agtunki? I really want my great-aunt. She'll find out things you can't."

I said, "Very good. Here, get into the warm pool. Sit down in it; you don't have to undress right now. Just get warm." I urged her along. Finally, dipping my hands in the water, I knelt on the tiles beside her and washed the blood from her neck and ears, gently checking the damage in a thin shaft of light. She didn't react to the pain much. I said, "Did he hurt you anywhere else?"

Her voice grated as harsh and level as before. "Yes."

"Shall I send for a lady herbalist?"

Her head turned. Her hand crept up and gripped mine hard, and she rested her forehead along my arm. Deep shudders jerked up into my shoulder from her. "Oh, yes, Pergo will be very brisk with me and my poor servant both, praise the girl and tell *me* I'm silly, and trot away when she's done as if nothing ever happened. Stay, please, I don't . . . want to be looked at by others. Strangers." Her eyes looked almost blank. Her words then were faint, tired, and extraordinarily gentle. "This is hard on you, too, isn't it, guard commander?"

I felt my mouth thin into a line. The faintness of her voice terrified me that she was sliding toward unconsciousness. "I don't care about that part of it! My friend was hurt."

For a long time she and I met each other's eyes. "You're very uncivilized," she said. "My brother won't like what you're thinking of doing to that—*that man.*"

I lowered my gaze. "You're right," I agreed, looking away at the steam swirls. The very thought of the political ramifications made my head ache. I straightened as the door opened; Rafai and a sturdy woman stood silhouetted against the light.

"My Lady," Rafai said, "may I suggest that my mother's family care for your servant while my wife attends you—" His hands made inadequate urging gestures, flapping the frightened woman toward us. "Noble-born, there are no other reports of violence as yet, but if you wish to supervise investigation from outside here, I can arrange it."

Rafai's wife proved to be equally efficient once she saw Girdeth's torn ears. "Clean cloths, the herbalist, boiled water," Iot told her husband. "Those should be numbed and sewn up, my Lady, and anything else he—" Then she hissed, "Rafai, will you get that—that bloody *creature* out of here, just upsetting her—"

"I'm *trying* to—"

Girdeth said in a thin, tired voice, "He stays. He's my friend and I want him here. Naga stays with me until I am satisfied with new security measures. Arrest my women."

Rafai's mouth opened in surprise.

I said briefly, "I don't think there will be any more assaults like this. Except for the maid who was hurt, the women did not come when Lady Girdeth was attacked. Nobody will tolerate *my* harrassing such court women, but I'd suggest the Lady of Fortress should begin investigating such negligence. Lady Girdeth asked for her Great-aunt Agtunki's help, who certainly has the authority and more impartiality to check such matters once she arrives. Has the prisoner talked?"

"Not yet," Rafai said in such a calm, glacial tone that I felt a chill run along my neck-hairs. Rafai was efficient. And Rafai was going to see questions were answered.

"By our Liege's rules for evidence," I warned.

"Noble-born," Rafai agreed, softly, gently, and left.

Limply Girdeth endured the rush of materials and the stripping of wet clothes and the bustle of being dried and dressed and moving arms and legs about.

Pergo and her bags of herbalist's mysteries arrived then. In a small lamplit room I held Girdeth's hands while Iot held a drapery above Girdeth's breasts for privacy and beyond the drape Pergo treated injuries. The herbalist merely gave me a sharp glance once, remarking, *"You're* a most irregular presence," and did something that made Girdeth gasp in pain.

I half-rose to my feet, glaring.

The herbalist lifted a needle to the best light, threaded it, and

bent again. "Hold her steady, youngster," she said crisply.
"And you thank Goddess he didn't get a longer chance at her."

Girdeth closed her eyes. "He broke off a metal band and—"

"Easy," the herbalist murmured. "I know. Easy. I've still to
look at your maid, my dear Lady, and the sooner the better."

When she was resting in a clean bed, swaddled in clean robes,
half-dazed with exhaustion, Girdeth allowed me to leave her in
Iot's fierce protection. I went to the corridor outside and rested
my head on my wrist on the wall for a few eons. I had to.

Pergo's voice said from a doorway, "A fine sight *you* are."

I lifted my head, blinking. "I thought you were done."

"Oh, I'll be in and out, checking on our two brave girls.
Quite a fight they gave him. What about you—*you're* the one
brought him down, didn't you?"

My fingers clenched. "Heard gossip already?"

"No. Look at yourself, you're a mess. Any of it yours?"

I pushed away from the wall. "I don't think so."

"Gone lame as a three-legged goat, and you don't think so?"

"I hadn't noticed."

"I had that impression," she said dryly, holding up washed,
wet hands. "I've taken the room adjoining Girdeth's. I want a
look at you before I put my things away. Anyone else besides
the maid hurt?"

I sighed. "There weren't any. You'd have to ask Rafai about
any new reports of fighting. I was occupied." Dangerous: The
place could have been overrun during my preoccupation with
Girdeth if Rafai had been any less competent. I went into the
small servant-sized chamber and leaned on a spindly table. Mechanically I stripped off my knee-guard and unlatched the re-
leases on the outside of my thigh leather. I laid off my weaponbelt,
unhooked the latches at the hip, pulling the lower cuirass flaps
barely up, pushed aside the folds of my corad.

"Not a trusting sort, are you?" She poked at the ax welt, at
bruise-stains spreading from my hip below the lower edge of my
cuirass. She told me to flex and relax muscles as she worked.
Strong, water-reddened fingers probed deep into the muscles.
She tilted her head slightly, concentrating entirely on her fingertips. "Should've seen to this before the inflammation got so
hard. We may have to wait for it to subside to be sure the pelvis
isn't chipped or taken a weakening fine break."

Looking down, I said, "What does that mean?"

She glanced up. Her eyes went to my harness and leathers.

After a moment she said dryly, "When the swelling goes down to where you can bear it—because you may find that inflammation radiating to a slightly painful elsewhere such as your testicles, Black Man—you exercise in a truss for men with hernia until the bruising is gone and I feel the bone, judge it sound. I know better than to think *you'll* take any bed rest." She slapped my shoulder gently and turned away, washing her hands from a pot of steaming water.

"Will Girdeth be all right?"

She turned back. Her eyes looked different. "If she doesn't find those cuts infected."

I stared down at my boots. "It's that bad?"

"I've seen worse survive," Pergo said calmly. "The maid just has a sore head, no concussion. I work in poor sections with the Women of the Harp. I've seen a great deal worse than Girdeth, not that it helps her much. I used my best antiseptic."

"Your experience helps," I said. "Will you testify at trial what he—he did to her?"

"No," she said levelly. "Not unless Girdeth herself gives me instructions to reveal it. You seem to have some power. If you care about her health, Black Man, you won't let anyone bully her about for quite some time. There's effects on the spirit, too."

"Yes," I said. "I know."

"Then you're one of the few men up here who do," she snapped. "Some women never get over the damage done them."

I stood up stiffly, aching, and strapped my armor on again. "Well, self-indulgence never got guards organized to prevent this happening again. Thank you for helping me. And Girdeth."

She snapped her fingers at my underclothes. "I'll let you prove your gratitude. *That*—that poor short-thread silk of yours is sign of a horrid practice, youngster. Cheap silk sheds doctor dried-out cocoons in a stink no one mistakes, and *no one* hires their stinking silk-girls for other work, so they're forever trapped out in the silk factory slums. You're ignorant of your tailor's vices, dealing with such corrupt merchants, or you'd never touch short-thread cloth. Never."

I lifted my eyes. "The *wool clans* want all my people sentenced to work gangs. So, is there a difference?"

She tilted her head. "Why give *any* of them good jade?"

"I'll remember what you said."

"I hear you're a judge in Commoner's Court since our Liege

left Fortress. Are you grateful enough that you'd ensure that
common women—even silk-girls—hurt just like Girdeth get a
fair Judgment when they come in? No one else can stop a
woman's kin, a shopowner, a head of clan, from exercising his
sick whims. Wife-beatings, assaults, slaver-sellings—Will you
order these maniacs thrown into prison?''

I smiled. ''I'll do better than that. Get the women's testimony
safely into court, give me proofs of abuse—abusive nobles I can
take to our Liege, commoners I can put on chain gangs in the
sewer channel, and I'll let you tend their shackle sores.''

''You're not nice.''

''Neither are you.'' I saluted her with a flick of my hand and
went out.

Strategically, the assault on Girdeth was a hideous proof of
someone's ability to penetrate Fortress at will, with Girdeth's
favorite earrings taken as proof.

''I see you've been busy, too,'' Rafai said grimly, coming
across the Great Hall to me. ''I've written a list of the trusted
men on my watch who volunteered for extra duty while questioning goes on and the women's quarters need extra outside guards.''
He held out the slate.

I glanced at it. Perhaps a third of the men could be trusted
with such a delicate assignment. I didn't ask about Girdeth's
assailant; he'd have reported any progress with that one.

Rafai said, ''Large improvement over last fall.''

He was right. In the past there were very few trustworthy
guards for the task. Commanding a watch, I insisted on complete
duty sobriety, background checks, and stiff tests of competence,
offsetting new recruitment due to increased pay and prestige.
Now, commanding the whole Fortress, it seemed I'd managed to
impress it on a few more men. Progress, I thought, and read
names. ''I'll remember the volunteers at promotion time. You
did a good job getting this written up so fast.''

Rafai beamed. He loved his drink as heartily as he adored his
food, his bed, and his new wife; but he'd worked hard to earn
and hold his place. People were often surprised at the hard,
stubborn core that drove him. Rafai, who seemed so big, so
relaxed and even-tempered, on his off-time gently worked sheet
metal for his aging father, the Head Armorer. Rafai, if he
grabbed me in anger, could probably twist me in half. If I said
the word, he'd gently wring the Cragman prisoner into little
pieces. It angered me that I would not—*should not*—give that

word. I smacked him on the arm and chose a tone that skated lightly over our shared rage. "Does a slab of buck meat and a few chickens speak to your stomach? My quarters."

Rafai grinned. I wouldn't intrude on his quarters; his wife's whole clan stiffly disapproved of natives, and Iot hadn't been reconciled one bit to me while caring for Girdeth. The last thing I desired was to make Iot unhappy with her new home and her new husband. I thought of asking to see Girdeth again under Iot's fierce looks, gave up on it, and sighed.

Sitting in my quarters picking over bones, I said, "Any trouble with the men? With Lado? He celebrated a bit too much when Liege came back this time."

Rafai shrugged. "Knocked their silly heads together, solved that. One fellow was so unwise as to call the rest of us a bunch of women for passing up Lado's ruin. Lado himself was—ahem—rather ill. Colorful, he was that." Rafai sniffed. I heard no sympathy in his tone.

I grinned wolfishly and opening a leather backpack, pulled out two goblets and a tiny cork-stoppered ceramic bottle. I poured amber fluid into the goblets. "Careful, Rafai. This is the stuff that Lado's clan has been trying to copy. It's not wine."

Rafai gave me a look. He gazed at it dubiously, sniffed it, lifted it to his mouth. Nothing happened in his broad face when he drank. He merely set down the goblet, flared his nostrils, and licked off his lips. *"Ahh,"* he said.

I grinned, sipping mine. My belly lit up like a coal.

"What *is* this stuff?" Rafai asked plaintively, sipping again.

I said, "Upai call it *a'afidir.* Distilled five times over, from a wine made of the dried pods of cupflower. It comes out raw unless you use the Upai methods; I don't exactly know the details myself. They know I have to enforce Liege's drug laws if I catch them working pods."

Rafai's eyes bulged open.

I said hastily, "Don't worry. It doesn't have any drug essence in it, none left by the time the pods go for wine. Lends a sweet flavor, that's all. This stuff is distilled so much it's pure wine spirits."

Rafai looked at his goblet. "That's what Lado's clan played at—does it have other names? Nobody will drink it by that name."

I snorted. "Snob. Does 'Crag rock-liquor' sound familiar? The Cragmen smuggle cases of it into Tan, if you recall. They use reject pods and distill by Crag methods, so it's not nearly as smooth as this. But very popular, I understand.''

Rafai leaned back. "Well, now. Noble-born, you remember Oldfield—Crag traitor! He used to make jokes about getting rich selling rock-liquor, aside from his flamed blatant drug trading. But somebody's trading in liquor just like him now he's gone.''

I nodded. "The market is still there and eager.''

"This—whatever you called it—is good. Give it a good Tannese name, it'd outsell Crag slop. Put them out of business.''

I tilted my goblet toward him in salute. "Yes, I thought the pleasure houses and taverns would buy this instead of the Crag liquor if they had a choice. This liquor is twice as strong as a Crag rock-liquor. To sell it, you'd dilute it four times.''

Rafai smiled. "I can see business might be profitable.''

"If we have Fat Nella's organization on our side, and I think we do, a new liquor source would kill off most of the smugglers who were bullying taverners. Let market forces work on them. *I* haven't been able to affect whoever's running Oldfield's old smuggling networks, but *this* might. You told me your wine-shipping cousins wanted to expand. Perhaps through them, with Lado's help at experiments and employing a few—ahh—expert Upai advisers, we could contrive to supply a crying need.''

"More rock-liquor?" Rafai grinned.

I didn't smile. "No. Putting Cragmen smugglers out of the rock-liquor business." Oh, I knew where to hurt Osa. The puppetmaster behind Girdeth's assailant would pay for his plots. I tilted back the last of the *a'afidir* in a quick toss down my throat and felt it burn away. Rafai looked at me with something close to surprise.

"I didn't know you could drink like that.''

I leaned forward, elbows on the table among the dishes. "Upai drink this at the important ceremonies. That's why so many are drunks in the refugee camps. They get introduced to it too young, I think—and, by Goddess, you learn to swallow without blinking an eye or it's a bad omen or some fool thing or other. They make it in small batches so constantly they've got transport methods down to an art, which should be useful to us. Remember one thing about *a'afidir*, Rafai.''

He cocked up one eyebrow, waiting.

"The skill to teach the making of a decent sipping wine is rare these days. You make sure your cousins keep my Upai safe. Smugglers won't disperse without a fight.''

Rafai smiled, holding up his goblet. "Noble-born, thank you. You've just improved a rotten day."

I cocked an eyebrow. "Only fair, after you got us through today without it blowing up into a scandal. And Rafai? I may confiscate any Crag rock-liquor sloshing up the officers' barracks. If you treat *a'afidir* with the proper reverence, I think it'll find a Tannese name for you—take that bottle to make friends with it." Then I warned, "Sparingly. It's not a drink tolerant of Tannese guzzling."

Rafai regarded the little bottle with respect. "Aye, Noble-born. Gladly I'll see if it tells me a name." He tucked the bottle away lovingly in his robes.

*A'afidir* was the legendary gold liquor of the Upai Imperial House. I gazed at the glimmering gold drops in my goblet, once restricted to the palates of the rulers of Empire. I felt very hard and very mercenary offering its secrets to the Tannese. Anything, I thought, if it defeats our enemies—kill the killers of Upai and Tannese alike.

Rafai shifted. He leaned over and told me, "I'll see if this little bottle of Cragman-killer might live up to your hopes, Noble-born. I think it will."

I murmured, "Or assassin-killer?"

Rafai's face went grave. "That I leave for you, Noble-born, when you deal with the likes of Girdeth's rapist." He saluted me and left me to a lonely contemplation of my empty goblet.

Yawning until my jaw muscles crackled, I unbraided my hair, stretched out on my proper, narrow bed, and stared at the stone blocks and rafters overhead: *a'afidir* made me sleepy. But it didn't numb the images in my mind at all. Burning away with me down into sleep was the blind, soulless, utterly destroyed look in Girdeth's eyes.

# CHAPTER

# = 8 =

I DREAMED IN that gray cold just before dawn: I flung out my arms. One arm scraped on the nozzle of the flamethrower, but did not deflect the barrel by one fingerwidth, though my hands burned wrenching on the heated metal about the igniter. I heard myself screaming for it to stop. Engulfed in those flames as in billowing clothes stood Caladrunan. He was not consumed, which somehow horrified me more than if he'd blackened and twisted in it. He said calmly from the holocaust of flame, "Wake up, Naga."

I let out a choked gasp and sat straight up in bed, clawing, raking something soft. My eyes focused on a face, a familiar face. Staring now into my eyes, Rafai rubbed his scratched, bloody wrist. I must have grabbed him. He muttered, "You were having a bad dream, Noble-born."

Great round beads of sweat stood on my skin. I stared up at him. My throat was sore; I must have been screaming down the walls. I blinked. Rafai, too, gave a start, as if caught, hypnotized, staring into my eyes. He backed a step and lowered his gaze, cleared his throat. "Some wine, Noble-born?"

"Yes," I said hoarsely. When I took the goblet my hand was shaking, bleeding from broad scrapes. I'd been fighting the sandstone wall next to my bed. I juddered the goblet to my mouth, gulped. "I dreamed they were burning Liege. *But he didn't burn*. I was trying to stop it."

Rafai's eyes grew very wide and still.

"He told me to wake up. That must have been you, speaking through the dream." I sighed, raking at my loose hair.

Rafai shook his head. "Not *me*, Noble-born."

I shivered. Rafai took a fur from a wall hook and draped it around me. "Never had a dream like that before. Not a reliving or a fit—dream-dancing was always awake—I know all of them, *always* the same. Not this one." I drew a deep breath, hunching my shoulders. "Sorry I grabbed—"

Rafai merely poured the goblet full again. "Liege required that I send a report of any dreams you might have, Noble-born."

I glanced up. "*What*?"

"Not merely for concern for your health, also for the benefit of the . . . the foreseeing they might bring."

I growled irritably into the goblet. "'Stupid stories."

"Liege ordered that I report it to him. Shall I write that slate now, Noble-born?"

I shivered. Of course he must. But it was hard not to see Caladrunan still wrapped in flames, his hands coronas of blue and orange. "Well, don't hang yourself pulling the bell ropes yelling about it!"

"Never," Rafai said lightly. He returned with a tray of food and slates and maps; he even dared give me a pat on the shoulder before he went out. I had the depressing idea that he, too, believed the dream might be a prophecy, damn fool.

Morning sun glinted through the narrow window-slit on the far wall of my quarters, striped across my bed. My vigor seemed to have retreated to a cold, fearful little knot in my middle. *Fear, that's all,* I told myself, and uncurled myself back into my body, forcing life and warmth back into chilled limbs. I was a Harper, a Sati of scaddas; I had work! I couldn't sit in a lump afraid of shadows like a child. Just a dream, I told myself. I slid my feet out of bed. Flame this shivering anyway, I thought.

As I read message slates, I heard the faint cries of refugees gathered in a courtyard outside to be fed and sent to the camps. Children made constant low keening noises as they were herded along through town. For a moment I lifted my head, listening; then I bent to the slates and concentrated more firmly on the war.

The situation delineated in report slates lay in a tangled mess in my head. While I responded absently to the guard watch changing at my door, I began drawing diagrams and timetables to link troop sizes, dates, and locations. Conflicting reports I resolved on blind judgment, testing my value as Caladrunan's strategic adviser. Strengham Dar was the only other officer given trusted access to the entire theater of war.

I frowned. Aside from problems with supplies and recruitment against a seemingly endless opposition army of starving bandits and malcontents, the real Osa had disappeared. New advances lay blurred within confused reports on Marshmen. The ragged swamp rats were recruited from their poor country and marched into Tan as decoys, screens for our enemies—who only armed such scavengers for mass battle, and once in the fields hardly fed the poor bandits. But Osa flamethrowers had vanished from our reports. They could be hidden in a dozen Holds hostile to Caladrunan, places where our spies proved short-lived and security tight.

I meditated over hiding sites and Osa intent. Fortress was a good physical site for resisting sieges and for inciting a war of possession in the first place. Aside from its harbor, six major roads and the Tejed River all braided together below our walls. The river's tributaries reached from all Tan's borders, the desert barrier ranges at the north, at the east slunk among the Marsh woods, and to the west, watered the rocky tongue of Crag province and drained from the high Plains plateau to build into a fan tightening across the entire fertile plain of Tan. No Osa would ignore this rock if he meant to hold Tan. And Fortress sat over an ancient gas well that fed eternally burning Altar Flames, the very fuel the Osa sought. Bitterly ironic, I thought, that our Devotee Elders had allied with the very men who, under sweet promises of respect, would plunder them. Perhaps the Devotees had been too greedy to learn powerfully secular uses for their divinely ordained property.

I showed my teeth at the slate. Our enemies showed a sudden clever bent. The Osa plans varied by the way I read skirmish reports. If I calculated their strategic aims variously, their recent movements also read differently, and so did my predictions—one of the finest examples of tactical outlay I'd ever seen, deploying troops for many different approaches, each one dangerous to us. We could not answer all their foreseeable threats. The skill of it provoked thought. And it suggested new military leadership.

I knew my trade. This deployment was unlike any Nando or Osa officers I'd studied in Histories and observed in the field. This abandoned the orthodox Osa advance protected behind masses of foreign screening troops. Instead, it disguised the Osa in small troops as scruffy hill-bandits. The whole thing was too assertive, too quickly planned and unified a campaign, to be within reach of any minor subordinate. Only an Osa theater commander could move so many different elements as he chose.

I felt cold crawl up my spine. The Osa, I thought, sent one of their real generals to clean up this tiresome brush war in Tan. I had an extremely healthy respect for such men. A new commander of allies to anticipate—I'd best warn Caladrunan of my suspicions. I stood up and paced.

*Fear,* I thought, remembering the icy terror I felt in the dream this dawn. The Osa general meant to make us fear—and if he was single master behind all the puppets, he had already used our fear. Assassins, hidden flamethrowers, the Crag rebellions, assault in an insecure Fortress, all made cowering Tannese sheep tremble in their sandstone fold. Better yet if such plots had killed the Lord of Tan, our only effective leadership, and incited Tannese civil war.

I narrowed my eyes. Because he used shaky smoke-and-mirror games, their new general revealed to me a serious professional prediction of Osa failure. Such a skilled general wouldn't bother with uncertain methods unless they'd sent him out—a genius—and failed to give him all the tools for a swift conclusion. The Osa must lack either resources or confidence in their invasion here. So for some reason the enemy hesitated—supplies, mechanical troubles, unreliable allies, internal politics. Caladrunan's spymaster must probe for the weak spot.

My fingers clenched white over the chalk. I still must penetrate their tactical charades. Where did they put their flamethrowers? That dream—Caladrunan's life might depend on penetrating the riddle tangled in that dream—flames enveloping Caladrunan . . .

I caught myself irritably, threw down the chalk in disgust. Just a dream, I told myself. Besides, he wasn't consumed in the flames, he was *alive.* I scowled. Then I thought, perhaps I've the right to odd dreams! Upai were reputed to be the most secret, feral, and Goddess-touched of all the native bloods. They thought me prophet in the guardroom, and their morale seemed better for it. Caladrunan said I must learn to use that. How else, this insidious part of my mind whispered, will Tan overcome the ants' masses of Nandos and Marshmen, those flamethrowers? The Osa can't guess or prevent the intuitions we bring to the field of battle.

I thought about mercenary Nandos achafe under the Osa yoke. The Nando commander, Manoloki, would soon fail his Osa masters if, pray Goddess, any cracks started to show; Manoloki meant to overthrow his masters when he dared. But he was never a charismatic leader like Caladrunan, and his mercenaries were rumbling and underpaid. To build recruitments, he offered fantastic contracts to Marsh swamp villagers—promises all still unpaid. Marsh nobles angry at economic ruin of all their villages, promptly declared war against him, which put them back in the perpetual Marsh civil war and prevented them from assisting us. That, too, promoted the Osa intent; they weren't stupid.

Different methods for different commanders. I glanced at the slates, wondering how well that Osa general did in actual battle. The slate reports murmured back, *Oh? We'll see what kind of commander you are, Naga Teot sá Inigrev sá Orena sá Kirot—can you fight me, who commands the Osa? What kind are you, Upai?* The image of me writhing helplessly in a fit made my neck-hair rise.

Then, pressing my lips thin, I leaned over and marked the spot where I felt the major flamethrower force would be found: the rebellious Hold nearest Fortress. A deep stabbing raid would collapse Tan's core resistance and morale; and it looked well within this strange new commander's skills to accomplish it.

I wrote down the passes and fords to warn of such an attempt, I sealed slate covers with melted wax and glued paper stamps, and I stacked them to go out by next relay. I stretched, aware of how little I'd slept, and traipsed out to an eastern parapet.

There I gazed down at the river Tejed, a silver glimmer among trees. The river made a lazy ancestral arc below Fortress, a natural line of defense, and lost itself in a delta of reeds at the harbor. People boated, fished, and picnicked on its shallow and placid fords on Feastdays. The Lord of Tan judged Harp competitions on barges there during hot summer nights. Firefly Night came on the river, too, for which boys wove reed cages and chased across evening fields in wild pursuits; a night when thousands of tiny lights glimmered on the water while precious conch trumpets blew.

Caladrunan had sacrificed nearly all of that to extend a barge channel into a major river diversion; to build an arc of water about Fortress deep enough to stave off besieging armies. Among the muddy raw scars of construction, masons now erected scaffolds to sheath the exposed bank crests in sandstone to resist sapping. Dray traffic from the cliff quarry clogged passage to the eastern Fortress gate. Pile butt crews drove bridge pilings into the mud at new gates in amazing din.

Above the workmen the eastern gate road doubled in a loop through a wall of heavy brush, a barrier built twenty feet high of felled trees; if we must, we'd fire this abatis in the enemy's very face. The way rose in switchbacks and became a narrow slot in a steeply paved glacis slope, exposed to machicolations in these walls above—siege walls caked with blown snow and yellow mud, and braced every four hundred paces with a gate or with round sentry towers. Inside, the walls dropped sheer to a sewer channel.

None of it enough.

The great massif of rock was not the imposing bastion it seemed from outside. Osa weapons had range enough to lob flames inside such defenses. The caves in the cliffs might also betray us to pirates up from a harbor assault.

A company of blue-clad riders clattered across a drawbridge below. Gate sentries clashed military salute. Fortress' usual pall of smoke, mostly from Devotee-sold kerosene, stirred; a breeze lifted stinking air from the sewer. I wrinkled my nose in disgust. While Rafai toiled up long stairs to me, bearing message slates, I looked into the blue distance past the river. A hawk spiraled over fields, folded its wings, and stooped, vanishing behind a clutter of town roofs. "Any urgent slates?" I asked Rafai quietly.

He handed over a slate about the northern gate catapult in repair for a beam cracked during a practice. Then he gave me the stewards' reports. I said, "Those figures there look a bit low, don't you think? Best increase the stock of bitter-fruits for scurvy medicine in case we have a storm-bound siege." I handed the slates back. Another hawk spiraled on the sky.

"Spoil easily in the damp," Rafai said. "Dried would be better, if less effective as medicine. We're short of iron, brass, and copper scrap, as usual. And the new Crag rates! Isaon got bored with court life; he's locating new sources."

"Cragmen ought to be rich, the prices they charge for virgin metals. I don't know where all their jades leak away to. I had noticed that as a metal merchant, Keth Adcrag—" my voice touched the words lightly, gently, "—suffered no signs of poverty in his house or person."

"*I* noticed how *close* he was when your beast was blinded in the street last moon, Noble-born," Rafai said, with distinct hard gratings in his tone. "I saw an interesting Crag invention in the market today: a sun dish, to cook without fire. Ships use them in the pirate islands. The merchant charred a piece of wood in its focus—near-scalded a fishwife who stuck her face into it. I wondered if changing the curve of such a mirror, using a very hot light, could blind a man riding like yourself. Perhaps from a window or rooftop? Maybe follow up with conventional attack.''

"How big a curved mirror can Isaon build?" I said abruptly.

"To blind a rider with?"

"No. No, I want it to focus like a burning lens out there—a good hard distance." I pointed my arm levelly at probable Osa assault sites across the river channel.

"To focus out there might be hard—the strength—''

I glanced up. "You've already talked to Isaon."

Rafai nodded. "Now he's got the replacement gas lines completed, I set him to fiddling and calculating."

"Mmm," I said, squinting at the hawks. Birds of captivity, those. It was a fashionable sport; far too many people wanted space in mews for anyone to care that Caladrunan kept none. Young birds gifted him went to expert country noblemen for skilled practical use. When such men toured Fortress mews, they disgustedly agreed with Caladrunan's silent opinions.

Nevertheless the birds were very beautiful, and I had learned to handle them for him. When a bird went out on *our* hunts, it was a haggard, adult at capture, or it had been retrained to the wild by the shy, wily old Sek falconer at Lake Hold; and it promptly got released. "Economics aren't everything," Caladrunan said once, gently. I never questioned it; *I* saw his face when he thrust a hawk up into the blinding clarity of the sky.

Riding back after such hunts, he'd look at me. His face would look anxious, defiant, scowling—a look that came of hunts suffered under his father Agaka Ún, the great hunter, hawker, and womanizer. While his father had been a collector, a grasper of objects, Caladrunan preferred to see hawks by chance in the wild. He collected only statuary, to set in gardens. Looking at me thus, he always asked, "Do you want to be freed of that Oath?"

I never laughed at his linking my Oath with hawks.

Great Oath was not a matter for laughter; its requirements were strict. As the Lord of Tan's only Oathswearer, my position was unique. Though he'd never make a tyrant, none of Tan's nobles cared to commit themselves to Caladrunan as deeply as Great Oath demanded; they'd learned distrust in the Red Tyrant's abuses three generations ago. I'd be a fool to give up its protection. It justified his trust in me; it proved I had a soul. It was more to my benefit than his, but he hated fetters.

Because he loathed all forced dependence, his demands in court life could be odd. He was too proud for bribery; if he must utter threats he felt his diplomacy had failed; he gave generous service awards and scorned giving court sinecures—a change from tradition which had earned him enemies. His noble friends were expected to run Holds without bucketfuls of his biased aid. For that alone, his government would be solvent, if there wasn't an Osa invasion to soak it all up.

All very noble and high-sounding, I thought, and baffling to courtiers. Most men tried to retain power, expand it, not to give it away with that wolfish smile of his. Early on, I told him that if my meddling made his position too difficult, I'd retire quietly to cleaning his saddles and weapons. He said that sounded a great waste of talent—but to escape my Oath, I had only to ask him. Merely ask. I'd be free to go, with all his military and political defenses clear in my mind.

And break his heart, too, I thought. I had no illusions about that. His simple offer required no more faith than did my mundane daily inspections—but daily work didn't shatter me with such stark evidence of trust. He was no fatuous innocent, after so many Judgments. Did he think binding my freedom troubled his own? I thought his in far greater peril than mine. He was Lord of Tan and could never lay down the burden. Burdens . . . neither of us dared drop war labors to do as we pleased, I thought, or *I'd* have been with him at war instead of watching a hawk above a field.

I always told him, whenever he offered to free me of the Great Oath, that he did one thing well: He knew how to ensure a man's undying loyalty. "Oh? How?" he asked, smiling.

"Smother the poor victim in work, make him feel appreciated for his trouble, and set a *big* meal table."

Caladrunan always roared out a laugh. I never failed to mention food. He teased that I was just like his dogs: I loved him for his food. Very clear in memory, I saw his face smiling up at the distant spiral of a freed bird. He said the magic of them lay in their splendid pride.

Odd. When I thought of my Oath, I thought of that.

I glanced around the wall parapet and then at Rafai, blinking.

Not like me, I thought crossly, to keep losing all sense of the present. Rafai waited steadily. He wore a faint, very faint smile.

Turning my back on hawks in grainfields, I growled, "Back to the training courtyards for both of us. Have to test more men for replacement and duty."

"Did you want to know how questioning Girdeth's assailant went last night?"

I turned my head. "Don't press my temper."

Rafai sighed. "Real gang-style resistance."

"So we'll use real Tannese-style justice," I snapped.

Ten days later, on a hot afternoon, I sat working on slates beside Girdeth's bed, as I had been doing every evening since the assault. She still had bandages and she winced, that hidden, reluctant flinch of real pain—a soft, ashamed little jerk of the muscles in her neck and face and arms—whenever she moved. She no longer wore a veil when I visited, for the day after her assault she had three guard watches assembled, and she said one electrifying word. She bluntly declared me *erdmuntoú*, acceptable in her most private quarters, and beckoned me to help her back to her bed.

It caused a huge uproar. Courtiers were alarmed about my wandering the women's quarters as I chose. The chaperone noblewomen had always judged Girdeth such an ungovernable child they abandoned her to me whenever I appeared; now she scorned to see any court ladies. Even Capilla sent polite notes and was, with equal politeness, refused. Girdeth admitted only her hurt maid, the herbalist Pergo, and myself. And the insult—such a public slap that I alone deserved Girdeth's trust!

Rumors were not helped by her seclusion. Some murmured that I was twisting Girdeth's mind; that in the poor child's pitiable state, someone should really step in and take proper care of her. She stirred very little when I was about, and less when I wasn't. No one else fought to take up the chore of tending Girdeth, since they all knew very well that Girdeth had always had the temper and language of a fireworks explosive—and likely still did. I hadn't seen much of it lately, which bothered me.

Girdeth stared at me while her hand fidgeted with slate copies of radically modern tapestry design; she'd been excited about those designs once. Her face was different in so few days—gone angular, paler. She was always staring at me now; I hadn't gotten used to it. She said that looking at me made her feel better. So I brought slate reports, and let her stare if she liked. I asked no questions.

"It's very soothing to watch you work."

I lifted my brows.

Her eyes half-closed. "When I was little, my nurse's husband sat with us in the evenings. He was a great, bluff officer in the Lake Hold garrison—pensioned off awhile ago—he always worked on his slates, and I sat on Nurse's lap. They hardly spoke a word all evening. It was all so perfectly peaceful. I never needed bedtime stories."

My chalk hand shifted. "Is it the slatework that reminds?"

"Oh, no. The scent—oh, he smelled of leather, dust, ganas, metal, like you do—and the way you glance around all the time. He and my nurse made me feel so safe." She laughed. "He was a tall, heavyset old veteran as big as Rafai. Gruff. He never said much, but I knew. I knew. He had the kindest, tiredest eyes."

I smiled back wryly. "Hardly alike."

"The eyes are the very same. I'll bet that's why my brother Drin just trusted you, for no reason. And he was right, wasn't he? And look how you trusted him, before you even met him! If he'd been like Keth, well, it wouldn't have gone well for you! He said he was friends with your brother at Redspring Hold—"

I looked sharply away at the slates.

"Sorry." She leaned forward, with more color in her face. "Do you miss Drin? Rafai said you were dreadfully lonely."

"Of course I—" I felt my lips tighten. It was possible she thought she was curing me, while I thought I was trying to help her, and both of us were going about in circles because Rafai had meddled. "I'm too freakish for most Tannese. I have a duty—"

"Mmm," she said, chin resting on knuckles. "I was never afraid of you, which is rather odd—but it took me awhile to get used to how you *look*. Oh, stop acting like you've got a pox. I just meant it was hard, learning a native face could look nice."

"I'm not *nice*-looking. I'm not nice."

She smiled. "Then why is half the women's quarters aswoon over you in the last few days? My maid says it's the fashion. Well, you *did* dispatch an ax-champion, you know, saving my virtue and all that." She spoke entirely too airily. It didn't fool me at all. Because of her wonderfully collected behavior, stupid young guards denied hotly that she'd ever been touched—let alone how. So she was allowed to keep some of her pain private. She seemed very much to want that. She had nightmares about eyes staring at her; I didn't stare at her. I lowered my gaze.

"There are times," she said slowly, giving each word its own careful weight, "you look monstrous. Like *him*." She shifted, wincing. "Oh, stop looking stricken. Everyone looks like him now. I'm tired of it. The whole thing. Most of all, the thinking. I never did thank you for—"

I shook my head. "Don't. It shouldn't have happened."

Her lips, when I looked up, were stretched into a strange, ugly, grim smile. Not a girl's smile at all. The smile became a painful rictus, and then flattened into absolute blankness. I looked levelly into her eyes and did not move.

She whispered, "I could have him punished in ways that—"

"Yes. You have every right."

"But you do object," she said, barely moving her blank face.

"Our Liege your brother would."

Her eyes were clear as the sea. "He hasn't come to see me."

"He can't leave the Army to Keth Adcrag!"

Her eyelids lowered as she thought about this. "Then did Keth Adcrag set this up, to destroy me? To stop me helping the Women of the Harp, the refugees? To get control of the Army away from my brother if Caladrunan came back here? Was that—that—axman good enough to kill you?"

I felt my jaw clenching. "I was lucky."

"But you're *always* lucky."

"No. It's rarely luck. I don't like depending on it."

"And you don't like his being so good." She looked at me sharply. "I should be terrified of *you*—you're the most dangerous man in Fortress, nobody could stop you if you—but I'm not. You're not like the others . . . the ones who *look* when they see me pass."

"You are very beautiful. The men idolize you even more since that happened. You are more precious to them since you were in danger, fool boys."

"Not *that*. The other ones, the ones who—they *look*: There she is, there's the one who got herself pronged; *they'd* like to be the one who pronged me—"

I narrowed my eyes. "Names, if you have them. Times, days, faces, if not."

She gave me those. "You don't think I'm hysterical."

"I was in the Nandos," I said dryly.

She drew back a little. "I suppose when you were Nando—"

I lifted my gaze to hers.

"Women?"

I shook my head. "In the desert, they say the Goddess protects Her own, and She does. Crazy I may be, stupid I'm not. I saw men die of Wasteland burns and diseases after, shall we say, they indulged in folly. Out there, *any* woman has wandered the Blue Sands a long time."

"It's not like that here," she said bitterly.

"No," I agreed. "But the court would flay me if I harmed a woman of rank. That's aside from *my* idea that a man who attacks an innocent is a coward. I don't feel pleasure when I dominate someone, when I fight." I shrugged. "Some men do."

Her eyes looked cloudy with intense concentration. "But you aren't a small man, inside. *He* was, inside. He was a twisted little thing." Memory put violent pressure on her voice. "There was nothing else in him. *His eyes*—he would make me dead, I knew it, but he was already dead inside, and he'd always got away with anything he thought of."

"They often do," I said. A flat wash of heat flared in my gut, jabbing through bruised flesh. Anger was dangerous. I took a shallow breath, stretching my neck to fight it.

Her eyes swung to me. Easily, quietly, she said, "I could make you angry."

"It's not that hard to do!" I said, struggling for humor.

She tilted her head. "I've never seen you angry."

"Girdeth, say whatever you need. I can hold my temper."

She stared down at her fingertips, pressing nail moons randomly into her bedding. "I'm sorry. It isn't fair to you. My maid told me I'm being cruel to everybody. But I can't—*can't—*"

"Shall I send off a note demanding for the sake of your health that the Lady of Fortress hop down here and wash your hair in her own lily hands without once uttering a word?"

Desperate, but it worked. She smiled. "There's worse things than washing hair. Rafai's wife Iot has been absolutely solid. She never complains. She gets a pinched look that means she dislikes it, but she doesn't say a word. Can I hold your hand?"

I reached out for hers. She stroked the back of my hand, across the knuckle scars; turned my palm up, felt of the tendons and harp calluses, pushed back the leathers at my wrist, ran her fingertips on the old Sati scars over the wrist-cords. Then she grasped my fingers in hers and pulled my arm taut and leaned her cheekbone against my forearm. I didn't move. She said, looking somewhere past me, "I was going to marry someone who was very handsome. He was going to be manly, and tall, and look wonderful in uniforms. He'd offer me jade necklaces and pearls, and tremble when I leaned on his arm. I was going to be the smartest adviser he had, and look demure when they all realized it, while I wore white brocades that'd make a dove swoon of envy. In my daydreams I was riding about at Holds and parades cheering our men, both of us very dashing and immaculate and terribly modern."

I said softly, "Still sounds good to me."

She gave a convulsive heave somewhere between a bark of laughter and sobbing, just once, and lay still again, holding my arm. "Well, my dear Sati, you don't know how Tannese loathe damaged goods. For disease's sake, royals are supposed to wed virgin like some poor pleasure woman assigned her life long to one stupid lord's bed. People might say I'm not—Pergo said that things tore a little—even if I lied, surely he'd *know*—"

"I don't know," I said. "Maybe not. Knowledge like that doesn't come by magic; that, too, has to be learned. And don't worry about rumors. News of the assault could come out later, but if it's handled right, you shouldn't have to confess anything publicly—you can just insist on choosing a husband for love rather than powerful alliance. Someone stable who can be told this privately. They will be privy to other dangerous things."

She seemed to slacken, to go thinner in place. "I don't know any noblemen I trust that far. Do you suppose my brother knows any other fellows with hearts like yours?"

I stood up. "We'll find one for you," I said gravely. "Properly trained and approved for our Girdeth."

"I've heard that hurt women—later—it's always like the assault all over again for them, no matter how careful—"

My fingers tightened on hers. "*No*. No, it isn't. Liege and Strengam and Rafai and I—and Rafai's wife and Strengam's wife—will work on finding someone you'll want and like. He may not come out looking wonderful in uniforms that way."

"I can always look at *you* instead."

I tugged her hair gently. "Tease. The better the uniform, the worse the brain, didn't you know that?"

"I'll tell my brother," she said lightly. Caladrunan, as she knew very well, looked wonderful in his official silks.

"I already did. Several times."

"What'd he do?"

"Put my arm up between my shoulder blades and spanked me." I tugged her hair again gently and slid my hand free. "Do you want me to bring anything when I come up this evening?"

She gulped, putting her hand over her eyes. Then she laid it on the cloth bedding and held up her head and said firmly, "No."

I inclined my head into a deep salute and swept out, before she got a better look at my eyes.

I returned that evening carrying a new stack of slates. Girdeth sat before her mirror table in an odd angular posture, elbows out, stroking her forefinger slowly down her chin. She spoke out suddenly without greeting or preamble.

"Do you know *why* they did it? The women told him how to get in. Rafai has found out; the women told him where I was. And he came and *he*—" she turned her head sharply away from the mirror.

"Why did they betray you?" I said evenly from the doorway.

Her fingertip pressed her chin. "I upset all the balances of power here in the women's quarters. The noblewomen who served me thought my politics too radical and my habits too improper, and they weren't going to obey me and help run any stinking refugee camp. They thought I needed a lesson in what happens to women who don't follow the rules. And they were jealous. Somebody else sent him, but the women helped. All of my women were widows, the Lady told me that: At the time I thought nothing of it. All those stupid young men *I* couldn't abide never looked at the widows, only at me. So the women helped him . . . they only meant for him to scare me. But he went too far, and they were found out along with him."

"We don't know what his orders really were."

She looked at the mirror. "I never felt I was beautiful. It was being in the succession that made those men look at me."

"Beauty, too," I said softly, regretfully.

She looked at me. "Do you have proof who sent him?"

"Not yet. Do you?"

Her head turned; she stared absently at tapestries. "Only suspicions. I'm sure Capilla was *horrified* when she found out what her women did to enforce discipline behind her back."

"Oh, yes," I said.

Girdeth heard the irony, the bitter amusement in my voice. She lifted her brows, one wrist propped under her chin.

I said, "She terrifies servants and courtiers who pester her for decisions, yet censures them if they guess wrong. A very distinctive style of leadership—if you call it leading."

"And you know all about styles of leadership," Girdeth replied, head turned away.

"Not all. Much, perhaps, but never all. Your brother is constantly surprising me with something new." I paced across the end of the chamber studying her back, the position of her arms, the sweep of her robes. She looked better, the stitches on her ears were healing cleanly; but she was vaguely untidy, rumpled, as if the finer details of dress were carelessly attended.

She picked up a gemmed comb, twisted her fingers around it. Quite sharply she said, "And what *else* did he teach you?"

I walked up behind her, set down slates, took the comb from her hand, and secured a stray lock of her hair. I brushed her temples lightly with the calloused tips of my fingers and said, "Gentleness. I had to learn it. Are you all right, Girdeth?"

Her face crumpled. She turned on her stool, rested her forearms on my belt, burst into tears. I cradled her tense shoulders in my arms. The sobbing muscled past enormous resistance. I slid down beside her, holding her, stroking her hair even if it knocked combs and pins awry. Her hands clenched knots into my robes at shoulder and back. "*Get him,*" she gasped into my twisted clothes. "Get him, the one who ordered it—if he did this to *me,* he'll do anything—promise me!"

"Yes," I said into her hair. "Yes."

She pushed herself back, shaking. "Do you know who—"

"I've only got suspicions."

She looked into my eyes, shaking.

I said gently, "And those, I think, are enough to begin on."

"You'll get him."

I hissed out a breath in agreement, teeth showing. Her shoulders twitched up and down with the effort to control her breath, to stop crying. I drew her back to me and said roughly, "Cry. You'll feel better. Cry all you want."

When the worst of it was past, the shudders diminished into small shaky quivers of her hands. Her spasms of hiccups eased to snuffling as she leaned against me. She mumbled into my wet shoulder, "You know something about crying, don't you."

I kept stroking her hair, long smooth movements of my hand, sometimes tangling and catching the fine strands on my calluses. "Yes," I said at last.

"My brother said once you were the unhappiest creature he ever met."

"Until he made friends with me, yes, that was probably true."

"Why did he make any difference?" she asked barely above a whisper. She lacked the energy for anything louder. "He isn't as brave and kindly and fatherly and all that nonsense as everyone says he is, you know," she said rather tartly. "Sometimes he's so stupid and stubborn and—" there were more tears wetting my shoulder.

I gathered her closer. "And you miss him."

She snuffled. "Don't you? Why did he make a difference whether you were unhappy? How could he?"

"That's a silly question," I said tolerantly, stroking her hair.

"Oh," she mumbled.

Amused, I said, "People do forget I'm human. I don't mind."

"You're the only man who ever held me," Girdeth said quietly.

"Shame," I murmured. "We ought to find you someone who'd—somebody who loves you with more than a dumb bruised soul."

"Right now I disbelieve *any* man's word," she snuffled. Weak joke at best, parodying her own fear thus. "Is that how you feel, dumb and bruised? I thought it was just *me* who felt that way since—since—"

I again stroked her hair.

"Naga?"

I turned my head closer.

"You didn't look when the herbalist—even when—?"

I rocked her a little. "No. I didn't look."

"I was terrified, I didn't want you to leave me! But I didn't want you to *look*—you'd see how awful I—"

"How could you look awful to any of us as brave as you were?" I said the words fiercely, protectively. My insides clenched and shuddered with anguish for her. But I held myself steady; I did not let it out. "Girdeth, we admire your courage. When you spoke to the guards, you were so strong, so crisp. No one calls that weak. They admire you."

"They'd admire me more if I'd beat him off properly, killed

him, *hurt* him, as you did. But I suppose that's wishful think-ing.'' She gave one huge sniffle, gathering herself together, and sighed. Slowly, leaning on me, she got up. I looked up from where I still knelt. ''I should get cleaned up and meet those people who've been plaguing to see me. Something to cover these messy ears, that's necessary.''

''I'll send in Iot and her hand-picked women.''

Girdeth laced her fingers before her. ''Naga. Thank you.''

At the door, slates under my arm, I paused, saluted her with a snap that crackled leathers, and went out. Rafai turned to me, questioning. I said gruffly, ''Send your wife in with ladies. Girdeth wants to dress for interviews.''

Rafai let out a whoop and yelled down the corridor. Until the investigation was done, trusted men guarded these corridors, further drain on Fortress garrison work. I distinctly saw one scarred old veteran's leathery face widen into a smile, and the even older man beside him looked almost teary-eyed. I turned away to avoid noticing it. I thought, perhaps I underestimated Tannese fondness for their golden, irreverent young Girdeth. Rafai said, ''She's really ready to interview again?''

I said, ''Well, let your wife dress her properly, and ask again if she's ready. No pushing her, is that understood?''

Rafai met my eyes. ''None of us wish harm to her that way.''

I glanced at the other men warningly. Then I looked at Rafai. ''We've got another piece of thinking ahead.''

Rafai's eyes gleamed. ''Finding the one who set it up.''

''How'd you guess?''

''My wife mentioned Girdeth was much set on it.''

I said between my teeth, ''So am I.''

Rafai said, hardly moving his lips, ''Adcrag?''

I tapped my nails on the pommels of my scaddas. ''Odd, how splendidly this mess could throw a lot into chaos. I think he'd like that.''

Rafai brooded a long moment, standing at parade rest before his squad of men. He looked like a great bear. He murmured something to himself, hunching his shoulders briefly, and only strengthened the impression. His belts strained to hold in his robes, as if cinched in against the weight of grain bags. Rafai, I thought, has stretched his bones up into a *very* large young man in these past moons. His voice rumbled down the corridor, uttering agreement with me. Then he held up a slate. ''Noble-born, this report—the street boys told my men that a big procession is rehearsing for tomorrow's parade near the Adcrag town residence. The boys said it'd be an unusual Crag wedding.''

I said, surprised, ''They turned in a parade permit, I saw it. Can't send any extra men down there—half the guards are stuck here already. I'll go by Fat Nella's and wander over to check on it. Think they'd start a riot?''

''They don't want their courthouses torched, do they? It's in their own section.''

I grinned at his cynicism; Cragmen only started riots in other people's quarters. ''It's been awhile since Lado and I dragged you into Nella's.''

Rafai blushed bright red. Since marrying he showed no signs of ever wanting to see the inside of Fat Nella's pleasure house again. I said soberly, ''Take good care of your Lady Wife, Rafai.''

# CHAPTER

# = *9* =

NEAR MIDDAY I left my gana and escort soldiers at the parade sidelines, ducking through Crag spectators. The Crag prisoner had disrupted my morning. After days of Tannese-style questioning— mild, persistent, endless, erosive as blown sand—Girdeth's assailant had yielded nicknames, the only knowledge he had. Rafai forced open those few cracks under the direst threat we had: My skills expended in total rage. In truth, I ruled myself rigidly in that chamber, venting just enough of my internal heat to reinforce Rafai's threats. Rage had been too close a thing; all that effort for nearly nothing—nicknames, *aphha!* When the guards next checked his cell, the man was dead, likely with the smuggled-in help of one of many Marshplant poisons. We couldn't tell if he'd suicided, with help, to avoid telling us any more, or if his employer—or some other internecine connection, gang plots could go stranger yet—had killed him. The hair still stood rough on my neck.

Tannese commoners mingled with excited Crag families for the pageant; parents held up children to see bright costumes. Mask-headed mimes danced mock battles, caricaturing both Tanmen of the past and heroes of Crag rebellions. Here Crag mimes won their mock battles, for in this alien enclave a different history held sway. Who was to say? A world with the Red Tyrant and the Osa long ago ceased to look so simple to me.

Grimly I hunted among the bellowing poets, tumblers, and actors doing festival dramas. At last I jumped a barricade and ran down the street. My escort shouted after me, trapped in the press. Costumed men and the clanging gongs never paused as I ran past.

Two figures at the procession's start made the spectators guffaw. A man on stilts towered along booming out parts of Caladrunan's speeches, flapping an enormous yellow false beard. A boy, painted black, capered and tumbled below him. Singing out of tune, he peered into spectators' faces and insulted them with clever patter. The boy did handsprings up to me, popped upright with an exaggerated snappy salute. His painted eyes went round. He let out a screech, clutched his face, and ran off down the street in abject mimed terror. That got a big laugh.

I sighed, looking past him. Nothing. No visible antagonist to the Caladrunan on stilts, nothing against Tannese parade codes. The stiltman roared jokes at the black-painted boy, who rallied with political quips and hid among the mimes in comic fear of me.

I'd become part of the charade: A Crag hero strode grandly up to me offering mock battle. A Tannese mime answered the Crag challenge with flourishes of his wooden sword. The eyes in the masks were not playful; and I suspected that, because the boy marked me out, the Tannese mime had shifted amongst the buffoonery to help me. They fought and jabbed awkwardly around me. The swords clacked; the Tannese mime's split and fell from his hand, which made the crowd laugh. The mock-Lord of Tan hid his masked head behind me in mock terror as his body swung neatly between me and a parade guard, obscuring me from sight. The Crag mime waved his sword—all his frantic action to call the guard.

I could go along with the fun. Acting disgusted, I grabbed the Tannese mime and flipped him over my shoulder into the gut of the prancing Crag hero. Both performers let out loud grunts and went down in a heap of painted heads; the Tannese discreetly kneed the Crag mime. I dusted my hands together and bowed to the crowd, who cheered as if it was all part of the show.

That it wasn't became clear when the parade guard ran off shouting. Already other green-robed men clumped along the street peering among the mimes. I was conspicuous with two masked figures in a heap at my feet. The guards marked my blue robes and my size. One pointed. They ran toward me. I thought, Caladrunan would tell you *not* to make a fuss. And he'd be right; this could turn nasty.

So I took six running steps directly at them, tripped the first guard into his fellows, and leaped sidewise, hurling myself bodily over the parade barricades into the close-packed crowd. I landed in a very surprised woman's lap. She had been standing up; now she was not. Now she sat in the lap of the equally surprised man behind her. Her mouth gaped into a cavern about to shatter my sensitive ears. Everyone crammed back, leaving a clear space.

"Thank you," I said graciously before she screamed, and scrambled up. I took two running steps, leaped, and grabbed the beams under a low house balcony. I swung there, kicked my boots up—and got myself up and balanced on top of a rickety alley wall beside the house. I ran along the top of the fence. People pointed after me, too densely packed to give chase. I jumped over one good-natured fencetop observer, who grinned after me. The guard's shouts faded behind me. The alley fence, with many changes of material and more gates, ran a good distance past the peering heads of the crowd. Long enough, at least, to run among people who hadn't seen me with the mimes. I hoped my escort had sense enough to avoid fights with the Cragmen parade guards.

I dropped off the fence behind the tallest country folk I could find: burly Tannese farmers. Because I was so short, I was completely shielded from view. Two of the puzzled men gazed round at me; caught in the parade crowd by accident, they knew nothing of court life and didn't understand half the miming. As Crag guards came shouting, running through the procession, I held my hand over my mouth. *"Tax men,"* I whispered, and the farmers smiled and closed ranks in front of me. When they moved, leisurely talking, I went amidst them.

At a good moment I took to another fence. When I saw the tail of the parade I understood the hostile alertness of the Cragmen: The sight jolted me out of my calm, out of my slouch at a wall, right out into the press of bodies. I shot through, furious. Exertion made me more alert to odors, sounds, and events, more easily enraged with the significance of this outrage.

I ran into the open, shouting, "Wait, wait," in Upai. Heads turned. The procession didn't even pause. But the cow-horned headdress turned in surprise, stopped; and the beautiful ivory-dusted face of a Upai woman regarded me with frightened black eyes before scurrying back to her place in the line. The noise of cymbals and gongs and wooden blocks resounded all around. The young Upai woman was being married. The richness of her

beads and headdress and robes proclaimed her becoming fourth
wife to a rich man: *to a Cragman*. Even now I saw more
green-robed men moving suspiciously along the fringe of gong-
pounding Devotees. Their eyes fell on my blue robes, my face;
they shouted. Again I turned and pushed past into the crowd,
evaded the guards among alley gates. How could a Cragman
marry a Upai woman? His clan would tolerate it only on some
pretense she was a slave-bride. Was it to prove Upai women
were whores available to anyone, that Upai were helpless against
Crag power; or was it to prove rumors about me true, to flout the
wealth to buy poor women's marriage contracts on whim—what
an insult these Cragmen concocted! I could not believe the
woman felt anything but terror. Keth's sort would like that.

Alone, I trotted along empty back streets several alleys away
from the marriage procession, my head full of the sight of the
beautiful Upai woman dusted with white to make her look
un-native, her lovely eyes rimmed with Cragman colors and her
headdress full of Cragman marriage symbols. She was desperate
to so abase herself to a contract marriage with such a hateful
family as Keth's; and so beautiful in spite of it.

I glanced up at slumping clay buildings. I'd entered the Sek-
blood section for a minor task. Here any ties of sympathy to
other natives were in my mind alone. And I didn't get down two
streets without rousing the wildlife.

Three Sek-blood toughs strolled around a corner and fanned
out before me. Their refined, narrow dark faces didn't at all
match their ragged robes. The biggest one drawled, "We wait
for you. You *stupid*, scribe? Bad, coming up here again. Hit
him."

The middle one said doubtfully in their blurred dialect, "Don't
look now like he did."

I tried hard to look like a harmless timid scribe: I had a
stranger's good name to protect. But it was not luck that my
robes hid my real accoutrements, nor that I wore ink stains on
two fingers, nor that Caladrunan's spymaster had sent me information on these Sek toughs. I backed up two steps and stumbled
against a wall. The biggest Sek walked forward holding his knife
in a deceptively lazy hand. He said, "Ah, he's the one, nobody
else stupid enough to cross here. Fancy new clothes! You gone
paid off? In the alley that night, scribe, your woman said was
*you* paid off, then you pay *us*."

I backed gingerly around a box into an alley door. "Can't

think,'' I stuttered. I had never stuttered in my life. ''No, my patron didn't pay me—''

The big one spat. ''Look, shaking so hard its knees knock. Here, scribe.'' He and his friends stepped into the alley after me. He grabbed my arm. I let him. He jerked me up close by the neck of my robe. ''Fancy new, these soldier clothes. See this?'' His knife flickered.

I nodded.

''Going to give me a reason to use it?''

I shook my head.

''What did you tell patron?'' He reached for my Harper's neck bag. That'd never do. I tensed my free arm and drove my fist into his middle. He lost his grip on my arm. I put my hand gently on his face, saying, ''*Surprise,*'' and snapped his head back before he had time to react. His friends, staring in horror at my hands, were next. They drove at me together, much good it did them. In the end they babbled what they knew—useless, all of it. I snarled down in my throat. ''That's for helping the man with the ax,'' I told the bodies. I straightened my robes and stepped out of the alley door. I closed it gently after me. My scadda blades never came out of sheath.

Some moments later I opened the back door of the big pleasure house beside the channel. I skidded a jade across the service table to the jade-keeper. Heads came up from fourpeg tables.

Fat Nella, owner of the most expensive pleasure house in Tan, set aside an ornate tapestry and walked up, spectacular sight—Nella's was an undulation of flesh like no other. She touched my shoulder with a pearl-garlanded finger, held out a wine goblet.

Nella had interesting guests and even more interesting information, none of it free: Nothing in her place was free. She had an underworld squabble with one of Keth Adcrag's cabal about a thousand jades in mislaid contraband; bodies were found from the fracas. She liked neither Manoloki nor foreign Osa plans for upsetting everything, thank you. Nella liked accounts paid on time, goods delivered intact. She liked order, if not law; so she considered that we had the same enemies, and passed her old friend Agtunki, Caladrunan's great-aunt, stolen documents.

Ironic that Caladrunan's just rulership was delicately upheld by two of the most infamous women in Tan. He slapped Nella with fines when her smugglers were caught—more than his father had dared—and Nella teased him for it. A moon ago, Lado and I got roaring drunk with her and serenaded the entire quarter. She said she liked my manners, or lack thereof; I never plagued for her patronage like so many other Harpers. Nella also hired dozens of my people, saying blandly to critics that Upai were cheap and quiet, unlike some folks. She protected her employees. She told me one time how a man hurt a house Kehran boy, and the revenge she took for it, which was horrible.

I touched water beading from the chilled goblet, not looking in Nella's shrewd eyes. I was safe: Robbing me wasn't worth the rift with my Liege. Yet he disapproved of the outrageous pirate queen; she made him nervous. Well, she made me nervous, too. Doubtless she already knew about the dead in the alley.

From behind the tapestries at my back came human murmurs rather than echoes off a solid wall. They were quite normal, unremarkable male voices but for the words. "Darling, if I eat another candy, slap me for it. I shall be out of my best robes and rolling in fat."

"Oh, stop it! Everything you've said today sounds like it belongs in a parody."

"You're just cross because that great lump of yours never showed his expensive behind in the place."

"He *promised* after he did some court business he'd come—by yesterday. He has some mysterious huge income; it's not like I should have to wait on poverty, for the love of— Oh, look there. My garter, what is *that?*"

"Not for you, that's what," the first one said crisply.

"Look at those thighs, my paints and feathers for—what does he do, throw pilings or something disgusting? I'm baffled. Too poor for a client, too tired about the eyes for a floor-boy."

"Harp, you cross old thing."

"Somehow I can't see a Harper working docks to eat."

"Oh, not exactly," the first one said with dry crackles of amusement in his tones. "The hardwear and harness isn't show gear, not like some of the guests *I* have to pamper. Can you believe it, that's a Blue Robe under the harpcase."

"My Goddess gone cross-eyed in praise of pearls!" the second voice sputtered. "*Not* the Lord of Tan's—ahh—"

"Oh, yes indeed!" the first said gleefully.

"Urr!" the second one said. "Oh, paint pots, I feel so out of date."

"I'm told, by a very good source, that all those cavalry Cragmen nobles who told the Council chairman how to vote, right there at that table, I heard it myself!—well, those thugs fell all over themselves with respect once they saw him fight. *Once* was plenty . . .''

"Oh. Bad-tempered?"

"Worse. A cold fighter. I've heard so extremely nothing about him, he blew up so fast—now nobody's talking. *That's* power, that is."

"Flames—he heard you," the second one said sharply.

I turned my head. "Took you long enough to realize," I said in snide imitation of their style. "Come out and face the worst."

A flurry of dismayed word fragments, and two rather rumpled Tannese in conventional dark robes appeared at the edge of tapestries. If there was anything suggestive or racy about them, I was too foreign to see it. With their mouths shut I couldn't have distinguished the Kehran boys from the other employees. Their hands fretted nervously, but I was used to that in new servants.

"Sit," I said, pointing across my table.

They sat so hard and fast it must have hurt; their faces were all strained eyes and tense muscles.

"Am I breaking any house rules?" I said mildly.

Negative head movements.

"Is my front view as interesting as the back?" I said in exactly the same tone.

They darted wild glances at each other, and then as one babbled, the other began to giggle nervously, hand over mouth. "But we only—"

I lifted my hand. Instant silence. *That*, I thought, was why Kehran boys were so popular. Instant obedience, whatever the virtue of the noble waving his hand—even better than a dóg. I was growing angry at the people who started this practice. I studied them, steepling my gloved fingertips. They didn't blink or twitch. "I think," I said dryly, "you'll have to inform me how one says 'at ease' to you."

They smiled and threw approving glances at one another, both for my consideration and for their own discipline. Of course if they'd been truly disciplined, I'd never have heard them talking. I said, "Do all the patrons deserve comment?"

I was granted equality in a conspiratorial sneer. "But *you* heard us, none of that lot ever has—"

"—we'd never knowingly disturb the great lord—"

"Noble-born, not lord," I said, correcting the title downward.

Modest, too, their glances said. They were beginning to grow interested and to lean closer. The second one was glancing down the length of me when I said gently, "You shouldn't invite trouble, if you're already committed to a noble. That is the system, isn't it, to prevent disease?"

The eyes flashed and the posture wilted. "Yes, Noble-born."

"For your lives, you should be cautious of patrons hearing your gossip and never reacting. Tell me your names."

They sat up straighter and produced absurdly coquettish words, whore's names. The older one leaned forward and said eagerly, "Well, *I'm* not promised yet. Or are you—?" and abruptly saw the chasm yawning before him.

The second one looked horrified. "You shouldn't be so rude, Jo," which was not the fancy name, "just because the Noble-born looks native and speaks plain, you shouldn't treat him like a snob."

"One should never make assumptions," I agreed, a touch of edges in my light tone. My eyes shifted between their faces, and my mood went to pity. Of course they saw it, and stiffened— which was better for what was coming. I could not believe these two had anything to do with what had happened to Girdeth; victims, debauched and prostituted by someone to a twisted childless fate, like sending a younger son to a border garrison which would never survive—and the two were not even as old as I was. There was little of the street boy in there; they'd been taken as children into the House. I said, "Iskapo, I came with bad news."

The second one, Iskapo, sat quiet, eyes absolutely still on mine. Only his hand groped out, and the first, Jo, took it tightly.

"Your Cragman patron will never come."

The eyes went white-ringed all around.

"He attacked a—highly ranked noblewoman and admitted conspiring in a cell of rebels to kill my Liege, Lord of Tan."

No more eye-white could show. But Iskapo was perfectly rigid in place, lips gone gray with pressure not to scream out. It seemed there was something, some bond of love, to show in this terrifying wreckage of a face. In another moment it was going to crumble into tears or some wracking howl of agony. And it was real shock, real grief. Amazing: That monster I'd fought had earned this boy's grief.

"Iskapo, I am permitted to question you and to pension you as his surviving Kehran if I judge you innocent, a statement which you may confirm by decrees proclaimed in the Great Hall every noon—"

"Of course he's innocent!" Jo said fiercely on his friend's behalf. "What did he have to do with that Cragman's stupid plots, Iskapo can't even keep his big mouth quiet, and the whole House knows it. Nella must've, the bitch, when she set you at this table!"

I turned my eyes on him, and still Jo blazed, protectively, but growing rapidly afraid. I looked back at Iskapo. Retired by the death of his life-patron, he must swear off all but the safest Kehran practices, at peril of his life; and if he worked, it would be in a trade he must learn for himself or apprentice among the very few ex-Kehran craftsmen.

Iskapo looked terrible, eyes staring inward at wreckage. And he was not, I thought, even looking yet at his own looming difficulties.

"There, there," Jo said, obviously distressed, "we'll manage something for you. I'll ask—"

I said, "Should you two wish to stay friends beyond this House, nothing stops Iskapo from signing your contract, Jo, and becoming *your* patron. Which would require some wealth."

They both stared, startled out of grief a moment. While I had their attention, I said, "There exist positions among courtiers which require a kind of artless sophistication which *I* distinctly lack, though I recognize its signs." I looked hard in both sets of defenseless eyes. "Positions which we would prefer to award to a loyalty born of gratitude rather than greed."

Iskapo was, unknown to himself, beginning to cry. Water ran unnoticed down his cheeks. He went back to staring at nothing again. Jo said angrily, "His patron was *terrible,* but Iskapo can't stand people going away—"

I looked at the tears and said softly, "I'm more sorry than I can say for your loss."

"Did you *plan* to put him into this—this—" Jo said, almost brilliant red with increasing fury, "—where he has to—starve out there or take whatever Nella gives him?"

"No," I said baldly. "I saw a solution to his problem when I heard you two speak together. I will not throw someone out in the street. I know something of what it's like."

My compassion made Iskapo lose his fragmenting self-control to sobs. For all the frightened jerks Jo gave him, warning him frantically to stop, he ignored all warning. I was impressed. A more fearful, manipulative, or greedy Kehran would have shut off the tears and tried to charm me instead of hurling my position back in my teeth with crying over a dead conspirator. "Go," I said. "You can send up a message to accept or reject my offer through Nella."

"Don't trust her," Jo hissed, and lifted his taller friend by one arm away from the table.

"Oh, I don't," I said dryly.

"She'll even bill him for his space here until he leaves!"

I looked at the bent head. "Yes, I know. I'll remember to see it's paid."

"Come away now," Jo murmured. "This way, come—"

"He killed—he—" Iskapo's voice rose loud.

Jo said grimly, "If I know anything about your patron, the Harper had no choice. I'll find out, I'll—" and they were gone.

Nella murmured, "Don't know how you do it. Recruiting right under my nose, and your hands right out in plain sight!"

"Practice."

"Not a pretty sight. They'll both be useless for days. But I'm betting the one who *caused* the whole mess was a worse one."

"I couldn't recruit them if you were known to take good care of boys retiring from your House." I tipped up the goblet.

"Sorry, I'm not *that* grateful to the flighty little things. They'd get hooked and eat it all up in drug syrup. Besides, the only madam who got a pox of radical social conscience was out of business inside a year. No thank you. Everything here pays for itself or it goes, even the kitchen cats. But enough about business practices. Now, Iskapo and Jo are lucky choices for you; I think they're stable enough to survive outside." She settled her bulk with deceptive grace. Powerful fingers massaged my shoulders. "Sad thoughts will put lines in your face."

I sat motionless, head turned slightly. No one besides me, fool that I was, had in the memory of man dared to threaten *her* person. She forgave my folly because I'd amused her. While Nella probed my shoulders, mime figures paraded before my inner thoughts.

I'd be seeing that Upai woman's face parading in my sleep, I knew it. Even painted white, that face followed me. Then I thought of Keth Adcrag. I could see Keth laughing, his red freckles whitening, as he suggested such a marriage to his kin, garnishing the insult with the stilt figure of Caladrunan. I kicked a chair. It spun around, fell on the floor, and smashed. I said quietly, "Cheap furniture, Nella. Just for me?"

Nella's fingers glided down my side. The hair crept coldly on my neck. "Temper! So—I hear my big bearhug friend Rafai got *other* names out of that rapist, but you can't touch *them*. Would you like us to bring you other chairs to break?"

*How did she know?* I told myself to be sensible. I gave Nella a look. "No."

"Good. You know you can't afford it, my dear."

"Ah, well, I had a worse temper before I was trained." I threw a chip of jade from my Harper's bag to pay for it.

Nella patted my crotch. I glanced into her face. Her eyes disappeared into smile-creases. "You're so pretty in a fight."

I thought of the Sek I had killed: mere errand boys for the axman who— I clenched my hand and felt the silver goblet inlay bend under my fingers. Nella's fingers stroked my hip. A cold wave ran over my nerves as I read it for what it was, a warning. My hand relaxed on the goblet. A long life in pleasure houses had robbed Nella of prejudices and desires, and vastly sharpened her lethal intellect. Survival was her rule. Other women left pleasure houses in loathing. Nella just said lightly that the House kept her from getting stuffy and outdated. She purred, "Too bad I left the trade, Sweetlegs, my service used to—"

I smiled, draining the bent goblet; she'd keep it for a trophy. "Nella, why you don't get jailed for your foul mouth—"

She ran her fingers up me in such a way that—behind leather armor—my insides flopped about, and I sat bolt upright in the chair. She said, "Now *really*, Sweetlegs, you do have the habit of insulting old women. I hear Capilla's *very* cross with you."

I laughed, plucked off Nella's hand, and patted her cheek.

She pinched my ear. "And the Sharinen alliance proposals?"

"All postponed again. The war."

"Fool Council." Her body relaxed into itself, a folding like a tidepool creature. "But factories, doctors, trade routes—just too good. Sharinen never give things away, you know. I wondered what they were going to wring out of us."

"Jades," I said flatly. "They'd make jades every time they turned their hands over once trade began. They'll buy iron ore cheap, sell it back finished and expensive. Our Osa war is a blessing, so they don't mind helping us; we keep the Osa busy here instead of warring at Sharinen borders. They've held the border against Osa for years; we need Sharinen help vastly more than they need us. This we were not so delicately told."

Nella said, "So we're Sharinen slaves, or Osa slaves."

I looked at her. "Which would *you* rather be?"

She looked thoughtful. "A very good point. Relax, child, you'll ruin all my hard work on those rocks you call shoulders. Some people in town here are making serious efforts to undermine you." She waved gently toward the street. "I took the liberty of making counterrumors."

"What?" I said fiercely.

"Not until I've had a little fourpeg. You so rarely indulge me, child." She lifted her silken bulk from the chair. Her fat ringed hand rested companionably on my shoulder as we went.

Servants piled a groaning table with roast duckling, pickle-stewed grain, and spiced dishes of vegetables; side courses of sweets, Nella's passion, kept coming and going. She fed half the Upai camps out of the house's leftovers. I still stared in amazement at her personal gluttony, and pushed aside my wooden trencher. She looked thoughtful, shifting back in her chair. "My new rumors need support. *Ercccchhh*, wife-choosing—your grandmother failed to pick you a wife. Negotiated like a simpering virgin."

I shrugged, savoring the fullness in my gut. "Neither of us has your experience in the erotic arts." I gave her a lewd look.

"Sheer business sense is what you need." Nella grinned. "I've got a Upai marriage contract. *You* must have a marriage to kill those absurd stories about you, and *I* want favor for favor."

"Fourpeg," I said in resignation, and burped.

We played fourpeg all day. I swept up the jades, and on the next play she swept them back. We were even players, my speed compensating for her greater skill; we both cheated, which amused Nella. Finally I pounced. "*You* outmaneuvered my grandmother on the marriage."

"She wasn't very firm. You must have heard of her—Kiroki clan Upai. The girl's wild as hill broom, and for some reason your grandmother doesn't realize *you're* worse. Now, since the woman's a knife-dancer, I think you two might do. She might even let you sleep with her sometimes, Sweetlegs; best you can expect of her." Nella held up a little wooden carving of a woman's face: the seal of the marriage contract. It waved in Nella's plump fingers.

"I won't kill for you," I warned her. "Nothing that hits my Oath, on Liege's honor."

She waved her hand. "You're a generous boy, under all that leather of yours. You told me about the Sharinen alliance, and I *know* you sent along those wine-shippers with their lovely liquor samples. Orena was *livid* that recipe's got out.''

One of Nella's soldiers slipped in and murmured into her ear. She murmured back orders, flawlessly twirling her throw; Nella ran her empire while she enjoyed the rest of her life. She decided it was time for a break when I held the jades. She confronted me. ''If you disposed of . . . well, you know your enemy at court . . . you'd save us all trouble. Did you know he runs with a Coteskani bitch now? She's after something—plans, dates, something—I have no doubt. Whatever the lady calls herself, *I* know her clan. And she incites him. He grows too ambitious. He makes mistakes that'll topple him some day.''

Twiddling pegs, I brooded. ''Liege won't let me assassinate.''

She sighed. ''That's never been the Tannese way: too upright for it. Bless the fools, that's why I'm on their side.'' At my glance, she laughed, waving me to take hard-won game jades.

I looked up at her under my eyelids. *''You* never hesitated.''

''Couldn't afford to dawdle over moral palpitations, dear boy, and you know it. If I had to, I'd sell your delectable hide to the highest bidder.''

''Rotten old woman,'' I said, without rancor.

''And don't you forget it. You'd be wise to rid yourself of your enemy. Consider this early payment for the job, if you like.'' She tossed me the marriage carving negligently, lounging back, and asked me to play my harp.

She always asked in a husky, respectful voice. She thanked me, after, in the same respectful tone. She wasn't always that way. Lado told stories about her hurling wine pitchers at Harpers who didn't meet her standards during house performances. She murmured, ''I await proofs of our mutual irritant's mistakes, reports which will please both our palates. I'll send copies to Agtunki. As for Tan's limping alliances, tactical problems—use your wits. I fear our Liege Lord will need them. Enough for one day, you fool boy. Get out of here, I'm an old woman. You've tired me out, you and your exuberance. Your escort is waiting for you outside.'' Nella pinched my ear and sauntered off, smiling. Rose and herb oils drifted after her. Grown enormous and dignified, her walk somehow still beckoned as sensuously as her perfumes did.

Outside, Rafai barked at the escort and glared at me. I fingered the carving in my pocket. The bridal procession had left a trail of bright litter on the cobbles, which, as I rode after it, led to gates in a walled compound. The glyph on the gate was a jagged line in a circle, iron set in the green paint.

I turned away, swearing. This was the local home of Clan Adcrag, of Keth himself. That clan had brought in a new wife to beat—one of *my* people! I remembered the woman's face had been nervous as a deer put to flight when she heard me shout.

The next three nights I kept seeing a woman's face. I thought of riding out to Caladrunan's war camps to tell him about it. Images filled my mind when I thought of her: My mind saw moonlight and the silhouette of plum branches across skin so smooth it shone like water on marble—skin so luminous it admitted of the slightest flaw, skin that would be dazzling against the darker flesh of my arms.

When I thought of telling Caladrunen, other thoughts always sprang to mind. I heard the sound of silks on a hot evening wreathed in the scent of writing chalk and lavender that meant cleanliness and order and calm restored in my world. Sometimes I wondered what it was that Caladrunan, majestic in his patriarchal brows and his great yellow mane, found in me who was shadows and darkness. I wanted to hear his voice rumbling round the walls. Friendly, and just as easily dangerous.

I rolled my head in my furs. He'd only call me to him when he had decided that this intolerable ache was something more than a convenient habit.

He conducted the war only four days' ride away, teaching new recruits how to march in formation. I knew I'd obediently stay in Fortress to do my duty, but I'd sleep very little, restless in the nights of my lonely term of service.

Levied soldiers, asked about their wives and children far away in the countryside, always looked surprised at my sympathy. I knew I was lucky; I could think of sometime rejoining the one person I thought of as family, the Lord of Tan. Rafai, careful, conscientious, duty-bound Rafai, was luckiest of all. *He* went home to his beloved in married quarters every evening and spoke enthusiastically to me of what to name the sons he might have. I did not crush his good humors by reminding him how unlikely it was that *I* would ever get sons—or, in Upai, to name daughters. I fingered the marriage carving Nella had given me. I thought, perhaps I should go to the Upai camps and find out if this was a good likeness of that woman's face. I slept then.

The next morning's training exercises were broken by a peremptory demand from the women's quarters.

"Lady Girdeth, you called for me?" I asked. Surprised, I stared at two slender veiled figures: one tall and young, the other weighted with gemmed ornaments, stiffly erect. Those antique silver-crackling robes revealed her age. *"Ahh,"* I said then, pleased and surprised. I'd not received slate message of her arrival—which had to be at her own orders, and she outranked everyone but her nephew Caladrunan.

*"I* called you here, young man." Caladrunan's and Girdeth's aged great-aunt Agtunki seated herself on a pillow in a rustle of silk, flourishing one heavy robe sleeve even as she threw back her veil. A waft of musky perfume drifted across the table. Agtunki poured herself mua, a brew as strong and black as Tejed mud.

"Don't look so scandalized, youngsters," she said crossly. "It's my only remaining vice, as you know very well, and I've ridden the worst road in Tan on your behalf. Girdeth, be off. It's rude of you to hang about embarrassing my guest with your melancholy. Health suits you better, my dear. Go get some sun in those overgrown play yards the Lady Capilla sees fit to call gardens—and do hold yourself up straight when you walk!"

Girdeth exited with a rather healthy crash of the door.

"Temper!" Agtunki remarked. "Sit, youngster. I recall I had trouble getting you to sit down for me once before. Do you think I'm a shrunken wrestler about to leap over this ostentatious table of Capilla's? Look at it, isn't it horrible. Carving all over—gouging the legs is more than enough. Ruin of good lumber."

"I thought so," I agreed, kneeling into one of the cushions opposite her.

Wrinkled lids moved; hooded eyes flicked from her goblet to my face. "Don't think agreeing with me makes me any bit less unpleasant. In fact, it makes me worse. No one agreed with me while I ran Lake Hold as a young girl, and I doubt humanity has improved enough to agree with me now."

I smiled. "So you'll enjoy terrifying Girdeth's negligent ladies."

*"You're* a thoroughly disagreeable young man," she said heartily, as if she approved.

"You thought I was pretty last time," I said dryly.

"Cheeky, too," she retorted, swigging mua. That mua would have put me flat on my back; Agtunki didn't stir. She growled, "Just what *is* wrong with Girdeth?"

I lowered my eyelids.

"Oh, come now, I can have that rude herbalist Pergo and that red-haired Devotee adviser daughter of mine run up here and questioned officially, but I expect that'd be a bit too public. At least I give you the compliment of assuming you're discreet. Read, then, there's the authorizations." Her hand snapped out.

*Slam!* The slate slid across the table. I caught it and opened the cover. When I looked up I said quietly, "Girdeth was not raped. She was assaulted with a strip of metal twisted off a brazier in her chambers. I heard noises and subdued the Cragman. He later died in questioning, of a poison either smuggled to him by sympathizers or forced on him to shut him up. The men who sheltered and supplied him before the assault died yesterday in a Sek-blood section alley. I believe all were paid to testify, if caught, that Capilla's women had planned the entire assault. The women themselves say they only meant to frighten Girdeth."

The old woman's finger tapped her goblet twice. "It can't be easy to get in here, I think. I've seen her chamber. Capilla isn't that stupid, it wasn't *her* plan. Still, an inside plot, not merely a madman's notion?"

"I believe so."

"Do you have proof of the one who set it up?"

I lowered my eyes. "No."

"Look at me!" she snapped.

I looked up. Quietly, I said, "Don't press my temper, Lady Agtunki. I have been . . . angry . . . since the assault. You are another vulnerable lady to protect. I failed Girdeth."

"No," Agtunki said harshly, surprising me. "That arrogant fool Capilla did, choosing such women as turned traitor so easily. What a scorched short-sighted act that was! The assault throws Girdeth's whole marriageability into question, weakens our future alliance possibilities—which might end up one day endangering Capilla's own venomous hide. Lucky you saved the girl at all. Certainly you've saved Capilla, sorting and squelching false evidence against her before it reached the court. And killing the witnesses who'd say so, too, if I read you aright. I talked to them both, you know, Girdeth and Capilla. All I hear is excuses from them both, Girdeth for drooping about—"

"It's been very little time since—"

"She's not going to get well by listening to depressing poetry, shutting herself away for days at a time and swearing she'll marry Keth for her brother's alliance sake, shouting that her body is good for nothing else now. Far more likely she's planning to murder the Cragman in his bed; she's a vengeful one when his name is spoken. As for that Capilla, oh, she's shocked, but it's curious what she emphasized." Agtunki gave a grim smile. "She certainly wallowed in your difficulties with pleasure. She talked about you and your problems and failings twice as much as Girdeth." Her gloved hand fluttered. "So utterly transparent."

"Few," I said, "have achieved the depths of your own subtlety, Lady Agtunki."

She snorted over her goblet. "I want to spank them both."

I looked down at the slate. Caladrunan's orders were unmistakable, and genuine. Slowly I said, "There were certain tasks to be accomplished here. As long as Girdeth is here, I should stay to protect her."

"Well, you can't sleep in *her* bed," Agtunki said, slurping more mua. "So, I'll sort out these ladies of easy politics and take Girdeth back to Lake Hold. These silly padded surroundings would drive a sane woman crazy in a tenday. What the girl needs is decent food, some fishing, some good rousing hunts, and plenty of regular work. She doesn't do a flamed thing here, do you know that? No duties!"

"The Lady of Fortress never assigned her any—" I began.

Agtunki muttered something rude into her goblet. She surfaced after a long sip, saying, "Too bad the girl had to fall in love with you. We may never get her straightened out and married to somebody worthwhile."

After a moment I closed my mouth.

"She has, you know," Agtunki snapped. "Flame it all. And the Lady's right about you—you're skinnier than I saw you last. You've no business stewing in this kettle of fishing worms. Set up the place so it can run itself, get out there blowing up the flamed Osa where you belong. By far the best thing for you."

I opened my mouth and closed it. Finally I said, "It wasn't given me to choose."

"An old mutual friend, young man, is hunting some information which ought to change my nephew Drin's stubborn mind. When I get it, you *better* have Fortress ready to stand on its own, because I'm going to bend that bitch Capilla backward if I must for your release. That flamed boy Drin—throwing away his own left hand because a certain coward Cragman insisted *he* wouldn't ally, obey, or lead troops otherwise. I told Drin, better ally with your worst enemy than a viper like that—that—"

"There is some suspicion," I said carefully, very softly, "that Girdeth is right in where she looks for revenge. I think she was becoming too popular at court, inclining too many younger lords away from the faction this man represents—"

"Well, my boy, what are you going to *do* about it?" Agtunki demanded, with the truculence of the impatient old, of excessive mua, of weariness.

"You are tired. I'll go and let you rest—"

"No. Stop evading my question."

"I promised I would . . . get the one who planned it."

"And what does that mean? Stabbing the traitor in his sleep, I suppose." She made a disgusted noise.

"That wouldn't punish him enough," I said quietly.

"Aside from putting you in a jail cell for murder!"

"Anyway I believe the Cragman dances to another man's music."

Agtunki tilted her head slightly, making one edge of her thrown-back veil fall comically across her ear. Her face, with its perfumed skin drawn in deep character-filled sweeps across the fine family bones, was not at all comic. I read there what Caladrunan might look like as a very old man. "So how will you punish the puppet-face?"

"The man I suspect," I said too softly for any listening ears in the walls, "is always very sensitive to public acclaim."

We both knew how badly Caladrunan needed Keth's troops, needed his generalship over those rebellious and very tribal Cragmen; no other Crag noble had a prayer of controlling the lot. We must retrieve something out of the morass of men pouring out of the Crag hills and pirate islands hungry for a fight. Agaka Ún's absurd policies, and those of other Tanmen, had bred for Caladrunan this generation of angry Cragmen; changed policy did not change injustices overnight nor assuage hatred. The Cragmen seethed under Keth, or they rebelled under insurrectionists and took to the side of the Osa; and of the two, Keth had been marginally better. I thought now that, in the absence of early, overt proof, Caladrunan had taken up the worst viper in the Crag nest.

The fallen hooded lids of her eyes stirred, lowered. "Do you enjoy destroying, killing men?"

"No," I said.

"You're said to be very good at it."

"Not fast enough," I said bitterly, "or Girdeth would be chattering about her tapestry designs right now."

"Girdeth is very young. Her brother was not a third so young at the same age. The way they teach girls these days—useless, all of it. I had to teach her to keep accounts myself. They're all like that, little idiots, and they dare call Girdeth rude!"

"Why do your nobles like weak women?" I asked her abruptly.

She said, with trenchant scorn, "Old fathers. Most of these young noblemen have no say in running their clans' businesses. They haven't fought a war, they've never proved themselves at much of anything. They're afraid an intelligent wife would incite jealousy—as obviously it has, in Girdeth's case—or make them look the very overdressed plum-brained husband-birds they are." She made a spitting gesture, waving her arm. Rings glittered coldly on her gloved fingers. *"Achh!* At least my boy Drin chose *you.* You're not weak."

"Flawed," I said gently.

"Aren't we all," she snapped. "In my younger days women picked up pitchforks and joined right in. We wouldn't have toppled the Red Tyrant otherwise."

I gazed past her shoulder at a red-splashed tapestry, a battle scene. "Tannese women fighting—it might come to that—against the Osa. We'll need every wit and hand we can muster."

She tapped her fingers on the goblet. "Now you send me some of Capilla's fashionable court-living nobles like the Women of the Harp, teachers Drin sent to Lake Hold. We'll see what we can produce in cooperage, joinery, weapons, and scribes, now the men are gone. We might get drovers! I hear of a new young clan of women drovers."

"They just affiliated with Women of the Harp, yes. Nasty customers in brawls, or so I hear," I said absently. "We could use heavy weapons, too—catapults, cannon—"

"Cannon?"

"A new thing. We can't duplicate small Sharinen guns; our barrels split unless we use thicker walls. But cannons need so much iron. We need the Sharinen iron-refining methods; we don't get the melt quality we need—"

"I don't understand a word," she said.

"I'll have a bombadier-smith sent up. And I'll have Isaon sent, too; he's designed an experimental sun-mirror that focuses to burn at far distance—"

"Good. And I'll keep Girdeth busy."

I said, "Will she be safe up there?"

"Safer than here," she replied, setting down her empty goblet. "People up there know one another. And love her. Up there she can hardly stir without an honor guard of youngsters trying to defend her. Even with the young men gone, she'll be safe." Agtunki's eyelids stirred, lifted. "I'm going to suggest to Capilla that *she* retire to a Devotee Retreat. She's made enough mistakes. If she chooses to stay here, taking personal command of Fortress—" Agtunki shrugged. "This rock won't hold long against Osa, however hard you've tried. An army in free motion is our only hope. With us safely away, you should be free to go guard my harried nephew from his plum-brained allies."

"I don't think my Liege had any choice—"

"Then help think him out of it," Agtunki snapped. "Allies who force you along are poison. *I* intend to leave with Girdeth in three days. See *you* get out of here inside a tenday." She gestured at the slate. "Drin shouldn't give me this 'all discretionary powers' nonsense unless he meant me to use it. For Goddess' sake, I could order you to jump in the sewer on such authority."

"Maybe this is exactly how he expected you to exercise your discretion," I said mildly.

"*You're* too subtle for your own good," she said. "Out! I've got Girdeth to upset, and a nap to take. Good day."

Outside I breathed deeply of the cold air drafting from the gardens. It was the first really fresh air I'd breathed for days.

# CHAPTER
# = *10* =

I SAW THE KIROKI woman a moon after Girdeth's departure—at the season's dance, the *estreka*, in the camp of my grandmother. Both as a test of Rafai's command and for time to speak to Upai and the Women of the Harp, I'd arranged myself several days away from Fortress in the refugee camps. Tuzo Kiroki was dancing, while her marriage carving rested in my robe pocket. My grandmother had not approved. Crazy Tuzo was not good enough for her only grandson.

Oh, she was tall, and wild, with eyes like knives and long black braids that lashed around her as she moved. And she was proud. She laughed at the camp men humbly offering to partner her, she insulted them and danced them all into the ground. Tuzo might be dancing the nightsongs, but she did not mean to share her bed tonight. Any man who won her challenge would not have an easy night of her—her bad luck that I was both good enough and crazy enough to try her.

Sweat dripped off her chin as she tossed her head and glared around in the firelight. My body ached with pent desire as I watched. My grandmother, standing next to me, sighed deeply. Orena said, "Mad, that one. That she dared come here, sanctuary at a dance or not! Against our laws she killed three Tannese strangers at Ringrock Spring. In midwinter our camp had to flee a killing mob in hunt to revenge it. What can be done with her?"

Muscles like rope rippled down Tuzo's arms as she threw back her ragged sleeves and began the next dance. Beside me, my grandmother said sadly, "Her father and uncles were killed in a Tannese raid, her brothers murdered by Nandos. You may know,

164

her sister was bought by Cragmen. No doubt the poor woman is beaten all the time. Tuzo's mother was Kiroki, her father Tarso, both of the highest blood but our own, and look what she has become.''

The woman tossed her head and gave a scornful laugh at a would-be suitor for the night. She flashed through a posture too fast for him to follow. He fumbled it, shame-faced, and shuffled away to his wife's furious shouts.

I said under the roar of the drums, "She would lead as a brothel queen, Grandmother. That is the spirit in her.''

Orena's robes heaved in a deep sigh. "My son, why do you stare after the shame of six camps? She takes no one but by her dances—and no one wins her challenge. She hates the world.''

"No. She is very like me," I said, and put my harpcase gently into my grandmother's hands. "I want her." Then I walked out into the firelight before the dancing woman. I saw people pointing at me under the roar of the drumming. She glared out of the curtain of her rumpled braids.

"Great Tannese lord," she hissed, and I saw her teeth gleam through the braids. "Great pale night-thing!''

"Outdance me then," I said sternly, and she laughed. She darted away and began the formal dance movements, taunting insults at me. I frowned. If she kept doing that, it might come to fighting for honor's sake. She carried many knives on her person, and she knew how to use them. Blood shed on the dance ground would be bad, but not unusual. Many Upai were dangerous when they let their emotions flow from them at an *estreka*. Held in the captivity of a Tannese refugee camp, in shame, made this the most dangerous *estreka* of all. I said quietly and clearly, "Don't insult me, sad woman.''

She threw up her head with a cry and shifted her dance to twice the pace of the drums. I followed her. Her body made a jerking blur in the unsteady light, snapping through each posture to stillness and back to life as fast as my eyes could follow her. Her braids flung around her head in wild nets. This was only the season's dance, not the spirit-calls before a raid. But so great was the woman's rage, she was dancing the *estreka* into a war dance, a revenge dance—and if I lost her, others would follow the furious killing-call, and I'd have a Upai riot to quell. Something flashed in her hands: knife-dancing.

*Not* a good omen. This, I thought, will be a bitter time: a knife-dancing at the spring *estreka*! My scaddas jumped to my

palms, and we twisted through the ritual knife postures. We spun
our blades in the patterns of antiquity, my double scaddas mir-
roring her many knives. Iron flashed around our hands and
spitted shards of orange light on the faces of the watchers. So
long as I matched her patterns, nobody could join.

I wondered, how terribly hard she has practiced! She danced
with the knives to release her emotions, not to exhibit—and she
was *very* good indeed. Her patterns I must mirror, then master.
Dance was our people's drama, our group release, and knife-
dancing was the most dangerous dance of all. She spun patterns
of light round her robes, once twirling the knives around her own
neck, spinning ox-wheels of light glinting high into the air and
back into her hands. Then she chose a new form.

She stabbed at the air, lunged, sliced, and attacked the air in
such graceful form that I knew a superb artist had taught her
attack disciplines—but in attack-dances she could not lose me. I
took away her lead, as was my right now, and added things. Her
eyes gleamed at me through the braids, no longer mocking but
full of intensity. Her lips drew back and she breathed hard with
the effort. It was her sixth full dancing, and my first.

At last, when the sweat ran down my face and my hands
began to go to simpler patterns, she staggered a step and stumbled, and nearly fell to her knees. Her breast heaved with great
gasps. From the first she chose ritual perfection, and she had
broken it first. She stood gasping until I finished the pattern,
modified it, and brought it spinning back down to myself in
mastery. She wandered out of the light like a wounded animal,
leaving the dance ground to other women. We all heard her deep
gasps fade fainter under the drums as she slipped away.

I declined the next woman's challenge. My grandmother's
face was grim when I took back my harpcase; she shook her
head warningly against the drums. Asking among the grinning
men, I learned that Tuzo had been forced away from all the
camps for her Ringrock killings. She kept her tent on the outlaw
edge between two camps. I went there after a decent interval.

She sat in the dark on a ragged goat-felt blanket, facing north,
outside her domed tent. In the light of the full moon she looked
distant, severe, and terribly thin. She had redressed her braids
and wiped her face of sweat. I threw down the marriage carving
before her. She continued to stare northward, eyes withdrawn
into shadows, as I waited. Finally, grudgingly, she said, ''No

light is needed between friends.'' But she shifted so I must sit in a band of moonlight.

I knelt facing her, my hands feeling over the ground in the dappled shadows. Against the stars I picked out her faint outline, then her glittering eyes. I said softly, "A magnificent dancing, Lady Tuzo." Lady Goddess of Larks, I had called her. It was her ancestral name, and I was the only one, besides my grandmother, who could call her by it. Two beggared nobles, kneeling between refugee camps, calling each other by glorious titles . . .

She said, "You suffered at the end, Lord of Darkness."

It was a faceted joke: mocking me for associating with pale Tannese; mocking my thin, high-bred skin among Upai; and mocking my courtesy. I replied with equal sharpness, "You can call me Night's Pleasure."

"You of the scars?" she laughed, a harsh, free laugh that rang out against the drums and the night. "More likely a night's beating, as it is for Pale People females."

I said soberly, "You know that is not true. Even a Tannese man doesn't fight by day and beat his woman at night unless he is crazy. You and I—fighting is for outsiders—we are soft inside."

"The voice of the bird moaning among the flowers," she mocked me. "So smooth and sweet-mouthed."

Stung, I replied, "I wouldn't be your first lover. What does it matter?"

"No, you would not be my first," she agreed calmly, and then she put in her claws. "Would I could take your flesh and put it onto the ribs of my child who died. You and your sleek tight skin! None of your bones show."

I lowered my head. At the *estreka* all the young men stripped to dance, and my ribs were by far the sleekest. Some of the women had felt of my muscles, my wealth. I said soberly, "Would that I could give my flesh to your child."

"But would you have, in your time of hunger?" she snarled. "You should have seen some of these brave, generous men! My own brothers, my child's very uncles, they repudiate their duties to me—*feh*, drug-heads! Don't plead with *me* about men's generosity."

"The father?" I asked.

"The father! Oh generous stranger—he gave where I did not ask! Why do you think I learned to dance knives, Dark One?"

"I didn't know." Nobody told me how Tuzo had had a child.

I hadn't grown to manhood among these strangers, my own people, to learn what was never spoken of.

After a time, she said, "I do not share furs with Nandos."

I lifted my head. She knew I was Oathsworn now and had never been a Nando of that despised kind. The most conservative Upai distinguished between Reti's Nandos and those of Manoloki. "A pity. I enjoyed your company."

"You humiliated me."

"You offered dance, and someone had to partner you. I have never seen a woman dance so hard, to that outer limit of skill." Privately I put aside dread of the omen: knife-dancing at the *estreka*! It promised an ill season. After a pause for thought, I finished, "What matter that I completed your pattern? I won after six others danced with you. And it was magnificent."

She snapped, "You don't feed a child on almost winning fights! You win, or it dies. That is all."

I lowered my head. "Truth," I agreed.

She tossed her braids about, smoothing her robes in the darkness. The sound of her hands brushing against the rough cloth came clearly and maddeningly to me: a noise more sensual than the hoarsest endearments. Then she said, "The young boys try to sweeten me; the rest of them sneer when they think I can't hear them. Dry mare and all the rest. Oh, I know."

I lifted my head. "You're barren?"

"The Osa," she said curtly. "They had me in a slave camp near the border for awhile. Thus the child. I've had other men since, but no child."

We sat facing each other, saying nothing. The feeling of helpless rage made me want to strike someone. The Osa sometimes sterilized women with wires, claiming that desert lands made them bear monsters. Mostly the Osa killed refugees, female or not. She had been lucky to escape with her life, let alone bearing or running with a child. My night desire had died in me like a frosted meadow lily in my lap. At last, I said, with a strangled little laugh, "I'm surprised the boys dare you."

Her teeth shone in the darkness. "I won't harm men who just *ask*—who don't take when it isn't offered."

"That's why you killed those men at Ringrock."

She agreed. "The stupid fools tried me." She made a rapid mothlike gesture with her hand, a blur of dark against darker trees beyond. Her scorn glittered in her eyes.

I said, "And would you kill me, too, when my belly was on you and my back naked?"

She laughed her harsh laugh. "You asked first. They didn't bother. I never promised to share any night with you, Dark One."

"You did—you danced challenge! But I won't ask." I sat listening to the drums. I felt tired and dispirited. Enough of fighting, I thought. "Good mother of the tent, let me sleep. I won't disturb your rest tonight."

She rose and held open the tent flap, eyes glittering. "Of course," she said in a dry, disbelieving tone. She poked the fire in the pit, spread a roll of furs, and sat down to watch me. She stared at my robe and said, "A Tannese gave you this, yes?"

I looked up into her face while I held the robe. Finally, with lips stiff as clay, I said, "Yes," and laid it aside.

"Tannese weave," she said, fingering it. After some time she conceded that I was actually going to sleep in her furs, not disturb her with male persistence. She opened a leather case and laid strips of meat on sticks over the fire. At my glance, she said curtly, "Dog meat. Dancers should eat."

I sat up among the furs, blinking. "My thanks."

She glanced up. Her eyes were the snarling, snapping black of the charred branches before her. "We hear about feasts in Fortress. Oh, yes, the pig-butchers like to taunt us." She shook her braids violently. "They throw the wastes of pig slaughters at us and laugh because we catch what we can."

I closed my eyes briefly. There was nothing on earth Upai scorned more about Tannese than pork, and the eating of pork. "Food is food. We have as much choice over our fate as the pigs, with the Tannese judging us at every turn." I pointed my finger at her. "If you kill any more Tannese, it is the end for you. Upai cannot go out alone and kill in the night for revenge, even a justice for murder, in this country."

She glared at me. "Oh, you like that part!"

"If you think that, you're a fool. If there is killing to do, leave it to me. Then no one can prove it was a Upai hand at the knife. For the sake of all of us, for your most distant kin, Tuzo, sheath that knife you grip in your heart!"

She lowered her head.

I said, "Swear to me, Tuzo . . . swear to me, as I am a Tokori, Warleader of the People, that you will not kill as you killed before, without anyone knowing!"

It was necessity in my voice, and she knew it. A promise sworn to a Warleader must be kept. It was her life and her soul if she willfully broke such a promise to me. She lifted her eyes. "I will keep my hands off the hilts," she said slowly, biting off the words like the fingers of an enemy. If a soldier must be taken prisoner by Upai, he should pray they were men. His end would be very slow in the careful hands of Upai women.

In my softest voice, I said, "In time, even your mouth will overflow with blood, and you will tire of slaying. We will fill your mouth with enemy blood, fear not. They are near upon us. But not now. The Tannese do us much good."

"They are fat and stupid!" she screamed. Her face and arms convulsed, slamming down a cooking stick. The green wood *pop-snapped* like a whip. She beat the earth in a frenzy. I stared.

I often struggled against the same frustration, the deep curdled hate of the refugee, with the complacent Tannese. Her fit of rage ended as quickly as it began; she must have been tired. She huddled over the fire as if chilled, shaking and shivering. I said, "Thus they learn more slowly. Be patient." I curled up tighter in the furs.

"Send us food," she said, shivering. "The camps go hungry."

"I have been trying," I said. "Would Orena's Council receive food better if it was stolen?"

Superstition among Upai clans prohibited eating food carried away from the site of the theft. In a time of plague, back in the Upai homeland, stolen food carried the curse of the rigid-swell sickness; thus arose the Upai habit of despoiling, rather than saving, raided foodstuffs. These days when raiders brought food home to the refugee camps, nobody asked too many questions. But my formal offerings of food had to pass the Women's Council, and stolen food was destroyed, and that was that.

Tuzo looked away from me and jabbed at the dog meat.

I said then, "Do you care so much for the child of a rapist that you cannot cease mourning, and you make the lives of your friends miserable?"

She stood up. The hem of her robe swept embers about. She cried, "She was my child—my *only* child! Friends? *Fehh!*"

I said, "Are you certain that the Osa made you barren? Pick someone you like, and find out. It would be better than fighting for every scrap you possess and competing against other men's hunting. And their sometimes generosity, as you might say."

"Who do you offer me?" she said coolly. "You take away all

the strong ones to be Tannese soldiers. These pitiful remnants, they can't feed *themselves!* I offered to go with the warriors—but no, they would not take me, they fear the big Tannese finding me out as a woman!" She shrugged. "Besides, I sold my marriage. It bought food. They call me married, so no fighting. Oh yes, I am a good Upai, I want children! But no man will take on the burden of acting both the stern uncle and easy father at once. Too much work for a silly husband! My brothers became drug-heads, they can't do the simplest duties to my children."

I jerked my thumb toward the tent flap. "There your marriage carving lies; I own it now. Orena speaks of taking a wife, as if being a Teot I have no choice. I must marry." Our gazes locked.

Tuzo's dropped first. "They sold my sister's marriage, and see what she has now: A trader bought her, off her fool-drunk of a husband. The Cragmen, they don't want a woman, just a slave to beat. I held the death ceremony for her. She is not Upai. They broke her. She is afraid." She tossed her head. "She should die, if she can't run away."

I said, "If I had known—"

"Eat the meat and let me alone. You, at court, what do you know? You just meddle in other people's lives." She went out, returned, and hurled the marriage carving down by the fire.

I shrugged and ate the dog meat she offered me. It tasted rank, which I did not remember. Such meat in the desert had been rich and strong and greasy, very filling, but not as rotten as pork meat. Yet this tasted horrible. Still, I thanked her. Then I turned my back upon her and the fire, and slept instantly.

Later that night, the sound of the fire brought me awake with a jerk, bolting me upright with the sleep still wild in my eyes. I was in a strange place, scaddas tight under my hands, and for a moment terror blanked out my mind. I must have cried out as I did when I was a child. My mouth was caked with sand.

Then I saw the fire in the pit, and the fresh log burning, and the woman's enigmatic eyes watching me. I did not think she had once closed her eyes upon me. Tuzo said nothing, turned away to shift another branch to the morning fire, and did not look again at me until I rose. Silently I left her.

When I stepped out of the tent I heard children shrieking and playing at the edges of the nearest camp. Girls darted past, peering slyly through branches at me, giggling and running away into the brush. I felt hideously conspicuous.

"Courting beads it will be now," Orena's voice rasped.

I whipped around. The old woman stood thin and straight, arms folded, at the far curve of Tuzo's tent. Hers might have been the voice that woke me. I ducked my head and waited in the proper respectful silence.

"What a pity, to waste such a handsome man on the likes of Tuzo." My grandmother's voice grated on the words like bits of broken rock against metal. "The very *image* of my daughter Inigrev, my grandmother Kirot—brave graceful women who chose husbands like lions—this handsome Upai takes no women. *He* is *anakri.* I hear it from his own big blue-robe soldiers."

I gaped at her. Lightning from a cloudless sky could not have stunned me more. I'd never expected such an accusation when I stood outside a woman's tent, embarrassed in the morning like so many other young men. At that, the tent of a woman whose marriage carving bound her to consider my merits and loving.

"You," my grandmother said, "are not of the People." She pointed her first two fingers at me, made a circling.

"Stop!" I said angrily. I gestured at her witch-signed fingers. What had set her off now! I said, "I am not—*that.* Why would I be here if—"

"So it sleeps yet, does it?" She sighed. "So only the first uncomfortable signs of it disturb you, grandson? The violence, the wild falling fits, the spewing of words you know nothing of when you wake—do these tell you nothing?"

"Tell me what?" I demanded fiercely.

She smiled, but it was not a pleasant smile. "The Council of Women is alarmed about you. If you dream-dance, you do not dance like our sages ever did. Oh, you are not Tannese either. *You* are something else in the flesh of my grandson. You are—" Her fingers moved in a defense against very great sacrilege. Defense against the likes of Osa priests.

"No," I said, in horror.

Her fingers paused, lifted lightly in the air. Then, in a terrible voice, not loud but thunderously clear, she said, *"On your face* before a Judge among the Sacred Women." My grandmother had never needed bullies to enforce her commands on the guilty. I sank to my knees and went down seriously before her.

"You reek of Tuzo's furs," she said, sniffing disdainfully.

"I returned her the marriage carving she sold away."

After a pause, Orena said, "That was an evil thing you have redeemed, which is good. It favors you, that kindness."

"Thank you." Oddly terrified, I asked myself, what *is* this?

There were established paths for disputes, and this was a far more serious business than any I'd ever seen.

Orena growled, "Few know. But to me, as to the Sacred Women, to the Council, you betray yourself in a thousand ways. You sniff about our camps like a dog, gathering warriors, but you are not of the People. You fight and slink about your Tannese lairs, but you are not one of their dogs either. You are not of any people! *You* came out of the desert, out of the death-rocks where my children died, out of the killing, out of the spirit-things let free that day by the filth of that evil time. You are one of the Goddess' wolves. You lap blood and rend hearts for vengeance where She leads you. No man dares check your frenzy. No woman gives you child, no man puts his hand on your head. We read it in you."

I felt the hair on my neck rise. *Kotoka' epopi,* the wolf of the Goddess: a man possessed with a wolf-spirit of vicious persistence and pitiless justice. A man insane—murderous if crossed—and just as she formally pronounced it, a man of no people at all. *Kotoka' epopi:* a holy force beyond the bounds of tribe or kin or clan. *They had no names.* And no Upai would so much as step in my shadow if she named me that. "Grandmother," I said, very softly, pleading, in utmost respect.

She said, "Do you show ritual attention to our ancient ways? Some, but not where it crosses your purpose. Have you friends of lightness, or silly humor? No, not among us. Who are your friends—Tannese soldiers who further your purpose! Though even you seem unaware of *why* you chose them. And the women ask, what is your chosen trade?" She pointed at my scaddas. "Those."

"I don't kill, I guard—" I bit my lips.

"You guard. What is it you guard?"

Very low, I said, "I swore the Oath to serve the Lord of Tan."

"And is *he* part of your purpose?" Her voice slashed at me. "When have Tannese lifted one hand for any other people—no, not them! They take and take, and make sly promises, but they never help any but their own pale kind. If you remain Upai, not a night stalker, then they used your Oath, and you are a fool!"

I glanced up. "He is a friend, like a brother, to me."

"*Kotoka' epopi* find brothers in odd places."

Goaded, I snapped, "He helps me fight it! I am not mad, because he—he helps."

Orena looked thoughtful. Wrinkles folded in patterns around her black eyes. "Friend, brother . . . odd words, with Tannese."

"I would not serve him if he rose no higher than being Tannese! As a *man,* he is greater than most."

"So I have always heard of him," Orena said curtly, and studied me. "Did he know just how you killed in your raids as Tokori Efresa before you came to Tan? Did you tell him? Did you tell him in your Tannese words?"

Again I bit my lips. "No. He wouldn't have liked that."

"But we've all seen the spirit in you when you go into seizures. Oh, I spoke with your Big Man. I called you a wolf-spirit. He agreed at times you slipped his leash and ran wild."

I cried, "But he doesn't know what 'wolf-spirit' means—"

"No. He only knows its truth. You hid it from him."

At last, humbled before the knowledge she had amassed and her vastly greater experience, I said, "Grandmother, I don't want to leave the People."

Orena studied me, tilting her head a little. "Get up, grandson. I want the truth now. The fits?"

"They're relivings," I muttered. "Of when the Osa . . ."

"The talking, the prophecies I hear about from Devotees, from these Women of the Harp swooning over you?"

"I don't recall anything like that, just—screaming."

Her face reacted briefly, flinching. She knew what it must be like if I screamed in those relivings. Upai were trained as children to be silent.

"And the other, the *anakri* part your Tannese soldiers gossip of?"

I looked away bitterly. Now she revealed she spoke Tannese. "Silly boys. They know only their clan rules and cannot see but by that light."

My grandmother sighed. She reached forward and took my sleeve, fingering the cloth. "Very fine, this. A gift?"

I nodded.

"From him, the Big Man, your friend."

I said, "Orena, my grandmother, I don't think that—I just—I have just—" I gestured at the silent tent beside us.

Her eyes focused on me: shrewd, hard black eyes. "Do not lie to me, grandson."

"I am not lying. I—" I struggled, trying to find words.

"Are you only partly thus, not wholly as the Upai know it?"

I felt oddly easier in my skin. "Yes. There are finer things than—" I made a distasteful gesture about *anakri* as the Upai knew them. "They could be more than Upai *let* them be. They could earn your respect. I've learned that much."

She set her hand on my arm. "This is difficult, grandson. Your mother chose her husband against my will, defied me. I'd learned that his parents had many kin dead among the People in bad ways—half of them lost their names in some way, taken of the Goddess. The other half simply went mad, and had to be destroyed."

"Lost their names," I said, lips dry, "as *kotoka'epopi* lose their names?"

"Many of them," she said seriously. "In the records I kept, I find it always returned. From one generation onward two, three, four births away. You have not progressed into it as far as your father's out-kin did. It passed among them in a frightening way, young; or suddenly, thoroughly. Not like you." She lifted her chin, gazing at me. "No—in you the foreign training has created a new thing. *You* are stronger, you have forced it to live with you. The wolf-spirit drives you, yes, but it has grown more patient, it is more cunning, it is more deadly, than it was in the others. You have forced the Goddess-spirit to learn some wisdom. But still, in a thousand small ways, we read it in you. It bides waiting, and breaks free in fits when it can. It dreamdances, and you are helpless before it. Yet you say the Big Man helps you."

"Reti did, too," I said, remembering how he had trained me. "He helped me. Then, yes, the Big Man, my Liege, Caladrunan."

She said, "Reti was once given a *kotoka'epopi* from your father's lineage. We could do nothing. Reti found it proper to aid that one's justice, and learned much. Oh, Reti knew what was in you. He knew what he chose when he accepted you in his camp."

I looked at her. The lines of her mouth were folded into bitter, severe disciplines.

Orena looked at me a long time. "Naga, my son, whatever you become of the Goddess' touch, we would not lose you. I do not condemn you yet as *kotoka'epopi*. If you can teach the wolf-spirit yet more patience and control, I pray you do, because our people will need you thus . . . or you would not be given to us." Then she pointed at me. "No more raids, child."

"But those raids proved that—"

She said, "Listen well. You proved nothing to *me*, grandson.

You care nothing for warrior's opinions; they tell me you never did. So if you lead another raid for your wolf-spirit purpose, grandson—risking your life, your sanity, and our Teot line— *then*, my son, the Women's Council will discuss *anakri* with you. And *kotoka'epopi*.'' She walked away calmly, leisurely. She was old—and too serenely proud to indulge in noisy shows of emotion now.

And I was shocked too numb for any tantrum. I stood dumbly as Tuzo threw open the tent flap. Staring motionless, her arms fell limp to her sides. Tuzo's chin was smudged and her robes rumpled. "I heard," she whispered.

I looked at her, clenched my hands. "Tuzo, I—keep your marriage contract. Do what you like." I waved awkwardly at the tent and strode away.

Some of the camp men were talking quietly over a sniffing bowl of cupflower, sitting by the last remaining drum-fire; not one of this group was younger than forty summers. Scarred like old wolves, they had aches no human should endure. After I joined their circle, a Upai-style fourpeg game, faster than Tannese, started up and ran into the dawn light. Retorts and laughter crackled along with the peg play.

"Productive labor," Tuzo snapped as she swept by that morning. "Is this how you feed your many begettings, O studbull?"

I looked up, surprised. I glanced around and saw their eyes on me. Someone chuckled softly, and someone else said, "Oh, he's been bitten bad. Must be quite a poison."

"Awfully young to die of it," an ancient remarked kindly.

"Throw the pegs," I said desperately.

They lay around lazily, these remnants of a vast Upai nobility, telling stories about their own amorous adventures, and teased me until I went down to the river to cool off. It was frigid water, and I came out shocked with the icy-hot bite of it. Nothing like lust to drive a man to absurd lengths. Tuzo was, of course, standing on the bank watching me calmly while I waded out, and told me frankly I was a fool. She threw an old ratty fur at me and told me to dry off properly, and called me horrid names when I did. Then she simply stalked away. For Tuzo, it was invitation.

Trotting to catch up, I went after Tuzo. She said nothing; even her face said nothing. We walked down through reeds silently, parting the branches and the cattails for one another.

I sat down on a rock by the water, glad of the wind to keep away the water bugs, while Tuzo belted up her robes. She waded across to a patch of ferns on tumbled wet rocks in midstream. Ice hung in sheltered crevices among the ferns. Water sparkled on the calves of her legs. "Do you need help?" I asked.

"No. I've got just enough arm—" she strained and grunted, "—for this clump." She came back with her leather bag filled. "For the children, for the coughing. I'm helping Ierné, the widow teacher, and her Women of the Harp."

I took off my thick blue outrobe and held it out to her. "Dry your feet. The water is cold."

She sat down on a rock, rubbed her feet on my robe, and put on her boots. "Your friend must love you, whoever he is, to trouble making that robe look Upai. And this belt buckle, too." She touched the new, woven-silver buckle. "Then you have a friend worthy of becoming uncle to our children, should it happen we adopt such strange patterns in this new country."

I lowered my head. Finally I leaned against the boulder and put on the robe. The hem was wet. "Yes," I said.

She lifted her head from rummaging among her ferns. She looked calm, attentive. Only the pulse at her throat belied her: that hollow at her collarbones surged unnaturally fast.

"I still feel like—" I began. "You wanted children. And I just thought—" I flung out my hands.

Tuzo looked me in the eye. "If you want to make me happy for awhile," she began, putting both hands at my hips. I put both arms around her and stopped the rest of her words; she put her hand to my cheek. Her fingers felt cold. When I drew back, she whispered, "Maybe I'll teach you a few of the things you missed."

"Mmm," I grunted, and we leaned against the rocks, slid downward.

Upai courting was nothing like the frigid manners of Tannese courting, simply because in a rough camp there was no place for formal clothes and artifices. There used to be some graciousness about it. Dreamlike bits, genteel customs, I recalled of the time before the Osa killed my kin. Part of it had been to stand and take whatever the beloved thought up.

Tuzo added some modern imagination to the present customs. It wouldn't *do* to make things easy for me. After her momentary softening, she tried to push me back in the river.

We wrestled around for quite a time among the cattails while she shrieked about my messing up the harvest of cattail hearts, and I shrieked about her grinding mud into my hair. She was as strong as her dancing, and uncanny snake-fast. I thought it time to quit when she beat me with torn-up cattail stalks in serious rage, hurling balls of mud at everyone within eyeshot.

It was a rousing defeat for the men's side when I politely conceded and ran away from camp, ducking all the way under her gravel-laden mud balls. I ought to have worn armor against her, the terror! Some old men came out and talked me into coming back, all the while nearly choking on suppressed laughter. When I finally returned to the fourpeg game, Tuzo whisked by and dumped a basket of gana dung over my head. I wiped my eyes, gasping, and blinked at the men. They and the children of the camp lay on the ground howling with laughter. I got up, gave Tuzo a glare, and went round and peed slowly and thoroughly on her tent doorflap. I got rousing men's side approval for this reply. Then I stormed off into the river brush peeling flakes of filth in every direction. That was the extent of my first courtship attempt.

But it wasn't going to be my only attempt with her. I started feeling stubborn. Vano, commander of my four-man Tannese cavalry escort, rode into the brush after me, looking patient and utterly sympathetic—and hard-pressed not to laugh at me. He saw me trying to get the slimy stuff off in a stream pothole, and he turned away with a tact that approached mind-reading. I began to calculate what this campaign would cost my pride. I wished I had an honest raid, or even a minor fight, to deal with instead. At least *there* I knew what I was doing. I sat out there sulking under an oak, collecting acorns into the hood of my outrobe, all that day. At least it was an escape from nagging Fortress duties.

When I returned to camp, I found a clump of Tannese riders waiting for me, surrounded by a ring of curious Upai—a much-expanded escort. I asked, "Why are you here?"

A slate was thrust in my hand. It was written in Agtunki's hand. Pitar had ridden back to Fortress, assessed that the defenses were adequately secured, and relayed orders for an ingathering of all the various generals for conference. Given no choice, the Lady of Fortress, Capilla, agreed with Agtunki's orders sending me as well out to war. Something took wing inside me, cried out silently in joy. I looked up. "Bed down in that southern tent, rest today," I said, knowing this would be a popular order. "We'll return to Fortress tomorrow morning."

That night, clean and tidy, I presented myself at Tuzo's tent as calmly as if the invitation of her challenge-night still held force. She merely gave an odd quirk of her lips and waved me inside, yanking the flap shut in poor Vano's face. The thick-set fisher-bred soldier sighed and trudged off to the Tannese escort tent; his crunching steps were the only sounds. Tuzo dropped a skewer of hot dog meat into my lap as she passed. I caught it before it scalded my thighs, that was all. I shifted to sit near her on her furs, and she only gave me a long, burning glance and went on punching her awl through rabbit furs . . . incidentally forcing me to jerk my knee out of range of her jabs. As the blaze of her cooking fire dimmed, Tuzo put down her leather work and sang the evening song. "Goddess of the Water, give me hope, give me life to live for, making our children many—" I shed robes, curled up and shut my eyes, following the melody in my head, and at some point I fell asleep. She woke me in the dark.

"Move over." She nudged my arm.

"Oh, your furs," I said, blinking, and sat up. I had taken her only sleeping furs. "I'll go—"

"No. They'll share out, dung-eater!" Fingers plucked briefly at my arm, pulling me back down.

I lay staring into the dark. Against my bare back lay Tuzo's bare back. She squirmed a bit and lay still. Then she turned over in the furs, dropped her arm over my hip, cupping her knees up behind mine like horn spoons nestled together. Her thighs brushed smoothly on mine. It was warm. I liked the warmth. I felt her breasts move against my shoulder blades as she breathed. It was . . . unique. "Mmm," she growled into my ear, like a purr.

I rolled onto my back. "Tuzo," I said quietly, wonderingly, and her arms slid around me, and her legs, and we did without words after that. She was kind enough to take me through it without complaining or yelping at my awkward caresses. She soon knew one thing I'd fought hard to keep when I was Nando—and something of the cost. And so it was damaged and bitter Tuzo who taught me about pleasure, touching my hesitant body with the kind of ethereal gentleness no one ever gave her. She rose above her past with a fierce giving so intense it made me ache for her. When Tuzo and I lay quiet again, she stroked my chest. I rolled my head toward her. "I'm so clumsy." I stroked her hair sleepily, knowing what honor it was to have touched her. The force, the courage in her, shone through every plane of her face as I looked at her. In that moment my soul yielded itself wholly.

"No," she murmured, "very considerate, Naga."

I felt suddenly shocked away like a chilled snail, and embarrassed; I didn't want to be compared to brutish others: I felt odd thinking about Tuzo's other lovers, her rape. An essence of those men might . . . remain there. Cowards, staining her forces, changing her until she danced knives and hated men. I felt abruptly squeamish, thinking about it. *Not my Tuzo*, I thought hopelessly. *Please not. No more taint of—*

She whispered, "I lied about my child. To make you go away."

My head jolted up.

She gave a dry heave of a laugh. "Oh, the Osa had me. I was a beauty then. I did my part so well I survived the death camp as an officer's mistress. Such a pretty little family! I let him make me a collaborator because I loved my life too much, and now I scream at my sister she should die. What a bitter joke! His child was so beautiful; he became *proud* to be her father! Ah yes, I took my revenge on him, stealing her and escaping. These poor timid camp Upai suspect me of it all, so they mutter and hate me. Oh, I saved the People in my officer's death camp when I *could*, but it was never enough. Nothing is."

I swallowed dryly, and felt my eyes spill hot fluid. Even this did not escape the hideous Osa taint—even *this*. Half-strangled by my thick throat, I said, "Do you admit being a collaborator because you still want to drive me away?"

"Poor stuff you'd be if that could do it. Am I too honest, and you not strong enough?" she said, harsh as dry snakeskins in the dark. "Poor boy, to love such a horrid stick as me."

I swallowed hard, stretching my neck up stiffly to make the tears dry away. "Will you *always* fear me getting close?"

She lay silent a long time. "Ahh, you. Honest one." Then her arm moved gently at my neck. Against my chest she whispered, "Give me time to believe, to learn, what you already dare. You need sleep. You have to ride soon."

"Perhaps tomorrow."

"I know," she said, and curled up away from me.

I lay staring up at open sky beyond the smoke flap. The easy sleep of my nights with Caladrunan did not find me here. Tuzo's breathing seemed loud. Odd, Caladrunan snored in a thunderous bass and never wakened me. The sudden and acute longing for his rumbling made me tighten up in pain. I thought, now I can be permanently unhappy, having given my heart to two very different people firmly rooted in separate worlds; always and forever I'd long futilely for one or the other. I knew too well that my affection had been given to both, like a flown bird, and would not come back to me whole. I rubbed my eyes, chewed harp calluses, and cursed myself for a stupid fool. It was well toward dawn when I fell into an uneasy napping. A dream of someone calling my name woke me up. I sat up feeling rumpled, sad, and out of sorts.

Lightly, so lightly, I touched the tail of her hair, but I let her be. While I dressed and ate some dry kinash grain from one of my saddlebags, Tuzo slept on. She had left the marriage carving by the cold firepit. If she wore it openly on her person the next time I saw her, then I'd know she was content to be my wife. Did I want her as wife? I thought of her pitiless honesty, of the soft heavy breasts moving with her breath, and of the fierce profile in the carving. I nudged the wood with my toe, sighing, and gathered my weapons. What would my people be if I became the Teot-consort to any *other* woman—if I chose a royal Mother who lacked Tuzo's courage? And what would my babes be?

# CHAPTER

# = *11* =

I RODE INTO the war camp five days later, well after dusk of a clouded and warm evening. The sentries, strangers, would have stopped us but for the sword-marked bags on our saddles. As I glanced at the camp's gana lines, everywhere I saw Cragmen— men with hostile watching eyes, lounging among the busy Tannese—yet I found no overt fault.

Pitar stood at his Liege's tent flap smiling, and promised food and freshly made mua. Caladrunan, massive and golden, was already reading my message slates. My tense body relaxed, for preoccupation was one of his common moods. Flopping on a stool, I sighed. Pitar grinned and proffered a bowl of kinash grain steamed with meat. I was wolfing it ungraciously with both hands when Caladrunan rumbled ominously, "Your judgment on that rock-liquor smuggling and murder case last tenday, Naga . . ."

I glanced apprehensively at Pitar. "What's wrong with it?"

"It is *not* proper judicial procedure to come down from your chair and bang the defendants' heads together and declare their teeth will be the next forfeit for contempt of court!"

It had been down in the cells with four loud barristers and other moderately impartial witnesses, but never mind. Innocently I said, "Well, it worked. They confessed."

"They were terrified of *you*, not the law—"

"Well, yes, that was the idea, Liege," I agreed, and dimly realized my mistake. He *never* allowed torture, or threat of it.

His lips tightened. "That is not law, that is intimidation. If you can't get soldiers to present adequate proof, you release

182

prisoners as innocents. That's the law! And our tradition. Confessions given under force are invalid."

"I never touched them, Liege!"

"Oh, I see—by *your* standards, you didn't hurt them. Naga, our ideas of law are so far apart we might as well be—"

"Well, they buy their witnesses in your court."

He stared at me. *"What?"*

"They do. I overheard a couple of plaintiffs and jurist advisers outside the door doing it, one day. They don't do it in mine! There—I wrote out a list of the paid commoners who keep witnessing under false names in different cases, I noted their disguises and their usual patrons. I thought you'd like to know."

He glanced at that slate. "Mm. I remember these first two."

"Oh, those two—they sell to either side; they're fair about it." I noticed Pitar had trouble controlling his face.

Caladrunan said a muffled obscene word. He pushed aside the slate. "Properly prepared cases never allow such witnesses to work. Don't you see, using force only creates bad law and bad judgments? Our men get sloppy presenting evidence, make no attempt to present a logical case. Lower officers follow poor examples—soon the whole process is no better than the Red Tyrant's flagrant—"

"I understand, Liege." He had an obsession about it, after having to clean up the courts left him by his father. He wanted systems of proof and punishment—along with a uniform jade-weighing system and secure well-laid roads. He didn't like me falling back on old-style hill-bandit justice in Commoners' Court.

"Not too clearly, you don't! And look at this case, the plaintiff insisted that you threatened to *freeze off his kukkies?"*

"Liege, I never! The bailiff bashed him, and he kept shouting. They had to haul the man out and bar the doors. His brothers told me he was crazy. They shouted a lot, too."

Caladrunan glowered.

I said hastily, "I just mentioned something about the Goddess blasting his—ah—goat's parts."

I heard an uncontrollable, hard-stifled snicker from Pitar. To cover it, I added swiftly, "Well, it won't happen again—"

The Lord of Tan glanced up with a sigh, waved. Pitar went out snickering and actually grinned as he let the tent flap fall.

The Lord of Tan put the rest of the slates aside.

"Girdeth—" I began seriously, but he lifted his shaggy head, running one finger over his sun-faded beard, and called for his son and his evening meal.

The last strip of sunset light failed. ''Girdeth was—'' I began
again. He waved me silent and listened to his son's chatter.
Large and beneficent as his lounging hunting cat, he said, ''Yes,
Therin, you may eat here.'' We ate by lamplight. Caladrunan
pushed aside his slates, devoting his attention to talk. The boy
listened as we talked over progress.

''Girdeth—'' I began yet again.

Caladrunan told his son gravely, ''Before she left for Lake
Hold, Girdeth sent up a slate offering to marry Keth Adcrag to
strengthen alliance. What do you think, Therin?''

The boy's forehead rumpled. ''But wouldn't he treat her
badly? She's so free-thinking, and Keth, he's—well, cruel.''

Impatience rose hard as rage in my throat. Looking at shadow
shapes, three times I snapped up my knuckles and dropped my
concealed wrist-knife silently into my fingers, then slid it back,
saying nothing. Caladrunan said, very low, ''He was different
when he first came to court. We were both—oh, a little older
than you, Therin—and friends. He always was a difficult friend;
he was so rough and so Crag, he had no other friends. We both
worked more and more duties; I had no time for him. He ran
with people who worried me; he said he was just watching them
for me, at first. If I chose now—'' He shrugged. Whatever he
knew or suspected, the Lord of Tan and I did not look at each
other; our eyes would have revealed too much. The memory of
assassins and all those tame Cragmen about his camp built up
around my soul like rime ice. Caladrunan went on, ''I thought
I'd already done every variant of tangling a friendship unpleas-
antly with ruling, but old friendships are the worst. Agtunki
cover-signed a second note of Girdeth's from Lake Hold with-
drawing the marriage offer.''

Therin said, ''Oh, good. They're safe at Hold now? I heard—''

I'd had too many angry days. I wanted to speak freely and
dared not, my feelings grew stronger the longer I stifled them.
They must have felt it in me, for I caught the flicker of
Caladrunan's eyes as his head turned to his son—quick glances
breaking that rigid posture of his. Now, when I most needed to
speak, I must contain my rage—and my fear for him—discreetly:
not what either of us wanted. I thought, send the boy away to
bed! Caladrunan must hear things I'd left unsaid because there
was always time before. We might die years from now and very
old, never having said enough.

I knew better than to give any sign of it. It was callous against

Therin's presence, and unworthy; but still the hunger was in me like the rage—*send the boy away*. Send everyone away.

Caladrunan said, "Yes, they reached the Hold safely—but that's private news only. See how late it is getting! Son, your bed's in here with us until we've got our perimeter firmed up."

I lifted my eyelids and stared at the Lord of Tan for three long heartbeats. That stare of mine had to make up for the whole frustrated night.

My jumbled emotions jostled too many stiff Tannese molds and fetched up odd readings. This time, for his son's sake, the Lord of Tan chose to refute rumors of that oddness by denying it. He looked firmly away from me, refusing to answer. And poor Therin shrank back in his chair and tried to pretend he hadn't seen something staring from my eyes like a murderer glimpsed through shutters, to pretend that he wasn't in this tent, that it hadn't happened, that I didn't exist. It was just too much. Rage boiled up in my guts.

I bolted from my chair, spun away to the tent flap—where my sworn lord at last gave me leave to vanish. I plunged out into the camp night, checking guards, learning about defenses, until I was cold rational again. The night was empty, answerless, comfortless; even the wind rasped harsh on my face.

When I returned, a tapestry hanging divided the tent, with healthy snoring beyond it; Caladrunan's bed had its customary privacy. He murmured, "The boy was exhausted. You may talk freely now, Naga. It's a risk, but I judge we're safer together near with you than one of us tenting alone. I ran into an interesting idea today, which is your fault. It came from a cousin of mine—a Devotee passing through some days ago on her way to check outlying refugee camps. I think *you* may know her." He could be as sarcastic as anyone.

"Oh?" Arrogantly sitting on his big armor bench, I took off and dumped out my left boot. A small rock fell out on the thick rug. I kicked it with an innocent look under the floor mats, which made him smile, drop his head into his fingers, and shake it in exasperation. Lightly I said, "Stir up some braindust in there?"

He said, "This Devotee told me about factions in the refugee camps and presented me with an extremely heretical notion. She told me, 'The early prophetic writings teach that we're reborn over and over.' "

"Oh, *that* woman Devotee," I said wryly. I stretched my toes with concentration. Then, at his expression, I said, "Yes? So?"

He stared back. "Is that all you have to say about it?"

"Of course not. Harper, after all." I grinned, peeled off my other boot; the razor inset on the built-in wooden fighting spur glittered blue lights. "I think it's a native belief adopted along with the Altar, the Goddess, and silk-making. Lado collected lots of Sek songs, it's common in that old stuff. Devotees ignore it, too horribly foreign—" I wriggled my toes, "—to pigheaded theologians."

Stroking the tails of his mustache, he regarded me as I threw down my right boot. If I adopted his light tone, it was because his manner warned me, in a virtual command, this was *not* the time to discuss problems like Girdeth. Then he smiled. "I wondered what it'd be like to remember other lifetimes, like living a quieter life. Be a back-court woman, embroider all day, that sort of thing. Play with children. Not have to worry about affairs of state."

I glanced at him quizzically. *"You?"* I snorted and got up, padding barefooted across the carpet. "Well, I find it pleasant to be able to aim when I pee." I said it over a white slushpot in its fancy stand.

"You're a rude one."

Retying my corad, I started an equally rude song about his own father, Agaka Ún, and a servant girl rather cleverer than the besotted old lecher. Caladrunan hurled a slate at me, and as easily I plucked it out of the air. When I sat down, returning the slate to him rather more politely, I shrugged. "Just because it's an old Sek-blood belief doesn't mean that *I* personally believe it."

He grinned. "Ah, my snappy feist-dog! You wouldn't say that if you were *really,* in your private mind, a native. The Upai used to insist that songs came straight from the Goddess, perfect, immutable—it's an article of faith, not a matter of judgment. Holding private notions on something is strictly a skeptical, intellectual way to look at things. Very un-Upai of you. Our Devotee friend sorts rigidly conservative natives from the Tannese-influenced with that one theological question. Thought I'd test it."

"That woman is even sharper than I guessed," I muttered. "Of course when insulted, *we* Tannese minds huff up *our* bristles and charge off solo like your fool sailor ancestors, discarding all tradition—once you drop the Devotee dogma off your necks and the elaborate court traditions you *must* preserve intact . . ."

"Oh, wickedness!" He narrowed his eyes at me and grinned. I gave him an innocent look.

"How long awake?"

I blinked. "But I haven't told you about—"

"Two days or more awake, by the look of you. Tell me about the Fortress-works, and then you're going to sleep."

He tapped my report slates as he cross-checked them with me on the defensive work I'd completed in the secret ways and my orders for completion of the diversion channel. He stretched his hands, grimacing. His fingers were cracked and red from too much chalk-writing, and stiffly curled. I told him sketchily Agtunki's orders to me; he did not mention the assault on Girdeth. I had no fresh knowledge, and I didn't choose to enrage him afresh. Lightly, I added, "I'm not done with Keth either, but that will hold awhile."

His eyes glinted amber lights. He said only, "I remind you, anything you do to him has far repercussions."

"Oh, I'll ask you." And I changed the subject. I told him about my grandmother's threats to me, then about Tuzo. He lifted one eyebrow at that, no more. When I had run out of news, he rose and propped his hands on his hips, looming over me. I looked up at him peacefully.

He said, "Did you sleep with her?"

I blinked at him, surprised. "My wife?"

"Wife? I didn't realize Tuzo was your—"

"She agreed to be my wife when she let me sleep with her."

He wore an odd expression. Finally, softly, he said, "Let you? I suppose she's some hulking great—"

"She is a knife-dancer of great skill. I worked hard to master her dance-forms at the estreka. I don't know many women who could test me so." I spun my scadda, sheathed it; spun out the right one from its sheath. It hissed past Caladrunan's knee.

His lips tightened. "So now you feel more like a man?"

I stared, puzzled. "No. It was nice, but I think—I hope—it will be better later. She was raped once, bore a child and—it must be a lot like your Lady Wife's feelings. Is there anything that helps—"

"I don't want to talk about her problems!" he snarled.

Shocked, I just blinked. "I thought you wanted me to set up a family, gut Keth's rumors about me. Why do you think—"

My tone must have been far too insubordinate. His hand swung down. I saw it in time to dodge aside. More in puzzlement than stubbornness, I stayed where I was. His hand made a dull *smack!* on the side of my face and bounced away. I looked at him. A dull red flush appeared under his clear skin, and his hand dropped, then slowly rose and rested on my shoulder. One finger brushed the place he'd struck me.

"You don't understand," he said.

"No," I agreed. "And I don't like being hit in anger."

"What will you do about it?" he challenged, glaring from my face to the naked blade resting along my thigh and back again.

I smiled. "Probably nothing. Keth needled you all day?"

He let out a long, long sigh and sat next to me on the bench. After a moment he rested his face on my shoulder. I put my hand up, brushed at his hair.

"I think you're even more tired than I. Can I ask you if I can challenge Keth—" I could ask permission to ask it, no more.

The words came distinctly: *"No—challenges—at—all!"*

"Even for the sake of Girdeth—"

"No. No fights, no challenges, nothing. Promise!" I did. He gave me an odd look and sighed again. "Didn't you understand the political implications of what Keth and I have been arguing in those report slates I sent to you? He insists that you're—well, that you should be tested for diseases of the insane—"

"I have a very literal mind. When a man is lying to me I don't always bother about the details of his method."

He groaned. "You choose odd times to slip from literal reality to *very* different ideas."

"Well, when you mentioned the smugglers' falling drug revenues, it rattled Keth just as I thought it would, didn't it? So I was right, odd or not, and *he* wanted you to ignore facts. Common fault; I knew a man who said soldiers reject large parts of reality at will."

"Who was the man who said that?" Caladrunan asked, chin on my shoulder.

I grinned, showing all my teeth. "Reti. My scadda trainer."

"Must I give you time off to be with your new wife?"

I lifted my hand and smacked his cheek lightly. "Tuzo wouldn't thank me for that. As I said, I don't think she likes any man that much. Tannese she is *not*." I angled my scadda to the light for corrosive fingerprints, wiping the long blade.

Caladrunan said quietly, "What exactly did you mean when you said you weren't through with Keth yet?"

I stiffened, not looking up to the face at my shoulder. My

mind poised a moment, turned to the side of mercy for his feelings, tonight. "I promised Girdeth something," I said at last, reluctantly. "When I have proof I'll ask your permission."

His eyes studied my expression.

I said, "I promise you the chance to consent—later."

I was uncomfortable meeting those eyes.

He said, "Consent to challenge? Never mind. You know my mind on that. No, tell me tomorrow. I'm too tired tonight. I've forgiven your ignorance of Tannese law codes before. I simply assumed you understood my wishes on violence because you understood so much else, I didn't realize that we had such divergent thinking, Naga."

I knew what he was asking: if another rift loomed in what I'd planned. I lowered my gaze to my scadda. "I promised."

"Beware conflicting promises," he murmured.

"They don't conflict," I said, lifting my eyes fiercely to his, feeling something hard and forceful flow into my muscles from some inner recess. Perhaps he felt the change; he drew back. I spun my scadda into sheath. "It is in your best interests, too."

He sighed. "And you think you're right? You're so tired you can't even think straight! Very well. If it helps Girdeth, I don't mind what you plan. Just inform me before you *do* anything. And don't turn that cold black stare on *me*. Save it for our enemies." He tucked his hands under my arms, pulled me to my feet. I was surprised when I staggered with my stiffening muscles and nearly fell; he caught me. Under his arm I went to a folding officer's bed. Someone always slept near him traveling. I sighed; tonight it was to be me, tired as I was. He said, "I heard your escort complain you gave them a hard ride."

"Yes." I flopped out like a cloth doll upon the bed—outrobe, riding leathers, dust and all. Brisk hands unhooked my robe belt, stripped me, dumped my harness and clothes in a heap at the foot of the bed. He set my scaddas under my left hand. I closed my eyes. Furs covered my legs.

"Sleep," he said.

I opened my eyes. Gazing up into his stern, almost frowning face, I felt tiredness eat into my bones. Awake for weeks, it felt. "Mmm. Where's that hunting cat of yours—need dogs, too—to keep you safe. Are you going to bed? I'm supposed to guard—"

His hand covered my eyes briefly. "No. You've been awake too long. Go to sleep."

"Can't disobey direct orders," I said, feeling my eyes close. I was falling fast into the embrace of the Goddess' mercy. I thought longingly, let the Goddess cover the busy eye of my mind, give me peace. "You should go to bed, too, Drin."

Such a warm night, I thought drowsily. Sometime ages later, beyond my closed eyelids, he answered, "Soon."

He held evening conversations, worked on slates, wrote out orders with soft scratching sounds, spoke with Rafai. Once his voice belled out into a laugh, rumbling round the tent. When Rafai blew out most of the oil lamps, pulling aside tapestries to let in all possible air, I came partially awake. "I've never seen him sleep so deeply," Rafai's voice said.

Caladrunan muttered something close above me, and a familiar chalk-scented hand touched my cheekbone. He said in a low voice, "We can let Naga sleep on. I'd rather not wake him."

I heard steps. Strange voices mingled with his voice. I listened drowsily to Caladrunan's step moving about, the clink of goblets, murmuring. Something was singing inside me as I fell deeper into the depths of furry warmth: *Upai, Not-Upai . . .*

Dry storm weather woke me a second time that night; voices, and the jingle of escort soldiers riding away outside, brought me full awake. I turned my head and peered about. Caladrunan's tent was silent and dark, and humid. I stole across to his bed. In the stark lightning light, slashing about the heavens outside and glinting through smoke holes and tent flaps, I looked at his face.

He was awake, one hand pulling at the ruff of his hunting cat. The big cat's paws dabbed lightly at his fingers, shiny black claws pricking into view against Caladrunan's light skin in the lightning, gone at the next stark bolt of brilliance. The cat purred steadily into the dark. The very night felt dense in the heat. The sentries outside shifted aimlessly under the heavy weight of the air, too oppressed to even snap at one another.

Caladrunan shifted aside. I replaced the dent in his furs left by his restless hunting cat with my own imprint. There was fur shed about from his petting the beast. The cat lifted its head and stared at me. I didn't mind the sardonic feline gaze; the cat let me touch its ruff, and rumbled a brief purr. The broad striped head turned regally and bumped Caladrunan's hand.

The Lord of Tan's eyes glittered with the lightning. For a long bell pass, we lay facing each other, stretched on cloth and under-fur for any breath of breeze, both of us stripped in the heat. Skin glimmered damp at his shoulders and knees. We didn't talk; grown into too hot a night for any effort, this was the kind of storm-dark in which sweat rose silently to beads on flesh. We lay motionless in the thunder and the rainless humid heat aware of each other as we were aware of the animals: the two guard dogs panted among the legs of the bed, and the cat sprawled irritably at our feet. All of us breathed choking thick air. All of us became animals waiting for the rain.

Other than the impressive crack and rattle of gear at each thundering shock through the earth, it was very quiet. I wanted to scream out against the heavy lowland air dragging at my lungs. Perhaps Caladrunan knew it. His hand gripped my right wrist, then fell away; in the heat that was close to unbearable. Too hot, nearly, to breath at all.

We heard the rush of rain coming in a sharp weather front over many road-cairns' distance, a soft atmospheric hum that grew louder with each passing heartbeat.

A sudden cold wind heralded the storm. The Lord of Tan flinched spasmodically, clutching my shoulder in the uproar, while I jerked up on one elbow. Wind tore at the tent, slamming kettles off tripods outside, throwing over insecure tent posts and wailing away with clothes hung on lines, escaping with loose tarpaulins. The nervous dogs nosed at the tent flap and whined. The cat leaped off the bed and disappeared underneath. Then it was over; there was rain, and cold air threading past the tent flaps, and sudden noisy peace outside. Hard, steady rain pounded like *estreka* dance drums—flooding Osa advances all over the region, bogging their flamethrowers.

Our bodies went slack in relief at the knowledge. I heard the sentries laughing and joking outside, prancing like fool boys in the downpour, boots smacking puddles. Cool air breathed over us. I let out a slow sigh, bumping him and then resting beside the damp cool length of his body, resting in the vitality springing from his pores. Tired, sweaty, even when irritable, he had it yet. Perhaps it was the aura of the rulership clinging over him like invisible cloth—the driving energy of history invested in him, a sense of memory longer than any man. I glanced down; in a dim flicker of stormlight his other arm moved, gold against my darker flesh. I stretched, arching my legs luxuriously under it, and relaxed.

He whispered, "I always forget how strong you are."

I grinned at him. "Now you're joking!" He threw out both arms and tumbled me down off the bed. I wrestled him back. I hurt him, teaching him where he must not get sloppy; but he understood my sometimes harsh devotion. If my body was a killing instrument superlatively trained and hardened, he was supremely capable of playing that instrument's owner to whatever music he chose. I knew he meant this wrestling as a simple practical test. But measuring strengths, testing our weaknesses, somehow he communicated his feelings to me: the humor, the impatience, ultimately his helplessness and his concern over me. He dawdled over taking his advantage. He refused to cheat—to gouge or kick or hurt me to win, though I'd taught him how and made him practice it on me.

I kept him to it; throwing a match was not good training. Of course, he used my old wounds against me, and defeated me. I cried out hoarsely in the end, yielding—the first time I ever yielded a match to him—loudly enough for the guards outside to hear. Instantly, I regretted the noise: They might think anything of it. He merely pushed aside my hands, checking that he had not injured me. I rolled over and smiled at him, and watched him realize how much he'd improved as a wrestler. Two moons back, I'd have him flattened in ten breaths—and in another two moons, he'd be pinning me unaided. He deserved his pride. As his informal trainer, I climbed back happily in the furs.

I lay panting. His hair ruffled softly under my breath. He murmured, "Goddess, I don't know why I always forget that set of muscles on you when we're apart. It's like holding a siege machine."

I chuckled, drifting despite myself toward sleep. "Siege, ha? Don't let me get too boring."

"No, I won't." He tickled me, grinning, but I only yawned and stretched myself into his ticklings. He propped up his chin on one elbow; idly, one finger traced patterns on my shoulder blades. I sighed in deep content. He asked, "*Kigadi*?" In the dark, in the sound of the rain, the kindness in his voice gave the question dignity. *Kigadi*, the shield-brother, should insist the right thing be done, should prevent his friend's mistakes, even against express wishes. I could have levered him with it to avenge Girdeth, but I had never abused that trust to get my own way, and would not now.

"*Kigadi*," I agreed. "Say it again."

"Greedy." His eyes were great dark moons in his gold skin, in the dim flickers of light, startling as a cat's eyes. And the eyes smiled, his gold face open and pleased as a child's bright Devotee mask. "I'm very glad you're here. Very glad."

At that moment I understood why the Goddess had not taken me away in a burst of silence and light when I was thrown from my mare, so long past: She had let me stay for this. I felt suddenly and passionately grateful for it from the bottom of my mean and wizened soul. Joy burst through me like shattered lights and halos of color. It was a madness from the regions of light, a gift of grace, undeserved, unearned—the breath of peace.

Caladrunan leaned over me. Sparks of Goddess-lights flickered lamp light splinters through his hair. His smile vanished. "What are you seeing, Naga?" I buried my hands in the wealth of his curly gold hair, arched my back, and cried out. White brilliance shattered in my head. Great happiness, like any great emotion, opened the gates wider to those strange realms buried inside me. Or perhaps it was just a fleeing-away, a weakness, a fear of happiness that ran with me away into a fit.

"Hold of the Red Tyrant—burn—it burns—"

Undoubtedly he felt the great muscular seizure that took my body and made my back arch back in a bow. I grunted and felt hot liquid run down my chin. Furs writhed, spiky with damp, around my legs. Something choked in my mouth—words, a shout high and clear as a bull's whistling, and as eerily wailing. Twice I felt my back muscles seize while words came screeing hard as ice-knives from the deepest roots of my belly, and something—hands, his hands—lifted me out of thrashed, rent bedding and freed me. My heels drummed on floor mats as the blackness came down full of twirling, darting totems, lightning dazzles, and the odor of red earth paint.

Rafai's voice said soberly, "Oh, yes, he's doing much better than he used to. He's returning from a fit seizure sooner, and he's going off into normal sleep instead of going unconscious. I've been keeping people away, to let him get some rest, after."

When I opened my eyes, it was night. The tent walls were lit only by lamps, and faces moved above me, words flew about as I stirred. The sounds made no sense, which somehow sparked an immense, instant rage. I growled, "Stop it! I'm all right, I'm getting up!" I staggered onto my feet and went out from the tent half-dressed and filthy, blindly waving off help. "Let me walk it off," I grunted, struggling free with stiff muscles. I stamped wretchedly to settle my razor-spurred boots. Humiliating, all of it. "Must walk. Work to do. Perimeter walk, yes. Stop fretting."

"Did we set off the fit? What did—" Caladrunan said solemnly, puzzled, with his hand out toward me.

"You didn't have to do anything. You made me happy."
Before I could move, Keth's step sounded outside; then his head
shoved in past the tent flap.

"What's this, Liege, about somebody else's trainees getting
positions in my top cavalry division—?"

Caladrunan turned to me. "I just wanted Naga's trainees to
ride with your cavalry tomorrow, Keth, but we'll wait. Keth,
you must get off to Pigeon Hold now, it's so close on the line of
march. I agreed that you could feast your brother's wedding
there later, but it must be now. There's no time later."

Keth's new-married brother was also one of Keth's top liegemen
in the cavalry, and for his pains had been made garrison commander of the troops reinvesting a Hold abandoned during Osa
attacks. Plush post, that, unless the Osa returned. I shifted my
gaze momentarily. Wedding. They really were dragging that
frightened Upai woman all over the fields of war so Keth's
brother could bed her, I thought. In an even tone I said, "All
good luck to the new couple, Keth."

Caladrunan's eyes narrowed the faintest degree. He knew my
voice, even when I meant to hide such things.

Keth snarled, "Not a couple. His fourth subsidiary wife.
Some Upai bitch brought in on contract. You might have seen
the official bride-parade in Fortress town."

I thought, you planned for that, you motherless cave-devil.

Keth looked me up and down. "I'd heard you had a fit
today—amazing how well you've recovered."

My Liege's mouth compressed. "I dislike contracts."

Keth shrugged. "The bride's broker offered her that way—
draggled goods at that. Farso, Arpso, Darso, I forget."

Caladrunan corrected, "Tarso-Kiroki. I negotiated about her
sister for Naga, but the broker insisted neither was available at
any cost." I shot him a glance. His face had gone stern. Nella
had tossed Tuzo's contract to me at unspecified future cost.

Keth shrugged. "Upai—they're all alike to me. She was under
blank contract. My brother bought it easily enough. Perhaps
another will come of age." And he smiled.

I felt a fine trembling come over me, but I held still. "If your
brother finds her so unsuitable, I'd buy her contract—"

Keth shrugged. "We couldn't *sell* you the woman, that'd be
slavery." His eyes squinted nearly shut with pleasure at me.

Dear price for survival, for a Upai family to barter away a
woman to strangers. Caladrunan must have tried very hard if

he'd trawled such muddy pools as those. I felt his eyes on me. The thought of that beautiful woman given to any of Keth's lean reddish brothers horrified me—cold, angular men with the same humors. There were kinder Cragmen. More civilized ones. At last, deliberately, I met Keth's eyes and stared him down; the man never could meet my eye. Then I left.

I paced the camp perimeter thoroughly, gathering my staggered muscles into order again, ignoring the men who followed me. Mostly, anyway. It was then that I heard, faintly on the night silence, drums. I growled at the stumbling soldiers to be quiet. I was listening so intently that I only hissed at a man who spoke.

*The rhythm*, I thought. That was a Marsh festival rhythm, carrying for cairns upon cairns' distance on the wind. It blew in snatches from enemy positions out there in the dark. Drinking and dancing with tramp women, no doubt, unlike quiet Tannese camps.

There was a brief flare of orange on the horizon, so far and so small I wouldn't have noticed it without being alert to the chance. I thought slowly, wonderingly: The fools are playing with the crippled flamethrower that Strengam had some days past reported seeing in a raid. And then, fiercely, I began to grin.

A guard spoke to me. I spun, scaddas in hand; poised for attack, I stared at him. He wet dry lips. "Upai are asking for you, Noble-born—something about a raid. We think desert Upai came in along with our scouts, but we weren't sure. We understand they found sign of a Nando drug-smuggling band. They asked you to go with them. Rafai told them to wait, but we don't know if they understood—"

I was no longer sleepy. "Those *fools*—I must go; they're not like Tannese, they won't wait."

The man called anxiously, "Noble-born, where are you going?"

I didn't tell him I was going on a raid. If these were desert Upai, I had to keep them out of trouble, for they wouldn't know their prey, Cragmen Nandos who smuggled. And Caladrunan must give consent to my idea . . .

Back at Caladrunan's tent I heard voices. I lingered a moment beside the flap, listening—they weren't being particularly quiet—pulled aside the flap, and went in. Reactions were very odd. Therin sat at one side, chalk poised over a slate, trying to efface himself. Caladrunan's face looked stern, and Rafai's was flushed. Quiet guilty glances . . . they'd been talking about me, I could tell. So I took it directly, hands on the bull's horns, and said, "What keeps me from doing the same trick on the nearest enemy camp as we suffered at Fortress? Easy to slide into their camp while they sleep and make a pretty mess of them all."

Caladrunan's face slowly paled. "You wouldn't."

"I would," I said. "I can do better than Crag assassins blindfolded on a foggy night. I *know* those officers over there, by description, some by sight. Our Upai scouts would enjoy helping me raid. The scouts found a sign of drug smugglers in the area, and I want to look at that, maybe do something about it, too."

Rafai moistened his lips, looking from me to his lord.

I said, "Think what a useful precedent it sets, Liege. Send assassins at us—lose thirty officers in turn."

Caladrunan looked shocked. "Thirty officers—"

"I'll take out the competent ones," I said crisply. "The nearest arm of Manoloki's army is Marshmen. They're playing drums at a festival rhythm, with orange flares—probably that crippled flamethrower Strengam reported today. They can't know what they're doing, playing with that machine. Keth's men reported a lost skirmish this morning, didn't he? I bet the half-trained Marshmen out there are celebrating it. Even if they're expert men, I can take one of them captive and learn all I need to kill fifty officers."

The Lord of Tan simply stared at me. He loathed this side of me; it didn't come out often.

*Let me go,* I raged in my inner soul. Let me go! Rafai had paled, too. Slowly, weighing each word evenly, I said, "Alone, I can give you the blood of twenty officers."

Caladrunan jabbed his thumb toward me, pointing Upai-style. "I should *never* let you! You get wild, Naga, you—"

Rafai said, "Liege doesn't allow Pitar or Strengam to go on raids."

I glared at him, while the Lord of Tan glared at me. Then Caladrunan picked up a wine goblet and said, "That's because I dared not risk them personally. I don't like murder, Naga."

Therin fluted helpfully, "You don't *have* to let him go—"

"Of course I don't *have* to!" Caladrunan growled, more at Rafai's questioning look than at his tousled son. "But I suppose as a practical matter, I will. Naga is not tied to any duties now. I suppose, given our present disadvantage in the field, I must let him." He gestured with his goblet. "Anyway, he'll pick a fight if I don't. All Upai are like that. Hurt their feelings and they'll kill you or drown you in a flood of tears.'' Another wave of the goblet. ''With him, you never know. Touchy little bull, it isn't hard to insult Naga, no indeed. Nobody can question his killing competence, so I can't use *that*.''

I slanted a look at Rafai, who was fighting to blank his embarrassed face. Security duty around Caladrunan was getting more privy and difficult than Rafai had expected. ''Begging pardon,'' I said, gripping my temper hard in both hands, ''but if you don't want me to— It isn't just ill-thought glory-hunting. I stay here if you decide so; no fights. And I'd come back on your word, if, once I rode out, you changed your mind and sent a messenger after me—''

He lifted his head, and his agate-yellow eyes stared so hard into my skull I wondered beams of glare did not shoot out the back like Osa flames. *''Of course you'd return!''* He reminded, by the grit in his tone, that my Oath swore me to it. Then he flung out one arm angrily. ''Never mind! I could kick you like a dog and you'd *still* come back, stiff and be-damned proud as ever. Oh, you always come back. You can't stand to run away from me for long. You *need* me, Naga.

''It's like one of those intricate little trinket boxes, with all the levers and gears and tiny parts twirling—and the Osa busted yours. I never know when I'll bump something loose accidentally— which is something you may *all* need to know about my fine Sati.'' Caladrunan swung round and glared at Rafai and his son. ''I don't treat him very well, do I? I work him like an ox and I make him behave. The man never knows how much leash I'll let him have. He waits on my will until he's half out of his mind, and then he's such a fool as to be grateful for it!'' He turned and waved the goblet at me. ''Why? For whatever reasons, he's twisted out of his broken head.''

It was Therin who spoke into the frightened hush. ''But Aunt Girdeth told me why, my Liege. Noble-born told her, once, that he loved you.''

That only made the Lord of Tan more savage; Caladrunan's hand slammed the goblet down on the table. He swung sharply away from us all and clenched his hands into huge pale mallets pressing down at his sides. The boy owned more courage than either Rafai or I did, to speak up; his father was in a towering rage and must have been long before I ever awoke from my seizure. *Why?* I glanced away toward report slates and hastily up

at him again. Deep rasping lordly breaths followed. At last he
turned.

Caladrunan glowered at me. In a soft, soft voice he said, "I
told you, son. It's all those busted gears in his head."

It was going to be a bad night for anyone who crossed
Caladrunan's eye. Beside him, the top slate bore my insignia
from the hardest report of my life: the assault on Girdeth. I
blinked. Therin had mentioned Girdeth's name. I looked at
Rafai, who made a single, assenting, clarifying gesture: *just
delivered*.

My reports on the assault had been diverted somewhere and
only now retrieved. Of course, in wartime such things happened
. . . innocently enough . . . Caladrunan had only just read the
news of it, along with the investigation reports I carried in
yesterday. Just as quickly, he connected the assault's effects to
Girdeth's marriage offer to Keth, and thence to Girdeth's desire
for justice. The slates I'd delivered to him reported only the bare
evidence found so far, which offered no source or intent for the
plot—so there was no focus for his anger. And he dared not
expose any bits of that shattering rage outside this trusted circle.
Apparently he thought my craziness was a safer topic for spies—
but then, he counted my fits a strength rather than weakness.

I said, "Was I rude or unruly or stupid to you, my Liege?"

Caladrunan's voice made my neck hair creep. Softer yet he
said, "No. It's not that. I don't think I've ever heard stupidity
from you. No. Those Osa broke something in your soul, Naga,
and whatever you might have been, it's all glittery broken little
pieces now. Proud, busted, skew-brained orphan. You forget: I
*knew* Upai as a boy, I knew your brother." He flung out one arm
toward me. "The Upai I knew lived in the land so gently they
could drift up to wild red deer and touch them. And what I've
got now is a creature who wants to strangle men in their sleep—a
Sati of scaddas, for Goddess' sake. Of all the things you could
have been! People warn me it's dangerous to consider you
anything but a lethal weapon."

I narrowed my eyes. Upai had changed greatly since the Osa.

Rafai said hastily, "Would we were all so able! We all
consider ourselves your weapons, Liege, just like your sword or
your spear." Therin added eager agreement, trying to ease his
father's distress.

Caladrunan bit off his next words in great bitterness, turning
away. "That's not how I wanted to treat my son. Nor my

friends.'' With his back turned, he said, "My friend deserved better."

Rafai said, "He doesn't enjoy killing."

Caladrunan snorted. "You haven't seen him in battle."

I said tartly, "Neither have you—"

He snapped, "I've seen Upai fight, Naga. And I've seen you practice."

I lowered my head. "My people—"

"I know a great deal about your people, more than you think. Therin's questions tonight reminded me how much I knew, and how much I tried to ignore. The signs are clear enough. If you lost me, you'd go completely berserk."

Rafai said, very quietly, "And if *you* lost *Naga*, Liege?"

Caladrunan flung out one hand. "Don't even say it. I don't want to think about *that* right now. I swore I'd heal Naga of the Osa; I really thought I did it! What a bitter joke, to have him revert like this now." He turned and stared down at his young son. The boy tilted back his head, looking gravely up; he did not seem afraid. "Therin, you should know that if I die, Naga will go crazy. If you think you can save Naga from madness, I pray you'll give it all the work it will require—hard work. But if it can't be done, if he goes murderously insane . . . my son, have the mercy to kill him painlessly. Quickly. I beg you."

Therin turned his head toward me; his were not a child's eyes at that moment. I lowered my head, face hot and shamed. Therin said, "I promise, my Liege."

Caladrunan sighed. "Naga kills to insure my safety, that's the irony. If I got him sane, then he wouldn't defend me so fanatically. We'll never find another madman so devoted."

Rafai frowned. "Guarding your life is our work, Liege. Like the Sati, we view it as good craftsmanship. We all attempt to work as well for you, Liege, as the Sati does."

"Goddess knows I give you enough work." Caladrunan sipped more wine. "There's enough to spare, certainly. You define—or excuse him—very well, Rafai." He gave me an ironic look.

"Perhaps as his trainee, I saw him from a different angle."

Both Rafai and Therin studied me. I was poking at my gloves, looking for worn spots. Therin said, "What did the Noble-born's brother used to be like as a boy? Did he really touch red deer?"

"We did. Together." Caladrunan turned, giving me a long, sad look. I could guess it was just such questions as these that— aside from the slates on Girdeth—put him in a rage. "His brother used to be a wit, a prankster, and practical joker, always singing or happy about something. He made everyone glad to be alive." Caladrunan grimaced. "They smashed you all to junk, Naga. It makes me feel sick."

Rafai said quietly, "Satis aren't exactly common junk."

"Neither was my friend."

I stirred restively. "Are you going to let me go or not?"

Caladrunan stared at me. "To kill twenty or thirty men—" he shuddered. "Oh, we'll give you praise for that, won't we?"

Rafai frowned. "Honor-chasing, you taught us, was bad for—"

I flicked a dismissive hand. "Who'll boast about it? Only Upai scouts will know. Liege, the death of a dozen ranking men *here* would be absolute disaster. I will hurt *them*. Your enemies let the Osa into our land, tried to kill us, assassinate you. Let them pay the cost of it."

"They failed in such attempts. But they'll keep trying. Why do you think I wanted you to *stay* here?"

I said crisply, "I assumed you meant to make use of me. Where there are Marshmen, there are sometimes Osa. Shall I bring them back if I find an Osa, or kill them?"

"I have *not* said you may go," Caladrunan said.

We looked steadily at each other. I said levelly, "Between your safety and my blood-debt as Upai—between these things there has never been conflict. There is no conflict now. You have the wider knowledge of the field. Command me."

*"Go,"* the Lord of Tan said harshly. "As well fetter a yedda, by Goddess. You'll keep us all awake muttering to yourself if I don't. Report here when you return, I want to . . . to know. Loudly, if it goes well. The men need the morale."

I looked sharply at him; his voice broke oddly on the words. I said, "I'll come back well before first light to resume guarding you. Manoloki's assassins tend toward dawn attacks. I take my gana, those Upai scouts who want to hunt smugglers, and one of Strengam's steadiest men, if I may. And your blessing."

Slowly he nodded. "Granted. The Upai are only to track smugglers off Manoloki's camps, *no* fighting with Nandos!" Caladrunan said. Then, as if dragged from him, "And if you're not back?"

"Then I'll be dead." I touched him lightly on the arm, but he did not move. "I'll post Strengam's man with my gana far enough back for him to escape and report." I gave both Therin and the Lord of Tan a long look. Then I went out to get my mare gana and Strengam's steadiest veteran.

Outside, I waved off Rafai. "No, don't call an escort. I don't want any but Upai. I'll just meet you by joining Liege's line of march."

Rafai's face looked white as a pond of moonlit water. "If you go without any escort, we'll be in trouble—"

I laughed and ran to my beast, robes flapping as I buckled my belts, and I snatched up a lamp carrypot with fresh coals. Rafai called furiously after me in the darkness. I took up the lines of my mare and swung up into her straps. Strengam too did not believe, until I was riding away, what I planned to do with his steadiest veteran, and then of course it was too late for him to do anything about it but yell after us that I was mad, taking off like this—too much time aback my crazy mare. I smiled.

From the lone scout awaiting me, I learned the Upai rode off meaning to ambush smuggling Nandos: These Nandos were men exiled from Crag and known to have shed Upai blood. Their trailsign read as a Nando band much larger and better armed than the Upai. But attack the Upai meant to do, even if outnumbered— and expected me to rescue them if they came to grief. They wouldn't give up the chance to fight; merciless knife-dancers rode with them, raiding women like Tuzo, who did not count lives.

No Tannese troop could move fast enough to rescue them. Nor would Caladrunan be pleased, I thought, if he learned of my solution to the dilemma. But as I flexed my grip with the hard gana traveling-jog, I kept remembering Therin's pale face looking up at me with large green eyes—Therin was no longer a child, with that taut look to the corners of his eyes. The resemblance to Caladrunan grew stronger with age. *For him*, I thought, *for both of them*. And I rode on.

# CHAPTER

# = *12* =

A FLIGHT OF CROWS flew up suddenly from the woods ahead—winged shapes visible against the veiled cloud-light about the setting moon. I heard nothing as I knelt in the brush, although the Upai raiders were all hidden behind me. Our mounts were in a cluster well back, heads high and silent; it was three bell passes since I left camp. We'd settled into ambush on the bend of a major trail. Because the Nando smugglers had automatically split into small bands to confuse any Tannese military tracking, we took our vengeance piecemeal.

"What?" softly I asked Hagavu, the best scout in the group. He could read signs that my senses, blunted by too many years among Tannese and other blind-faces, would not pick up.

"Ten riders," he said, bent to the ground. "The last of them will come soon. See, they disturbed the crows. Careless."

I frowned, scraping my razor spurs silently in the dirt as I squatted. A tall, stiff Tannese could not have done this. This was the last and biggest bunch of smugglers; the others were dead or prisoners answering Upai women's questions. They were very persuasive, those women like Tuzo who went raiding with men.

Hagavu said, "Why do you hide the blood? Won't your Pale People read other tales on you?"

"I doubt it. And they have rules."

One of the younger men said sardonically, "When we go back, shall we put on nice faces for all your pale friends, Tokori Efresa?"

I said crisply, "Don't scorn them. They gave us refuge."

"On land once *ours!* We need no help from blind-faces—"

202

I said, "O ignorant one, this was Sek-blood land before the Tannese invaded them, and the Sek would have offered you only the red hand of war. It was our land so long ago you would never know them as Upai at all."

Hagavu remarked, to the melodies of argument cascading around us, "Are we *all* children?" Vollies flew in reply.

I murmured, "I'd forgotten how we argue about everything."

"*We*, O great pale Tannese lord? Dry white bone!"

I turned. "Women's Councils decided upon exile in Tan, as is proper; it was not *my* place as Tokori to choose it for you . . . I offer all assistance as I can, which is also proper. So be silent before our Tannese hosts, curb your willful tongues, or face all your Councils for imperiling children and the place of children."

They shut up. They knew I'd *do* it. They felt I ran them like my hands and feet instead of respecting them as men. I spent half the time of most Upai leaders in my organizing of work; and for my domination these men had survived the night better than they deserved, for the risks they dared.

"Soon," Hagavu announced. We all heard the faint faraway clink of gear—careless smugglers, so careless. Fierce melodies flickered about me as I waited. A word here and there, rising from the general Upai music, flew up intelligibly.

"Ghostface swine-eaters!" It quite spoiled the flow of tones. I sighed, glancing toward the shadow-bulk of our ganas—ears up to approaching riders. Then, crunching of brush and rattles of rock silenced us; the night lay all the quieter for small betrayals of an alien presence. "Go," I breathed, and black shapes glided on black beneath starlight-silvered brambles.

They returned bent under lax and awkward burdens. The screaming would come much later and far away.

The Upai rode away. Alone, I rode onward toward Manoloki's war camps, to the bigger task I'd promised to Caladrunan. Strengam's steadiest man had proved equal to my test of patience: He told me what he'd seen of enemy movements, and I gave him new signals and stationed him with our pair of mounts over a stream. There the wind blew steadily from the enemy camp down to him; his scent would not set off alarms in the enemy's long gana lines.

I looked like a dark Marshman in drab clothes—I meant to use that. As moonless late as this night was, no sick, footsore recruit could look for the difference. Two years of service, spying among Manoloki's hated Nandos before Tan, even gave me the

voice for it. The tired swamp-rat foot men weren't dancing and
feasting—they had fluxes of the bowels, as in all raw, new-
marched troops. A man lingering near the latrines deserved no
attention. Farther in, I went to belly-crawling stealth.

At the trench of the inner officers' camp, I watched.

Everything favored me except the odds of killing so promised
many—nothing ever went so perfectly. So far I'd found very
little new information; I'd just crawled over foul terrain, lost all
my righteous anger, and gained an enormous glacier in my
middle.

The small inner camp was set on the slope of a ridge. Through
it, the stream flowed down to where Strengam's man waited for
me in the woods. Marsh sentries shuffled about the inner camp.
Set mostly to guard officers against their own unruly troops, the
sentries were neither numerous nor particularly skilled. I watched
two guards arguing; a third one accidentally dropped his sword.
The camp showed few torches. The only real noise came from a
large central tent where men reeled about carousing—and then
closer, from a set of footsteps.

Stumbling latrine drunks would find me sooner than if I hid
among those dark officers' tents, but crawling forward now
would alert the approaching man. On elbows and toes I ghosted
sidewise into deeper shadows and flattened again. At the contin-
uing careless crunch of gravelly steps, I realized the folly of my
hatred and my promises. I had to do something about this noisy
man.

I stiffened at one side of the ditch, wondering if I'd gone mad
to try this. I lay flat on my belly, trying to breathe softly through
the stinging stench, with my head aside a misplaced pile of
dung. I shut my eyes to mask the whites. My fingers and feet
were relaxed, poised, ready to drive me upward like a lunging
black-fang lizard. Still the steps approached. I thought of rock, I
thought of sand dunes, like a viper among the cold rocks. Every
grating footstep was more carelessly arrogant. *Vanity and rage,* I
thought mournfully, while my heart jerked in my throat and the
steps paced closer.

I never used to feel fear like this when I'd been Tokori, on
Upai raids; but then I'd done nothing this rash. Ambushes were
one thing. One-man attacks on an armed camp were another.

The steps paused . . . I heard rustling. Warm and pungently
wine-scented fluid ran under my taut fingers in the cold dark.
The man grunted, thrust a boot at my inert body, as if I was a

muckpile. When I gave way gently under his toe and did not otherwise move, he turned away scuffing his boots at loose soil beside me. I saw his head turn in outline against the farther torchlight and the stars.

He was drunk. His Nando-wrapped head bobbed too much against the stars. But I still knew his distinctive walk. He'd been a Sati escorting Manoloki when that evil old fool dared show up in Tan. This squalid camp was a shocking fall for such a high-level Nando: No wonder he was drunk. He lurched.

A chilling force jolted through me. I found myself up, on him, and wrenching at his head. My left scadda rose, the pommel finished the attack before I could even sort my jumbled impressions. Reflex, all of it. Something *cracked*, ridiculously simple in my hands, like the neck of a chicken; the head waggled loose in my grasp; the heavy body slumped over my knees.

Smells rushed in on me. I rolled aside, bile choking hot in my throat. I lay stiffly on my back watching for alarms. Finally I felt over his body with my hands, praying for the man's soul while my fingertips searched his pockets. I wished squeamishly I did not have to handle the dead. Upai avoided the dead.

I took a scroll from his jade pouch, tucked it away in my robe, and got to my feet. I crouched and trod quickly and quietly to an officer's dark tent. I felt the standard beside the tent, identified it by touch in the dark. I wouldn't need captives to direct my attacks. I went around behind the tent and dropped to one knee, listening. From the trench I'd watched a man snuff a torch and pass inside that tent as if to stay; he hadn't come out.

Within, I heard regular soft sounds of snoring. I felt for the rear tent pegs with one hand. I glanced around before I untied the loops from the peg and lifted the side of the tent by degrees. A sharp draft of air might wake the man inside, and he'd know the tent confines as I did not.

One of the tests given me at Sati ranking was to slip the lines of a gana mare, newly foaled, from the hand of her sleeping owner. Mares with new foals were rightly feared for their ferocity and alertness. Her owner was just as dangerous; so I had planned it carefully as any raid, slid the leather as gently as owl's feathers from the grasp of the tired man, and tied his lines to a nearby bush in proof. This was no different.

I felt with my fingertips inside the tent, slid my body inside, and lowered the tent wall gently after myself. I crouched in the dark, waiting to pick out the faint outlines of objects against the lighter tent walls. I squinted, and swept the area before, above, and to each side of me with my fingertips.

I touched a leather box with my right hand, but nothing in front. I crept forward a pace and tried again. My left hand brushed something soft. Cold chills leaped on my back: I'd touched the sleeper's hair. I edged forward another pace and touched again, lightly as I could, moth-feet. Harsh cloth met my hands. The man lay in his blankets on a raised bed parallel with the side of the tent. A low-hanging cloth flap hung over him; mosquito cloth, which Marshmen packed everywhere with them.

I reached behind my ear and drew out a garrote cord, feeling the icy surge of fear rattle my insides again. This man was too far gone to deserve moral uncertainty of any sort—but fear, yes. By reputation I knew the man I crouched next to, and if he woke I'd be in trouble. I used the cord quickly, twisting it down hard against the straps of his own bed. The man gave a grotesquely soft gurgle, clutched my wrists in a final paroxysm, and died.

I felt macabre as I yanked free from those clutching hands. I covered my mouth with my hand, gagged silently behind cold stinking fingers, and listened for alarm sounds. I had known and fought men to whom cold murder was the only joy; but not for me. I wanted to throw up. Killing Osa and their allies rose from a sickening berserk grief for me, not fervor or courage. I felt myself a coward. I lowered my hand, sick, and prayed for the souls of the two men I had so secretly released from life. Hot-blooded kills of impulse or fury were so much easier than this. A very cold and unpleasant part of my mind remarked: *and so much less useful.*

Presently I got my nerve back. I searched the corpse, finding nothing, and likewise nothing worthwhile in the pouches and trunks I dared fumble into. I slid under the back of the tent by degrees, listening and watching in the starry dark. Finally I fastened the loop over the peg again and crept to the next tent.

Going into those tents did little good for my peace of mind. It was not magic in any way. I used basic Upai stalking techniques to avoid the sentries, narrowing in arcs toward the higher ranking quarters. As I went, I learned better which tents to enter, and to skip, and I moved faster. I was not proud of what I did. Few of the officers ever woke to know what was happening before they died; and those few were so surprised, their struggles were brief.

The faintest noises set my heart jerking wildly in my chest, but nobody seemed to notice when a man *did* manage to stagger up under my weight, or gurgle, or grunt. The biting, rational comments bursting into my head were new, and strange, distant; the thoughts frightened me more than the small agonies of fresh alarums. Every time I felt the gagging sick terror, I prayed, glided to another tent, and made myself go through it again. I would not have the fear rule me. *Coward, guerrilla bully,* the Lady of Fortress had called me once when she thought I did not hear. She and her courtiers would have called this very act of war cowardice by Tannese rules. *They* know nothing of the real thing, I thought grimly, spreading my hand with yet another face under my fingertips as I struck.

Stiff with the fear riding me, I crept along into the eastern side of the inner camp. Here, most of the tents were empty. The enemy command tent was still brightly lit with torches and lamp racks within, raucous with laughter and women's voices and the music of Marshman drums and flutes.

But the air smelled of spilled Osa flame-fuel, of sulfurous soot.

A bulky box shape loomed in the shadows behind that tent. Nearly the height of the tent itself, the armored box bore a long horizontal nozzle; chains of interlinked metal plates ran over toothed rollers as a carriage along each side. It was a flame-thrower. Aimed toward the south and lit by two paltry torches, one roller was absent—a raw black socket. Tracks in the churned dirt told me that drunks had climbed on the machine, kicked violently at the damaged treads, sent its flame shooting up well into the air like a beacon.

*This*, I thought, is a night of possibilities. I fingered my chest-knife, looking at the flamethrower. I wondered if there were any engineers capering within that tent. The machine was too crude for true Osa work. Likely built of stolen and impro-vised parts—and no less dangerous to us—the Marsh-bloated Nandos would not want true Osa to know of it. Careless as the smugglers had been, I thought. I stepped from my pool of shadow.

A voice barked at me. I spun, chest-knife tucked along my arm, and barked back. I was shouting at a dull-looking Marsh sentry. He didn't even have his sword out nor his bow to hand! I answered with classic Nando procedure: I shouted a string of abuse for his slovenliness, I swore at careless latrine-diggers and stupid sentries, perfectly loud enough to wake everyone in camp. I had filth on my robes to account for, after all. No one came

out to check the uproar. It was standard procedure in a camp of
sick sullen Marshman recruits.

"Don't know you," he grunted and backed away mumbling
as if to walk away, but I saw tension in the motion. I was ready
when his legs tensed and his body drove abruptly sidewise like a
frog into a shadow. I collided with him at a counter-angle and
added a thump of my pommel to quiet him. In the same motion
as killing him I swung him into the pool of gloom behind a
one-man tent and let him down.

I slipped inside the dim tent. It was empty; a small oil lamp lit
a table as if its owner just left—more carelessness. I read the
slates stacked on a small scarred table and replaced them exactly
as I'd found them. The camp's flamethrower was indeed built of
scrap parts, secretly; the slates were requisitions for more "guerrilla thrower parts" direct from Manoloki. His Nandos meant to
try it on Tannese before they rose up and used it against the Osa.
I slipped out and continued my ugly tasks along the arc of five
darkened one-man tents.

The sixth tent was lit. After I listened to conversation between
two men of intelligence and planning ability, I walked around
and went straight in: I couldn't ignore such competence. I pulled
the tent flap shut and gave them an old Nando-sign: *quiet*. The
quartermaster and the infantry trainer simply blinked at me.

A scaddaman's real talent was hitting two simultaneous tar-
gets. I gave them no time to cry out. The oil lamps burned on
serenely while I retrieved my blades. Then I searched the tent.

The noisy command tent was next. I wrapped myself in one of
the dead men's robes and strolled behind the command tent to
the shadow side of the flamethrower. An oil lamp went with me,
tucked under my stolen robe. The fringes of the robe began to
singe, stink, and burn. My hand stumbled over metal flamethrower plates, at last turned a stolen key correctly in a lock.

The thrower guards never noticed me. They were peering
through a back tent-slit at the festivities within. I heard a dancer
announced within the large festival tent and the roar of drunks:
Yali of the Sixteen Bells. It seemed Yali was very successful
with her bells and dances, because the guards were groaning
softly and scrabbling, arguing to see, and doing all the other
things soldiers do at such provocation.

I felt up under the flamethrower lock panel for the type of fuel
crevices that could destroy Osa flamethrowers. This one was a
fair copy, wonderful luck. I stuffed burning rags from my stolen

outrobe into three fuel vents and dropped the oil lamp into the main fuel tube. The rags smoked. A flare of fire started up like a tongue from different holes in the metal armoring. My heels drove at the ground. Away!

I was moving in the slow dreamlike state I'd felt in other attacks and raids: I spun and ran out of that place for my life. As I plunged past, I heard the soldiers swearing softly at each other by the tent and wrestling one another for view of Yali.

*"Fire!"* I screamed, to panic them. Two men turned their heads in surprise at my passage, then I was past. I dove into a dead man's tent for better shield.

The night roared into fireballs of brilliance. In that scalding glare I saw a man start up from blindly shaking a corpse inside the tent. His mouth was outlined, shouting, in that lurid glare. My left scadda spun at him. In the next heartbeat all was black night again, and my ears rang with explosion shock. I swung my head, searching for any movement before me.

A second fireball shook the night. In that light, the shouter lay on his back beside the other corpse. I groped forward on my knees into a hot puddle of fluid, wrenched free my scadda, wiped it, and ran outside into reddish light licking down to darkness. Men ran wildly past. I jostled into the crowd, all of us stumbling toward the billows of fire. I shouted panicky Marsh dialect words and slipped off toward the east, plunging down into meadows among the picket line of screaming ganas. I swung my stolen robes, charred blood-soaked rags, at the beasts, and increased the panic. I jerked ropes free, shouting in Marsh dialect that the commander and all his Nandos were dead.

Herdmen ran everywhere about me, dragging officers' ganas, erratically changing direction, while only one man in the lot shouted for order and tried to keep us bunched together under command. When I stumbled close on him, shouting and peering over a lamp in the dark, I gripped his arm, babbling as if panicked; he patted me soothingly. Then he saw all the splashed blood . . . Competent man, I thought regretfully. I took away his lamp and killed him.

The ganas stampeded when I took the lamp and torched some brush alight. I walked carefully away from the burning brush into the deep grass, sensing ahead with eyes, toes, and thin bootsoles for dry brush and branches that might crackle and betray me. I'd scrambled one of many gana lines, but stampede could shatter this camp—which might topple other parts of Manoloki's army.

Marshmen clattered through the woods and rode along shouting at each other, loosing off arrows at shadows in the grassy brush. I sat quietly under brambles and watched. When three men made to ride right through me, wild arrow flight leading, I gave the scream of a wounded redbuck nearly underfoot and scattered them. They fled back toward camp.

I would have fled, too, if a wounded buck started up under my gana's hooves screeching like that; wounded bucks, with their nocturnal sight, and in this season still carrying their breeding-horns to fight wild dog packs, were dangerous. I adjusted my boots and climbed slowly through deeper wooded ravines, seeing by starlight; the dappled shapes were faint and confusing. Once I fell loosely, quietly, over a deadfall and rolled through mud; I'd reached my stream. I came up screaming yedda lion calls, a snarling, rising whine that ended in a grunt.

Strengam's man screamed back a reply as I crossed the little stream. Yedda calls should stampede any followers I might have picked up; but it also spooked our ganas. He had to drag the beasts along. We met in the open, in the cold running water.

"Glad you waited past that explosion," I said.

He said dryly, "I figured it was your way of announcing yourself. So I got the beasts ready to move."

I chuckled, bent over and drank deeply in cupped hands, then wrestled my way onto my nervous mare. The yedda calls wouldn't fool skilled woodsmen, but I thought it helped increase the confusion. The camp uproar was audible this far away and getting louder.

No point in getting *caught* in their chaos—so our ride back to Caladrunan's camp became a reckless crash through ravines. I rode low in my saddle, shadows and dappled light flowed over our backs. Branches cracked across my face and back, but I didn't care. At one point I charged a confused Marshman patrol. I shouted news of their disaster and left them scattered in a panic behind us. Safely away, Strengam's best man laughed out loud triumphantly behind me. His relief was nothing to the wine-headed rush I was feeling.

I pulled my mare up to the fierce shrilling of our own perimeter ganas, challenging us. My beast barely checked, let out the herd-call like a squealing kettle, and lunged through their startled line. I laughed when my escort soldier started shouting our exploits back at the sentries.

"Stay clear," I roared, warning, over the shrill whistle blasts

of my mare. She charged down the trail into camp, straight at a
knot of officers. They stood gaping beside the mess tent. For the
sheer thundering in my chest, I screamed a yedda lion call,
tweaked my beast's nose-lines to curb her—and my gana shot up
on her hocks before them, climbing the air in parade display as
pretty as the fanciest cavalry. My filthy robes flew back, my
Upai boots flashed beaded lights under the torches. Clods of mud
and grass flew back off my harness as the mare whirled on
hindquarters, forelegs thrashing the air and all the while screaming like a howling spirit.

"*Hai iro huuup,*" I shouted, free hand slapping her neck in
praise. The mare shrilled like a showy parade beast and lashed
out at nothing with her forehooves. I laughed.

Rafai stood shouting to one side among archers. Bowcords
drew back. Grim giant, Rafai gripped a naked sword. Proper
herd call or not, I could have been *any* crazed rider on a stolen,
mud-spattered Tannese beast; and he meant to stop me.

"*Huup hupo io,*" I shouted at the mare, and along with her I
gave the thunderous bass territorial roar—which was seconded
by their own tethered beasts. The officers looked shocked: Well,
it *did* take a Harper to get the rumble of it to curl the toes like the
genuine call. My mare dropped to all four legs and snorted,
shaking her horns threateningly, while I caught three fast breaths.
Then my beast backed and hooked her horns and spun about
twice, reared, lunged—and spun to a brief stop in a scrape and
snap of dirt. I'd expected that. Instantly my air expelled as a
shout: "Rafai, message to Keth and Strengam. Tell them the
southern enemy camp is disordered, running for the pass!"

Rafai stared up, mouth open. "*Naga?*"

But the mare was bucking again. Rafai must have seen me
only as a shapeless dark mass in the mare's saddle. I was
covered with dung and grass and mud from my crawling circuits;
leaves from the woods stuck to me; there was blood on my belly.
There seemed to be more of it as I moved, but I didn't think
much about it. I shook the mare's neck to make her behave, but
she rolled a wild eye at Rafai's voice and took a notion to hump
and buck and thrash among tents, tearing her horns at tents and
ropes and washlines. Men scattered back from her horns.

"*Askap io Teot!*" I shouted down at them, slapping her
shoulder. That beast was no more ready to be tame than I was.
Between locked jaws my molars clicked each time we shot up
into the air and jolted down. She thundered up and down tent

rows roaring the bass territorial cry until I pulled her up in a long
dirt-purling skid before Caladrunan's tent.

"*Io Teot!*" I shouted. My beast climbed the sky, screaming,
and danced down side to side until she came to a sudden, jolted
stop, whuffing. Iron hands gripped her nose-lines close.

Caladrunan straightened, grasping the head leathers, and held
her by main force. She jerked, grunted, her horns quivered; she
whuffed air fiercely and sighed. Then she tented one hip up,
resting on the other three legs, and stood still. Docilely she
accepted the lump of datefruit the Lord of Tan offered. She knew
him well.

Round eyes stared at us from all angles. Really, she had been
about to stop bucking anyway, but only he and I knew that—and
his success vastly impressed the watching eyes. He patted my
mare's greedy nose. "Rafai, that message to Strengam and
Keth—make it an order to attack the southern camp at will." He
turned and put the lines of my beast into the hand of a guard . . .
and he crooked his forefinger, once, at me.

I slid down in front of him. The Lord of Tan wore blue silken
bed robes with Devour strapped to his waist in its black war belt.
While my beast was led away, jerking proudly at her lines and
snorting, I handed Caladrunan the scroll I'd taken. I pointed
northward. "You could kill the rest of them tonight before the
other camps reinforce them." From some distance my mare
shrilled and kicked, and then the night was quiet. Eyes stared at
me from all sides. "I blew up a flamethrower in the middle of
their camp."

"Indeed." Caladrunan snapped his fingers at two rookies.
"Bring clean clothes for the Sati, water, and wine."

I slapped my chest. "A little mess, a little blood."

"Whose blood?" Tanman asked gravely.

I didn't answer him, only slapped my clothes gleefully and
grinned. The stains on my scadda pommels were obvious. Therin
appeared, all sudden bright curls, behind his father; the men
were not so absorbed in *me* that they impeded Tanman's Heir.
Therin asked, "How many did you kill?"

"Oh, I lost count. I'm unsure how many the flamethrower
took out—they were having a party in front of it. With any luck I
took out lots of senior men from *all* their camps." Blissfully
unmilitary report, that. I saw Pitar standing at one side, a slate
dangled from his lax hand. I snatched the slate and chalk from
him and began writing. "Liege, I doubt we will have trouble

taking that camp. Now *these* names, I killed by hand. We won't likely have trouble with Nando assassins for awhile; they'll be busy fighting each other for new ranks! And I saw *this* in a tent, and overheard *this* in a tent—'' I scratched chalk across the slate, jigging from one foot to the other because I could not stand still; my body itched and tingled all over.

Devour's pommel and quillons glinted silver as the Lord of Tan tucked his thumbs in his belt. I laughed at the sight, tossed him my slate, and shouted gleeful quotes about his sword Devour from Histories—which made the Tannese glance uneasily at one another. Caladrunan gripped his hand firmly on my arm and gestured me to go into his tent and sit down, but I couldn't sit. Officers crowded in after us. I paced around answering questions; about a bell pass later, Strengam Dar came riding in personally, grimy with soot stains and dirt from riding.

The leathery old man said, "The pass is clear, Liege, if you care to advance."

He added in his grave soft voice, "Approximately three camps combined forces to put out a fire in the southernmost camp. They were failing in that when we fell upon them. We—*ahem*—also managed to capture two flamethrowers in the eastern camp as it weakened. The enemy is now a disorganized mixed body the size of one camp derived from all three. My outriders report the enemy flees northward into difficult burned-over terrain. A third of Keth's cavalry took up pursuit. For the sake of his beasts and short supply trains, he said he'd halt chase and establish camp at the debouchment into the burned lands, with your consent."

Caladrunan looked up at the tall old man and began to laugh softly. "Oh, that's good enough for tonight, yes." Strengam gave a long, slow grin. Keth strode in then, shaking off dust and cursing. He reported that his outriders told him the way was clear as far as we cared to ride. Since Keth used no advance Upai scouts, we'd get no helpful further details. For a moment all was silence. Then Caladrunan said slowly, "Therin, would you pour these men wine and Naga's—ah, rock-liquor. I think it appropriate to celebrate now. *Lightly.*"

Keth's eyes glittered once at me and turned aside.

I let out a whoop and laughed, *"A'afidir for me!"* and Caladrunan's hard fist punched me in the shoulder, and I punched him lightly back, and Rafai was slapping my other shoulder. Then we all sat down to talk tactics. But at no time—I was still clever in my giddiness—did I forget Keth's pale eyes watching me.

We moved supply wagons now, using torches, ahead of the troops. The faster infantry would catch up all too soon in daylight, pass them, and promptly slow down. Better to keep speed up. The men began breaking camp around us as we talked. Whenever I walked out of Caladrunan's tent for a breath of fresh air, the night was still as a virgin's veil. The noises of men talking, the humming of movement, excitement, and kicked-up dust rose against that starlit stillness.

In the predawn watch, during which I was slugging *a'afidir* straight from its bottle, Pitar told me, "I love you handing me a camp reorganization in the dead of night!" I laughed at his disgusted expression, and then footmen and underofficers and messengers and trainee boys, they were *all* standing around me outside Caladrunan's tent asking questions. Rafai had to fend off men clustering too tightly round me. Everyone knew what had happened. Caladrunen had to send them all back to work. And he dragged me inside and gave me stern orders.

It was just dawn when I bathed, dressed partway, and sat down on clean rugs. At first light, when gray crept through the slit between the tent flaps and across the carpeted floor, he knelt beside me examining a cut across my ribs. A steaming bandage lay on a clean table next to him. He frowned, probing. A metal fragment, perhaps thrown by the flamethrower, had gone through my robes and leathers and embedded itself between two ribs. I hadn't even felt the impact in the tumble and tussle of the moment—nor later.

But I felt it *now*! Caladrunan probed and lifted up a thread of coarse silk from the wound, then another and another. The thick silk fibers woven into my robes did not break or cut under impact, only buried themselves in a wound. If these fibers were drawn out carefully, they captured all the shrapnel within the threads. That was their purpose. "Now," he said, holding the threads.

I breathed. They'd given me a bowl of cupflower for this, a disgusting weak dose. Now I swigged the horrid, badly-made Tannese *a'afidir* with my free hand. I spluttered at the taste and wiped my mouth. "All right," I said and stopped breathing.

Therin held my shoulder and arm braced hard back for his father to dig my ribs. The boy could *never* hold me against a real flinch, but I didn't wish to injure him, and so I held still. I refused to let anyone else at those ribs. Not even Rafai qualified for digging at my ribs. I was drunk with victory and *a'afidir,* but the Lord of Tan had shamelessly encouraged me at it. He refused all my offers to stand guard, but truly he should have warned his son about me and drink.

Poor Therin had asked me, some time ago but still a long way past sobriety, if I felt anything for the men I'd killed this night. "No!" I had shouted, laughing. Weaving on my feet, I recited a history of crimes committed by the men I'd murdered. During the worst ones I had pointed at their shocked Tannese faces and laughed hysterically. Caladrunan told me, firmly, that I was ruder drunk than sober—and sober was bad enough. I laughed myself silly at that. It was later they made me sit still for their amateur herbalist efforts.

Caladrunan passed a knife through a lamp flame and bent again to my side. Therin tightened his grip. I swallowed the mouthful of liquor sloshing in my teeth, and I thought, I've felt wounds as hard as this before—they both look entirely too somber about the whole thing, I should cheer them up! It's not nearly so serious as they seemed to think. So I began a song, a favorite of Lado Kiselli's, the old song about a pig, a farmer, and a traveling pleasure woman; I knew at least thirty-five verses. It was also the foulest, smuttiest, funniest song in Tan.

Caladrunan's lips twitched. He put down the knife. *"Naga,"* he said. He looked pointedly at his son. I looked the Lord of Tan right in the eye and sang on, and drank.

Therin said, "Liege, I've heard it before. From Lado."

His father started to laugh, and finally wiped his brow and picked up the knife and flamed it clean again. When he paused, I sang more. He finished his probing between verses. When all the last silk strands were gathered into his hand, he pulled, and the metal sliver slid neatly into his palm, captured on a patch of silk stained red from my body. He bound a pad of silk over the hole. Instantly I pushed away both their hands and staggered up to my feet.

I blinked. Voices filled the tent. Concerned faces—a lot of them, all different—swam queasily about in space. I drank the last strong resin-scented drop of *a'afidir* and tossed the bottle aside and walked forward, untidily dropping the stupid, badly fit clothes impeding my body. Nobody would dare attack me, not now; I was that far from using any brains I had. I stumbled down on the fuzzy furred end of Caladrunan's own bed and grandly waved all the faces to go away. Vaguely I felt Caladrunan pull furs over my nakedness. I must have muttered something irritably as I closed my eyes, but I couldn't think what I had said. I slept the sleep of the just. Dreams dared not come to me *that* day.

Reti had taught his trainees that drink hit hard and never held a skirmish line against an enemy. All over again, I learned he was right. When I woke up, I was jostling about rhythmically under a blinding glare.

"What in the Name of the Sixteen Whips of Sitha's Torture Chambers!" I said strongly against this outrageous condition. I had a sickening hangover, my ribs hurt horribly, and I had to relieve myself now. I sat up before I lost all will to do so.

That was a mistake. A vast mistake. I clung limply to some shuddering wall, eyes shut. I was being jostled by the lurching of a clumsy contraption only vaguely of the cart persuasion.

The Lord of Tan said, out of hazy glare, "Not feeling well?"

My hands bumped against things. I mumbled curses and crawled the length of the cart over a bulky load, banging up hard against a leather sack of intolerant materials. I tried not to clutch my ribs and howl. After awhile I squinted open my eyes. I was looking over the end of a cart at a grinning escort. They hailed me enthusiastically with loud salutes.

"Bastards," I said, wincing. I peered round and saw Caladrunan's bull gana prancing alongside the cart. The bull was decked out in full victory regalia; so was Caladrunan; so was the cart I rode upon. I was naked, except for a bandage around my ribs. I cursed them all, peed over the end of the cart, crawled back to my furs, and tried hard to make the world go away again.

It was impossible. The cart jounced, shuddered, bobbed, and heaved sickeningly. I mustered strength and indignation to demand, "Who put me in this thing? Where's my gana?"

Caladrunan's voice said, "I put you there myself. You were so drunk you fell all over, honking like a bull in a rut and mashing your claws in our faces. Wasn't I considerate? I kept you from making a public spectacle of yourself when you sleepwalked—or drunk-walked—through the officers' mess at dawn this morning."

"Ah no." I groaned and rolled over, and squinted my eyes tight shut. I knew I was lucky to get into this wagon; anyone else would have had to shift for himself or lay with screaming wounded. The thought didn't make me feel better.

He said, "For the hero of the day you seem very unhappy."

"Shut up," I mumbled into my furs, but not very loud.

"Is it possible that you mixed doses of cupflower, rock-liquor, and distilled wine spirits—and noisily ignored *all* advice against so doing? Is it possible that you ignored the herbalist's advice completely and drove him off, publicly, threatening him with a gana strap in great comedic wit? Is it possible you refused to be treated by anyone but a royal amateur—dare I add, that you loudly challenged anybody else to dare lay hand to you? Or that in front of everyone you defied me—*me!*—to guess what you did with my Upai scouts, and *still* they haven't returned from whatever caper you put them to?"

I uttered one of the purpler and rarer Tannese curses, and he laughed at me. The jostling went on longer than any human body could endure. I said, "No wonder the wounded scream. Where's my clothes? Where's my gana? This is—" Several rude and explicit words finished it off. Cupflower and wine spirits, chased with *a'afidir*, would do that to anyone. Of course, Caladrunan had to make a show of scooping me out of the cart, getting my robes on straight, and plunking me, limp as boiled potweeds, in my saddle.

Tannese soldiers loved to see their heroes properly treated and feted and made much of—a mood that did not allow me any merciful quiet. They loved outrageous heroes, and all their noise would make me act that way. They *should* have seen me drummed out for dereliction of my duties. Drunk as I'd been, I could no more have stopped assassins than I could have walked through any idiot mess tent—no matter what *he* said I'd done. The escort soldiers were all grinning until I could count back teeth. Ah, Goddess, everyone must have seen me like this. Especially Keth Adcrag. Ahh, stupidity. Mess tents, no less . . . I closed my eyes.

When I finally squinted my eyes open to look ahead, I saw that Caladrunan rode on one side, Therin on my other. At the look on my face, they burst into guffaws. Well, I'd been stupid enough to drink alone. I rubbed my forehead tenderly, fearing my head might fall right off my shoulders. Caladrunan was right: I had been an utter idiot. But I could have sworn that he put that *a'afidir* bottle into my hand, told me to drink it . . . a direct order . . . A wry voice in my head snorted: Never again. *Never*.

Tannese merely thought it funny when a man drank and acted silly. Mess tents . . . By now, the whole thing would be all over

Caladrunan's army: that Caladrunan's Sati came back from a raid
and got raving *drunk*, with exact details of what silly things
Caladrunan's Sati had *done* while stone-blind out of himself.
Now they'd retell what that Sati did when he woke up *sorry* next
day. Keth Adcrag would make every bit out of it that he could. I
groaned.

Caladrunan glanced over and said, "Don't look so sour, Naga.
You were doing all right until you took off your clothes."

I groaned again.

"I think the officers forgave it when they saw the bandages."

I groaned louder. That meant enemies knew where to hit me. I
said sarcastically, "Medicinal numbing, you told me, eh, Liege?
I suppose you'll get to tease me about the mess tent part that
came later."

"No—that was earlier. That's why the officers saw you naked. You made a ruckus of it, and I needed their help. When I
carried you out of the mess, you were *not* pleased. And they had
to help me sit you down for bandaging."

Therin smiled at me as he rode. He had a good seat on his
mare despite his lack of real Plains-style training. But I didn't at
all like the smirk on his face. He said, "I think they forgave
you, Noble-born, after they saw the flamethrower crater."

"I don't remember any crater," I said glumly.

"You were snoring," Caladrunan said.

Messengers rode urgently to Caladrunan then, and the humor
went out of his face at the tone of Strengam's message. With
forty soldiers as escort, we rode the rough merchant road past
footmen trudging in clouds of dust.

My gana jolted along beside Caladrunan. I breathed carefully,
settled my legs firmer in my saddle braces, and turned my mind
from pain. I could guess what we'd see—for in the northern
borderlands, the clear Tejed River grew black. Where the Osa
burned, it ran utterly, completely, sooty black.

# CHAPTER
# = *13* =

THE DAY, HOT and airless, did not feel like early spring. The light grew dull all of a sudden, tainted with an alarming orange filtering over the sky, like a soot cloud from a grainfield fire. We rode along the river to reach Strengam's camp, and left the last of the famous long limestone river plateaus behind us. The trail climbed red clay bluffs which rose high above the riverbed.

"There," Strengam said. "*That* was prime oak and pine woods the scouts now call the Forest of Ash."

"In the gray rain that melts people's souls," I quoted grimly. "Tie cloth over your faces and the beast's mouths."

We stared at a broad swatch of black spread over the land like a stain, hill after hill beyond the Tejed. Jagged tree stumps speared the sky along the hillcrests. Logs lay fallen like broken black straws on the lower ravines; already rain gullies and deep gouges dug into the flanks of the ridges. As our mounts rolled their shoulders to climb the bluff trail, our sightlines grew into many cairn's distances over the depressing ash drifts of the far bank.

Ash and blackened stumps rose mutely eastward to the highland border with Marsh. The horizon was a flat black line; the river was ink-stained as far as we could see it to the north.

At the ford we stared at the remains of a village. On our side of the broad Tejed River, birds sang, grass grew between mounds of blown ash. On the far side, the earth lay bare but for rain-packed gray drifts, scatters of cracked masonry, heaps of rubble. The heat had been so intense that only shards of bone showed the position of bodies strewn in defense of the place. Good clay bricks had melted and shattered under the heat. We could all see the great scored slag-arcs of flamethrowers charred deep into the loamy earth. Caladrunan grated, *"When?"*

I coughed. "Before that big storm—the tracks are rained on. The last report from here was dated two days before the storm."

Looking outward, the Lord of Tan's eyes flared yellow a moment, and hooded. "They drove away in their machines laughing."

I leaned forward in my saddle. My mare whoofed; she didn't like the smell that hung funereally close. "The Osa could have run down from Pass of Bones in the time between the ford report and the thunderstorm. I wonder if they planned this burning to keep us from turning eastward. You see this orange light—new ash in the wind since the storm. They still burn. They march and burn."

Caladrunan said to Strengam, "Your scouts did excellent work to find this so far ahead of the main column. I was concerned when the local reports weren't coming in." He turned his beast, glancing at the sun. "We'll water and camp at a cleaner site than this." Then he looked at me. "Not a word," he warned.

I rode silently. He would camp beside Keth's cavalry. Crag troops moved at our east edge, still stiffly part of the Army; for all his plots, Keth Adcrag expected politics, and the Tannese Army's need for numbers against the Osa alliance, to keep him immune. Looking at the evidence as impartially as Caladrunan did, Keth wasn't even involved. He saw an isolated cell of saboteurs here, a raid there—ordered from outside by the likes of that wily new Osa general. Nothing I'd done made a difference—either in camp or here. I glanced at the ashlands and shuddered. My small raid had been petty revenge against the kind of horror this fire had wreaked, raging on for cairns upon cairns' distance. Violence beat like a drum-pulse in my ears.

We turned northward parallel to the blackened river, unable to cross where we'd planned. As one bell pass of march and the next passed, Caladrunan took his escort scouts in sharp, darting forays up the bluffs and to the river, but the eastern hills rolled past unchanged. The fire damage thinned only at western river's edge to show patches of seared life, small green sprouts struggling through layers of muck.

Men attempting to ride scout along the far bank threw up choking clouds of ash until finally they gave up. Fine particles of ash drifted on the wind and got into everything. The next ford was the same, lashed with arched charred marks in the soil, broken bricks, and bone remnants. Detachments stayed behind to bury the dead. I squinted into the dull brownish afternoon light. This broad fire started somewhere too distant to be sighted from our camps at the time; and until today, the wind shed its ash the wrong way to warn us. The Osa might even have planned that, checking prevailing winds.

Too late to help any victims, we just followed and read the treadmarks that rolled north toward the Osa root-hold at Pass of Bones. Constantly, new batches of Upai scouts rode out of the brush in scattered groups, silently joining both Strengam's scouts and our own contingent. I glanced at Caladrunan. He did not seem to notice the scouting groups had grown in size, nor recognize past their face cloths who these new Upai were. His brows were smudged with sweat and blown ash; his features set hard, turned inward, as if he fought some deep, acute pain.

I turned my head at a noise. The brush acquired movement. Two Upai stepped into the trail before our lead pair of soldiers.

No Tannese had spotted them until then. The lead escort riders jerked about in their saddles, further startling their otherwise calm beasts. The ganas whuffed and reared a little; but the dark, watchful Upai neither stirred nor blinked before them.

"Liege Lord of Tan," they said in drawling, blurred, singing tones. "Smugglers told stories to us."

I thought, so *that* is how I sound to Tannese ears.

Caladrunan rode through his troop. He said to the scouts in stilted Upai, "You were only to track them! Who told you to *attack* smugglers?"

"Tokori Efresa," one of the scouts replied slowly, as if speaking to an imbecile. "Ask *him*, Lord of Tan."

But I'd sidled away into the brush to ask my own questions.

Caladrunan squinted back at his Tannese. "Where'd Naga go? I—need a translator." He knew exactly who was the Upai called Tokori Efresa.

Tokori Efresa's name and neck bore a large Cragman bounty.

I thought, Goddess preserve my hide and hooves, *now* I pay for helping Tan in my particular way. I finished whispering with Hagavu and stepped out again. A freshly startled Tannese rider swore at his nervous mount and growled, "Where did *he* come from—?"

Caladrunan hissed at me, "These Upai attacked smugglers. You went off on that camp raid *alone*—"

I laughed, thinking what the Upai would say to that! Not a
pleasant laugh. *Blind-faces*, these scouts called the Tannese. The
varied muck on my leathers that night told all. I heard the
Tannese shift uneasily in their saddles. The Lord of Tan snapped,
"Don't laugh like that! Some wondered if you were out witching
on that raid."

"Witching," I said, amused. In Upai: "Bring the sack."

Hagavu, stolid-faced as stone, opened a stained leather sack.
One by one he lifted out captured Nando face cloths. Each scrap
of cloth, mantle of Nando anonymity in that mercenary's broth-
erhood, was marked with a Upai death symbol scrawled in
blood; some were already too red-stained for the marking to
show. I murmured, "Manoloki *was* actually with these Nandos
awhile, but the old bat himself got away."

Caladrunan looked at the blood mark. "What does this mean?"

I laughed again. The Tannese behind him sat in their saddles
in odd rigid postures; two young soldiers lifted their hands in
witch-warding signs. I said, "Blood taken for blood spilled in
the past. After we take that proof of kill, warriors do not handle
the dead again." Then, over the violence pulsing in my fingers,
I murmured, "But the living, they take longer . . ."

"Why do you keep these—trophies? That's not Upai!"

"Since the Osa murdered my clan at Redspring Hold, it *is* our
way. The Women's Council keeps count over the years: When it
is equal, blood for blood, then peace can begin. There was a
great debate—I should recite it for you—over the allotment of
ten dead allies for one murdered Upai."

"How will Upai ambassadors argue this quota to me, now I
know of it? How will the *Osa*?" Caladrunan said, oddly stilted
even in Tannese. "I would see these Nandos. As they fell. For
myself. *You* go on to setting up camp."

"Hagavu will guide you." I wasn't pleased, but our enemies
were in such disarray, that the Upai and his Tannese escort were
sufficient protection against any scattered Nandos. "Women are
burying the dead—their leader will be a lady of bloody lips
called Tuzo, my wife. I don't know how they've cleared the
camp-of-questioning. Hagavu won't go into the killing ground;
he'll just show you the way." I explained to Hagavu what the
Lord of Tan wanted, endured the scout's shocked protest. Hagavu
thought such a Tannese request perverted: to want to examine the
dead! Then I told Caladrunan, "We do not harm innocent outsiders. The Osa allies do. Manoloki's Nandos attack children and

old people in villages, in camps, asleep, when they can. But among Manoloki's men we are greatly feared—*we* prefer to take his prime officers, his smugglers. They are prouder and go down harder.'' I looked up at him in the dusk. ''I don't think you're going to like looking at the Nandos, Liege.''

He said, with bits of iron rasping in his tone, ''I don't worry about the dead. The *living* disturb me now. Set up my camp well away from this ash-land and *stay* there until I return. Does your guide speak Tannese, to explain things to me?''

''No, he doesn't. This will prevent misunderstanding among words. Few can translate Upai for tender Tannese opinions. Upai don't like stories of the dead dragged into the private life of their tents.'' Hagavu knew Tannese, but he'd never linger over dead enemies, and he would never show sign that he *could* speak to people who asked such things of him.

A muscle jumped in Caladrunan's jaw. He turned his beast to ride away after Hagavu, who had mounted up as stolidly as ever. Caladrunan's face had gone as dour and grim as his Tannese sandstone walls. I stood aside as most of the Tannese escort rode past. I thought, Caladrunan already *knew,* when he asked, that he would hate what he found on the killing ground. I sighed. Undoubtedly my wife Tuzo would exult in her revenge and dance hideously before the Tannese soldiers. Oh, she had taken enemy blood, as I'd promised she would. But bloody and savage, whoever she chose for her bed, she would not sleep this night with me: I set up Caladrunan's tent with the straggle of tired escort.

The Lord of Tan looked even worse when he rode up to the camp and his tent a full bell pass later. He spoke to no one. As he dismounted, his face looked so drained it was gray, a pallor under his windburned face. He looked once at me and strode past. His escort occupied their hands with gear and looked away. I ducked inside after him, dropped the tent flap shut, and stood waiting.

The yellow eyes stared into mine—whitened as pale as noon summer's sun with fury. His hand hovered beside my face. His whole frame seemed to vibrate. *''I will not,''* he gritted at last, ''succumb to striking you for what I saw.''

''It might make you feel better,'' I said calmly.

His hands closed on the front of my robes, and he dragged me up and shook me, rattling my bones. His face congested to dark in a way I had never seen before. He picked me up, bounced me down onto my feet, hard—and violently spun away with his back to me. All his muscles under the robes stood out, gnarled taut.

I was impressed. *Now*, he turned his back to me; now, after what he'd seen on the killing ground! He must know what roared in my ears yet. That rage had not left me—not once since the raid, stoked hotter in riding those ash-lands. In the back of my head, I still recited chants for the control of temper, a thread of calming melody.

He snatched up a slate and smashed it down in a smack of shattering stone. His hands clenched: He was still struggling not to hit me. Caladrunan spun around to glare at me. "Vicious ridgerunner murders—" he said, jabbing a forefinger toward me. "There must never be such a sight caused by your hand in Tan. Never! Swear it."

I folded my arms, turned partly away; I stared into the middle distance past him. Chant murmured in my head. He picked up a slate, breathing heavily, extending it toward me: report on what they found out there. Arm extended, he spoke at last—in a raspy voice. "Do I have to send you back to the desert? Could you not stop the Upai at this . . . this monstrous ferocity?"

I said softly, "Blood for blood is the Upai requirement."

"Not like that!" he shouted. He tossed away the slate on his bed, a slap of flat on fur: Both the sound and his expression were eloquent with revulsion. He almost collapsed onto a stool.

"Naga," he groaned, with his head in his hands. "What have you done? Oh Goddess, those bodies . . . Keth sent me a slate reciting rumors; *he* knew before I did, before your murdering Upai ever came out of the brush! Maybe some Nandos escaped to their once-kin among his men for help. The Cragmen already have wild rumors. They exaggerate, saying Upai—especially *you*—go out murdering anyone in your path. They'll use such things as proof of all their stories. Is it true? Are there other such things you never told me?"

I whispered, "*No* smugglers escaped. Traitors among the Upai—or Upai misled about who they're helping—talked, that is the *only* way Keth could know." I turned carefully, half-blinded with the rage I strained and struggled so strongly against. Slowly, stiffly, I knelt by him. I touched his hands. "Drin."

"Get *away*," he cried. His fingers tore at his hair. "How could you do—"

I bent my head slowly, stiffly, painfully. "If you war against

Osa successfully, then I will not offend your laws, Liege. The tortures were not at my wish; the Nandos didn't know enough to justify it. But it was my duty as Tokori to help my warriors, to preserve their lives. We grow fewer, of raids, of hunger, of illness. And they are my people," I said quietly. I was very, very angry.

"But knowingly you have offended against my laws! If they require such things of you, you must renounce it. Prove you're still human; renounce that title." He spat. "*Tokori.*"

Softly I told him, "It won't help. That is what I am, Drin. *I am* what you saw out there."

He moved so fast I simply let it happen. His arm caught me under the collarbones and swept me away toward the tent wall. "Go away!" he said, in a voice that shook and rose unevenly in pitch.

I hissed a little as my back rolled across saddlebags on the floor. Then I was up again on my feet automatically, hands clenched. And my rage melted in amazement: Caladrunan sat with his head in his hands, while tears flowed down his wrists. I straightened tiredly. Long past, I made the choice to swear Great Oath, and I would not change it. Whatever sacrifice the Upai wanted, in my life *kigadi* came first—and I had transgressed against him. I felt heartsick. All I wanted was for my friend to be at peace. Not *revolted* like this. "Drin—"

"Don't call me that." His voice stumbled out between hands.

"*Kigadi*," I murmured.

"Nor that!"

I said, "Liege. All right. What promise do you want of me?"

He squeezed his fingers hard into his face until the tips went white. Finally, low and harsh, he said, "I've been a judge for years, Naga. I've seen some bad things in Judgments, in evidence, in the last few skirmishes out here. I thought I understood you. Understood the Osa." He made a muffled grieving noise, wiped hard at his eyes, and straightened as if his body hurt. At last, he continued sadly: "I never saw anything so inhuman. And you . . . how could anyone invent such things? If you want to do such things—if the Upai *want* you to do such things—"

I said levelly, "I can always be not-Upai."

He lifted his head with a jerk, staring at me. The tears had reddened his eyes. "They can't expect such monstrous—"

I said softly, "Yes. We have changed, *kigadi*. The Upai *you* knew, the Osa murdered them—those Upai are a people you will never see again." I spread my hands, clenched them. "I *would* unname myself. But it affects your alliance with them. They could call me *kotoka'epopi* for it, and deny all ties."

"They're monsters," he whispered.

"No," I said. "A very bitter and angry people, that is all."

"And what are you?" he cried out. "That you can allow—" his hand gestured wildly toward what he had seen out there, on the ground of testing, among the broken bodies and questions.

My head rose high. "I never meant you to think I was safely tamed when I am not, *kigadi*."

"Tamed!" He gave a rough choking noise.

I said, spreading my fingers, "I have shown you *malat*, the snake-trap noose. The rope here, the cut-brush spring to noose and lift the prey. I also showed you *mala*, the man-trap: the harmless noose, the thread-trigger, the weight to hold him high." My fingers diagrammed these things on the tent's brazier. I thrust my hands into stronger light, one finger bent like a claw. "This is *malavatu*, the trap with prong. The noose rises strongly, yanking up the man, but the rigid prong catches, guts as he moves past. Do you see?" My fisted right hand snapped past the claw fingers. I drew a line lightly from chin to groin.

Caladrunan looked strained and white. "Yes, I see."

"I am *malavatu*. I'm not a soldier as Tannese know it, never was, never pretended to be. I'm a trap set to kill Osa and those who serve Osa. Do not set aside use of my skills. The Osa do not abide by any rules you know. Do not let them use your honor and your grace against you!"

He looked down at his hands. "Recently Orena warned me about . . . purposes. Of forces in you. I promised I'd try not to cross your purpose."

"Try!" I clutched my head. "Don't risk your country with such enemies by refusing to use me, or raids, or anything you can lay hand upon to help you, Liege!" At his expression I shouted, "If I thought you were Osa, I'd cut you in half, *one strike*, snap, like the sand-death viper. It is in my bones, it is bred in the blood!" Rage pulsed in my head.

"That would stop me feeling sorry for myself."

I gripped the lid of a locked traveling chest. Slowly, in a thick voice, I said, "Do not jest that way."

Oh yes, I had had dreams of him lain out like the rumpled corpses after a raid, his body no longer animated by the Goddess' silly magic jugglery. The traveling chest's wood bowed and cracked with two sharp reports under my fingers. My hand groped out, gripped the split pieces, crushed them together. I gritted, imploring him, "Do not jest about your death. I dream-dance, I see too much—I—"

His eyes flew up to mine.

I knew only one final way to avert a reliving born in such rage. I released the splintering pieces. Heavy, thick-headed and half-blind with emotion and rage, I lifted my open hands and turned slowly, deliberately, toward the hot brazier.

Powerful hands locked about my forearms: His hands would touch the metal first. I went rigid. He pivoted us both and plunged our arms into a bowl of washwater away from the brazier, gripped my hands there. I bent my head silently over the water, over rigid, tension-locked wrists. Visions of dried grain sheaves danced in my sight. *Pray,* she had said. I prayed. Hard.

Caladrunan's eyes looked like huge black holes in his shadowed face when I finally looked up at him. The scent of sweat and leather came up strongly from his robes. I drew in a deep hissing breath and straightened. "Better," I said.

He freed me and muttered, "So the stories about Sati rages were true."

"Any rage, at this stage, is a Sati rage. For any cause that can anger you. I was angry during the raid. I was angry at the ashlands. I did not say it lightly, that I was *malavatu.*"

His hands gripped around my neck, cupping my head, "Naga, promise you will *never*—"

I closed my eyes.

He drew in a deep breath, let it out in a long shudder of a sigh. "At least get those Upai women sent safely back to the refugee camps where they ought to have been all along. And contemplate changing yourself from *malavatu,* for my sake."

I looked up. "*Kigadi,* you will need *malavatu.* You will need me thus. There are not many of the breed, and you will need it."

But he was silent.

Five days later, Keth spoke loudly at me outside the officers' mess, acting a less than humble supplicant. It seemed his brother's new Upai wife had rolled herself into a fetal ball in a Pigeon Hold courtyard and refused to move, still in her wedding finery. They were most annoyed over the finery. Keth asked that I go reason her into decent wifely behavior: Persuade her to learn

Crag dialect, to dress Crag, to be less wild. He sneered over how difficult, insane, and filthy the woman was.

I thought, *yes*, wifely behavior: I'd tell her to drive her private knife in that husband's flesh, and then escape!

My shocked fellow officers clearly thought the woman at fault, like a dog that savaged children. Keth seemed unashamed to say these things publicly to me. He might wish me to go see her under their tyranny—or, on the road there, ambush me. Caladrunan nodded permission, with a concerned expression. Out of mercy, or simply desire to see her, I went. But I warned both Caladrunan and his guards what trouble there might be in my absence, and I took an insultingly huge escort of guards with me.

Keth's new-married brother apparently found nothing in Pigeon Hold worth his time; there were no signs of work on the defenses of the place. To call the place a Hold was to ignore the inroads of squalor on a once-gracious keep. We saw neither Keth's brother nor any noble of rank; inside, my men were not offered so much as well water. Otherwise, all was exactly as Keth described. The woman was rolled up in fetal despair in one muddy courtyard corner. Her face was still powdered with white, but smeared, and the powdered Cragmen colors around her eyes were run over her face with tears. Rafai behind me said softly, "Poor child."

She flinched. I said to her, in Upai, "I am not able to take you away, but I would if I could. I will try my best for you."

The woman began to weep, shielding her face. In another time, she'd have been the jewel of a Upai Imperial court, her blood second to mine in succession to rule. Now I wore road-draggled Tannese robes and knelt in a courtyard with her, while her tears dampened the dust—a woman trained in the desert way, she didn't make a sound. I questioned her. She whispered between her fingers, "The women, the women in that big town were terrible. They fought each other; they wanted to poison me, to beat me with a whip; they screamed and flew like hags, such women—"

"Has anyone hurt you?" I asked.

"Only stones, here and there, by the man," she whispered, and fell silent. Tannese noblemen would not dare take a pleasure woman over such virulent objections at home, let alone a wife. It made life intolerable in cramped Fortress quarters. Matriarchal Upai did not confound the peace and order of the tent that way.

Lost to fighting, men were few; if they must, Upai women chose dance-lovers for the sake of bearing children, and banded together as aunts to one another's youngsters. I said, "Would the man give you back? Could I ask the bride-price, and undo this thing?"

She turned her head toward me and saw my blue robe. She gave a squeak of horror and flinched away, muddy hands over her mouth. Her eyes went to my belt, my scaddas, and her body shook like a wild deer tied live to a rock-lion trap. She would not speak again. I told her how to escape Pigeon Hold, how to reach the nearest Upai scout camps cross-country. All this I whispered in Upai to her, and got no answer of her. When the Cragmen grew impatient, I told them curtly they had best send her back home to a Upai camp and put their other women in better order.

Their faces expressed scorn.

I sneered back. The greasy seneschal pointed at the road out, turned his back on me, and walked away. Rafai growled. I looked up at the archers marching the walls instead, and got my men into saddle. When Pigeon Hold's gates were locked shut after us, I looked at my escort soldiers and thanked Sitha I'd brought so many. I'd have died of an "accident" else.

Rafai said grimly, "Those Cragmen, they're animals. Close, that. Three, four less men with us, we'd be in chains. Or dead."

I agreed, calculating ambush sites on the road back. Futile to plead the woman's plight to Caladrunan; under Tannese contract law he could do nothing. It depressed me. "What did Keth want to hide from me today? There are simpler and less obvious ways."

Rafai looked back over the line of riders, scanned the terrain. "Maybe Keth wanted to pick a fight back at camp. He's such a child, he'd do it for Liege's attention."

"Nasty thought."

Rafai recited the roster of movement in the day's schedule; we'd rejoin Caladrunan eight roadcairns from the campsite we'd departed this morning. Nothing sounded especially suggestive.

I scowled. Keth's movements could never be called accounted for, not with the sort of verbal reports his officers gave the record auditors. Though promising young Tannese trainees had been sent to him, writing was beyond any of Keth's inner cabal. No one understood exactly what *happened* to trainees put in his cavalry.

And Keth really wasn't smart enough to know how the Upai

woman's slavery would rattle me. It had the smell of a clever man giving orders from afar, acting through a clumsy tool. Possibly a tool too stupid and ambitious to realize he was being used.

I mused out loud. "The honor guards are on high-density watches to protect our Liege in our absence. This trip might be just harrassment. But I don't think so. It's possible that cabal of Keth's spread fights or rumors in the mess tents while our best officers were at the meeting we've missed. We can find that out."

"Then why did he make sure *you* were gone? You haven't even got a command out here yet," Rafai said.

"I'll bet officers who Keth doesn't even know made odd suggestions in the tactical briefing, trying to push Keth's plans on Liege. Or just reinforcing certain parts of plans. It might be large-scale strategy the mastermind behind Keth wants to change." I looked up into Rafai's eyes coldly. "On *that* I have much to say." We watched for ambushes.

Nothing happened on the road. As expected, we reached camp too late for the tactical meeting; Caladrunan, looking harrassed, beckoned me aside. "Did Girdeth send anything new to you about that marriage offer that Agtunki talked her out of?"

Something unholy cold washed and prickled over my skin.

He raked at his hair and beard, squinting out of his tent at passing officers. "Keth insists she sent him a direct request to marry her dated only two days back, and the seal looks real enough. Even preliminaries would give him horrible prestige."

I touched Caladrunan's sleeve lightly. "One or the other would die on their marriage night."

"Yes, yes, that's the whole flamed problem!" he snapped. "I don't feel like gambling on Girdeth's skill with a knife against that lady-butcherer. Even if she lived through it—killed him— his troops would rebel. Try to think up a good excuse for me to refuse the marriage."

"He's distracting you with nonsense," I said. "Either that, or that Osa general's spies forged Girdeth's sigil genuinely enough to convince Keth she really did send him that slate. Call it what it is—nonsense that can wait."

"Deadly nonsense," he said, and waved me to go drill rookies.

The next ten days stayed hot and airless, very unlike spring. We left the river and the ash-land, turning to Keth's alternate route; the Cragman was insufferably smug. The conservative clans among our own officers were depressed, which meant dangerous, for lack of battleground contacts despite chasing enemy tracks for so many days. *Nothing* I said conveyed to these men the monstrous speed of the Osa.

Under my eye at midday rest, a new brace of ganas were harnessed and the morning's escort brace were fed, watered, and groomed while I went through a translation exercise with Therin. I kept the other eye on the sky. It was brassy brown, and the wind came off the east stinking of ash.

In the middle of the rest period a whip of clouds appeared on the horizon, heavy and very low. In one half-bell pass, just as I released Therin to his escort, the sky clouded over completely and the light went dim. Thunder rolled between the river bluffs in sullen echoes, though the air stood stifling hot and still. Not a leaf among the willows of the western side moved; not a twig, not a blade of grass. Great flares of light shot through the clouds. Officers barked orders; men scampered about gathering in loads, tying down tarpaulins on wagons, grabbing picket lines of animals, putting out cook fires. Herdmen fanned among the spare mounts and held nose-lines, offering sweets. Off-duty or not, I went for Caladrunan.

The wind came down on us in a solid sheet and carried away dust and ash in driving masses. I wrapped my face in a cloth and tucked it down in my hood. Large warm drops of rain hurled through the whirling dust, pounded on my robes. Therin ran past me with his guard-friend Esgarin, shouting, "It's just like a summer storm, isn't it?"

As an omen, I thought, this equals the strange fog that filled Fortress when Caladrunan first rode out to war. I made my way to him, clutching my harpcase tight under my arm. My scadda scabbards caught the wind and thumped at my legs, straining at my harness. I stood with him under the officers' mess tent awning, while the wind slashed sidewise at our legs and big drops of rain pelted like eyes into the dry dirt. The tent boomed and cracked against its guy ropes. I thought, was it wise to stay near any tent?

"I love it," Caladrunan said, peering round excitedly. "The Osa must be cursing their machines now! What, does it scare you?"

I looked at him. "You've never been in a desert storm. It would teach you great respect for this."

He clapped me on the shoulder; no fear in *that* man. "Cheer up. We're going for a ride."

First, he set Rafai and a ten-man guard on his son, to keep Therin out of trouble—already Tanman's Heir had been dragged away from the river by Esgarin, where he'd been trying to see what strange fish might rise to the storm. But the rascal's lordly father told me calmly that *he* wanted to ride around because the soldiers would want reassurance, would want to see their generals out getting muddy along with them, giving directions and helping. I kept my mouth shut; I had reports that Keth Adcrag was in his tent with a girl bought fresh and frightened from kidnapers, frantic to escape him and the attentions of his men. None but Cragmen dared go far enough into that camp to hear the shrieking. There were bets among Rafai's men on what the girl would dare say when she was thrown out again, if she was ever seen alive at all. I doubted that Keth would come out in the rain to act the general for very long, whatever orders were given him.

I had not yet passed these reports on. Caladrunan still hoped that Keth had reformed as much as promised; and I knew well how such foul news would affect my lord's mood. The soldiers needed better of him.

The rain came down in heavy intermittent sheets, a long drenching wash and then only a few drops, then another downpour. The heat left the air; I was cold in my wet robes. I thought, squinting at the clouds, that it might turn to sleet if it got much colder. We'd got back to the normal season.

Caladrunan's beard hung in little damp points as he talked with officers and with me. His eyes were bright and excited; the Osa would be bogged by rain. He shouted once to an infantry unit. "This is better than staring out cold stone holes back home and swearing about being bored, boys!"

They raised their fists and shouted back to him, while he grinned proudly at his muddy footmen. He reached out suddenly and lifted up my left arm, and the men shouted my name, too. And nicknames. They couldn't shout things like that at their Liege Lord, but they could tag *me* with puns and jokes. My habits, my temper, even the mares I rode, my raid and my spectacular drunk and my fits—they quipped at me for all of it, fearlessly, inventive in the shelter of a crowd. I made myself smile and throw back puns on their names as good as I got. They seemed to like that even better. Caladrunan laughed at clever exchanges.

He turned to a grinning messenger then and lifted the leather cover of the slate. "Good news, boys. We've a Hold to stay in, if we march. Two days at most for steam baths and hot food—and that after a good rousing fight and a bit of plunder! We can get through a little rain like this."

He drafted more crews to move stuck wagons; he sent off directives to Strengam Dar and to Keth about—because it would make a convenient depot—taking the rundown Hold Keth had peevishly insisted was dangerous and could not be left untaken behind our lines. Well, that was the conventional wisdom; perhaps Keth was just feeling less secure than usual about that new Osa general, who'd become the topic of several major briefings of late. The Lord of Tan rode up and down the line of men, putting his own shoulder now and again to a particularly stubborn wagon. With his strength, he could shift a wagon tail, and half a load, like a great ox-gana straining at the labor. The men cheered him for that; it was more like a village holiday than a forced march. We ate a soggy meal on the march; the drovers and footmen sang work songs to pace themselves down into the dusk. I heard Therin in the line giving cadence. The boy sang some of my own rude songs, too. I grinned at Caladrunan as I reinforced the spread of it. "Good spirit," he approved, proud of his men, and his eyes were full of happiness.

At full dark I went to the tent that shielded Caladrunan's sand table map, a map rebuilt by a young officer every evening after tents were bivouacked: This was doubling as my new staff tent. Somebody had already put up my banner in front, a white sword insignia on blue ground with the three wavy black quillon bars of a general of unconventional forces. I snorted at the banner and got to work.

I was nearly done when I heard a familiar step grating across the rutted clay ground outside the tent. I lowered my head, hoping it would go another direction. It was the stranger's step accompanying the known stride that made me frown. Just in case . . . I adjusted map sticks with quick care, and lifted my head. Keth Adcrag swept in, saying to the lovely unveiled lady on his arm, "Don't worry, that's his habitual expression. Probably an unfortunate scar in a painfully delicate place that—" He shrugged. "—the best of us risk these things. I did figure out that baffling Tannese interest in him—as a phenomenon, he invites the same sickening fascination as a really gruesome murder tried in full court. Hardly to my tastes, but with Tannese . . ." He shrugged.

"Strange. *I* have always found Tannese fonder of practical competence than of nauseating spectacles." The woman's gaze darted eagerly over the sand table markings; she must have maneuvered for days for this opportunity, while Keth laughed at her stratagems. *Not* his usual tearful abducted deminoble dragged about and thrown aside if she grew too tiresome. When he uttered her name I knew how badly he'd been led about and flattered. *Fool, Keth,* I thought savagely.

I said, in my most even voice, "You are excused, Lady."

Keth said, "But I'm escorting her."

I lifted my eyes. "You stand in my staff tent. She goes."

The woman purred, "Forgive me, I didn't realize you felt so badly about women."

I said, "I don't keep company with whores, nor do I permit them in my staff tent. He can pay you elsewhere."

I saw Rafai, standing unusually close to the tent flaps, let his breath out in a soft, startled, farmer's phrase. I read it on his mouth.

Keth said, "Perhaps your Sati scars affect your talents to appreciate such charms as my lady possesses."

I raked shut the leather cover over the sand table. "Those who care to try my talents—" I rested my hands on the table's edge, "—have already satisfied themselves. Discuss it with those who've bouted me."

Keth's eyes flickered. He had never dared, in practice or in challenge, to bout me. He said, "I never impugned your skills at any *job*, Sati."

I jerked my left hand. Rafai advanced on the woman. She whirled petulantly to go.

I said dryly, "Leave Keth his jades, *Lady* Coteskani. He won't like being left so unceremoniously impoverished as *that*."

The woman turned back, snarling, but Rafai gripped her arm. The jade bag dangled indisputably from her sleeve. She'd picked Keth's pockets clean, along with whatever object or document she'd been sent to pick off him—greedy mistake. Coteskanis were like that, no matter how beautifully disguised, whatever name they borrowed. Keth's face contorted. He ripped the thongs from her wrist, spilling the contents. She spat. *Her* version of his manly prowess was fascinating. Rafai turned a deeper red than Keth.

Vano, impervious, hustled away the squalling bundle of raking nails and threats and spat oaths. When Vano returned he reported the lady was being escorted back to Keth's camp. Keth, all the outraged noble, refused to bend for his own belongings. Vano picked up the bag's contents and returned them. I said smoothly, "Many of the Ladies Coteskani forget minor things like *asking* for other people's property."

Keth visibly flushed. One of a commander's duties was to keep secrets secret; and running with pickpockets was not the way to earn respect among officers. Snatching the bag, he said in a cold, rasping voice, "So it's true, you're as sharp as a housewife choosing melons in a market."

I set a sand stick in the storage slot at the table edge. I wondered what was in that bag to provoke such rage. Pity I hadn't dared pick up the bag myself. I said, "You and I have never bouted. We should. You'd find it good practice."

Keth's face, mottled with magenta hues, faded beyond rage to a dreadful white which looked worse than his madder red.

I murmured, "I'm sure it was all a misunderstanding with Coteskani. Nothing *serious*. I beg your pardon, I didn't hear—"

"I don't have to endure this! I came to consult the map."

I smiled, rolling back the table cover. "I've set up markers to show what I suggested in my messages—" Rapidly I rearranged most of the sticks, gesturing and talking. The woman never saw my real plans. Close . . . but strategically misleading.

"Leaving that rebel Hold intact behind our advance—the Hold of the Red Tyrant—that is extremely unwise," Keth said, still in that cold, dangerous tone. "Liege planned to take it, you know."

"Waste of time," I said, surprised. "The place is falling apart and badly supplied; it'll fall. If we leave an engineering crew to undermine the walls, and a company to take it when they do, then we can get on farther to Green Mill. There—"

Keth said with trenchant contempt, "You flamed eunuch— you're *afraid* to siege that Hold, on your own name, as a general. You've never run a siege—"

I set down markers. "Wrong. I planned the nine-day attack by Reti's troops at Ox Mouth Pass—which set back highland Marsh rebel lines for three years. I was eighteen summers at the time. I should hope I'd learned more of my craft since then." I smiled. "That was part of my level test for Sati."

That war was also famous. Keth looked unhealthy. "You—"

I was still smiling. "If you knew my scars as well, you'd know I am not a eunuch. Ask my escort what I couch with—

knife-dancers! Not whimpering *children* raped in a street and passed like whores among a troop of big, brave, armored men."

He never heard. Keth raged on carelessly. "You're *afraid* to take that Hold. You refused every challenge offered since you came to Tan. You always were a—"

I said, "Challenge, Keth? Is *that* the word you uttered?"

A large figure lowered head to enter the tent flap. Others, like Strengam Dar, followed. Caladrunan rumbled, "I have forbidden the Sati challenges without my express consent. I grudge the time it wastes."

Keth pointed at the map. "He thinks he can leave the Hold of the Red Tyrant to engineers. I wouldn't, were I you, Liege. It could become a site for rebels and *disaffection* from your cause." His voice emphasized the words peculiarly.

The Lord of Tan regarded him. "A hunch of yours, Keth?" he murmured in the mildest of tones. I heard barbs beneath.

Keth said, "Leaving Holds untaken was never *our* tradition."

Caladrunan glanced at me. "That's true, of course. There is the matter of time to think of, though."

Keth set his jaw and ran through the traditional arguments. I stared at him as Caladrunan's dogs did, movement for movement, while the words slid past. Keth's voice was even more impatient than normal. I mistrusted it.

"That Hold the Sati would've left untaken—" Keth persisted.

I couldn't resist temptation. I said flippantly, "How is your brother doing, Adcrag?"

Keth looked up. His face became ugly.

"Oh, you mean his *wife*," he said, and a silence fell in the subdued noises of the officers around us. "You want to know about my brother's new wife? It seems the whore Upai was pregnant before the marriage."

"You mean he didn't notice the contract terms whether she was virgin? *That* surprises me."

Caladrunan gave me a sharp look: He knew I said nothing casually. But he'd only impose his formal presence if he must.

Keth turned away fiercely. "He aborted it, said he'd return her with a striped back. The broker will have to repay the contract finances."

"Invalid," Strengam Dar remarked, in his dry tones. "That reform law a year ago, you recall. No welts, not even bruises, or assault charges are laid against your brother. The abortion is simply heinous. And her broker won't repay for rejection of the bride once she's taken by the groom's agents.''

"Expensive joke *that* turned out," Rafai murmured, knowing I was the only one who would hear it, and hear the purr in it.

I looked at Keth under my lids. Perhaps he thought the Upai would kill the rejected woman the way shamed Tannese and Crag families had been known to do; I thought they would welcome Tuzo's sister back as from the dead. I said, "Returning her will make your brother's other wives happy."

Keth suddenly sighed, as if he was simply too distracted to bicker, too tired to keep up a front. "If you fret over begetting your precious children so much, why'd you sell her off after you put it to her and got her pregnant, Upai? Is it because your own clan says you're crazy, and they don't want it passed on?"

I said, "*I* married her sister. It seems she already picked someone for husband, until your brother's unnatural, racial lusts and her poverty interfered."

"Ah well, whatever she did, now it's all speculation. She killed herself five days ago. Put a knife in her guts before my brother could beat her for ruining those fancy wedding clothes."

Caladrunan's hand snapped up curtly; for a long moment I did not move. Finally I pulled my lips back over my teeth.

In the meantime Keth went after me. "You see how much he cares about the woman since he ruined her."

Strengam murmured, "It hardly seems pertinent to—"

Caladrunan signed a swift, imperative dismissal at me. Mentally I repeated chants for clearness of head as I inclined my head to the Lord of Tan. I said mildly, "Excuse me, my Leige, while you discuss this matter freely." He waved me off. He knew the limits of my temper. As I passed Rafai—standing watchfully outside the tent flap—I muttered, "Excuse me to wipe ganamuck out of my ears."

Rafai didn't even crack a smile. Nothing. But his eyes slid over to me, and the side of his face nearest me curled a lip. Twice the usual number of men stood outside with him, to guard Caladrunan's person while Keth was there. A lot it'd help. I smothered a grim laugh and joined them.

Vano, next to the tent flap, looked stony-blank. He edged over and murmured, "Got a look at a scrap of reedpaper out of Keth's bag. Names of wine-shipping families who have begun selling that new rock-liquor. Keth wasn't afraid or hiding it. A set-up?"

I nodded stiffly. "Threat against the wine families," I said

from a dry mouth. ''Warn Rafai to send off message of it.''
Something cold and ancient and far back in my head murmured,
just how much *does* it take to force me to act against the
Cragman and disobey my Liege? Keth cannot be allowed to go
on thus. And the Osa general must know that, too. *It will be
soon now.*

That day's messenger had slates from Lake Hold. Caladrunan
handed two sealed slates to me and went on reading his own
messages. I broke the first of Girdeth's wax seals and learned
what Agtunki had found to absorb the girl's idleness: evidence,
accumulated with a ruthless eye for detail and the help of
Caladrunan's urbane genius of a spymaster. The second slate,
she wrote, was an indictment signed by her, countersigned by
Agtunki, sealed and ready to my hand if I should need it.
Unspoken was her trust that I'd use such proofs on her behalf, to
fulfill my promise to her.

''Anything important?'' Caladrunan murmured, glancing up.

I got up and paced. ''Not yet.''

His eyes glinted. ''Do bother to *warn* me, if you can.'' When
I stared at him, he only went on reading slates.

When I looked at the rookies that day, I could read lines under
their eyes. The whole camp seemed to be caught up in a frenzy
of boastful celebration, melancholy, or fear before the army's
first major assault on that rotted Hold of Keth's delight. I myself
kept seeing the face of that woman in the courtyard. As I
finished drills, I overheard youngsters whispering at the back.
''—what's chewing the Black Man—real monster!''

Rafai's voice barked and silence fell; at dismissal they went in
small clumps, looking back.

I scratched out a circle of challenge size and took off my
outrobe. I stretched, warmed my muscles, and ignored the soldiers who lingered to watch me.

I first took up my prayer stick, then fighting spurs, then
chest-knife, and a wooden practice sword. I kept seeing the face
of Tuzo and her weeping sister, then the frozen eyes of Girdeth;
it interfered with my fine control. I let the rage possess my body.
I trod that dangerous line between control and mania which
brings a fighter to peak ability and force. I flung myself into it.
Finally I shadow-played myself against a tall fodder-stack. Un-
armed, I ran through cat-dance, sand-dance, snake-strike—the
formal training dances. Run this fast, the dances acted like a
razor whipping in and around and out from an enemy.

I was sweating and flinging drops of sweat when I completed the dance. I felt full of power; like a glowing lump of iron in the heart of the forge. All the rage had concentrated in my middle. This was a royal rage, outrage, a righteous wrath. At the center of my mind, like a seed wrapped within the images of the women, within the image of fire, was an image of tall, crop-haired Osa, flat of face and skin pale as mua stains next to Upai. The clever Osa general had set all of it into wild motion, set all of his puppets dipping and bobbing. *There* lay the deepest inner rage, glowing, radiating fury: Osa, through all these years, true source of these atrocities.

I stripped off my inner robe. I was vaguely aware of soldiers watching from a low wall of straw bales that divided sword practice court from tent areas. I drew my scaddas, snap-snap, by a hard strike-draw combination—and saluted the empty air in a flourish of edges. In that air hung the enigmatic face of an Osa. An Osa general of great skill. Yes, clever man, with his priests whispering behind him.

I began the Bloodstorm dance. I was tired, and that drove me to it at an even faster pace than Reti used—which was foolish. The scaddas whined in the air with a sound I had never heard from them before: the droning whine of the legendary Bloodstorm of Reti's own teachers. Bloodstorm was for a suicidal idiot whirling in a light-footed fight across the slipfaces of dunes, over loose rocks, in the unstable scree of a cliff, among multiple enemies. An error in timing or breath control with the whirling blades made a dancer slash himself. Such was the concentration required that a dancer did not bleed from cuts. There were stories of dancers darted, bowshot, gutted, and gashed with poisonous blades, and never noticing it, never stopping, until the end of the dance—when they dropped dead over their shredded victims. The skill and focus required made it the most fearsome of the attack-dances. No counter defensive dance was known for a true Bloodstorm.

The grips of the scaddas slapped my palms lightly, spun and reversed hands and rose in salute to the air, and I was done. I stood there blinking a moment before I could break myself from the rhythm. My breath came in great regular heaves now.

The mob of soldiers kept on staring. The air felt too thick for breathing. Somehow my body, arrogant at the sight of so many eyes, pulled itself upright. I sheathed my blades and reached for a rag to wipe the sweat from my shoulders. To me, the sound of

my breathing was deafeningly noisy. I looked along the faces on
the wall of fodder. Therin stood among them; he seemed very
quiet and pale and impressed. With wonderful solemnity he
brought me a goblet of boiled water, and I, as gravely, thanked
him. Soldiers spilled out into the practice area, chattering wildly
around me; three of Rafai's guards timidly held out my robes. If
the clothes seemed to have too many pockets, and to weigh
abnormally heavy, none of them said so.

Then Rafai spoiled it by saying, "Liege wishes you to appear
at general staff meeting with him."

I growled, "A bit rash of him. *I'll* show those idiot Cragmen
really meaningless demands, wasted time, and pointless talk."

Rafai just grinned. "Lead us, Harper, to that joy."

In thick unseasonable heat, loaded with a highly displeased set
of Cragmen, the meeting did not go well. I expected that. The
Lord of Tan had resisted what Keth's cabal wanted, and Keth
had decided to force more meetings until they did get it: not
merely marrying Girdeth, not just altering the Army's course to
attack the rotted Hold of the Red Tyrant and delaying the attack
on Green Mill, but calling an inquiry—on unstated grounds—
that required all the senior officers.

As clouds rumbled outside and heat lightning flickered, the
Crag general sat down stiffly at a table. Caladrunan sat down
stiffly upon a two-step board platform behind his own table; both
tables were piled with slates. The Lord of Tan said coolly,
"Your objections to march position have been answered in my
slate messages, Keth."

Keth muttered, glaring at me, for *I* stood between him and the
Lord of Tan. Caladrunan gestured; I sat stiffly on a stool on my
Lord's first plank step, a promotion that still rankled Keth.

"You demand to know why I insisted on an inquiry? Naga
knows! You've all heard of the tortures he committed, raiding
those Nandos—methods so shocking our own Liege was offended though they were the enemy! Do you know what his
people call him? Madman. His own grandmother called him
possessed, insane, murderer. He's repudiated by his people, his
own kin want to drive him off. He has always been mad.
Prophecy has never had anything to do with it; even *he* keeps
saying that. As for all that vaunted training, it seems he does not
remember his own history while becoming a Sati, or will not tell
it. So *I* will—"

When I opened my mouth, Caladrunan signed me to wait.

"The real story," Keth jabbed out his thumb and first two fingers at me as he spoke, "is that Reti threw you out *twice*. When the Master of scaddas found out your insanity, he put you in Lady Yoyu's orphanage. Later he took you back—and found your faults hadn't changed, so he tossed you to Manoloki's Nandos. You survived that. Reti took you up again with your whole training Hand—maybe he saw something to make him think he could cure your problems. But it got worse; all his officers advised him to stop training you, that you were crazed. But he kept at it, kept making you more dangerous and wilder all the time." Keth waved at me and turned to the assembled officers. "Reti had this madman living like a witch on snakes and rainwater out there—and when officers questioned, Reti told them he was tooling a new weapon."

I rolled my boot idly in a circle. Keth *had* studied me, it seemed. I flicked a glance at Caladrunan and back to Keth.

Keth went on ranting like an orator. "Until this . . . *this monster* he'd created lashed out during a fit. Oh, Naga already killed some of his own men—he blew up a flamethrower Reti's men built—but Reti forgave *that*." Keth smiled thinly. "Not the death of Reti's best friend, his Harper. Reti threw out his mad favorite for that, sent him off in raggy Marsh gear, alone." Keth turned and looked at me. "Maybe we should consider Reti's final judgment before we trust Reti's mad creature in any more conferences."

Caladrunan gestured sharply for my reply.

I leaned back, stretched. "Reti sent me out in rags to spy on Manoloki, as he meant me to do all along. That was what he aimed for."

Keth shouted, *"You killed your own harp trainer!"*

"I killed him, yes. Twice."

# CHAPTER
# = *14* =

MEN SHIFTED ALONG the benches, blinking in surprise. Well, I *was* a Harper, after all. When Keth moved as if to interrupt, he was glared down. I said, "I damaged his brain. I was in a fit, yes. I repented of it all the moons I fed Tomu and nursed him and washed his clothes. Tomu died slowly, for moons, in constant pain from an internal growth taken from a tour of duty in the Wastelands when he was younger. He suffered. So Reti granted me the right to give Tomu the mercy. If I struck him straightly, moons before, instead of slipping the blow—if I'd let the fit take me wholly—Tomu would have been spared that pain." I sat back, studying faces. "Reti sent me to work within Manoloki's Nandos to defeat them, with a reasonable cover to protect me. Ask Reti's men. They work for us now."

It was then I realized that Keth must have squandered too much spying entirely on me—for our recruitment of Reti's officers, shocked him white and silent. Nothing else had touched his sneer. And Caladrunan was smoothing a smile from his mustache before it showed.

The air in the war tent seemed thick and dead in the silence. There were very few times I'd actually stared into the eyes of a person who hated me, whom I intended to kill. Such a study was usually inconvenient, and I never liked to let them get a good look at me. But the very first time I'd met Keth, he spoke words matched—more than matched—by the sheer corrosive lava I read in his stare everlastingly since. Instant, irrational, and unmistakable repulsion: Intense, mutual hatred had taken moments. He hated me with as much force now. For all the various political reasons—including my increasing belief that Keth only did the bidding of my real antagonist—I hadn't killed him. Yet.

"*You*—" he spat it before the assembled general staff, "—are mad. Like any other Nando, you're used to selling yourself, perhaps that's where traitorous word has leaked to the alliance before cavalry raids. And sea raids."

I said, "Are you hunting for an excuse for bad luck, incompetence, or poor security?"

"*You're* unfit for civilized noble company—you hang so close to the bed of the Lord of—" he caught back reckless words unspoken and went on, "—kukkie-sucking little Kehran boy unfit for military duty—"

Under his breath, Rafai muttered, "Ah, but he must be too good a Sati, or *you* wouldn't bother trying to remove him."

I propped my boots up on an extra stool and circled one toe lightly in the air, which made the razor-spurs at the ankle glitter. "Do you lay charges?"

Keth turned, fists clenched, and screamed his refrain at Caladrunan, who looked blankly impervious, and then at Strengam Dar, whose face was pale. Not good, that. Not even a titter rose from the back where the younger men clumped together. Not good at all. Keth shouted, "Nobody else dares call you witch to your face, Sati, but witch you are! You use that Devotee Order—Women of the Harp—as a front to pervert the Goddess' will to your damned seizures! Well, I refuse to endure whoreboys jumped up in fancy dress—"

I sighed. "Can't you be more imaginative than that?"

He should never have tried to outshout a Harper. My voice cut through his as through the buzz and noise of a tavern. Harpers had need, at times, for the art of quelling mobs. I waved one hand. "How about something like accusations that I collect dancing bears, or throw extravagant binges in some dockhouse flop, or some interesting scandal about . . . oh, say, an interest in propping smugglers' declining revenues. A couple of murders of tavern owners were *ordered* on the Tejed River docks and foiled by good dock gang security. Two murderers in Commoners Court told tales about the complexities of rock-liquor sales, Keth."

Eyes moved among the Cragmen.

My mouth drew down in a flat line. "*So* much easier to yell '*traitor*' at some foreigner like me than a cozy inside courtier closer to home, isn't it? If you like accusations, how about some for you, Keth? We learn certain cavalry officers knew about the burning eastward when they pressed for permissions to use a westward route that did not put *them* in danger. Strange they failed to warn anyone higher than their own division. That negligence let the Osa finish murdering everyone in the ford villages.'' I looked down with burning eyes. ''Children.''

Keth's tirade blundered on. ''I've got proof that you—''

''Produce it,'' I said coldly.

''Proof so confidential is cleared only for top officers—''

''If you mention witch fits and kukkie-sucking here, you may *prove* slanders to all this noble company. If you can.''

But Keth didn't need to have hard proof to cause damage in an army built of loosely allied clans with lots of inherited bickering. Top Tannese officers, mistrusting Keth's shaky discretion involving the Lord of Tan, would let Keth do just that—avoid direct proof—in a frantic effort to avoid scandal. Whatever my supposed crime, the most important part of the Army—the multitudes of junior men—would be convinced of guilt just by the obvious panic among Caladrunan's higher ranks. If Keth's accusations ever came to trial, some poor dupes would stand up and testify that I'd cracked their stiff Tannese codes like a pot-iron sword in every possible way. That Keth had never held to such codes was *excused* by his Crag nobility—and his begged-for numbers.

I could prevent Keth's uproar one way: keep them all here. Only hard proof would stand before the entire, skeptical general staff and those irreverent younger men. Keth had to stick near the edges of the truth—obvious fabrications would be laughed down here. Or so I hoped. Keth knew I'd freely produce proof about my own collection of scandals, or I wouldn't have suggested it. Keth and I shared a good, long, hateful look.

Strengam called for order, making distressed noises aimed toward dismissing junior officers—*not* what I wanted at all. Subtly I signed a request to Caladrunan. I stayed in my relaxed posture, but I was glad I was wearing full leathers under my robes: My sweat didn't show. Caladrunan signaled to Strengam; the meeting continued unchanged. But the old general, in taking up a goblet of wine, hissed at me, ''Are you trying to split this Army, Sati? How are we going to repair this—?''

Keth shouted a name. ''Proof, you demand—I give you proof!''

A skinny young man stood up, pointing at me. ''Lord Adcrag, Eurstas and me were in the Teot's escort; we heard the Teot talking with his kin, his grandmother. She was angry, she accused him of being—of being like a Kehran boy—of being a mad crazy thing that they'd outlaw from their camps. She said he murdered and raided without *their* wishes *or* the Lord of Tan's, that he did *horrible* things. He heard us—so we hid in a wagon escort, came out later—''

I snorted. Leisurely I crossed my ankles the other way. In Upai I said, ''Is that all you've got, Keth, some blubbering child?''

They all looked blankly surprised.

The boy caught up too late. ''Eurstas knew Upai!''

In Tannese I continued, ''Then at the very best your Upai report comes second-hand and unverifiable.'' Bitter it was, too, to find some Upai traitor had given this boy information for money—but not surprising.

There was laughter. Keth looked furious. He was glaring at the young man as if glaring him quiet. Mistimed accusations, disarray among the ranks, I thought whimsically.

Keth bellowed, ''We have testimony of captives taken and tortured by you—''

I leaned forward, hands lightly together. ''Very interesting, because none of my captives *ever* escape me alive. Along with testimony of enemies, *this* is your reliable witness? A boy who was certainly never in my escorts and who only served—outside your Crag troops, Adcrag—two days' duty at Fortress, and that six moons ago. Which, by the way, was three moons before *I* ever came to Fortress.'' I gently dropped the last block of truth. ''A boy who, of late, hasn't done his slated turn at mess duties even among *your* troops, nor done *any* wagon escort duty since he went to you, Keth. Wagon escort names get tallied to reduce pilferage.''

A lot more faces turned pale. Keth favored younger men by letting them out of onerous tasks; another big mistake, not to check that evidence of the boy's movements.

''Come now,'' I snapped, ''or don't you remember your rotation rosters? His corps insignia doesn't match either his uniform or his real name, or his original assignment. From a squabble during intercorps bouting, I judged this fellow might one day make a swordsman if he didn't whimper so tiresomely when he gets stung. Or did your instructors bother to tell you that, youngster?''

''Abusing this witness—there's others—'' Keth snarled.

I said softly, "This isn't a trial. *But we can make it one.*" For a moment rage lunged in my chest so fiercely I stared down, eyes stretched wide open, as close to striking at him as to breathing. Then I snapped, "You want interesting scandals? These officers might be interested to hear what was found outside your Crag encampment last fall at Lake Hold—one day after a poisoning attempt on Liege's life!"

Keth shouted, "The Lord of Tan nearly died there of your incompetence and that old man Pitar's, everyone knows that!" A lot of the Tannese present there bristled in outrage at that. He roared on, "You *whoreboy,* you know nothing about any business of war nor court nor judging—you're a witch!"

"And you're indicted." I smiled. "The accusation slate, evidence direct from the Lady Girdeth, rests before you there. You can answer questions before my Liege Lord of Tan in a full court trial." Caladrunan shot me a look none the less horrified for its speed and subtlety. I waited while Keth shouted at me. I went on, "You could redeem much guilt in the matter by supporting his march plans as my Liege asked you to do. Stop shouting or you'll miss all the fun parts. You'll have to enforce discipline on your partisans in here, Keth." I stood up, stretching my fingers in my black metal-banded gauntlets. I looked between my spread fingertips. "As for *my* competence, no whining Kehran boy ever had the courage to face *me* in a bout. Let alone in a challenge."

Keth's eyes were pale ice-green discs with pinpoint pupils. I'd never seen the color of his eyes clearly before. Hatred constricted eyes like that. Not once had he taken up the offer I kept flinging at him. Smart man. I'd beaten his best ax-champion off Girdeth—though only he and I knew it. To earn the prize buckle I gave away to Lady Yoyu's orphanage, I'd beaten the boasts from Keth's previous pet, a swordsman with as weak grip on his temper as his master.

I'd have respected Keth if he'd *tried* me, just once. We could have learned something together, endured something, that way. Keth didn't think I was human because he'd never fought me, and never would. He meant to wipe me away much as he did Fortress garden caterpillars under his boot. And I didn't know if, through some stratagem, he'd found a way to do it. So I grinned slightly, showing off the gold inlaid by Sharinen in my back teeth. And I said the one word that no officer with Keth's sort of troops could stand for. I said, "Just proves that you're a *coward*, unlike these other Crag lords."

He lunged. Other Crag officers grabbed Keth, held him back. He screamed, "You crazy witch, no sane man fights sorceries—*nobody* else dares challenge your witching the way I do—"

"It was your men who tried me and failed," I snapped. "But not *you*, never you! You lack the honest courage for it. Only your paid assassins—your own witch-made monsters—ever challenge *me*." My voice went soft. "In the street, at night, in mob numbers, then they dare it. Big, brave men. Men just like the bandits who terrorize the villages your divisions pass, the night raiders who've tortured, kidnaped, and killed. Rafai, from those slates before you, read the victims' names of this past tenday, as Liege's records list them."

"The Lady Yalt of House Birch, guest of Orogoroni, abducted by men in green and vanished. The Lady Puagatai, throat slit—"

Everything got horribly quiet. Upai scouts had found a lot more bodies than the Cragmen had thought possible.

I said, "We have descriptions of victims discovered, those kidnaped in the course of march, where it happened, what happened to them as judged by their discovered bodies. Peculiar: Women of royalist nobles' Houses suffered terribly, but Houses of doubtful commitment in the very same reaches did not. The trail clearly follows *your* line of march across Tan, as we will demonstrate during your trial on maps of—"

Keth sputtered at the Lord of Tan, "I demand you ask your crazy Sati what *he* did to innocent people, sneaking about after us to lay off the blame!"

Caladrunan's face was not just immovable. It had become granitic. He said quietly, "Then you won't fear Judgment on it, Keth. Or on rock-liquor murders either. Or on your troops' failure to report on the burned lands. We will see who *did* order these things. At this time, you hold to your directed line of march, or stand immediate trial under martial law for defying *me*! If you correctly support our assault on that Hold—which *you* insisted must be taken—I'll grant you showed genuine goodwill."

"It's *the Sati* who's the murdering witch—"

Caladrunan stood up, cold, lofty, and dignified in his blue robes. "Strange crime for a man my sister declared *erdmuntoú*."

"*What?* How dare—" Keth heaved and yelled in the midst of his men, apoplectic. The place was in chaos. Everybody was

practically popping veins in screaming at the other side. It
looked like a fistfight was in full course at the back.

The Lord of Tan said, for the sake of the sour Devotee scribe
still scratching away on record slates between Strengam and the
tent wall, ''I know something of the matter of the murdered
villagers. When I offered clemency terms to those who could
testify on it, in a general Army-wide report, the attacks only
escalated. The most renowned victim is the Lady Birawered,
pledged to become a Devotee under the Elder Safanio before her
murder three days ago when a group of Women of the Harp were
attacked—''

Through infighting or brute ignorance, one faction of the
idiots had murdered one of their own—the best court informant
and patroness of another faction's Devotee Elder. She'd gone out
there secretly to collect proofs of some sacred transgression or
other among the women she died with. The murder was committed mistakenly, or to silence her, not as a Crag-style rape, as the
Lady Birawered had been neither lovely nor young. The Osa-
allied organization did not pass on information clearly or rapidly—
side product of fear, perhaps. The Elder Safanio and his lot
would take skins for that mistake. One contingent of Cragmen
roared in fury and launched themselves at other Cragmen. The
place erupted.

The outer zones, the younger men, flew wildly at one another.
The older officers stood back eyeing one another in taut postures. Keth was pulled back and away by his own bodyguards,
while we of Tan stood tensely around Caladrunan, weapons in
hand. Among the heaving knots of men in the tent it was mostly
knives and fists, too close and rapid an event for swords.

My sight blurred, instantly red.

*No,* I thought. The Osa general's stupid Cragman tool will not
escape. *He will not.* I walked slowly forward, standing before
Caladrunan, even between Rafai and the rioting. Each footstep
required hallucinogenic care. Space wavered and distorted at the
periphery of my vision. Music whispered there, where totemic
animals bent fiercely to their drumming, lightning-shot eyes
turned like pools of darkness to me.

*Dance!* their voices echoed fiercely in the shells of my ears.

Fit coming, I thought, but could not find words to warn my
Liege Lord so—and this was not the usual sort of fit, the familiar
reliving of bad memories. I dropped my weaponbelt near
Caladrunan, for the safety of my friends, not my own; I knew if

in hand during this dreaming, I would dance scaddas as deadly ever I danced them in war. I turned toward Keth's knot of men and my arms extended, two first fingers pointed like blades. Reverently, rhythmically, words rolled from my mouth: huge sounds, rich and round as voices of the ancients' great iron bells.

"*Keth the Adcrag,* you are sworn upon the honor of the bones of Crag, upon My flesh that land—and We shall see upheld that oath, or life shall blow like locust husks from the flesh of you." Heads turned, startled eyes glanced over, weapons dangled. The words tolled on. "*We* call you to account! Think long and long upon the damage traitor action has done your own cause. Tool, manipulated and tricked and bullied by a force that would eat you alive and never notice the loss. Yes, look your deepest fear in its face and read the lineaments of truth! Repent—and you *will* repent at length the horrors done innocents—then time may grant healing among you and your true friends. But *flee* your many promises upon the breath and bone of this land, Keth the Adcrag, and the loins of you will *shrivel* and the fruit thereof shall be spilled upon the dry and burning wastes—"

Cragmen shouted and pointed at me. A Cragman hurled something shiny at me. Instantly it was flicked aside off a long gray sword flashing up before me. I neither nodded nor blinked at Vano's fierce protective motion. My hands opened into arched claws, pointing yet. The Cragmen about Keth, struggling beside the tent wall, fell still, staring at me. Keth stood frozen-quiet, looking up with an open mouth as if at some nightmarish horror of a creature.

"—and the innermost being of you shall writhe in torment with monstrous delusions, the gut of you shall grow large as with child but its only food and substance shall be unnatural flesh—"

To one side of me Caladrunan's face looked pale. "Where in Flames did you learn a curse like that, Naga?"

I took another step toward Keth, my hands poised like claws overhead. "—As Keth the Adcrag clove to evil like unto that of the Old Ones when they warred with one another and cast us down from the sky and gave unto one another the death of races, give he one lie—*one lie*—with his face, lying against what he planned in his secret heart, *then* be he now gaunted as they were gaunted, be he eaten by putrifactions as they were, be he caused to lose his scheming will to the rot of the ages as *they* rotted within their metal shells, peeling all their skins—"

Rafai and Caladrunan looked at each other. Rafai said, "I think I overheard a bit like that once, the Women's Mysteries—"

"Yes," the Lord of Tan said grimly. "And I don't think Upai men know such words any better than we do. I don't know where he's getting it. Stay out of his way. I don't think he sees us."

The words came with exact ritual care, rolling out in the long rhythms of the great curses. I found sunlight glowing into my eyes, perhaps from a rent in the tent. There seemed to be a lot of knife-cut light-holes and lots of sunlit spaces among the storm clouds outside. My arms lifted into a dust-mote light beam as stiffly as if the shaft of light were planned for; and somewhere inside me, I felt a deep, cold terror. Some object fell from one of those holes in the tent, I heard it—automatically my hand opened, and into it fell a stalk of kinash grain. The dry inflorescence of round reddish kernels glowed in the sunlight like red wine. The bits I kept in my robe for praying over were never so perfectly intact. Vano gave a sudden tight little grin as he saw it. "Good timing, Esgarin," he muttered, though only I seemed to hear him clearly.

"—see you the truth? Even as Her light calls to examination this foulness of the Adcrag, this corrupt profit in flesh and fear, this sewer trade in defiled gifts of healing, in surgeries for pain, in medicines for torture! Even in repentance the Adcrag be cursed with pains so long as he shall remain within his body, for evil created upon Our child of the womb called Girdeth, called Mirob, called Isado, called Betath, called Ondine, called Cuusk—" Names, more names, poured from me with pitiless clarity. I was helpless to stop the flood recital of the wronged.

Keth screamed, "Not true—*never*—I never—"

Pitar rasped, "Those two names, Isado Iralad, Ondine Wef, those were murdered Women of the Harp. I'm not sure of others—"

"I am," Caladrunan said. "Can you find some rational officers to control this riot? I know I'll either be fighting Keth tonight or he'll be begging me to forgive him and take him back!"

I turned directly to the Lord of Tan. "Do you, Heart of Iron, Ruler of this *Our Land*, refute the justice of this claim of abomination, in the sight of *She*? Do you, Ruler, choose such a tool of the Cursed Ones as any hand to the righteous?"

"I don't even understand what you're asking!"

The stalk of kinash pointed out at the staring Cragmen, ringed about their chalk-faced leader. "Yes, at the task of war he shall indeed pay what he promises you now, Ruler, but *beware*—" My eyes ringed white all around in fear, something took my body in a seizure of power larger than anything I'd ever felt before. "—this the Goddess demands of you, Ruler, choose! Choose to smile on the hand of the Cursed One, and the loins of you shall blacken, even as his shall do—" I choked at that threat, gasped, shook my head violently, spun about, refused to admit the curse. My head jerked like a curbed beast. "—mmmhh—"

"He's mad," Rafai whispered.

"No. He's fighting. Keep everyone back."

I gasped. "There is a death in this place. There is Death. I smell it in this place." My hand flung down the stalk of kinash, and there was a flare and roar of flame on the dirt, as instantly gone, leaving nothing behind. It looked just like gunpowder, dropped by someone in the press and just sparked off by the heavy stalk, but nobody had thought to search for a pouch or twist of gunpowder, any more than they thought of someone dropping it. They all just screamed instead. Somehow, without knowing how I'd reached them, I was among the Cragmen officers, my hand stiffly outstretched, fingers spread as if to grasp the sun. Men cried out and fell back from me, screaming like pigs at slaughter: high panicked squeals.

I turned blindly, glancing right and left, crying out in a tolling note, "Smell the death in this place—with the hand of the Cursed One blackening upon the breast of those of Our children you did not protect—see you not the Shadow? There, *there* rears a Death to shrivel the face of horror!" Most of the Cragmen broke and fled, pouring in streams through the rents in the tent. My hand arched up, pointing. Softly, softly, that tolling voice said, "And the Death follows you."

Then I smelled the panic-sweat in the air along with churned dust and gana leathers, and sharp stabbing pain ran from my eyes through my head, jolted like a glacial spike down my spine. I staggered then as if drunk, stumbled on an overturned bench. Blue-robed soldiers swayed back ridiculously onto one another to keep clear of me. I stopped, clutching both hands at my roaring head, and felt a huge grip seize my left arm. Another different hand, just as large, gripped my right arm. *Brave men,* I thought dazedly. I couldn't get enough air.

Caladrunan said gently, "Is it over?"

I gasped, "Think so. Didn't mean to—no air—"

"Let's get him outside, Rafai," Caladrunan snapped, dragging me along. Pitar walked Caladrunan's other side, sweeping a
hostile gaze over the remaining chaos. But no one jostled us.
Rafai found a slit in the tent wall, held it courteously for us; we
staggered out together.

"*Down,*" I gasped, and felt my legs give way under me. My
insides felt all hollow and strange, and my hair prickled all over
my body. They let me down on my knees, and then, slowly, on
my face. I lay there in drying muddy ruts. "All going round," I
gasped, my fingers crushing wagon rut crusts.

I cried out then. Something like a cannon shock wave grabbed
up my body, as if I was in the grip of eagle's talons, and rolled
me. A broad blow as of a fist of air slammed all against my face
and chest. My body was flung away wildly, flew—flapping like
a tarpaulin blown in a sandstorm. I tumbled over and over,
thumped to a stop.

Scrub brush grated into my neck and hair. I lifted my numb
face out of a spiky clump of grass, and blinked. The air stank of
storm and charred green tree and burned animal hair. I heard
cries, rustling noises, grunts. Footsteps grated up to me, a
shadow fell across my flung-out arms. "Naga?"

I blinked up at him. He seemed very far away. "What happened? Why'd you hit me?"

"I didn't," Caladrunan said. Dimly I heard shouting, panicky
voices, the uproar of officers among troops and the shrieking
ganas. "The air hit us. I think."

I looked down at crushed ruts. My flesh shuddered.

He said, "What did you do? You called it down." He looked
at the sky. Huge splatters of water dampened the clay crust on
the ruts, thumped my hair and the back of my hands, clattered on
my leathers. "You called a lightning storm! You were shouting
in some ancient Upai and you—*you called*—"

"I did?" I sat up, rubbing my head.

He looked at me. "You just cursed Keth with impressive
thoroughness, Sati. Would you mind explaining—"

"Oh, that." I squinted.

"*Oh, that!* he says calmly—after lightning just killed a tree
with Keth's own mount tied to it!"

I glanced up, twisting my neck painfully. Shattered and smok-
ing remains loomed on the ridge above us: One scrubby tree
blazed against the horizon. Beneath it, blackened hooves stuck

straight up from a balloon of hide. Two other ganas with strange scorch marks wandered dazedly about, whistling. Men were pelting headlong away down that hill. "Best stay low till the storm moves away."

"And where did you learn that—that *curse* you recited?"

I rubbed my head. "The Old Ones of the cave of machines, the same ones who built your stupid Fortress gas mine." Then I remembered he did not know the ancient dialect—the only one that came easy to my tongue just now—and that I must use Tannese. Well, I tried to. My mouth stumbled over it. "The Old Ones were not like us, you know. The cave, it changed me. I don't remember well—it's scrambled in my head—"

"What's he babbling?" Strengam's voice asked. There was a ring of faces about me now. "That isn't even Upai, is it?"

"I can't understand him myself," Caladrunan said, and leaned down. "No, it's not Upai. Here, I'm taking your arm—"

*"Down,"* I said clearly in Tannese. "Get. Down. Now."

Bodies hit the ground with speed.

Somewhere—not at all far off—there was a brief sparkle of lightning in the clouds and a tremble in the air. That was the only warning: A shattering glare gouged at my eyes through my shielding fingers, the earth jumped under my face with a dull concussive rumble. Trees crackled suddenly, explosively, on an eastern hill. Caladrunan stared into my face. "Naga," he whispered. "Those were Cragmen there. They all ran for heights, and the lightning hit—"

Another glare of light. I blinked and grinned crookedly into all the faces. "Don't need them to fight Osa. Got me." As a joke it failed. We flinched at another bolt of light and concussion; this sharper shaking threw some men off their feet.

Caladrunan muttered, "At least it missed Keth. Maybe I can patch something together now you've put the fear of righteousness into him—" It was true we all heard high squealing Cragmen pleas, all begging to be allowed obedience, pleading to tell all and anything they knew, *begging* to return all as it was before. The Lord of Tan asked, "Can we get up now?"

I looked at sunlight glancing in shafts through clouds igniting sheets of rain to waves of falling icy glints, then down to the rainwater glinting on my wrist. My body shuddered. A drool of blood ran down my lower lip. "Yes."

Then the babble enveloped us like a plague of stinging flies. Keth's voice said, "Liege, if your Sati discovered information I

never realized might be important to you, I beg your forgiveness—
ready to supply whatever knowledge you desire—no idea my
adviser officers might conspire with the Osa our enemies—yes, I
spent too much time worrying about Naga. I honestly believed
that anyone who acted so strangely—witching fits or true prophecy, how could I tell—very worrying, what if he was one of the
top Osa spies—''

Caladrunan snapped, ''Enough.''

I felt hands upon me, lifting me, restraining the twitching in
my body. I writhed, hating it, trying to climb free. I had no clear
notion of how far they carried me. Words dribbled crazily from
my mind; I didn't know if they heard any of it.

Caladrunan growled, ''Take him in my tent. Bring his
weaponbelt.''

When the sunlight went, the light left my mind, and the
power, and the mad jab of knowledge and imperative. Suddenly
I was choking hot. I fell back gasping on the furs and cried out
hoarsely, ''Oh, Goddess, take us, we dance the death—the
death—'' and passed out.

# CHAPTER

# = *15* =

BY CONVENIENCE AND vagaries of the terrain, a nervous and much-humbled Keth still got his former way, three days later. Keth *insisted* that none of his demands about the place had ever come from the plots of the officers arrested as traitors. His reasoning was and remained the conventional Tannese wisdom. We had to take the Hold away from the Nandos who held it, of course—mostly poorly trained Marshmen. From the crest of the ridge above, Caladrunan watched his Army demolish a panicked enemy. The Nandos had no catapults or flamethrowers. They hadn't even tried to make chevaults-de-frise or dig in stakes to hold off our cavalry. But for the ash-lands diverting us, we'd never have marched here.

Mud sucked under the hooves of the ganas with loud popping noises; half the Army—including Keth's cavalry—waited behind us in case they were needed. The enemy acted so inept Caladrunan grew suspicious of ambush. Therin stayed back with Pitar in a safe position. Too much danger, the Lord of Tan said firmly to his son, but *he* sat more exposed on this ridge than I would have liked. He sent out a messenger to shift our line of foot back, to pull the defenders outward by subtle degrees and then smash their attenuated lines. The walls were rotten with openings for a force our size. I asked, "Why put a Hold *next* to a hill?"

Caladrunan laughed. "You've never seen what quarrying out hills costs, have you? And the water supply is down there. But the real reason is that Ser Gavan wouldn't pay work crews to cut the stone. He got wall stones, and left it at that. He had other uses for his treasury."

Rain trickled down my back. "Ser Gavan was the Red Tyrant."

"*This*," Caladrunan said with irony heavy in his voice, "was his very first Hold. We all begin as Holders, you know. The ruling dynasty has been in my family long enough, everyone thinks Lake Hold is the Lord of Tan's special province."

I said lightly, "I hope when you say *we* you don't often put yourself and the Red Tyrant in the same breath."

Caladrunan gave a grim, wry smile while his eyes roved past me over the field. "It may come to that. Despite how frantic he's been to keep his men to my march orders, Keth's been panicking about and half-ignoring my orders today. Probably his alliances in his officer corps are coming apart after *your* deplorable efforts to scare him into religious obedience. And his brother's message from Pigeon Hold was openly insolent—Keth will be messing his saddle straps when he sees it. I'll have to take firm measures over that insolence—perhaps cut the grain-cost subsidy for Pigeon Hold's garrison and troops." He pointed. "There, the final push. They think they've broken our front line. Come."

We rode right down into it. Behind us the standard-bearer unfurled the great sword banner. The silver embroideries caught the dull rain-gray light. Caladrunan meant his movements to draw attention to the front line, away from the rear attack of Strengam's men. He needn't have risked his own person, but the soldiers loved him for it. Caladrunan's hair and breast embroideries caught a gleam of sunset light from under low clouds. He gave a roar and charged the ragged enemy lines.

My mare gana rode on his left side, shoulder to shoulder with his bull. We met the rebel rush with a crash of beasts and metal meeting that hurled lighter ganas off their legs. Hostile herds of ganas did not mingle lines as the ancients once recorded of their flying war machines—strafing their enemy in passage. Ganas charged in a mass and crashed like rams, head to head, horn to horn base, with resounding gunfire cracks.

Swords dinned together. The sword Devour flicked bits of light like a gem as Caladrunan spurred his bull and crashed a rebel beast. The slighter animal staggered from the impact, the rider lifted a mace; I impaled the man. The blade bound on rib armor. He fell into me, entangling my body. Past helmet slits I saw-felt-sensed a Nando swordsman was extending at me.

In a sharp weapon-*chop!* Caladrunan lowered the edge of his huge shield, knocking away the man's blade. I threw out my left

arm and killed the swordsman even as my previous limp burden
slithered away, freeing me. The Lord of Tan bellowed a laugh,
pulling back his shield for himself. His sword arm moved Devour in great figure-eight scything blows.

Wild arrows flew everywhere. One stuck in Caladrunan's
saddle; he snapped it off and fought on. Rafai calmly grabbed up
our falling standard with one hand from the dead bearer, and
with the other hand spitted a foot soldier on a spear like a fish.
Calmly he handed off the standard to another banner boy, jerked
his spear free, and used it again. Caladrunan roared approval like
a yedda lion. I yelled, "Liege, there ought to be more escort
with us."

Caladrunan laughed, spinning his bull to join my mare, presenting some sort of line to a loosely strung corps of pikemen. As
they charged us, they grew yet more ragged; but still, any rider
of sense would have run away. He shouted, "We've outrun
escort, Naga. You take that one—" and we were in the midst of
the poles, fighting as a pair to break and tangle thickets of
pikeheads.

Had they been a tight-packed phalanx we'd have had no
chance. Strung out and isolated, they had no chance against our
armored fighting ganas; we hit them like a cannon shot, exploding their lines. The Lord of Tan had a slash-stab parrying
rhythm, while I used a faster double-speed technique with two
scaddas and no shield. When a man lunged in off-rhythm against
Caladrunan, I could take the strike and parry it, hurling away the
lone man at the pike's end with sheer gana-mounted driving
mass. At times Caladrunan's shield would jolt-stop and shatter
entire clusters of pikeheads. He seemed to sense pike clusters
and heavy arrow flights and got his shield up before they reached
my lighter weapons and armor—while I darted out of his cover
and blunted his fast-jabbing opponents before they picked open
his slow, heavy guard. From riding together so long our mounts
worked as well together as we did.

With the pikemen in a shambles, Caladrunan roared, "They
don't know us, boys! They don't know we're knocking at their
gate!"

The answer ran back over the battlefield in a ripple, mouth to
mouth. The footmen advancing in steady ranks chanted, "Lord
of Tan," in long even calls that rumbled like the sea.

We took the walls as night fell, swept away the defenders.
Engineers could have sapped it, giving the defenders time to

grow afraid and desert: much more economical than this pitched battle. But the Red Tyrant's crumbling Hold was ours by ninth night bell.

Caladrunan shouted for light by which to inspect our capture. There was some sporadic fighting as soldiers rooted out pockets of Nandos and townsmen, and captured the last defenses. Squads of defiant rooftop snipers still held two sites, but at daylight our catapults would pick them out; in the meantime their zones of fire were kept cleared. When we got to the main halls our men had already broken the doors into storage. Officers called out stocks of metal, grain, wine, wood—a much larger store than the garrison in the place warranted. Resupply Hold on a convoy route, I thought.

Caladrunan and I began inventory on upper levels, the largest. Strengam took the middle floor and Keth the lower caverns—rather a punishment duty, that, but Caladrunan was in no mood to have his whims questioned. Keth sent up a slate that he'd secured the lower caves against entry from the river, in case the Hold was meant to trap us for an Osa guerrilla river-launched ambush. Keth's inner command cadre would get hit first in *that* event, another grim whimsy of Caladrunan's.

The defense here had shown classic Manoloki-Nando incompetence, from the very size of its garrison downward; an Osa army rolling up in flamethrowers was the only thing we need fear.

I went around organizing sentry watches, checking that weaker wall zones were protected by extra men, while reserve troops dug hasty entrenchments before full dark. Caladrunan, sitting down at a table in the main Hall, sent out orders about supplies, water, and enemy wounded and dead; our casualties were already in surgery or the burial yard.

At the same time Caladrunan went down to talk with Keth alone—ostensibly to check the quality of the water coming in, but really to check on those cave inventories. He saved himself grief by going while I was busy elsewhere.

I waited for him, furious. When he returned, he looked at my face, shook his head, and told me to hold my tongue in my hands if I must to silence it. In the next breath he ordered wood set to heating the Hold's big bath hypocausts to smoke any infiltrators out of the pipes beneath the bathing rooms. This had one practical benefit: Like us, squads of tired men used the baths in turn, all night long. We also visited the Altar room, kneeling clean and damp on the pitted dusty old stones. Sitha's Abode had been neglected during the Nando occupation. The Devotees muttered when Tanman dismissed them from their cleaning tasks.

Caladrunan knelt in front of the Altar slab and the Bowl of Flames—a blaze he lit himself. I knelt three paces behind him. When I glanced up, it was to the hair curling damply over his collar. "Thank you," Caladrunan said at last to the Flames, as if his burdens had lightened. He rose to his feet, patted my shoulder as he passed, and strode toward the door. I saw him safely to the guards of Rafai's watch, then I went down into camp.

I found the grumpy old guard-watch herbalist resting beside a surgery tent. "Ha, dead-alive, you," he greeted me. The man looked deathly tired himself; we never had enough skilled hands to work at feverish speed saving lives during battles. I sent the tired herbalist up to Caladrunan, for the Lord of Tan had several cuts on his arms. So did I. A new thigh scratch and my old rib cut from my solitary raid were pulling painfully. But with work still to do, I waved off the herbalist to my Liege's needs first. Through the next two bell passes, I checked on stabling for the guard's mounts, on our Upai scouts, and I glanced into some of the barracks and tasted the food, once hot meals had begun. Satisfied, I went up to the main Hall.

In the private Lord's chambers, Caladrunan had been busy as well. While the herbalist dressed Caladrunan's cuts, the Lord of Tan dictated message slates. When the Devotee scribe, as sour-faced as before victory, complained of weariness, Caladrunan blandly sent for Strengam Dar and his son. I grinned. The Lord of Tan stared at me and levelly ordered me to submit myself to care. I scowled.

While the herbalist washed the cut on my thigh, the scribe muttered indignantly under his breath. Keth Adcrag came in with Strengam, carrying a pitcher, and ignored me; he seemed to be far away in some frozen fearfully uncertain place in his mind, as if he couldn't remember quite whose saddle gear was trustworthy and whose was dangerous. Something whispered chants in the back of my head, flickered like warning. Then Caladrunan waved absently at the pitcher. The scribe poured out gobletsful of dark fluid. The Lord of Tan looked up, noticed the scribe's resentment, and watched with that mild, serene look I recognized as Caladrunan at his most dangerous. I, too, reached out, though the Devotee looked insulted, and took my time tasting of my Lord's share. My Liege Lord said lazily, "Rafai tested it."

"Not bad, for a mongrel blend of rock-liquor," I drawled, and got a flash of Keth's eyes for the barb. Still not as good as *a'afidir*, I thought. As I slouched on my stool, Keth poured more for both Strengam and himself. Half-seen reddish forms flickered at the firelit edge of my vision, capered vague warnings of a fit to come if I relaxed my vigilance. I blinked them away. We analyzed the day's battle; Strengam wrote it down. Preoccupied with his own distress—the rows among his officer corps were enough to keep anyone awake nights, waiting for the odd slipped poison—Keth complained. He saw no point in plowing over what couldn't be changed now, and *he* wanted to sleep.

"After some battles," Strengam remarked dryly, "commanders didn't sleep at all for two days. Be grateful. Did you ever learn what your disguised spylady—that Coteskani woman that Naga recognized—was after?"

Keth sulked. "Find out exactly what we *didn't* know, *that* was her job to learn," he said curtly. "I don't know any more than that. Died in questioning."

"Of course," Strengam said.

Keth didn't notice any sarcasm. He kept glancing at me surreptitiously while my leg was sewn and bandaged. I said nothing; but I was not pleased that he saw my wounds. The Cragman dropped his eyes from mine if I met his gaze, and stared in a different direction. The Tannese all looked blank, shuttered, when they glanced at Keth. *Alien,* I thought, staring at him, *Keth* is the foreigner here—not me, who by rights should be. The feel of it was clear; *I* was welcome among the Tannese, and Keth was not, anymore—if he ever truly had been. The herbalist departed with a smoked redbuck quarter from Tanman as fee. I longed sleepily for *a'afidir* instead of this liquor, and for bed.

Keth tossed his drink into the back of his throat, gulped and muttered something about sleeping for a tenday. As he rose he gave Rafai a sudden, brief, ugly look. Keth slammed the chamber door so hard after him he made the bar fall inadvertently in place. I closed my eyes. My wounds ached, old and new. It had been a long day.

I held out the royal goblet and Strengam refilled it. They poured out all around. They talked. I listened numbly. Out of a hazy spiritous glow I watched them talk, and talk, and talk. The battle over again, old battles their fathers fought together in, planned battles, possible ones. They talked until the torches had to be changed. Therin wandered in once, sleepily knuckling his eyes, alerting his father to time. Both Therin and I dragged off obediently to bed while our Liege kept talking.

"We charged into this territory killing all these poor fools," Caladrunan's voice said, "might as well let them run away as fight them—" He sounded as if he was talking to himself. Then their voices went softer, and I lost them between the hiss of the torches and the noises of stones settling in the cold night. Presently the torch in the inner chamber winked out, leaving a strip of dusty floor lit at the top of the door. I blinked at the shadows, and sank softly down to sleep.

I woke in a vague lamplit cool. Caladrunan moved my body around in his furs and made room for himself, but it was far away, and I felt impossibly drowsy. He said, "Does your leg hurt?"

I grunted. I scrubbed my eyes open, fumbled for the gold pitcher, and shoved it in his hand. "Drink," I said, shoving aside the hunting cat's lazy bulk. "Two battered drunks trying to cheer their wounds and getting more holes. This stuff is dangerous."

"Horrid aftertaste," he muttered. "We fought well, paired today. First battle together."

I put down the decanter, turning to arrange myself not to strain his arm wound. "Warm," I said into his furs. The hunting cat leaped off the bed, nosed at the chamber door, swatted the nose of a guard dog with a hiss, and vanished into the clutter of furniture in the next room.

"It felt good to have a shield-brother there, Naga. No one ever kept up with me, fighting, before. Guess you're so light-weighted your mare matches my bull's pace."

"Pig-farmer," I said without temper. "Not *that* small."

It was to be a broken night. I fought my way out of a bad dream and came up thrashing in the dark. I had a sickening headache. "Hush now," he said drowsily, pulling me closer.

"Drin," I said sharply, for I was still half-asleep, and the intimate name came easily. "Drin, listen." I sat up, struggling out of the furs. I lit the bedside lamp from a flint and looked around. Caladrunan opened his eyes. "What?" His eyes looked blind with sleep. His hand knocked over the pitcher on the bedside table. Black fluid splashed over the wood. Black!

I pounced on it. Small black particles floated in the bottom of the pitcher. Someone had dared to drug us. The sleep left his face like clouds clearing a sky. His eyes narrowed at the edge of panic in my voice. He sat up, stared at the black stain and then at me. He was all cold alertness now. He said, "Rafai tested the wine spirits, what I gave you was very diluted. And we *all* drank some, seemed harmless. Maybe the drug was put in the bottom of this pitcher—you told me once blackened cupflower leaves have this slow an effect. You said you couldn't taste it either, only see it after a few bell passes."

I kept smelling smoke, dimly, like blood in my nose. But there was no hearth fire, and the inner door was tight shut. I saw none of the animals—there should be animals. I held my temples. My head throbbed as if I'd taken cupflower. I hadn't drunk enough to make me so confused; and the wine spirits couldn't have been fuzzing my brain after so long. "Drin, *get up!*"

Then I hissed when I threw careless weight onto my cut thigh. I turned to Caladrunan, holding my aching head, unsure I'd heard anything at all. The thumping came again, and both of us jumped. I grabbed my scaddas out of sheath. "I've heard that— I've heard that before—that noise, that's—*Osa!*"

I flew to the door. It was barred; I pushed the bar free, but the heavy wood refused to give way. The Hold was built of stone blocks reinforced by joists, rooftrees, and pillars of old dry pine—no real effort to make the stone support itself: cheap, quick building. Such timbers burned well. I spun, shouting, and ran back to Caladrunan.

He was already nearly armored up. I threw boots and robes and armor on myself, cocking one ear for the groaning of falling timbers, and snatched up what I dared, grabbing and stashing small things in pockets. Timbers creaked above us. I ran across, panting. *Fire-fire-fire!* chanted my mind. Impatiently, I flung aside a tapestry and ducked into the Hold-ruler's escapeway.

That door stood rigid against my attempts, too. I tapped the panel, backed up, and kicked. Wood broke under my foot, framing gave way. I pushed aside wreckage and stared down at a heavy iron grid fallen on the floor mats amidst a tangle of dead guards—a grid strayed from an entire rusted old pile of iron that barred the secret way into Therin's chamber. The only torch had nearly burned away, but the smell of oily smoke here was thick and acrid. The center of Therin's chamber floor was a broken pit full of low, sullen flames. As I stared in, floor stones dropped into the burning cellars below. The boy's bed sloping downward at one wall looked rumpled and empty; I saw neither clothes nor weapons about. A table slid into the pit and vanished in a sudden eager roar of sparks. The secret escapeway went with it. The only way out now was Therin's front door.

We skated about the creaking perimeter walls, found the door completely unlocked, and plunged out into a fight. The main hall was full of dark forms thrown among the fallen stones and timbers, messy, crushed things slick underfoot, men locked together in heaving groups. We dodge-danced between the knots of bodies, spinning and running through the debris. Some of the Tannese recognized us, threw up a sword-block, grabbed at an enemy, to help us through. Others simply stumbled into our way. Caladrunan kept stopping in distress, and I kept dragging him onward.

I shouted over the crash of destruction outside, "Therin's gone, we have to see outside there—"

We ran through empty Devotee passages out into the Hold's main Altar. Fires sprang through cracks spreading in the floor. Voices vanished in the fire roar; mutely I pointed out a path in the increasing rubble to the back of the Altar toward Devotee quarters.

Then Caladrunan whirled in alarm—and slumped, leaning on me in relief. Rafai and his underofficer Vano, the rookie Esgarin and a squad of guards, spilled into the Devotee quarters from another door and slammed the door shut on licking flames. Sooty-faced, they bent over gasping, their hands and clothes burned. What armor they wore was blackened. Some of them had been out in the chaos of the Hall fighting for their lives. Rafai waved limply and trotted to us. Because I was panting harder than he was, unable to speak, he gasped, "We're the first reserve guards, Liege. Bad all over out there. We fought off a Cragman squad trying to take our garrison doors; came fast as we could, couldn't get near your chambers at all for the numbers they had. Where's the rest of the men? Dead? The dogs?"

"Just exactly what *I* want to know," Caladrunan said grimly.

"Don't know," I heaved out, and explained about the route through Therin's chambers.

"The rooms up to the Hall were all empty; maybe the watches are all in that pile at your chamber door. We expected you were gone, too, just chance that we came this way—" It was clear Rafai's wits did not suffer our drug headaches; so *we'd* succumbed to leaves put in the pitcher after Rafai tasted the contents. In terse words Caladrunan explained it. Rafai looked

furious, a ludicrous fierce sooty expression that almost made me
laugh. Water stung in my eyes at the same time.

Rafai's men were recovering. I strapped my harpcase tighter
under one arm for my rib-shield. Caladrunan grabbed my wrist
and dragged me over to a half-fallen rafter, pointed up at an
upper level arrowloop. The second-floor balcony that once ran
along the wall's inner face had skidded down the sloped, fallen
rafters into a heap—useless now. I scrambled up one long timber, which shuddered and danced under my weight. At the top,
gripping the rafter and its splintered corbel, I stared out the hole.
Hot air exhaled from the building past my body.

In the night courtyards outside below, orange-lit and sharply
outlined by their shadows, men ran about. Osa and Nandos and
Keth's men were all mixed up together out there, and they were
*not* fighting each other. I strained to see all the top bailey. Its
outlines looked odd: Then, in root-cold horror, I understood. To
a group of men robed in white—*Osa priests*—men in Cragmen
helmets pointed out prisoners among a roped-in pen full of
blue-robed soldiers, robes nearly black in that light. A heap of
gear lay on the ground. Someone in Tannese armor plunged
forward wildly from the back, grabbing up a pike. From one side
a cone of white shot out, spattered horribly along lines of jerky
dancing prisoners, and left my eyes dazzled, near-blind. The
white-robed Osa priests still calmly observed, gesturing gently to
one another. I spun about and ran headlong down the timber,
hands flung out. *"Drin!"*

I couldn't see him or the others in my dazzled blindness. For
some moments I held my wits, calling quietly and peering,
despite the wild red figures capering warnings all about the edges
of my sight. If Caladrunan had taken cover against the bright
Osa light, it was out of ignorance of the real danger.

Then the Hall joists jumped and juddered beneath my feet, and
the roar of thrown Osa flames boomed in through the dark arrow
loops overhead; white light barred among the remnant third-floor
rafters strained overhead. I spun side to side in the Hall's thick,
dim flickers of orange light, and cried out unheard. A wall stone
split overhead, shrapnel *whanged* in all directions. Everything in
my abdomen seized taut so hard my throat convulsed, but no
noise escaped.

A flare of white ran up a pile of shattered wood in front of me,
igniting hot blue and orange points like a torch. I stumbled aside
into a dark hall pillar, grabbed it; it gave way and pitched me

forward into heaved floorboards. I crashed against sharp edges
even as I tried to roll. Small embers glowed evilly in my face.
The heaps vibrated beneath me to distant machines. Shattering
through the air came another bellow of Osa flame, as abruptly
snuffed, outside.

Something grabbed the back of my belt. I twisted violently in
the grip before it got good purchase on me, lashing out blind.
Cloth rent under my hands, blue cloth, and my fingers were full
of torn light hair. Vano's bearded face drawn into pale rictus
screamed at me—and a gobbled noise left my mouth in reply.
Rafai's ringed hand grabbed my left shoulder. The Hall boomed
and shook with Osa strikes outside. I felt my knees give way,
and then I was heaving up my stomach helplessly onto blue-
tasseled boots like a wretched hound. Caladrunan gripped my
braids, shook me, gave up on getting sense of me, and simply
lifted me by one arm onto my feet. I hiccupped and cried,
smearing my wrist at my face, while he dragged me stumbling
along through the chaos. I was profoundly shamed even as I
wept. "Drin, *oh, Goddess*, Drin, I thought—oh, Goddess—"

The Lord of Tan did not even notice. He forged ahead in great
strides through the debris, head up. After a moment my legs
found the same rhythm, and my hand locked on his wrist to
complete the climber's grasp he'd begun. It helped. I took deep
breaths, fought against the shimmers of concussion-pain, the
totems jabbering madly in the starry darkness in my skull, and
the terror that had soiled body and mind. Slowly the red panic
drained from the inside of my head. For all his not-noticing, he
felt the sense come back into me. He shouted, "Did you see any
loyal men outside fighting?"

"Yes. Oh, Goddess, it's no good, Drin. The Nandos have the
men out of the west barracks; I think the Osa said to disarm or
they'd flame prisoners down. So they dropped arms. I saw one
whole line flamed down after a man went wild and attacked
them." More tears leaked down my face . . . futile, already-
shed tears.

In a low servant's passage he jolted to a stop, grabbed my
jaw, turned my face fiercely up to a bar of firelight thrown
through broken walls—and I as fiercely let him look. I told him,
"I fight! The panic is *gone*, cured—I never run again, never!"

"Yes," Caladrunan said harshly. "Where do we go?"

I led the way into the cooler garrison barracks among the
lower level river caves. Doors opened on nothing. It was five

frantic doorways before we saw anyone, and then they were
running figures in a cross-corridor far beyond our reach. We had
to duck and run past a fire roaring out of a door in one narrow
passage. *A trap, this Hold was planned as a trap!* I thought. My
wet face dried brassy-tight and hard as my mouth.

"Come," I said, and urged them on eastward.

Floorboards crumbled under us, showing gaping furnaces below, as we ran into servant's quarters. I jumped a gap and
grabbed Esgarin to keep him from sliding into a live red hole. I
gasped out a question, but the boy had no idea where Therin
might be. I yelled at the others, "Maybe Strengam took Therin
out first. They might've got out."

Caladrunan nodded, and yelled ahead, "Which way now?"

As we plunged through an eastern kitchen door into a smolder-
ing meat locker, Rafai yelled back, "East-running tunnelways
might get us out. Naga's right. Every open way is blocked at the
curtain wall. Just missed getting caught in the garrison tunnels
myself—everything went up in flames." The far door of the
locker smashed open under his boot.

The Lord of Tan shouted, "See any organized Tannese muster?"

Vano spoke up beside us in sturdy fisher-accented shout.
"No, Liege, not a one of us. I asked my patrol. We met Rafai in
the Hall—only muster *we* saw were prisoners getting killed
outside."

The crash of stones echoed noisily in the narrow way. The
thump and roar of fire grew louder behind us as we ran. The
tunnel struts were all of timber too, of course.

Caladrunan panted, "They ran flamethrowers up close after
dark, troops hidden close all day, to attack so quickly—well-
planned. Those Nandos and those Osa didn't drop out of the
sky."

Rafai was swearing fiercely and with extreme foulness under
his breath.

I said, "They climbed through the river caves. Osa general
must've bribed a lot of people in various ways. Not enough men
or time for us to check every cavern down here."

Caladrunan coughed. "Impossible." The others ran silently
after that. We burst out of a minor servants' hall into a woodshed, and then into a slop courtyard. I looked wildly around,
coughing in the smoke.

Flames threw up a glow at the southwest, reflecting orange
and brown off the clouds and lighting up the night like the

torches of a god's Feastnight dance. While we stood there shin-deep in garbage, a great crash shook the ground. Visible flames sheeted the western sky, lighting the buildings around us. Sparks glittered on the roof of the woodshed behind us. I flinched back against a wall, covering my eyes. "Fuel dump," I gasped.

Caladrunan grabbed my arm so tightly his fingers bit into my armor straps as we all watched the flames climb the western skyline of the Hold.

Vano said in a shaken voice, "That wasn't like that a moment ago! It wasn't like that before we ran up to Hall, trying to reach Liege's chamber. Goddess Above and Below!"

Everyone there, including Caladrunan, made averting signs in renewed horror. We couldn't hear any screaming over the moaning and roaring of fires, over the wind streaming upward, hot past our bodies. But we all knew we would, if the Hold were not falling in a continuous rumbling and crackling of exploding hot stones. Vano's brief moment, in a fight, could've been anything from split instants to many bell passes. I knew my own time-sense was gone.

"North," Caladrunan shouted then. He kept putting dents in my arm leathers with his fingers as we ran—first one of us leading and then the other, pulling one another in a mad chase like a child's game. Deeper in the town, within the curtain walls of the Hold and away from flames, we heard running feet, chaotic mobs, and screaming. I couldn't see faces, only shouting mouths. We blue-robes all linked arms. At times our wrists were strained nearly to breaking apart in the crush, and always we drew back toward the Lord of Tan's bright golden hair, a banner of a head glowing above the others. It started raining in the streets, while the Hold's dry interior burned hot and heavily. Fires hissed like lizards at the raindrops.

At Caladrunan's tight-gripped gestures, tugging up my wrist, we all scaled a wall and broke from the crush of bodies. We ran along the walls of dark merchants' quarters, dropped down into a just-ignited stable—for the beasts were still inside, abandoned to die. Only one boy had got there before us: A frightened rookie in blue robes was trying to pull the terrified ganas out past burning hay. He had got them harnessed somehow, but they held their horns rigidly high and refused to leave shelter. The boy was crying without knowing it, all streaked soot and burned hands in the sullen glow. The Lord of Tan yelled for all of us to mount, beckoning the rookie too. Caladrunan yelled, "If *Naga* can't get these out, nobody can,'' and we mounted up, Caladrunan pulling me up before him on the stable's lone bull.

The bull kicked and screamed at the weight and the stench. I gave the poor beast savage slashes on his dewlap with my fighting spurs until the maddened animal charged out of the stable gate. I set the bull at a low wall, aware of Caladrunan's weight leaning with me. Other beasts leaped after, and then they were all coming, a terrified loose herd screaming like children in pain. Between us all we kept them in a loose ring, driving them from the stable courtyard through the confused darkness of the servant alleys.

We ran toward the north side of the Hold town through crowded towerlike poverty quarters where nobles never went, where fewer fires had begun as yet. We collected more riders: young cavalrymen, grim Tannese strangers who ran and fought beside us like brothers, and a noble lost from Strengam's entourage, who shouted that he had not seen the old man since the end of the day's battle. The streets scudded with figures running in the fireglow and shadows. Even occupation by *two* armies had not rooted out all life from these back quarters, where no one who wore fine robes went alone. Skulkers exercised old skills even now.

On the beasts, which we had to fight bitterly to keep, we outran them all, clearing the way through Nando invaders twice. Whenever we reached open courtyards away from the tall, narrow, unstable stone buildings, we saw progressive waves of burning rubble—flames advancing north and eastward after us. The Hold's curtain walls went down along with the interior ones. The shocks of falling stones and earth tremors made the narrow poverty ways dangerous with flying stone and broken timbers. Nothing could be heard over the fires and screaming din. When we hit the north gate, we led hundreds of grimy servant quarter refugees. Even the rats were driven out by fires whipping into the streets from the southwest.

I squinted ahead in the dark. Someone had torn their way out of that gate ahead of us: There were piles of Nandos and red-haired Cragmen tossed about an overturned flamethrower aglow with sullen remnants of fuel. The gate-leaves hung awry and the locking bars hung smashed as by an Osa tank; no one tried to stop us on our charge toward it. Was it Strengam who got out, capturing an Osa tank with his men? I wondered. The bull under my legs flinched at something and picked up speed yet again.

A lance of flame sizzled to one side of us and snuffed out in a billow of smoke. The west pylon of the gate exploded in a shower of stone and flame as we flew toward it. Stone shards swept the running beasts and refugees like a ragged scythe all around. I shouted. Caladrunan shouted back.

The eastern pylon exploded then. I heard the *whang!* of a ricochet, the explosion, and something punched me on the right side—knocking the wind out of me and almost sweeping me off the saddle. Only Caladrunan's hand clenched on my belt kept me up, for alone I would have gone over gasping between our bull and Rafai's beast beside us. Then Rafai was riding beside us and pushing at me. The Lord of Tan shoved me back onto the bull's neck with a sharp wrench. Then we were away from the walls, free. I lay forward and clung onto the bull's scored neck, sobbing for air. My harpcase tugged and bobbed oddly from my harness, beneath my right arm. The bull, too, shrilled and faltered a stride, and cried out in piercing shrieks.

Behind us a gold flare scaled the night, rising into a roaring column of fire. When I looked back under one arm, the whole gate was gone: It was a mound of rubble surrounded by an eerie greenish fire. Only a few dark running figures followed us outward, of all the refugees that'd jostled about and after us. Another lance sizzled out, reaching past the gate. We rode for our lives. An Osa flamethrower advanced out of tower shadows, hosing down that gate section and the rubble beyond with brilliant bluish streams of fire. A lance of fire touched the wreck of the flamethrower buried in the rubble. It exploded in cascades of white and deafening barrages, subsiding in concussive rumbles.

We rode on blind. The whole time, crazily calm in the midst of the uproar, I kept thinking that *someone* got out of that gate. A troop had killed those Nandos, overturned that flamethrower, and saved us, if unknowingly. Someone had to have escaped. Keth and the Osa can't keep an entire Tannese Army captive, I thought.

Caladrunan took the nose-lines from me. I couldn't hold against the beast's tugging. My weak right side had begun to cripple me—for sensation I felt only blooming feathers of early heat—as we left the road. The rib injury from my raiding was compounded now to a misery of awkward, incapable weakness: My body wouldn't serve me. When the bull heaved about, I felt no pain yet, which bothered me. We turned east across unplowed fields to the river.

When we paused in a thicket of willows to rest and assess ourselves, I looked around in shock. Half the Hold lay crumpled into a pit, all brilliant live-orange coals. The cave-combed bluff below the Hold, the stone hill over it, the fields around it, were bright as daylight with scattered fires. Outside the devastation the entire country swarmed with dark ant movements, black against black. People had escaped; they were still running, lit here and there by the firelight. Men ran past our thicket calling to each other in panicky Marsh dialect—deserters running away. One of them fell into the willows beneath the bull's feet, gurgling, and died clutching an arrow in his belly. Esgarin lowered his bow and said, "Sorry he got so close, Liege."

Caladrunan sat quietly in the bull's saddle, his hand gripped on my belt. He was staring at the Hold. I gasped in a breath and answered, "It's all right, boys. We're up and fighting, all that's important." The bull continued to moan with wounds, but we could do nothing—such severe injuries would never stay bound up. "Need another beast—does Rafai have the extra beasts—?"

The Lord of Tan slid down and away to take the new mount's nose-lines. His voice spoke softly in the dark as he moved around to each man in the group; his unseen night-large presence seemed unreal. The bull's moaning disturbed his new mount, made it shy about. The willows dripped rainwater. I told him very quietly that I was bleeding from the ribs and couldn't shift my right arm strongly enough to fight. He gently pulled aside my flopping harpcase—which I would not yield up, even to him— and he opened my armor, feeling with his fingers for broken bones. He cut strips of rag from his robe and bound them around my chest and under my harpcase, building a sling for my arm. He said *he* hadn't even been scratched. I grabbed his wrist in my left hand and kissed it, in sheer relief. He gripped my hand hard, told me to hold position briefly on the wounded bull, because the mount distinguished me in the dark from all the men on foot, and rode into the thicket with Rafai.

In truth he wanted me to rest. It was the oldest leadership method recorded: speak in the disorder, give sensible orders, calm the panicked ones with work. It shored me up, too, and I was grateful. If unhurt, I'd be doing the same. Instead, Esgarin sat his beast nearby, watching me. While the bull shuddered under me, I watched the Hold's outerworks fall in slow waves of fire. A Tannese voice called. Startled, I listened to a Tannese voice whisper my Liege's titles out of the darkness beyond the thicket; then more voices reported timidly, streaming in from all around the willow shadows. We could retrieve some of ours in the flight from the burning!

Soon I had six rookie footmen standing with Esgarin and me, all asking questions with chattering teeth in the cold rain. One wept in fright; he'd almost been hit by a fire blast. The stink of us all in the rain proved they'd fouled their clothes, too. I kept talking to the weeping boy until he stopped whimpering. At last Caladrunan rode up and set a cavalry man in my place, and took Esgarin and me deeper into the thickets. My bull stumbled, jolted me and my twirling brains, which wrung a groan of a curse from me. In a hollow among tree roots, where he dared talk loud enough to be heard, Caladrunan asked questions, piecing together what had happened to us.

Keth.

The Osa general's plot had been far more intricate than any expectations. Keth hadn't even realized, probably, exactly when he passed the information desired of him. When he began to worry about it, perhaps he persuaded himself it didn't matter. And certainly when the Osa showed up, Keth would've mustered up his dignity and told himself *that* was the side he was on all the time. I knew Keth even better than he knew me. *I should have realized.*

Almost a stylish betrayal, I thought; perhaps the first time Keth managed to live up to his braggadocio before those court dandies and the few brave Ladies who openly scorned his uncouth Crag manners. "I'll show you, I will!" He had.

Caladrunan chewed on bitterness for awhile, rousing at last to give orders. Caladrunan had the spare ganas driven to water and then onward to more secure clearings deeper among the willows. He selected calm men to go out as pickets, to scoop up loyalists and kill enemies who stumbled onto us. He sent out the steadiest men of all to get information on enemy positions to the north and about the Hold itself. The spies began trickling back in twos and threes; with plans based on their reports, he sent out an attack force of fifty men to ambush the flamethrowers that advanced slowly, destructively, upon our thickets from the south.

The force he sent out never returned to us. We heard some small explosions and saw balls of fire rise on a bluff directly south of us, and we hoped that some of the men would make it back to us. It was not to be. A massive red and black storm-ball rose up northeast of the Hold—a ball that uncurled like a flower with majestic slowness and lit up the world. Bluffs arrogant from the beginning of time were humbled to dust, to clouds flying, tumbling rock. The hill where we'd spent the battle afternoon above the Hold became a red coalpit image branded on my eyes.

The crack of it blanked out my brain with pain. I held my head curled into my good arm. When it eased, I saw Caladrunan turn his face into the intense glare, and his mouth moved, but I heard nothing. As the last of the glare subsided gently, I saw other men holding their ears or tugging earlobes. Oh, I understood why: About me shadows wavered and shimmered and roared with pain. It was hard to think past it. *May the Osa suffer from their own weapons,* I thought savagely. That was a fuel cache blown by our retaliation, I had no doubt of it. If *we* had suffered, the enemy was closer yet. And the closer the clever Osa general had been, the better. But, knowing that elusive enemy, he was safely far away, and taking quiet progress reports.

For awhile none of us could hear. We used signs when we could find a bit of firelight, stripes of light glancing into the thickets. I wondered dully whether the hearing loss was permanent, on top of all my past ear damage. I set my teeth against the jolts and lurches of my staggering bull. We moved north among the willows and birch groves; Caladrunan thought we might have been illuminated to enemies in that moment of glare. I couldn't hear his theories nor anyone else's, but his hand signals were enough to inform me. It wasn't until we'd stopped to rest in another dense clump farther from the Hold that anything got into my ears.

The first noise was the basso chuffing of my bull. Then I heard Caladrunan say, "Our advantage—Osa—actually slower—outrunning—supplies move slower than—" He seemed to be yelling. I saw Vano's smudged dirty face move in the shadows among the saplings, a face striped by the faintest orange light, apparently shouting. In the center of my vision, some of the men worked under torches. At sight's edge, the lights shimmered away like fish-kites on their lines. I wondered what Vano and Esgarin were trying to tell me. He tugged at my knee and pointed. I looked down.

I felt stupid and thirsty. It took a moment to understand why, in the dark. Blood was draining down into dark patches across my leg, and the gana under me staggered along bleeding from a

ozen places as badly, though in my growing foggy pain I had
ot noticed. Esgarin pulled Rafai over, who went off and re-
urned with Caladrunan; the Lord of Tan shouted inaudibly at
1e. At last he got off his own beast, reached up, and dragged
1e off by the waist, yelling something at Vano. The short burly
oldier bent down and unbuckled my cuirass and slashed my
obes and looked at my ribs. I thought fuzzily, *oh yes,* somebody
nce told me Vano had doctored ganas and dogs and all kinds of
nimals. Caladrunan held up a skin of water and squirted some
1to my mouth. "More," I gasped. I drank heavily. Snatches of
ound got into my fuzzy head as they talked. I drew a breath,
ormed out words, and felt something resonate in my throat and
cullbones, though I could hear nothing. "Where are they driv-
1g us?"

Caladrunan heard me. He nodded, pointing westward. "Fire—
oread from—quickly—"

I tried to sign that I understood, an effort which made my head
che badly. Frustrating, how thick my thoughts worked. We
vere being driven eastward toward the river and the ash wastes
f the far side.

"—need—gathering place—Rafai second commander—sent
arn—Fortress—"

Vano bound my arm in a new sling after wrapping my midsec-
on like a burst pig sausage. Someone else waited there for him
o work on them as well, and he turned away.

Caladrunan said, "Almost ready—slip past—"

He'd been deeper in the hollows than I when the storm-ball
ose; I was thankful he could hear now. Caladrunan turned, and
vo new ganas, harnessed and ready to ride, were brought up by
smudged youngster: I blinked stupidly at him. Yes. Esgarin.
etween the ex-stable boy and the Lord of Tan, they lifted me
p into a saddle; Esgarin put the lines into my left hand. He
ooked up, saying something.

I spread my fingers as sign I understood. The gelded beast was
o calm at my bloody smell, it *had* to have been trained to battle;
it was, I could ride one-handed, pressing the lines against the
east's neck or away. Vital to me in my state! Caladrunan
1ounted up, also, turning his head. His mouth opened in calls,
nd his arm waved in the orange-flickered dark. Formless dark-
ess, torches, we all moved. Scouts reported to him as we rode
long—they were a mixture of men, some of them Upai, fading
1to the brush ahead. They rode the freshest ganas Caladrunan

could give them. As for us, at a tired walk we led a startling
large rabble of footmen, mostly men who'd bivouacked outside
the Hold walls: the least privileged and lowest ranked. And
Goddess' ironic justice, the safest. I estimated we marched with
two hundred men, and the number grew as we picked up more
shivering fugitives fled into the woods beyond our own belated
flight.

We went north in hopes of squeezing eastward past the slower
Osa advance—and the Osa troops were slow only because they
were clearly hunting food and supplies and then burning whatever they left. While they slowed to destroy empty villages and
hiding places, we merely ran. I rode beside Caladrunan and
drank from his waterskin, passing it back when he touched my
arm for it. Water and air both tasted of soot.

A little before full daylight we reached a village at a ford on
the west Tejed riverside. It had not been burned, but it was
empty of people. The men hunted ravenously among the houses
for food. Those of us who'd been officers checked that they
settled into hiding away from searching daylight eyes and Osa
distance lenses, but where they could run away freely should
flamethrowers roll up.

My hearing had improved; I could hear some of what the men
told me. I posted a batch of soldiers among the ganas, crowding
them together in the warmth of a shed that had seen such stabling
before. But half these men promptly left their post to walk me
back to Caladrunan's chosen house. They ignored my swearing
at them for idiots; they seemed more afraid of Caladrunan's
temper than of mine, the state I was in, and they meant to be
sure I returned to him on both feet. Politely, they said I was
staggering. I was *not*. Much.

We found Caladrunan sprawled on an abandoned strap-bed in
the headman's house. The soldiers looked at him and crept out.
Caladrunan lay staring up at the torchlit ceiling. Mildew lines
and spider webs across roof plaster marked its abandonment.
Leaves lay blown in corners. It didn't seem like a good moment
to report my inadequacy for duty; I brought out the dry little
journeycake I'd found, sopped it in water, and pressed it in his
hand. His eyes stared far past me. He ate with slow mechanical
gestures. His face looked utterly exhausted. When he pressed
over half the cake back in my hand, I was too hungry to protest.
I gobbled it.

He startled me in mid-gulp. His hand grabbed at my leg.

dragged me down beside him, grasping at me and hanging on, a man desperate to get away from his own troubles. I fumbled at him awkwardly, like patting a dog. At my touch, his eyes returned from some far distance to me and became aware, and contrite. His grip relaxed. I curled up, eased my injuries, and gentled my body about to ease both our wounds; I leaned against the wall. Silently I held out my good arm, and felt him slide in under it. He put his face down to the hollow of my good shoulder. I lowered my cheek to his hair, and closed my eyes. My fingers tightened on his arm. It was the only consolation I knew to give him: a silence, asking nothing.

At last he said into my shoulder, "Last night I set men to watch the caves on the river. I mistrusted, I thought the cave watches might smuggle in stuff—and of course, they did. Invaders. One of our men told me that when he escaped he found bodies thrown in a heap near the south gate. Our own *Devotees* came up to our men, sent them running off to all kinds of wrong places, even into ambush. *Of course* Keth was frantic to stay with us, to be obedient, until his planned moment. I didn't listen when you warned me; I thought it was so absurd for him to betray us!"

"It was. He got maneuvered into it," I said.

"His alliance with us could've worked if Keth gave it a real chance, if he just once saw we were right about the Osa. He was never so stupid about Crag plots and politics as he's been about this Osa's manipulations. O Goddess—Devotees, or Nandos, or traitors in our own troops, killed my cave watchmen, and the Osa put Keth's men in place while we were drugged to sleep and then barricaded in, unable to sort out disorder. I found out from one man that they even put out the hypocaust fires and the Hall torches, let invaders into the main buildings from below. I think the men on watch outside our doors were attacked so fast they had no chance to wake us, let alone get us out. Rafai said after that men were just piling in from both sides so hard and fast—perhaps we were meant for captives for questioning or ransom—"

I said, "They'd have come in and taken us if they knew we were still alive in there. Maybe our watches piled in on the invaders so fast they never found out."

"The Army is shattered, we've lost most of our officer corps; nobody knows what happened to Strengam or my son. I hope Strengam took the boy out that gate we used. I hope my son got out."

If there were tears, I did not look to see them, and he made no
sound. For long and long I just gripped his shoulder with my
fingers. When I did peer around at his smudged face, his eyes
were closed in deep gray-lined hollows. He was asleep.

"Not your fault," I whispered at last, in a voice no Harper
would have admitted to owning. "Mine. My fault. I hurt the Osa
as hard as I knew how. I went after Keth, and it drove him
crazier than he started out; he couldn't see *anything* clearly. I
should've killed Keth. He has hurt you every time, to hurt me."
I tilted my face low against his hair.

I said to the sleeping Lord of Tan, "Goddess knows, I'm
sorry for what I did wrong, if I ever had a choice about it. Oh,
Drin, if the Osa—if Keth—hadn't hated and feared me so much,
they would've been careless, they'd never send such a strategist
to Tan, and we'd never have been tested like this. And failed
it." My throat ached. "Drin, I was never defeated before.
Never." But my eyes were dry as a sand-death viper's scales
winding away upon dunes, and nothing watered the grating
drought inside me. Perhaps curing me of fear, in the fallen Hall,
had cured me of the humanity to cry. Where it had been enough
in the Hold just to *survive,* I felt too much pain now to be
grateful for my mere life. Or for his.

I turned my face against his hair and shifted my hand. I closed
my eyes. *Goddess rot it all.*

Eventually the torch burned down and snuffed out. Gray
predawn light replaced it. Stained cloth and snagged silver em-
broidery threads caught at my calluses, and mud crumbled away;
under it, the sword symbol glittered clearly and recognizably
between my fingers. In a few days the unpolished threads would
tarnish green and vanish against the dark cloth; now the muddied
surround just made the silver symbol look more pristine. I
watched light fracture into rainbows off it.

My gaze traveled past that, past the curly glimmers of his hair
to the dawnlight pinking the far wall, echoing in shadowed
reversals all the cracked and broken shutters above me. The
ragged lines of light between the shutter lines grew from blush
pale to golden and crept down the plastered wall, while
Caladrunan's body breathed in regular slow rhythm against mine.
"I have a responsibility," I said into his hair. "You don't know
yet how to survive as an exile in hiding. Pray Goddess I don't
fail that duty as badly as I did anticipating the Osa's maneuvers.
Maybe it was all my fault. Maybe the Goddess doesn't like

revenge. But keeping you alive through exile, retake Tan, that's the only hope for your merchants and pig-farmers and little girls—Goddess preserve their stubborn necks. Nobody else will take pity on them.''

A rumbling vibrated suddenly under my arm, startling me. The Lord of Tan said, very low and clear, ''But you do. *You* take pity. You told me once, pity is due when you have the power to change something—and we *don't,* now. First we have to survive. Just look.'' And he lifted one hand from my side, holding up a broken tangle of smashed harpstrings, pale wood, and leather casing. The smashed harp lay along my wounded side—shield, life-giver. His yellow eyes lifted to mine over the wreckage. He had loved my music.

I kept looking in his eyes because it hurt too much to move anything, including my head. ''Oh, we'll *survive.* I can make another harp like my first one, out of thornwood. Now, you know, I think we could link up with some of the Marshmen who wouldn't join us before because they hate Cragmen; I have a location for meeting them, I remember those last few dispatches we got—'' Life was coming back into my voice. ''What's so funny? They knocked us down, but we don't have to *stay* knocked down just to please our enemies!''

''*You're* back to normal,'' the Lord of Tan grunted, and sighed. His eyes rolled shut. ''Goddess help us all!'' And he dropped instantly to sleep.